ONCE IN A
RED MOON

ONCE IN A RED MOON

by

Joel Townsley Rogers

RAMBLE HOUSE

Third Ramble House Edition

ISBN 13: 978-1-60543-402-5

ISBN 10: 1-60543-402-7

Published: 2004, 2005, 2009 by Ramble House
Cover Art: Gavin L. O'Keefe
Preparation: Dixie J. Whitted

To
OTIS JOEL ROGERS

from whom I have consciousness
of all tremendous Visions, the
eternal Mysteries, the abiding
Laws, the dreadful Awes, the
cruel dog-driving Fates, and
with that consciousness courage
to meet them all, and death,
this book is respectfully
dedicated.

ONCE IN A RED MOON

PROLOG: THE BLOODY MOON

Here, within the blood red shadows of the moon, a man lies dead. A knife has pierced his breast and heart. The knife's haft quivers. On that silver haft a golden serpent is wound and wound around. Its emerald eyes twinkle and gleam with the fury of the moon.

Who did this thing? Who killed this man?

Minutes pass. Take count of them, for a soul has passed with them.

The red moon sails in cloud and clear. Over the sea, over the shoal, over sand and rock and marsh its nocturnal keelson journeys.

Shadows crawl in the darkness. The flash of a blade, a strale of steel, an arrow of disaster—a knife! Breath of murder!

Clear and cold, her blue eyes somnolent, a woman stares at the sailing moon . . . A girl is crying in the night: "Gay! O, Gay!" Lovelorn, whimpering: "Gay! O, Gay!" . . . Shapes running in the darkness. "Halt! Halt!" . . .

Now let the moonlight die, and come again. Horrible night rolls round. The shadows are one with it. All seem asleep.

The crimson moon falls far upon the marshes. The dead man in the moon has bloody eyes. Watch! He is laughing.

Who did this thing? Who killed this man? Who struck that serpent knife?

Here a man lies dead. Think of it! Last evening he drank the wine, he kissed the lips, he threatened death. Yes, he threatened immortality to his enemies as fiercely as any little god. Now his limbs are flaccid. His brain holds no more thought than the colon of a worm.

Where are gone all those inchoate thoughts, those desires, fears, passions, memories? What is this which lies upon the narrow bed, this lump of clay?

Only last evening a marvel more intricate than the multiple involutions of the stars—more nuclei of force in him than there are suns in space—a reservoir of aeon-toppling potentialities which could (did we but know) grip creation by the throat and unarm the weeping angels.

This was God's own image, this the promise of divinity, this clod.

Nothing left now which would fetch above a dollar five cents as charcoal, fat, phosphorus, iron, sulphur, salt. Yet he was worth ten million dollars. You can read it in the newspapers.

One tick of eternity's clock sufficed to end this life—to cheapen ten million dollars' worth of man to a junker's dollar, five—to smash this divine machine—to strew to limbo, wind, and the dark night this intensity of dreams and passions which was once a human soul.

One tick of eternity's clock. Scarce would you have time to yawn. What is life? What is time?

Dead. Dead for a ducat. Spitted through the heart.

Who did this thing? Who killed this man? Who struck that serpent knife murderously through his heart?

Now let the vengeful mobs howl forth! Now let the cruel men who hunt for men turn their dread eyes upon this circumstance! Now let the hounds be loosed, baying up the crimson moon!

Who did it?

"I," says the red moon. "I did it with my bow and arrow. I killed Cock Robin!"

I. EIGHTEEN DOLLARS FOR DEATH

OLD Tim Grady, the movie millionaire, sat in the Alhambra Palace with his son Padriac. The Grady super-picture, starring Rose Dawn in "Sin" was on the silver screen. Those lovely wistful eyes of beautiful Rose Dawn! Certainly they were worth fifty-five cents of any man's money, including war tax.

Police Lieutenant MacErcher leaned over the theater's back seat, his legs crossed, lowly conversing with Solemn Ike Duval of the Argus Agency (private detecting neatly done).

"That's a cold un, that young Padriac Grady," MacErcher said with a jerk of his head. "Always figuring. Look at 'im now. Smart business man, I guess."

"Not much like old Tim," whispered Ike, softly moving his jaws. "But then, though they don't look alike, in a kind of way they *do* look alike."

"Ain't it the truth? Young Grady seems like the old man's shadow."

In close-up ten feet high the screen showed beautiful Rose Dawn. Round pearl tears upon her cheeks. Mist gathering in her large eyes. Her mouth trembling as though she yearned to kiss each man in the Alhambra Palace who had paid his fifty-five cents. Thoughtfully MacErcher rubbed his stub nose. Solemn Ike kept silence; his small, cold eyes softened; he coughed behind his hand. Yet he was a man who knew no love of women.

Old Timothy Grady, sitting far down front, shivered through all his giant frame. He clasped the chair arms. Erotic music, how it quickened hot blood within the heart. And old Tim had taken liquor.

In simulated love delirium the woman on the screen threw her arms about her screen lover, clipped him close, drew his lips to her shut eyes. Throb! throb! throb! pulsed orchestral minstrelsy, drowning the high theater hall in floods of deep-noted music.

Screen tricks, screen tricks! Only a painted passion for the camera.

Old Tim Grady growled an oath, his voice raspy with brogue. "I wish she'd act like that for me."

Padriac Grady didn't answer his father. Deliberately he looked at his watch. His gray eyes were expressionless. He had never seen Rose Dawn in the flesh. "I want to catch the Knickerbocker for Chicago," he said. "That picture's going big out there. We ought to make a mint of money from it."

Rose Dawn still lingered in the arms of her screen lover. The packed house was mute. Only Padriac Grady seemed bored.

And one other man. He arose, stumbling over knees, stumbling up the aisle, staring at the carpet. The Gradys did not see him, nor would they have known Anthony Anthony of the Argus Agency.

Ike Duval straightened up, giving a curt salute. " 'Afternoon, Mr. Anthony." But Mr. Anthony was still looking at the floor, intently, pondering something. Without a word to Ike he passed through the doors out into the cold gray day.

"That your chief?" MacErcher asked, rubbing his nose again. "Smart looking fellow."

"No, he's no fool," said Solemn Ike. "But he's a man with damn' queer ways, MacErcher. Sometimes he's almost beyond me."

A screen villain had seized beautiful Rose Dawn, haply purporting to kiss her holy lips, haply to strangle her. Her gold curls raveled free. She fought madly till her dress was torn. No one of the thousands watching her took full breath. They clenched their fists. Spencer, the physician, pulled his beard. Bellbender, the minister, tugged at his collar band. Todd, the lawyer, passionately mopped his bald head. The orchestra beat bass chords.

Over a table the villain bent Rose Dawn. She seized something, a knife, a paper-cutter, a pair of shears. She struck. Tearing at his throat, the screen villain toppled heavily. He raised his arms. He spun on one heel. He fell; and so died.

Rose Dawn stood with arms stretched, as on a cross. She shook her curly locks. Something of the tiger's fury in her eyes! A flame; a holocaust. Quick the light died. She was cold again, beautiful Rose Dawn, perfectest of actresses, as she knelt to look at the dead screen villain.

In that heavily breathing house no one applauded.

"Well done!" whispered Padriac Grady.

Old Tim took deep breaths. "You'd never think she could look so fierce that way," he said unsteadily. "She's a queer gir-rl."

Solemn Ike Duval put on his derby hat, preparatory to leaving the Alhambra Palace. "Them movies!" he jeered. "Did you ever hear of a woman killing a man like that, MacErcher?"

"Movies aren't what they used to be. I liked her better in her first plays, 'Hearts Afire' or 'Mexican Love,' eight—ten years ago. Too much of this trick acting now. She used to be the real thing when she was playing with old John Dawn."

"Dead stuff," said Ike with a yawn. "What's a good place to get beer?"

The Grady car was waiting when the Gradys came out of the theater. Old Tim was not yet entirely accustomed to his vast wealth. He surveyed pridefully the car's dark green gloss, with the tiny harp and initials on its door panels. He made loud show of drawing on his gloves of staring around him, of giving commands to his giant Negro chauffeur as he stood with a foot on the running board. Padriac was nervous, impatient of the observant crowds. He urged his father inside.

Tim looked about for some acquaintance he might patronize.

"How are ye, Thorn, boy!" he shouted to an elderly gentleman approaching through the Broadway throng.

A slight frown appeared on the gray, supercilious face of the man addressed, but he made no sign.

"How are ye, Thornwood?" Still Tim Grady got no answer. "Good afternoon, Mister-r Clay!"

Mr. Clay lifted his grave silk hat. "How do you do, Sir?"

"Well, I do pretty dar-rn well," old Tim muttered as he climbed in the dark green car.

He rolled away, proud of his car, proud of his giant black chauffeur, mightily proud of having been saluted publicly by a Clay, than whom, God knows, is nothing better.

Citizens on the sidewalk stared after the Grady car ten minutes.

" 'S Mr. Grady himself," said Citizen A. "Tim Grady!" cried Citizen B. "I don't believe a word of it!" said Citizen C. "It ain't possible. Why, that fellow walks or talks just like you or me."

Black Tom, the chauffeur, swerved the green car west through traffic to Eighth Avenue. Tim ordered him to a halt before a small pawnshop. Above the doors a gilt sign: "A. Bliss"; in the windows mandolins and toilet sets; the entrance iron-barred, looking exceedingly black within. This was a place much patronized by actresses, jobless men, and by persons who had become possessed of pawnable jewelry and silverware in queer, mysterious ways.

Padriac waited in the green limousine while old Tim strode through the doors. Mr. Gus Bliss, the shop's proprietor, left his iron-grilled cage and came with haste to meet Tim Grady. Tim's mottled red-gray face was furious. His lips clapped open and shut, emitting only harsh hisses.

Bliss was a small, soft man. His doglike eyes were frightened. He belonged to a trade accursed; a pawnbroker is insulted, threatened, hated and despised by all men; none is more truly of the tribe of Ishmael. Gus Bliss was wary. Like the kicked cur, he was quick to show his teeth. It does not seem possible (perhaps only Anthony knew it) in his Sephardic heart of hearts Gus Bliss wanted to be a gentleman and a poet.

"Where'd ye get that photo?" roared old Tim, pointing a shaking finger. "What do ye mean showing the face of Rose Dawn to all the war-rld in your dirty rabbit-den, ye louse?"

The pawnbroker did not dispute a matter of mixed metaphors. He rubbed his hands. Tim was pointing to a large silver frame which enclosed a picture of Rose Dawn, her head lying on her two palms pressed together.

Old Tim made furious gestures. He tore off his hat and rumpled his red-gray hair. His hooked nose quivered. The purple pouches beneath his eyes inflated like small balloons. By a head he topped Gus Bliss as he leaned over, swinging his right fist in short arcs. Old Tim Grady was a fighting fool, especially when confronting small men.

"Well, Sir," the pawnbroker stammered, "a very fine gentleman left that with me, as pledge. Many fine gentlemen have dealings with me. Mr. Gay Deleon—"

"Gay Deleon, the notar-rious gambler?"

"Well, Sir—"

"What does he mane selling the photo of my intinded wife to ye," old Tim foamed, "like as if she was a common wench! I'll have him hanged! I'll have him jailed! I'll give him a kick! Give it here!"

He made a lurch for the picture, wrenched it from its shelf, smashed the glass with his fist. "Ouch! O, mother Macree!" Old Tim sucked his knuckles. He tore out the picture of lovely Rose Dawn, stuffing it in his overcoat pocket. He threw down the silver frame, jumping on it. In swift cycle his wrath had passed from Bliss to Deleon to the silver picture frame. And now that the frame lay stunned and lifeless, old Tim Grady's wrath was calmed.

He smiled grimly. "How much do I owe ye?"

Death lingers in a second. Gus Bliss hesitated twice a second. In that time old Tim's quick roving eye had passed around the shop, over the cheap suitcases, the clocks, the stacks of blankets. In a glass case he saw the serpent knife.

A heavy-bladed weapon, steel and silver. Around hilt and haft, marvelously intricate, was coiled the gold-green serpent. Its rattles were clearly marked. Its scales shone. Its emerald eyes winked and blinked at old Tim Grady, venomously hypnotic. Apparently it stirred and moved.

"Be Jasus!" said Tim Grady, watching it strangely, "I'd like to have that thing! How much 's it cost?"

"Well, Sir," said Gus Bliss. "That'll cost you pretty high."

Outside the green car waited. The evening grew darker and colder, but Tim Grady did not come out. Padriac had drawn forth a note-book; with a pencil-stub he busily figured costs and percents. Tom Jefferson, the giant black chauffeur, beat his breast for the cold. He drew up his coat collar till only his great white eyes shone in the gathering night.

A girl, passing hastily down Eighth Avenue, thought those white roving eyes were for her. She halted stock still, planted on her stumpy, fawn-colored legs. Her dry red hair frizzled with anger. She clasped her imitation sable coat about her breast. Shop lights now flashing on shone in the eyes of Tom Jefferson as he met the girl's stare.

The girl stuck out her tongue. "Go ahead and get a eyeful, you big baboon!" She approached, putting her hands on her hips. Provokingly she stared through the limousine windows at Padriac Grady. "Make your nigger keep from looking at me!"

Padriac glanced up, rubbed his chin, then resumed his calculations. A half dozen street loafers sauntered up. "What's the coon doing to you, Dot?" Their weak, white faces scowled at Tom Jefferson. "Don't you try fooling with a white girl, black boy!"

Tom Jefferson looked stonily ahead of him. Apparently he had not heard. But beneath his fur coat his giant shoulder muscles rippled. Cold, hard, immitigable as black granite.

The slow approach of a policeman drove the loafers and Dot away.

Within the pawnshop old Tim Grady and Gus Bliss yet bargained over the price of the serpent knife. Keenly they fought. Old Tim was shrewd. Liberal as the wind in his gifts, but tight as a Scotchman in a bargain. His glances brightened. He would make the bargain hard, even for death.

"This here knife," said Gus Bliss, leaning over his counter, his soul warmed by converse with such a fine gentleman as Mr. Grady. "This here knife was left by me by Mr. Pete Lopez, the gentleman who reads fortunes."

"Twelve dollars!" growled old Tim. "Not anither cent, if I bar-rn for it!"

"Forty-eight, and I lose money. This here knife was used by Mr. John Dawn in the movies. He cut another gentleman's throat in 'Hearts Afire.' "

"Far-rteen dollars!" old Tim said, banging down his fist. "I'd not do more for my own mother."

Mr. Bliss threw wide his palms. Tears trembled in his soft brown eyes. Lovingly he fondled the serpent knife, broad steel blade, light silver handle.

"Thirty-six dollars," he said gently. "This here knife is one beautiful piece of work. It would be a fine thing to give to a lady."

The pawnbroker balanced the weapon on his palm. Old Tim's fingers itched for it. The weighty blade slipped from Bliss's nervous hand. Point deep it drove in the soft pine counter. The serpented haft vibrated to music inaudibly fine, as though the snake's belled tail had begun a warning poisoned song.

Old Tim pulled it out, but it cut the pads of his fingers; again the knife dropped, again stuck point first in the wood. Tim Grady cursed.

"A heavy blade," said Gus Bliss, "and sharp." He stroked the weapon once more. The artist's fiery passion was evident in his glance. "Thirty-six dollars," he said, softly.

"I'll split the difference," old Tim roared. "I ain't a nickel nurser. Eighteen dollars!" He flipped out a large wallet and fished through it.

"Split the difference between what?" asked Mr. Bliss.

"Between thirty-six and nothing," said old Tim Grady. "Eighteen! Count it. Smell it. Bite it." He slapped down the dirty bills.

Gus Bliss intoned the dolorous song of the Babylonian captivity as he wrapped the serpent knife in an old copy of the *Morning Mist,* strong twine about it. Its heavy blade could not cut through, nor its golden serpent sting. Old Tim watched with the pride of ownership, glorying in a bargain.

A blow upon Grady's shoulders. "Well, wad the divils look? It's auld Tim Grady!"

Old Tim turned furiously. A fat man had come in the shop, an illy-wrapped bundle under his arm. His nose was snub, set in a face round and red as an orange. He reeled, leaning heavily on Tim's shoulders. His breath was beery. Foolishly he winked and laughed. "Pawning yer pants, Tim?"

"Git off me, McGinty, ye drunken mick!" old Tim said with dignity, giving a blow to the fat fellow. "Don't ye know a gintleman when ye see one?"

McGinty's laughter faded. "Why so uppty-duppty?" he inquired. "Do ye think I'll take an-ny airs from ye, Tim Grady? Ain't we fri'nds?"

"We do not belong to the same class of society," said old Tim Grady, brushing the sleeve McGinty had polluted.

"Ay," said McGinty, with half a sneer, watching the wrapping of the knife. "Up to yer auld tricks, Tim!" He nudged old Grady.

"What do ye mane?" Tim roared in thick brogue.

Winking often and drunkenly, McGinty leaned over and whispered close to old Tim's ear. McGinty was tall, yet he had to stand on his toes. Gus Bliss listened, but he could not hear what words McGinty spoke.

". . . The bloody moon. . . ."

What whisper was it in that darkly lighted pawnshop from McGinty's drunken lips? Old Tim Grady clutched to the counter. His knees sagged. Why did old Grady's jowls fall slack? Why wilted the fury from his face? What ague of terror made his body shake?

"Ye can trust yer fri'nd Dinnis McGinty," said McGinty, giving another poke to old Tim's ribs.

Blood came back in old Tim's face. He turned in a fury, waving his fists so viciously that McGinty was sobered. Bliss crouched behind his counter, muttering: "Gentlemen! Gentlemen! Pleasant gentlemen!" McGinty stumbled backward, his arm over his face.

"I'll turn ye over to the police, Din McGinty, if you open your mouth! I'll get you!"

"Try and do it," said McGinty. "Try and do it."

Old Tim Grady snatched up the wrapped serpent knife, hurrying out to where his son and black Tom awaited him. Even through the thick paper wrappings the heavy blade felt cold.

And his heart felt cold. It was the ebb-flow of alcohol.

II. THE DOG-FACED SPHINX

HERE you see again that dark and silent man, Mr. Anthony Anthony, organizer and head of the Argus Agency (private detecting neatly done). He sits in his hotel room thinking of several things, while his ears are filled with the chattering of one Wigley Arsen, star reporter of the *Morning Mist.*

Arsen talked of prohibition, the income tax, women, and the movies, all of which are very important things these days. Rose Dawn's photograph, standing boldly on Anthony's table, brought up talk of the movies. Arsen's words (Arsen was a wit) buzzed here and there, bright little bees in flowers.

"Men like the movies because the heroines are silent," said Arsen, pulling at his watch-chain, and waiting for the expected laugh.

It was not clever. Anthony did not laugh. Arsen tried again.

"When God speaks on the movie screen," said Arsen, "He always speaks in old Gothic caps." That brought a smile. Arsen was pleased. "When a movie matron is shown sewing little silk diapers," he said, hysterical with his own laughter, "the orchestra makes music to imitate the rustle of a stork's wings."

And so on.

Anthony's rooms were adorned in bizarre fashion. Old weapons—rusty guns, swords, pikes, hung on the walls or stood in corners. There was a sea-rotted gray ship's plank over the fireless mahogany mantel, its lettering—"777"—dimly illegible. A mounted giant flying fish, stiff wings outvanning, goggle-eyes popping, smirked like a winged Assyrian devil, a Tiamtu of abominations.

Queerest of all was the floor rug, an intricate design embodying the essence of nonsense. Arsen thought it interesting. "What does this fool design mean, Tony?" Arsen asked Anthony Anthony.

Seven blue pyramids beside a winding yellow river (or perhaps a winding snake). A three-humped green camel bending elegantly to drink the river, if it was a river, to bite the snake, if it was a snake. Set in this scene of rural Egyptian placidity, a dog-faced Sphinx slept on its paws. Its chin lay on the sand; its brow was wrinkled with mysterious canine thoughts; its very ears were portentous. Now it seemed to raise its head, and listen. Upon its square dog face was hateful, sardonic laughter.

All this Arsen saw woven in the rug. And the journalist, curiously, was sober. As he peered, and watched that grinning face, Arsen fancied the rug held some secret meaning, portrayed a mighty truth just beyond his comprehension. The three-humped camel meant something. The snaky river meant something. Yes, surely that loathsome mirth meant something on the face of the dog-faced Sphinx!

The mystery tantalized Arsen, and in the midst of a word he became silent. His bright glance flickered. Some magician of the East in ancient ages had bewitched that rug, had labored over it in the sweat of his soul, for centuries long spinning into it his occult knowledge of the meaning of life. Bewitched it was, for the dog-faced Sphinx opened its eyes, and yapped.

Over the left shoulder of the Sphinx six tufted threads of deepest red formed a full round moon.

The riddle of existence! And used for a rug. The feet of stupid generations scuffled it, their placid rockers plowed it, their blind fat eyes looked full on it, ignorant and dull. Something terrible in the weaving of that rug! Arsen was superstitious.

Leaning over curiously, Arsen took from the table the photograph of Rose Dawn. Unmistakable her clean, piquant, almost boyish face, her drooping mouth, fair curls, marvelously clear eyes. She was dressed in Spanish costume, with black cobweb lace mantilla, tall tortoise comb, and a rose in her hair. Hers was a face known to millions, known better than the face of any other woman was ever known before, than even the countenance of the Madonna, than even the fabled beauty of that queenly harlot who razed great Troy.

"I'm not what might be called a youngster any more, Tony, nor what might be called a fool." Arsen paused, but Anthony did not agree. The reporter was irritated. He would allow no man even tacitly to admit him a fool. "Well, I'm not! You can take my word for it. But if ever I could be a fool for a woman, *this* would be the woman!"

Arsen looked long at the photograph.

"So she is going to marry Tim Grady," mused Arsen. "I think I could—if I were that sort—kill a man to have her for just one night. Though that's a Hell of a thing to say."

Anthony opened wide his black, startling large eyes. He sneered. "Some time," he said, "some man may." Then he laughed, but not happily.

Wigley Arsen was looking at the dog-faced Sphinx, the riddle of whose meaning would never cease to fret him till he solved it or he died. "You know Rose Dawn?" he asked. But Anthony shook his head.

"Old Tim Grady is a fool to marry her," Anthony said morosely. "*I'd* not do it."

"I would," said Arsen,

"And you would die happy," said Anthony.

"Of course I would."

"So will old Tim Grady."

"Grady will do what?" Arsen asked.

"He will die."

Wigley Arsen glanced at his toes, and from them at the dog-faced Sphinx. Mystery in the Sphinx's smirk, as in Anthony's words. Or again, there might be nothing.

Announcing himself by a knock, Ike Duval tiptoed in. His jowl was set like bitter stone. His small eyes did not blink. He gave a half salute: "Evening, Chief." He rolled his derby on his forefinger, flashing suspicious glances about him. His eye on Arsen seemed to say: "That man bears watching." On Anthony: "He's a queer un." On his own face in a mirror: "I've seen him in the rogues' gallery."

If there was anything secret about Solemn Ike, it was an open secret that he was a second-rate detective, some dogger of suspected spouses and peeper-in at keyholes. His very shoes were in the police fashion. But he was sharp and shrewd, and he was tenacious. His surly mind could bear hate for long.

"Everything's pretty good," Ike said, in answer to a question from Anthony. "Grady's moved out to Dawnrose now. We get good grub. Christmas Eve's coming soon, when he'll be getting married. A big blowout. By the looks of the wind, it'll be full moon."

"Is Grady still harping on that?" Anthony asked alertly. "Does he want me to assign another man?"

"No need, Chief. Grady's got a big black hope now, name o' Tom. And *I* ain't a-scared of no moon."

"Funny," Anthony told Wigley Arsen when Ike had gone out. "Grady has some wild notion that the full moon is bad for him. He's superstitious as a goat, you know. He's asked the Argus Agency to guard him. So I've assigned him Ike Duval."

Arsen was not giving attention. That curious rug fascinated him. He wanted to ask Anthony its meaning again, if Anthony knew. Anthony's remark hummed in his ears: "Tim Grady will die!"

Tim Grady, the rich man! It did not seem plausible. He was a millionaire. Well, well, indeed (thought Arsen); but we all die!

III. REMEMBER YOUR SINS, TIM GRADY!

A CRYSTAL globe clear as water, round as a giant dewdrop, was throned on a black velvet pedestal. Shiwa, God of Faces, blew incense smoke through flaring nostrils. Lamps hung and swung like little ruddy jewels. Curtains pasted with gilt stars and crescent moons shut out all light of the cold December day. By the wall on a tripod rested a hemispherical bowl of water, to which a nickeled pipe led. Occasionally blue fires flickered on the surface of the water; flamed, danced, died down without a glow.

Old Tim Grady strode into this sorcerer's den of Pete Lopez, who passed as clairvoyant. Tim strode; but fear was in his step. His heels were cold; his spine felt brittle. He pulled and pulled at his gloves. Pete Lopez, sitting curled up in a chair like a little shriveled spider, watched old Tim cunningly, quite a little amused.

"Ye are the fellow they call the Sear Nit?"

"Le Sieur Nuit," murmured Pete, pulling at his ragged mustache.

"All r-right. I don't need to tell ye my name, since," (cunningly) "if ye're as smar-rt as ye think ye are, you know it already. And if no, 'tis no harm. I want you to understand in the beginning that I think all this is non-sinse. I don't believe a war-rd of it!" Tim pounded fist into palm. "Feed it to the fool women, but you and me are too smar-rt, huh?"

Pete Lopez, small as a monkey, and with face nearly as dark, waved a gracious hand. His speech held a slight Southern slur which can't be duplicated. "Of course, of course, Mr. Grady. Have you come to see me about your marriage to Rose Dawn?"

Tim Grady sat down sharply, feeling his knees. "So ye know my name, do ye?" he roared, somewhat frightened. "How did ye do that?"

Lopez closed his beady eyes. "You were born in Ireland—" he began carefully. ("County Car-rk," old Tim nodded, watching Lopez strangely.) "In eighteen-sixty—sixty—" ("1863," gasped Tim, excited. "The ilivinth of July, to a dot. How did ye know *that?*") "I know all things," said Pete Lopez drolly.

He spoke slowly, groping for words: "Very intricate planetary aspect. . . .Warring stars. . . .Influences of Jupiter, Mars, Bacchus. . . . Love. . . ." ("Married twice by church," said old Tim Grady. "And many another woman besides.") "Great wealth. . . ." ("I reckon I ain't bankrupt," said old Tim Grady.) "But troubles, troubles. . . ." ("Ay, I've had 'em," said old Tim Grady.)

All this with many pressings of his brow, many long fits of brooding on the part of Pete Lopez. Occasionally he opened a hidden faucet, causing blue fire to lick on the face of the water-bowl. Now he arose, pacing up and with quick catlike strides.

"A night of full red moon when you were born, Mr. Grady!"

"What do ye mane?" Old Tim's tongue was thick. "Don't speak to me o' the bloody moon!" he cried.

Lopez spread out a chart, crinkling and black, on which astral orbits were marked by white ellipses and dots. Like an angel in flight from star to star Lopez's lean brown finger pointed. Tim Grady breathed slowly. His complexion was pasty. He held a handkerchief to his temples.

"Your son and daughter will give you trouble," whispered Lopez, watching old Tim to see how his words were taken. "And the stars do not speak well, Mr. Grady, of your marriage to Rose Dawn."

Old Tim's lips muttered foolishly. For a long time he could not speak. His hooked nose quivered in some passion too vast for other utterance.

"They don't? Ay, no! I see 'tis an evil sign. O, damn—" He breathed heavily, smearing his paws over the chart. With an oath he dug his strong fingers into the paper. "O, damn to all the star-rs!"

He leaped up, tearing the black map strip by strip, growling at it, mad as a dog. "I don't believe your dirty nonsinse! A trick's in it! It's a lie!" He stamped and kicked the torn paper on the floor. "The curse of Cromwell on ye! What are ye after-r being after-r?"

Lopez watched calmly, still amused. "Look!" he said sibilantly.

One of the red ceiling lamps was reflected in the crystal globe. It shone upon that convex, gibbous-imaging mirror in a round red fire.

"The full red moon," Lopez said with a sneer. "Your evil sign. Watch out for it!"

"What do ye know?" howled old Tim Grady, swaying, falling to a chair. "What do ye know?"

Pete Lopez, known also as Greasy Pete, called up a private telephone number when old Tim Grady had staggered out. He got Gay Deleon, the gambler, on the wire.

"Old Tim Grady was just in to have me read the stars. He's afraid for some reason of the full moon. . . . Thought I'd give him a scare. Told him he is a fool to marry Rose Dawn. . . . All right, all right. But he is a fool. . . . O, no. I don't wish him that, Gay. . . ."

Pete put on his greatcoat and went out, no doubt to consult another astrologer. For though he knew himself a fake, yet he was a believer, and there are stars.

IV. BLACK TOM JEFFERSON

MA HIGGS, mother of lovely Rose Dawn, was a whale of a lady. She had creased, blubbery arms, breasts, and chins. If these be beauty, she made the most of them. Her hair was gold faded to hideous brass. She had once been prize beauty in the Harvey eating-house, Moline, Kansas. Had married the snappiest drummer who ever ate fly-specked pie at Moline while the old Santa Fe local waited, and snorted, and took on water. Had been paramour of a traveling actor who traveled with her to Evansville, Illinoy, and pursued his travels alone. Had made her living by cooking, scrubbing, and by putting her daughter in the movies. She thought her life had been hard, which was true; and often wept over it, which was not pleasant.

For the past fifteen years, since Rose Dawn (then Rose Lovely) at the age of ten had entered the movies, Ma Higgs had lived according to her desserts. Her nails were manicured as often as she pleased. She stuffed herself with greasy sweets until her tongue fermented. Her diamonds were probably the largest and ugliest ever dug from the dirty earth. In short, she enjoyed the varied satisfactions of being rich.

Out of the clay, the poppy. Out of the mire, the lily. Out of Ma Higgs, out of a snappy drummer and a traveling actor, out of Moline and Evansville, beautiful Rose Dawn. Could anything so fair and sweet come to earth that way? Did not an angel bring her here, unborn of flesh, wrapped in the pinfeather down of his wing?

Ma Higgs answered a telephone ring. Rose Dawn, beautifully marcelled, gowned, and tinted for the afternoon, sat on a divan. Her legs were thrown sideways like a mermaid's tail, if mermaids' tails were ever clad in spider-web hose. Her head rested at an angle on both her palms. Her great blue eyes, staring past the outer window, were softened with a hint of tears. It was a pose in which she had been often photographed, and which gave full value to her fair, exquisite beauty. Each of her poses and gestures was always like that, perfection of grace, of an artful artlessness which was true as life. Two interviewers (male, stammering, frog-chinned and titwit-voiced) had just been dismissed.

Even as she swore over the telephone, Ma Higgs admired her daughter's pose. To be sure, Ma Higgs loved Rose. In her she dreamed of her own lost beauty. More, Rose was a meal ticket.

Ma Higgs shouted: "Get off the wire, you loafer!" She slammed up the ear-piece with a bang, continuing to mutter. "Gay Deleon ringing you up again, dearie," she said. "You ain't got any business fooling around him, now we got old Grady hooked."

A thin frown was on Rose's clear forehead. She tossed her head, but said nothing. She was afraid of her mother.

"Deleon's only another good-for-nothing like that John Dawn," said Ma Higgs spitefully. She had always hated Rose's husband, could not forgive him even now that he was dead. "And it was only God's own mercy you ever got rid of *him*."

Rose Dawn put her hand to her mouth; it might have been an acted gesture. She did not reply. She arose, going to her room. A quarter of an hour later Mrs. Higgs found her in the bathroom, washing her red eyes. But a touch of powder, a touch of paint, and that was soon mended.

Old Tim Grady came in. He looked about him with a large air of proprietorship, his hands in his pockets. And why not? He paid for these expensive hotel rooms. He would pay for Rose Dawn. He was rich, and his money would buy anything.

"Arrah, Rosie, me colleen bawn!" he greeted with jocular brogue.

Rose gave him her fingers, but did not kiss him. She hoped she would never kiss him. Now he smelled of alcohol, and his ragged white moustache was dirty with cigars.

"A week," said old Tim, pressing her hand, breathing thickly, bending close as though he would gobble her up, bone and flesh, between his strong yellow teeth. "Only a week more, Rosie! Think of it!"

Rose Dawn tried to smile. She had thought of it, many and many a night alone. But all her thoughts could not let her deny that old Tim Grady was rich. Mrs. Higgs smiled fatly. She folded her porcine arms on her breast. Truly that light, however dull it was, which shone in her round little blue eyes was light of motherly love. She loved Rose, wished all good things for her. The greatest good she knew, here or in Heaven, was to marry Rose to a very rich man. Her daughter would never know, God willing, even with children of her own, how Mrs. Higgs had schemed and worked to bring this marriage to pass. Thinking of her own tribulations, Ma Higgs sniffled.

Grady's flaming, hard eyes passed about the room. "You're well fixed," he said with satisfaction. " 'Twill serve for a week. I've moved out to Dawnrose now. Everything's ready for you, Rosie. The painters are still about, but the mess of the carpenters is being cleared up by some dirty dagoes. I've got a surprise for you, Rosie. Wait. Close your eyes. I brought it with me. 'Tis what the old imperors used to give their imperesses."

Old Tim essayed a jocose tone, but his normal snarling voice broke through. He put fingers to Rose's arm, which quivered at the touch. Mrs. Higgs smiled; she would have liked to dance and whoop. She rolled her eyes to the ceiling.

Once before a bridal home had been built for Rose Dawn; none such as Tim Grady's great new Hudson mansion, Dawnrose. "Red Rose," John Dawn had called that little Hollywood home. She had been more easily pleased then. Her heart had been younger, not so old and hard as it was now at twenty-five. Red Rose was gone to smoke and flame. Over John Dawn rolled illimitable oceans.

The ash; the drowned; the dead . . . forget them! But thinking of that old time. . . . Thinking of the dead. . . . Old Tim Grady was genially talking.

Old Tim's quick glance rolled about him. He started towards a small snapshot lying on the music cabinet. Mrs. Higgs made a motion to snatch it, but Tim forestalled her. Mrs. Higgs was panicky.

"Who's this?" old Tim growled, snapping the picture with his thumb.

It was a tiny photograph, faded by sun, frayed at the edges, of a young man. Through the haze of a cigaret he smiled. Half of his torso was visible; he was sitting on a horse. Old Tim's fingers trembled. Surely a dead man had never looked with eyes so keen and bright!

"That's that John Dawn," Mrs. Higgs said nervously. "That's him in 'Hearts Afire' eight years ago."

"I never set eyes on him before," said old Tim, looking darkly at the snapshot. He twitched with jealousy, the curse of libertines.

On a pretext, Rose had gone. Tim flopped down on the divan, spreading his knees apart. Mrs. Higgs seated herself beside her future son-in-law (who was her senior by a dozen years). She coughed; she bustled; finally she nipped at his sleeve with her fingers.

"I believe in being practical," said she, looking over her shoulder to see if Rose was within hearing. "That poor dove is so romantic."

"What poor dove?" old Tim snarled, drawing away from her, whom he thoroughly hated.

"Why, Rose."

"O!" Tim gave a hard, sly laugh.

"She flung herself away on that Dawn when she wasn't no more than sixteen or seventeen," went on Ma Higgs, "without a thought to the morrow, or the roof that covered her, or her poor Ma who had worked so hard to make her what she was, and give her a chance, and let her live a life where she wouldn't have to do scrubbing on her bare knees. . . ."

Her talk rambled on and on. She could talk more, saying less, than any other woman in captivity. It would be vastly wearisome to chronicle her circumlocutions, for they caused a sickness of the flesh, a dizziness of the ears, a vacuity of the medulla oblongata. Old Tim scratched his red-gray hair, paying no attention.

Higgs lengthily arrived at the point. "You've got your son, and your daughter, and no doubt they think they're millionaires, and go throwing your money around like drunken sailors, and spending it here and there. And they'll have children, and get married, and come to you to feed them—"

"My boy Padriac will spend no money he don't 'arn," old Tim said drily, breaking in when he could.

"I've known him to buy orchids for Rose," Higgs lied, slyly nodding and nudging. "If she wasn't too sensible a girl to marry a young fellow dependent on his father for his clothes, and his shoes, and his neckties, and—"

"What's that?" roared old Tim. His red eyes glittered. "Padriac's been seeing Rose?"

"Ah, I thought you didn't know of his going-ons," said Higgs, with low pleasure. "It's a wise farther knows his own son."

"I'll cut him off without a copper! I'll drive him to the street!"

"Be that as it may," said Mrs. Higgs, secure in the satisfaction of a perfect liar. "But with things as they are, and the wedding only a week away, and you and Rose about to be married, and she expecting and intending to be your wife—"

"What in the name of auld Ireland are ye driving at?" yelled Grady, reverting to his native brogue.

"There ought to be a settlement," Mrs. Higgs said, firm and defiant. "She and hers ain't going to be deprived by you and yours."

"Listen to me, woman! Are ye asking me far-r money?"

Mrs. Higgs withdrew a hitch. Old Tim was raging red. Higgs had always known him as a most liberal man. She did not understand that at a demand for money, or a demand for anything, he shut up tighter than the mountains.

"We only want what's right, and just, and square, and—"

" 'We want!' Who do ye think you're after-r marrying me to?"

"Rose, I trust," the woman faltered.

"Thin Rosie can trust me! I'm not marrying you, and don't ye forgit it! I'm marrying Rose, and nothing will stop me. But if ye don't watch your step, ye'll be left on an iceber-rg in Bar-rneo. If I wa'n't a gintleman, I'd say what no gintleman says, and tell ye to go to the devil."

Mrs. Higgs indignantly panted. Her small eyes closed, so tight the eyelids screwed in. She gasped; she wheezed; she snortled; expressing her emotions in all the ways a lady can without swearing.

To himself old Grady thought: "I've star-rted ye right, ye old yellow crow! Ye'll not be after-r going after-r me again."

To herself Mrs. Higgs thought: "Just you wait we're married to you! I'll make you jump over the grand pianny when I sneeze, you loud-mouthed old mick!"

She retired in billowing spasms. After whispered words beyond the door Rose Dawn returned to pour tea for Tim. Tensely Tim watched the soft movements of Rose's shoulders, his huge hands clasping and unclasping. She will be mine, all mine, fire and light and heat, the flawless woman! ran the voiceless burden of his ecstasy.

Rose was uneasy beneath that fierce gaze. Hot were Tim's glances, yet her spine shivered. Little words: "Cream?—How much sugar?" ("To Hell with it," growled old Tim Grady.) Little gestures: the turn of a wrist, the quivering of one eyebrow. Little ticking of a clock. Little pulsing of hearts.

"You said you have a surprise for me, Tim."

Tim smote his hands together. "Bejabbers, I forgot!" He went to the outer door, calling loudly out the hotel corridor. The door was filled with an enormous shape. Obedient to Tim's imperious beckoning, Tom Jefferson, the giant Negro, came stalking in. Hat in hand; his shoulders heaving; his white eyes half closed. He seemed to bend to get beneath the crosstree of the door.

"What do ye think of 'im?" asked Tim Grady, grinning. He gave Tom's breast a thump.

Startled, Rose glanced at Tom's hands to see what gift he carried. "No," said old Tim, understanding her. "This is the surprise—him, Tom Jifferson." Another thump on Tom's heaving chest. "Ain't he some black fellow?" Grady asked with high pride.

Tom's impassive face showed a fleeting expression of contempt. His skin was so intense in blackness it seemed a ludicrous paint. He stood looking at the carpet.

"The law says you can't have slaves," said Grady. "But howsoever that be, Tom Jifferson is mine. Three hundred a month I pay him, which is more than nigger iver got before. And he's mine! Turn around, Tom."

The Negro obeyed, heeling slowly. His black rosewood countenance was fierce. A Thor in sable. Stupid, stolid, iron power.

"Bend up your arms, Tom!—Rise on your heels—Take a good breath!—Did ye iver see such lungs?"

With childish delight Grady pointed out to Rose the strength in that body; impersonally, as though Tom had been an elephant.

"And more, he's highly iducated," boasted Grady, jamming hands in pockets and rocking on heels. "He's been to the Univarsity. He's a doctor, and knows his Latin and his Greek."

Tom Jefferson stood patiently, awaiting what next.

Rose Dawn nervously pulled at her handkerchief. The giant terrified her. The whiteness of his eyes was like white heat, and in his stolid air was hint of terrible, chained devils! And when those chains should break. . . .

"I'm going to give him to ye, Rosie," said Grady. " 'Tis what the imperors did for their imperesses. He'll serve ye honestly."

Rose Dawn laughed with hysteria. "What on earth!"

Now Tom Jefferson's half closed eyes lifted from the floor, looking full on Rose Dawn. The woman twisted a ring on her finger till her flesh was scored. She did not meet that glance. Tom's nostrils quivered. He looked away again. One glance. But Rose Dawn would see that full glance upon her once again.

"Send him away, Tim!"

"Women are fools," Tim Grady stated from the depths of his wisdom. He was sulky because his gift had not been better received.

Long after old Grady and Tom were gone Rose Dawn sat alone, watching a little fire which burned in the grate. On the hot bars lay, white and an ash, but still glowing, the little snapshot of John Dawn as he had been in "Hearts Afire." Old Tim Grady had thrown it to the consuming flame. Dawn's features were gray and cherry. Had that curling crisp paper been touched, all would have faded to dust. But his deep black eyes were yet two points of light.

"I was peeking through the door," said Mrs. Higgs. "Grady's big black nigger give me the creeps."

She moved her jaws eternally. Rose did not listen. She watched the fire. Its black smoke arising seemed the face of Tom Jefferson.

And in the deeps of coals burned her last token of wild John Dawn, consumed to utter forgetting. Thus to old memory, thus to love, thus to the dead. He and she had once, Rose Dawn thought, played "Hearts Afire" together when all the world like that was flame.

V. ALMS FOR THE POOR

EVERY rich man gives to causes not always written down in the books of the Associated Charities. These may be poor relations, old servants, old masters, or ladies who, once paid for their beauty, are now paid for their more precious silence.

To Mr. Todd, second or third member of Todd, Todd, Todd, and Todd, old Tim Grady's personal lawyers, two men presented themselves on the afternoon before Christmas. Both came for money. The first of these two men, old Thornwood Clay, wore a silk hat and received a stipend from Tim Grady. The second, Dinnis McGinty, wore a cap and received blackmail. He, of course, was not a gentleman.

Higgleson Todd was a square man with a square bald head. He appeared to be constituted of something heavier than mercury. When he sat down, it was as though he were anchored and cemented to his chair. Higgleson Todd was cordial to old Thornwood Clay, for Clay was of the ancient and honorable Clays, and quite as good as a Todd. He was less suave to Dinnis McGinty. Why those two came to him on the quarter for their doles from Grady, the lawyer did not know. He suspected some sort of blackmail, and did not want to get mixed up in it. For, looking at it baldly, blackmail is an unpleasant thing for a gentleman to get mixed up in.

"How are you, Sir?" he bubbled to Clay, discreetly sliding a check across his desk. Todd did it with an air totally absent. His soul might be in Tahiti for all notice he took of the check held lightly in his fingers. "How is your son Thornwood?"

"Very well, Sir. He's in Florida."

Old Clay spoke drily. He wist not of the Todds. He put on his gold-rimmed glasses, gazing vacantly about him. Over the head of McGinty he stared as though McGinty were a louse, a creature not recognizable by the Clays. Five years or more, four times the year, Thornwood Clay and Dinnis McGinty had met in the offices of the multiple Todds, and taken their checks, and gone. They had never spoken, but their breath had been like snorts. Nothing so devilish proud as your beggar.

"Miss Dubby! Miss Dubby!" Todd boomed, hammering his desk. "Show Mr. Clay to the door," he ordered the frail-haired girl who appeared.

The lawyer watched old Clay stalk out the door, thin and crackling as an old dried twig. "He'll throw that away in the market, or in some gambling hell," the lawyer thought. "Bet he's tossed away a million in his time. Well, he can afford it."

Todd could not tell, no one could tell, that only Tim Grady's charity kept Clay from the breadlines and a couch on a park bench. Clay's back was stiff as though made of gold.

"Well!" Todd slapped his thighs, turning brusquely to McGinty.

McGinty was a fat, marvelous red-faced fellow much bloated by drink. His eyes were red, too; his nose a positive purple; his teeth green. Since Tim Grady had begun to make money, McGinty had done no work. Idleness had wrecked his strong frame more terribly than forty years of slavery in Siberian mines.

McGinty laid his paws on the desk. "I want me money!" He wiped his nose with his sleeve. He'd take no uppishness from anyone. "Me money, Mister-r L'yer."

Todd waved a check as though it were not quite dry. "Mr. Grady tells me, McGinty, that you've made threats to him. You've been after him for more than your regular allowance. Mr. Grady'll not stand for it."

"He *will* stand for it," McGinty lowered. "He can affar-rd it. Put that in your face and chew it. Ain't him I and me auld fri'nds?"

"He has consequently instructed me, McGinty," Todd said coldly, "to tell you that hereafter all funds from him will cease. You can expect nothing more."

McGinty wasn't listening. "What's that?" he demanded dully, scratching a hairy ear.

"I say you'll get nothing more!" Todd slapped his ringing thighs. "I don't want to see you in here again. Clear out!"

McGinty gulped. He laughed hoarsely, his mirth increasing till it swallowed his face. He leered at the big-headed lawyer. "Niver s-spit in the wind," was his sage advice. "Tim knows better than to tr-ry anything like that on his auld fri'nd Dinnis. What's the matter? Is he saving his money for this pitcher woman he's after-r marrying?"

"You heard me!" The sneer at Rose Dawn brought blood to Todd's big face. "You get out!'

"Ye 're damned right I hear-rd ye! And ye hear-r me!" McGinty smashed fists on the desk. "If you're fri'nd to Timothy Grady, tell him he's putting r-rope around his nick—"

"Careful, care—"

"Will that rum-soaked hog tr-ry to ditch Dinnis McGinty? Half of his is mine! If he but tr-ries to double-cross me—double- cross *me*—" McGinty closed a great hairy fist so tight the fingers seemed riveted—"I'll strangle him!"

Leaning back in his chair Todd listened to McGinty foam. He was rather pleased. "Do you know," he asked, breaking into McGinty's roars, "your threats can send you to jail for a year and a day? I have no compunction about sending you to jail, McGinty. One more crack from you, and I will!"

McGinty growled his laughter. "Ask Tim Grady before ye tr-ry that, Mr. L'yer. Send me to jail. But if ye do, by this duke," (a shake of his fist) "Tim Grady will hang!"

He stalked forth, proud as an Irishman.

VI. THE UNINVITED GUEST

WINTER night. Eve of Christmas. The moon is round and red as a tiger's eye.

Lights and violins bubble bright from Dawn-rose-on-the- Hudson. Old Grady's wedding night. The mansion is new, the violins, lights, guests are new, and the most expensive money can buy. The Hudson alone is old within this newness, and black with a scum of ice.

The wedding guests are those not too proud to know a rich man, and not too rich to be proud of knowing a rich man.

There is Dr. Russel Spencer, Grady's private physician and specialist on alcoholism. A lean man with tortoise-shell glasses and sandy beard. He has a droll turn of mind and putters when he talks.

There is Captain Peter van Chuch, a short-legged Dutch dunderhead, plump, full-faced; a man not yet old, though he is eating himself to death. Van Chuch was once of the fighting Navy, Annapolis and the rest, but found the going too rough. He skippers Grady's white yacht, the *Thorn*. The brass and trumpery of the Navy are on his face, but not the gray glint of the guns.

There is Higgleson Todd. There is young Buddy Schermerhorn, known as Squirmy, who would go any place for a drink. There is Mrs. Tiffany Bonnell, whose husband's cousin married a Sir. There is Mrs. Wiggs, whose grandfather was a gentleman.

Other guests. Large noses; lumpy panniers; dewlap jowls; gentlemen like barrels; ladies like potatoes. The aristocracy of the Republic is gathered, the hope of culture, many of whose immediate forebears could write no more legibly than a crow. A scene of fashion and disdain. The queen of beauty marries the king of money. If on this Christmas Eve you took the whirlwind's wings, seeing all gracious gatherings of the elect through all the universe from Beacon Street to Lakeshore Drive, from Canopus to the throne of Heaven, you could happen on no vaster assemblage of wit, fashion, money, pride, and astounding facial ugliness.

A famous event, this. From coast to coast it will be bruited. Mrs. Weinvoll, of Milwaukee, Wis.; Mrs. Dusty Hoag, of Waco, Tex., will read press accounts of the Grady-Dawn wedding with sighs, thinking such things a great deal finer than Heaven. As they likely are.

Wigley Arsen, who has already written about it for the *Morning Mist,* talks to Ike Duval. Ike is close by old Tim, watching him solemnly, following him from buffet to cellaret. Being unable to speak to Grady, Arsen addresses himself to Grady's shadow. A University man, a society scrambler, a snobbish sort of man is Wigley Arsen. His little brown moustache quivers but for the great; his restless eyes are continually flopping. His vice is to wag his tongue in the first person. He loves to couple his name with mighty names. At that, he is no fool.

"I understand from a friend of mine who is very close to Mr. Rockefeller that Mr. Grady is worth ten million dollars," says Arsen to Ike, with affable condescension.—"Yes, Sir." Ike speaks coldly. Arsen is a friend of Anthony Anthony, for which reason Ike thoroughly dislikes him.

"Young man!" old Tim bursts forth, having overheard, as Arsen intended. "Young man, ye can set it down in your paper-r I've got more than that!"

("My intimate friend, Mr. Timothy Grady, told me confidentially he is worth a cool twenty million," Arsen will repeat it in the city room of the *Morning Mist,* tilting back in his chair to listen to the whistles.)

Dr. Bellbender, of St. Cecil's, will officiate. A nice-voiced old gentleman, correct as a silk hat, generous to beggars, essential at reputable weddings. He is orthodox, but liberal; no theologian. Always condescendingly pleasant to Methodists; the yellows quote him as having said Jews are human. Solemn Ike, who esteems himself a physiognomist, does not trust Bellbender. He thinks Bellbender has the face of a baby- murderer.

"I come from a family of bachelar-rs," old Tim says, quite without humor. "But I ain't given that way. What do ye think of my third, Spincer? Speak up! I don't mind what ye say."

"Remarkably beautiful," Spencer murmurs thoughtfully. "She must be very healthy." He nods his eyes, thinking medical thoughts.

"I've outlived two already." Grady speaks with certain grimness. "I'll outlive her."

Dr. Spencer surveys Grady curiously.

Rose Dawn will be married in black. Close at her side, her fat old mother watches henwise, ready to cluck at the hawks. Mrs. Higgs knows the high worth of her daughter's virtue. Rose cannot afford to play with flame, as do the daughters of the rich. Only when Bellbender has pronounced his theoretically unshatterable words will Mrs. Higgs cease her maternal watch.

At the outer door, the porte-cochere entrance, Saltpeter, the button-faced butler, answers a ring. A bloated individual, purple of overcoat and nose, stumbles and tries to force entrance. "Auld Tim Grady live here? Tell 'im Mister-r McGinty wants to see him—see him at once. I'll brook no no-say!"

McGinty's breath was alcoholic. Saltpeter stood like stone. Uncertainly fumbling in his pockets, McGinty produced a card. "Me and me friend want to come in. Me fri'nd's card. I'm Mister-r McGinty."

"I heard you." With disdainful fingertips Saltpeter took the pasteboard. He read, holding the card beneath his nose, pencil jottings on a white, square card—

"Rose Dawn, you can't go on with it. John Dawn."

The butler tore the card, crumpling its shreds in his fist. "You're crazy," he said smugly. "Who gave you this?"

"A man outside. Ye call me cr-razy?"

"I said crazy."

"You're crazy yersilf!"

Saltpeter bumped McGinty with his knee, forcing him across the carriage drive. Shadows were in the lawns without. Saltpeter closed the door, shutting out all ghosts and demons.

VII. DOLLAR FOR DOLLAR

GAY DELEON, the gambler, when flush had chambers on Park Avenue. Luck running ill, he crept into some disastrous hole like a spider, there to hide and abide. He could spend more money in ill taste, and live on less money in good taste, than any other bounder in New York.

A young man, this Deleon, handsome, tricky, with a glance fatal to women. Famed as a man about town, if that's fame. He could spice you tales of any of the sacred women of Broadway as easily as he could point to cobbles on the street.—"In love with Marjorie Deveau, Squirmy? In '15 Marjorie and I—No, I've got that mixed. *That* was Rose Dawn. She gave me—" His thin, complacent drawl would foul an alabaster saint.

Old Thornwood Clay gambled that Christmas Eve. His face white as chalk, with silly, shaking hands, he played the money Todd had given him that afternoon. It dwindled. It was last; and it was lost.

Thin, austere, scion of a line of sportin' gentlemen, he played the game according to the code in a world which has lost its codes. Something pretty decent about him, too, though his gentility is now but a foolish form.

His black hour. He stroked his hands repeatedly. The face of Deleon was flushed and jubilant. There'd been high play tonight. Tonight. The night had come, on Park Avenue and the sky. Old Thornwood Clay had a vision, a dream of death—

He saw the old, proud house of the Clays toppling. It was a house of cards. He, last of the very ancient and honorable Clays, sank into quicksands without foundation. Still and dead as a scummy swamp all creation about him. Serpent eyes rimmed him round, a green light which did not flicker.

By God, the last dollar!

"Before we forget it, Mr. Clay, I hold a couple of thousand of your old IOUs I'd like to have you settle. Twenty-two hundred, to be exact."

"To be exact!" Old Clay mutters stupidly. He empties his pockets. Pens, smoking things, letters, a watch, wallet, but no money.

Deleon picks up one of the letters, making no bones of reading it. "Huh! So they bid you to the Grady wedding." Often, being drunk or sober, Gay Deleon has boasted that Rose Dawn loved him. Yet God help her clear blue eyes if that be true! For in ways unspeakable, Gay Deleon is lower than a dog.

A nasty fury arises in the gambler, compounded of many thoughts. He understands from old Clay's fumblings that Clay can't pay. With a low oath, whose occasion is unknown to Clay, Deleon raps his knuckles. "I'd like my money, Mr. Clay, and I'd like it now!"

Old Clay stutters, palely flushing. "I'm afraid I haven't got so much on me." He searches diligently again, though he knows it is vain.

"Is this how much a gentleman's word is worth?" Wisely sneering, Gay Deleon crumples the worthless IOUs. "They'll do to start a fire."

"Do you question me, Sir? Be assured, Mr. Deleon, I pay my debts! Always! I say, always! It is insulting, Sir, to question me. It is not gentlemanly."

"Either you pay me, or you don't. If you don't, you know what you are. You're a damned beggar, that's what you are!"

Clawing at his coat, fumbling with his eyeglass cord, shaking all over, Thornwood Clay gasps. "Sir? What did you say to me?"

"O, why don't you wring old Grady for the money?" Deleon is not willing to meet Clay's cold, furious glances. "You've got some sort of hold on him. Everybody knows you've been blackmailing him for years."

"Sir! Sir! I'll pay you dollar for dollar! Dollar for dollar!"

Old Clay is righteously indignant as though from his old claws even now he planked down dollar for dollar. A very ancient and honorable Clay has spoken. Who dares doubt him?

"Dollar for dollar!" he repeated grayly. "Dollar for dollar!"

"Get it from Grady? I wish you luck. If I had your hold on him, Clay, I'd wring him dry."

"Dollar for dollar," mumbled Clay. His lips mouthed emptiness.

"All right. All right. What I want is my twenty-two hundred. For the rest, you can dollar for dollar the world to death."

"You will receive it tomorrow. This debt shall not stand!"

On Deleon's plump face, a wise, a subtle smile. His little pointed black moustaches bristled like cat's whiskers as craftily above his cards he surveyed old Clay. The old man's anger was worth money to him.

"And never will you see my face in here again! Never!" Clay buttoned and unbuttoned his coat. "Dollar for dollar!" he sang his chant.

Old Thornwood Clay had played the game, and played it out. The honor of the Clays demanded that this debt at cards should be paid, though the universe be riven, though, murder come of it. There was no alternative.

Clay sat mute for a moment, staring ahead of him with dead eyes. He surveyed his recourses; none was left. His son was likewise a wastrel at cards; no good could come from him. Friends there had been to the house of Clay, but they lay beneath the unkempt grass.

A fine pass for the scion of the very ancient and honorable Clays to be come upon! For a long time, and oftenest in the night, Gay Deleon would remember the face of Thornwood Clay as then he saw it, the cheeks drained of all vitality, the lips twitching as though with taste of tears. Deleon would remember on *his* black night, in his dreadful hour!

Now it would be well for you, old Thornwood Clay, could you lay your head on a woman's breast, sobbing those tears away. Too late, too late. The world is a hard place and lone for old men, who are hard and lone. They have no tears.

"Going to Rose Dawn's wedding?" Deleon asked more cheerfully. "I've half a mind to wipe scores clean if you'd go out there and break it up. Don't scowl at me. You can't scare me. Grady's not worth killing; nor she. I was just joking." Deleon named Rose Dawn with a foul oath. "That's what she is! I know her."

Thornwood Clay stumbled out, muttering the incoherencies of insanity. "Dollar for dollar!" And now: "An eye for an eye!" Gay Deleon, who had watched many losers go out those dismal portals, knew well old Thornwood Clay was done.

For the winner, the fatness of the earth. For the loser, the asp's tooth. It is a gamble.

Gay Deleon did not look up. On the white face of Thornwood Clay was the dreadful mask of a man who whips his soul to murder!

VIII. THE FACE AT THE WINDOW

AND now Mrs. Higgs stands up to give the bride away. A bride in black. Her mourning night.

Here is old Tim Grady, sobered suddenly, wrapping an amazed dignity about him. The Irish (God bless them!) are always actors. Old Tim is of the tall men, of the race of kings. The high nose, the scornful lip, the martial eye—pure Nordic! Tim's sires have all been emperors, though their empiry have been but a pig-sty.

Here Rose Dawn. Her golden aureole of hair is uncovered; old Tim's money will coronet her. Her countenance is virginal as snow, in contrast to the blackness of her gown, her breast lustrous as ice. Beware, for such semblance of cold lies often in white hot heat.

Some people, being smart and making pretense of traveling with the go, whisper naughty things about Rose Dawn. You may hear them all if you lie down and put your ear to the gutter. Who is free of such? They say—They whisper—But They speak much, and They are fools. Sure her face is fair enough, her eyes incredibly blue. Many the brave man who has loved her.

And now she is to be married to old Timothy Grady, who is nothing holy. It is a wonderful thing to be a bride to a man with ten—twenty; who can set the price?—millions of dollars. And old Tim Grady will not live for long.

Near to old Tim she stumbled. People looked at each other.

"If there be any man," rolled Dr. Bellbender, in his most sonorous tones. . . "let him now speak, or forever hold his peace. . ."

Easily he spoke the name of eternity, though *forever* is a mighty word. He paused, for he was dramatic. Once before the forever was spoken to you, Rose Dawn.

As they knelt, a pendant globe made old Tim's mottled face look ruddy, added respectable sparkle to his red-gray hair. Rose bowed her head; the curls upon her neck brought queer spasms to Bellbender as he looked down. The lights gave to her death-black gown a living glow.

". . . Let him now speak. . . ."

Beyond Bellbender an alcove of windows. Beyond the windows the darkness. Beyond the darkness the sanguine moon. Round about, and round about, whirled the waste winds of the void.

Upon the downcast, exquisite face of Rose Dawn shuddered some dreadful thought. A thought, call it; or memory; or vision. She seemed to sway, and Bellbender put down his hand. Just for a second, that was all.

Mrs. Bonnell sighed, it was so appropriate; and Mrs. Wiggs felt she could sob, if her grandfather had not been a gentleman. Mrs. Higgs looked up and out of the windows. Through the soft silence rang her hard whisper: "My God!"

Bride and groom looked up, following Mrs. Higgs' frozen stare. Nothing to be seen beyond the alcove windows but the cold out-of-doors. Old Tim stared long, bending back his spine. In those unshaded windows he caught the glimmer of the sanguine moon. He trembled as though he would catch hold of Bellbender's knees.

". . . Or forever hold his peace. . . ."

"Go on! Go on!" Tim whispered thickly.

Dr. Spencer bobbed up, anxious, professional, suave; and bobbed down again. Mrs. Higgs regained her equilibrium; she set her jowls. But the pupils of her eyes were still dilated, looking larger than her small, cold blue eyes. Tim Grady looked no more at the window. His hand over that of Rose Dawn was heavy like ice.

"What was the matter, Ma?" Rose asked her mother when she had opportunity.

"It was nothing. I thought I saw something, dearie. But it was nothing."

Nothing? Is a ghost nothing, old Higgs, though it come back through the shadows, far as to life from the everlasting, far as from Heaven to here? Less than dust on the wind, less than a dead flame.

IX. MIDNIGHT WATCHER

RAGING wind, and the cold shine of Christmas middle night. Brooms of storm have swept the skies clean, with pale white streaks from east to west. At such a sky on such a night a weatherwise sailor might look aloft, and say: "There will be hurricane by morning!"

Dawnrose is a thousand-eyed pumpkin goblin, each window reflecting the carmine of the moon. At the door beneath the porte-cochere stands the butler, Saltpeter, stealing a whiff of a cigaret. Within, close at all times to old Tim's side, are Ike Duval and black Tom Jefferson, to protect him from the horrors of the moon. In there may creep no crook or spook, wandering houseless in Westchester County.

Up and down the drive, deep in the shadows of bushes, out of sight of Saltpeter, walks a solitary man. He waits a message that does not come. Rose Dawn is at the dance.

Coats and reefers so wrap him that if he be young or old, fat or lean, or whatever manner of man at all he be, is not apparent. His eyes seem preternaturally bright beneath his hat's low brim. He has the appearance of height; but that may be due to the night, which casts long shadows.

His step, if you listen, is lowly audible. Slow as a clock; something Hamletian in it, something of the tragedian, something staged. A moody man, a conceited man. A man conscious of himself. He is his own audience in his own silent drama. The weighted hemlocks bend, the wind pauses, for they expect to hear him speak.

From his air he may have been so pacing all night. Again, his vigil may have just begun. The moon rides low.

Along the river road and up the drive between Dawnrose's gates, with blur of lights and creaking brakes, comes a taxicab, slowing to a halt beneath the porte-cochere. Saltpeter has closed the door. Old Thornwood Clay, chattering and shaking, climbs forth from the cab.

"B-r-r! B-r-r! Sure this is the right place, driver? Don't bother about waiting. Mr. Grady will send me home. Have Smith put this on my bill."

The chauffeur spits sullenly, wiping his mouth with the back of his hand. No tip on Christmas Eve. Because he is an American and a Christian he mutters gloomily. Having unloaded his Americanism and Christianity, he turns his car with a shriek and races the wind southward.

Clay is left alone in freezing shadows. The solitary watcher has come up, standing at Clay's elbow. "Is this Mr. Grady's home?" Clay asks, for the man bears an air of authority.

"Yes," the stranger replies, drawing out the word long and slowly. "But the wedding is over, Mr. Clay."

Clay raises his dogged eyes, striving to peer through glasses. "I beg your pardon. I didn't recognize you at first. My eyes—You are—?"

"Yes," says the unknown.

Clay fumbles for words. It is not remarkable that a man he does not know calls him by name, for he is Thornwood Clay, of the very ancient Clays, and likely the whole world knows of him. His heart is warmed.

"So he's married? Is she pretty? I suppose so. Grady always had an eye for women."

He feels his way up steps to the door. The stranger is close at his back as a goblin, and about as full of speech. Something disastrous in his presence. Saltpeter, cigaret cupped in palm, nods sleepily just inside the entrance. Music from the ballroom above drifts and drags.

Glancing back, Clay sees a light haze of snow on the lawns. It looks colder than snow, cold as wet cotton. "I'd like to see Mr. Grady," he explains.

"What did you say?"

"I'd like to see Mr. Grady."

The stranger draws his ulster collar up to his forehead, seemingly immersed in reflection. His fists are clenched. "I'd like to see him in Hell!" he whispers with terrible voice.

He goes back slowly to the dark. Old Clay stands still; the man is vanished. Clay thinks he has talked with the dead.

X. BLACK BLOOD

"LOOK at 'er," stuttered old Tim Grady. Very thick his tongue. "Ain't she the prettiest thing you ever saw in skir-rts, gintlemen? Or without 'em!" A cackle; a nudge in the astounded abdomen of the Reverend Dr. Bellbender. "That damned van Chuch! If he looks at her again that way I'll wr-ring his neck! She's mine! She belongs to Timothy Grady now, and no man will come between!—Stand closer up to me, Ike Duval, and ye, Tom Jifferson. I feel a cold wind on my back. Pour me something, Tom!—She's mine! I will—I will—"

Old Tim grew wantonly obscene. Dr. Bellbender, being a bachelor, listened in anguished placidity; Dr. Spencer with the glint of a smile behind his sandy beard.

They stood at the edge of the ballroom floor. Grady had gathered a few male wallflowers about him; he talked to them as was his pleasure. Deep and thunderously beat the drum of syncopated song. Sweat riveted in the eyes of the Negro musicians.

To the barbaric tomtom tremble of the jungle Rose Dawn danced her bridal dance in the arms of Peter van Chuch. Dr. Bellbender reflected, curiously trying to find the implication of it, that the known rites of Hymen had gone askew these latter days. While the bridegroom stood and watched, the young men scrambled to dance with the bride—van Chuch, Wigley Arsen, Buddy Schermerhorn, Spencer's son Laurence, even bald Higgleson Todd. Higgleson Todd most of all. He pressed her close. His moist eyes were rapt and ravished with music.

"She's mine!" cried old Grady; yet it seemed he lied. "Not love nor learning nor looks got her for me, gintlemen. I'm no fool. 'Tis money talks, as I've told my boy Paddy often. Paddy wanted to be a l'yer. 'L'yers enough in the world,' I told him, 'with Todd, and Todd, and Todd, and Todd, and God knows all. Git to war-rk like your old man did, and make money,' I says to him. ' 'Tis money talks.' Those were my very war-rds. ' 'Tis money talks.' "

"A very acute observation," suggested Spencer, in his queer puttering way.

"This is an economic age, Mr. Grady," Bellbender began genially. "But I think we should give credit to other things, such as breeding and family—"

"Ain't I well bred? Ain't the Gradys as fine people as iver war-r shoes?"

"True. True. Of course I didn't mean—"

"I've got blood behind me, don't ye forgit it! We have our coat of ar-rms. We could wear a crown, was we minded. But I ain't proud or consated over it. It's nothing."

" 'The rank is but the guinea's stamp,' " Bellbender quoted soothingly.

Fortunate that old Tim did not know the words. Scotchmen may not be quoted to an Irishman without disaster.

"And, speaking of learning, what's it worth?" Grady continued, besotted with loquacity. "You will be surprised, gintlemen, to hear from my own lips that I ain't what you might call highly iducated, in the book sense of the war-rd. I come from a family of highly iducated gintlemen; not one of 'em but knew his letters, and some of 'em beyond. My old man wanted me to go to Dublin Univarsity and study to be a bishop. He was a student his own self. If my old man was living, he could quote you Latin like a book. Much good it did him, with his *hic, haec, hoc,*" old Grady added grimly, "when he stood in the murderers' pen!"

Tim teetered on his heels, hands clasped behind, neck stretched, red face thrust forward, loudly talking. Spencer glanced shyly at Bellbender and, meeting the minister's uncomfortable gaze, turned his head away.

Old Grady paced away, his guests and bodyguards following him in a flock. He strode into the library, pouring out drinks.

"Now, Doc Spincer thinks he's pretty damned smar-rt cause he's a doc. Don't shake your head and grin at me, Spincer! I can read what you're thinking like a book. It's a gift which, comes from handling men, what you call phisychology."

Tim dilated on his knowledge of practical "phisychology," full of wise saws and modern instances.

"You think you're smar-rt. But with all your learning, I hire you, and I fire you. I could affar-rd to hire the smartest man iver lived to black my boots." The air was growing thicker; Tim's head swayed. "That's what money'll do. It'll buy iducation, like it'll buy Ike Duval's strength or Bellbender's high society name."

Tim smacked his lips, highly satisfied. And sat down, and stood up again. Some devil of drink goaded him on to trouble.

"Stand up here, Tom Jefferson! Stand closer yet. I'm feeling of a draft; and a cold wind's coming in some place. Here's something to chew on, gintlemen. This black fellow is my man, body and soul, if he's got a soul. And why? Because my money hires him." Grady smacked his lips again. "I hire him. Yit so far as iducation goes, he's got more'n me, maybe."

Solemnly Tom stood beside his master. Spencer had a glimpse of uneasy glances cast right and left. Tom's hands were clasped in front of him. And now they opened, and he smoothed his waistcoat buttons with sooty fingers. A study in moving marble. Above him a square dome of light shone full on his shaven, polished head, gleamed in the whites of his eyes.

Jungle minstrelsy beat from the ballroom. Tom's skin seemed to crinkle and crisp; his nostrils widened. He stared at nothing. Grady's guests looked him over with insecure boldness, as they might through glass look over some huge sleek snake.

Feeling a silence, Spencer spoke. "Surely the blackest fellow I ever saw," he pondered, as though Tom were deaf. "Pure Zulu, I'd say. Our niggers are mostly African West Coast stock, flat-nosed, peaceable, good-natured cowards. The slavers got them because they were easy to catch, and they'd bear the lash. But the Zulus, by God, are the same race that ruled Ethiopia! Straight nose—thin lips—unusual dolichocephalic skull," he diagnosed. "Where do you come from, Tom?"

Bellbender looked Tom over with more humanity and less science. "So your name is Thomas Jefferson? Do you know, my boy, that one of the Presidents of these great United States was named Thomas Jefferson? You should study and work hard and behave yourself, so some day you will be more worthy of the name. It's a good one. Here's a dollar, Thomas."

Tim Grady surveyed his servant maliciously, his head at a slant, his lower lip curled. "Ay! He's studied hard. There's a black fellow claims he's the gr-reat gr-reat gr-reat grandson of the sicond President of these United States, Tom Jifferson of Virginia. Like enough it's so."

Tom scuffed the rug. Grady took whiskey neat.

"And I," Tim continued, patting his lips with a handkerchief, "Timothy Grady, gr-reat gr-reat gr-reat grandson of Terence Rory Grady, who was lord mayor o' Bally by Donegal Water, hire 'im. He's a smar-rt coon! Tell 'em how iducated ye are, Tom."

Grady was in a fine, fierce delight. He caught up a chiffon scarf from a chair, twisting and winding it till was a rope. With the same proud glance of ownership he would have directed on his new bride, Tim looked his servant up and down. Idly he snapped the wound silk chiffon, like a lash.

Tom spoke without Southern slur: "Four years at Howard University, in Washington, getting my B.A. degree. Four years at Columbia Medical, with, an M.D. That's all, Sir. It's not so much."

Spencer tugged at his sandy beard. Tom a doctor of medicine! Spencer felt curiously shamed. "What—what—" he sputtered. "A physician! Why haven't you entered professional practice—kuf! kuf!—Dr. Jefferson?"

"I give him three hundred a month," Grady said. "That's good reason why. It's four times as much as he could 'arn feeding pills to constipated niggers. Eight years it took him to git that iducation, and I buy it for a far-rthing. I've bought him, like I could buy ye, Spincer, or ye, Bellbender, was I minded to make the price big enough for ye!"

Dr. Spencer sucked his cigar. Took it from his lips. Thoughtfully surveyed the point, which was burning enough. Bellbender wiped and wiped his glasses, as though they were too dim for vision.

Old Tim flicked the silken scarf. Tom's lips were thin as a scar; his eyes deep as charred wood, but light in them like the light of smoldering fire. In spite of his prattling, Tim had respect for the giant's sullen strength, if not for his vaunted learning. He did not intend to strike Tom. But the scarf in his hand leaped out too far. It curled about Tom's waist, harmlessly, but shamefully.

"Don't you dare to hit me, you old fool!"

Tom growled deep menaces. His sullen face twisted with mad pride, with fury, with the blood lust of the great black kings! Again he growled, deep as a tiger. Civilization, education, all the white man's sleekly copied ways, fell from him in dust. Snarling, Tom crouched on his heels, wrenching the scarf from Tim's frightened hands. With strangling, silent grip he tore the silken scarf in two, shaking it like a snake.

That ripping seemed to bring interlude in the orchestral music. Tom's forehead was greasy; his broad shoulders heaved. Ike Duval tried to grasp the giant's wrists; but though his hold was hard and in the best police fashion, Tom shook him contemptuously off. He stepped back.

Tim Grady regained his voice. Of ghosts, of devils, he might be afraid; but never, be it said, of a man.

"Ye damned—damned black baboon! I'll kill ye for this—I'll smash ye!—I'll fire ye!"

He kicked furiously. His big dancing pump flew off, striking Tom on the chin. It was absurd. Tom's anger departed; he laughed with all his teeth, heaving great guffaws. Tim sprawled back against a chair, puffing and blowing and threatening, yelling about the ingratitude of servants.

"I'll fire ye without a letter of ricommendation, Tom Jifferson! I'll hound ye from the country, if the word of Tim Grady's anything!"

Tim sat down heavily. He waved away Bellbender's soothing words.

"Gi' me my shoe!" Tom picked it up. "Put it on my foot!" Tom knelt. "No—I'll keep ye and make ye pay for this, Tom Jifferson. Ye'll call me an old fool! Ye iducated ape! I'll put ye where ye belong. Hark ye! I'll remember this, and ye'll pay!"

In the ballroom dancing music swelled, as gin inspired the jazz saxophone. Growling yet, Tim walked toward it, Tom Jefferson following him close and silently. Two tall men, red and black, sunset and night, they stood at the ballroom door, watching Rose Dawn.

"The black fellow will remember!" said Dr. Spencer to Dr. Bellbender.

XI. FALLEN FLOWER

WHATEVER the terror which had overcome Mrs. Higgs on looking out the window, whatever man or ghost had wrenched from her that frightened cry, it was now forgotten. Rose was married to old Tim Grady. No mischance could alter that.

Higgs sat at the ballroom's edge, looking stuffed. Her diamonds were proud as eggs.

Maveen, old Tim's daughter by his second wife, was dancing with young Schermerhorn. Maveen was in gold and green, which set off a little too brilliantly the cherry lights of her hair. Soft blue, even maroon, would have made her face look less flushed. For all that, in her own way a pretty girl.

Young Squirmy, being stultified with that which bubbles in silver flasks, stepped on Maveen's ankles, and sprawled, kicking her shins. Squirmy was the better part of seven feet, and thin as a sapling. His ambition in life was to grow a moustache.

This night was not pleasant for Maveen. She was silky and sullen of eye. Her father's new love was her new hate. So filial was she that all his loves became her hates. Moreover, Laurence Spencer, the doctor's son, was whispering in a palm-bower with some young half-bodiced female. Maveen was raging jealous, since she nourished a most partial passion for Laurence's thinning blond hair.

Squirmy stepped once too often on her feet, reeling with foolish laughter. No manners these days; no one apologizes for anything. Maveen disentangled herself, muttering a word not nice. She sat down by Mrs. Higgs, fiercely wishing for a cigaret.

"O, I say," muttered Schermerhorn, following her over. "I say."

He didn't say what he did say. Maveen looked at her injured feet. With an unsteady shrug the beanpole young man dandled himself away.

Fanning herself, Mrs. Higgs looked at Maveen from the edges of her fat eyes. She barely knew old Tim's daughter, but was suspicious of her. This night had given her authority as step-grandmother to Maveen. With her instinctive combativeness, she resolved to exert that authority at once.

"Where's your sweet brother, dearie?" she asked, stroking Maveen's gown. "I ain't saw him. Or is he that young fellow you was dancing with?"

"Padriac is only my half-brother," Maveen replied with great distinctness. "I am *sure* I do *not* know where he is."

"Him and your farther had a fight?" demanded Higgs. Maveen answered nothing. "Don't like your farther a-marrying Rose, don't he?"

Maveen tossed her bobbed red hair, giving Higgs lofty glances. "O, yes, Padriac's crazy about it. We're all crazy about it."

46

"Just as well you are," Mrs. Higgs said briefly. "You couldn't be nothing else."

Silence developed, but in Mrs. Higgs's vicinity no silences grew old. Maveen seethed; she stayed for trouble. Wigley Arsen ambled up, asking her to dance in his voice like nice ice-cream. Maveen waved him away.

"What a pretty dress, dearie!" The Higgs creature grasped a fold of Maveen's gown in her pudgy hand. "This green is the only thing you can wear and look anywheres decent, ain't it? Red hair is so hard a cross to bear. Arburn, I suppose you call it. Some call it arburn, and some call it henner, but *I* call it red."

Maveen wrapped herself in her brief skirts. Ladylikely she tapped her foot.

"My own Rose can wear anything and look like the Queen of Sherbet," said Higgs, folding her hands in her tranquil lap. "I've saw her take a tasty little piece of rag that wasn't hardly more'n a dish-cloth, and wear it at a dance with all the fellows crazy about her. She's the sort don't need clothes!"

Maveen squirmed and yawned. She refolded her knees, propped her chin in her palms, slapped her calves; with her feather fan, turned her face from Higgs.

"The night Rose met up with John Dawn—only sixteen she was then; ah, well I remember!—she was wearing a little gown didn't cost a cent more'n a dollar and a half. Worse luck for her! And it happened things turned out, and as eventualities came to pass, 'twould have been better for her she hadn't been wearing anything.

"Was he the sort of fellow to marry a girl like Rose—?"

"I didn't ask," Maveen broke in curtly.

"But I'm asking. He was not the sort. Always a go-to-the- devil, wild, rough-riding sort of moving pitcher actor, thinking as much of hisself as if he was Douglas Fairbanks. And he never had no money. You bet I did my best to make Rose see him in his true light! You may talk about the war all you want to, about the artorcities, and the torpeding of the Louvain, and the rotten dyes we got to use these days, but there's *one* good thing it did. It put an end to John Dawn!"

Lawless Western grimness lay over Higgs, that hard-lifed lady. Maveen flashed a glance at her. Maveen was a little frightened.

"*He* never could buy all the perty diddles a young girl likes and wants and desires, and which your farther'll get for her. Hisself to me Mr. Grady has said: 'I'll pour out money like water, Mrs. Higgs, to make Rose happy.' "

"Father's a good talker," said Maveen, edging away. "If he'd said he'd pour it out like liquor, it'd mean more."

Mrs. Higgs thought Maveen was disrespectful to her elders, a crime the Higgsian conscience could not abide. "I know it's hard on you and your brother, dearie," she said grimly, "that's growed up since the time your farther began making his money with the expertation of having it all to yourself. But you'll have to swallow it. If I have anything to say about it—"

Maveen sneered, almost sticking out her tongue.

"You're right! I got a lot to say about it!" shouted Higgs. "And I'm going to keep on saying a lot about it, for any lip you hand me! Rose married your farther to get what John Dawn couldn't give her. And we'll get it!"

"You make me sick," said Maveen, furiously conscious that her voice was loud, that Laurence Spencer was looking at her.

"You may be sicker yet, dearie. We're married now, whatever comes of it! As Bellbender said: 'What God has joined together, let no man put to slumber.' "

Maveen's temper, fierce and mad as that of her father, overwhelmed her. She seemed ready, in the purpling of her face, in the clawing of her hands, in her muttered words, to tear out Mrs. Higgs's honest eyes.

What deaths might have come of it can't be known. At once came a noisy silence in music, a swirl and scuffling among the dancers, a cry. Bravely Rose Grady had danced with Todd, van Chuch, Arsen, and the rest; while her face grew whiter and whiter, till it was whiter than paper, and no blood seemed to pulse from her heart. Yet through it all hysterically gay.

Laughing at Todd, or trying to, she fell. Todd's arms could not seize her quick enough. Her curly golden head cracked heavily on the scuffed waxy floor. Full length she lay, eyes closed, her funeral black dress like a shroud,

"Poisoned!"

Todd stood still, too dull of thought to bend and lift her. Laurence Spencer carried her away in his strong arms. "Nothing serious, nothing serious," Dr. Spencer puttered. "Fatigue, or excitement. Young women will go the pace. Well, well!" he stuttered. He flushed at his son as his ear lay on Rose Dawn's slow stirring breast.

In half an hour Rose Dawn was with her guests again.

XII. CONSTABLE BURKE

IF records be kept in Doomsday Book, they will include something of good and something of evil which Tim Grady had done against his salvation or damnation. At one place on the record will be a red line like blood.

In Ireland a price upon his head. Suns of forty years have not obliterated his photograph from handbills in the files of the police. "Wanted, for murder!"

Ah, murder is a dreadful thing! It graves a crimson cross on the temples, say what you will. He who slays with his own hand another man, though he believe not in God nor his own soul, yet will be palsied at a strip of paper blowing down the street, will bite his fists at the sound of wind, will wake and cry aloud at night when the lone dog howls!

Is Cain's sin no cosmic sin? Are the lives of men so thick that the tearing off of one of them stirs no passion in the stars? I'd not like to risk it.

For the good he'd done, Tim Grady had made money, if that be good; and children, if they be good. Now in his old years his money-bags were become nests of vipers; his children were to him as the spawn of hate.

Women and whisky and wrath—old Timothy Grady went the way of the flesh. Thinking of him, these words are a refrain. *Women and whisky and wrath*—which was the greater passion, I don't know. All gave him delight. All were (as men say) his soul.

The flesh is corruptible; and it perishes, the desire of it, the fairness of it, the strength of it. Its ways are thorny ways to go, and lead to the alkali deserts of Gehenna.

For Tim Grady those deserts were near. Within the night, upon the black sea, Timothy Grady heard the voice of God prophesying to him of death. Or was it only his own Fear, which serves each man for God?

Now is old Tim more drunken. Now are his hands shaking. Why is he so dreadfully wary of the innocuous moon, which burns its pathway west across the Hudson? It works no harm, save to lunatics.

"Listen, Ike! I think I hear a noise above!"

"The wind," says Ike Duval,

"Then 'tis a cold wind."

"The winter wind."

Tom Jefferson says nothing. His somber eyes are still morose. He is blood of Ethiopia, a king! He remembers Tim's blow.

"Don't you be worried, Mr. Grady," Ike says in amusement. "With your sets of burglar alarms, and me and Tom to keep an eye open, you couldn't be bitten by a bedbug. No one can break in here."

No one. But up in Tim's chambers a man walks softly around. And the speared light of the filling moon breaks in through an unshaded window. Red moon! . . .

Ah, long ago it was—forty years—in County Cork, in Ireland. Young Tim Grady and his auld man sat at night to drink the world under. A bottle of the water of life was atwixt Tim Grady and his auld man. Which bottle passed to a gurgling grave— and another—and yet again. Stars blew that night, planets flamed, comets wheeled. Burned a crimson moon, sent, I doubt me not, by the English.

The spirit of the red-headed man arose in Tim Grady and his auld man. They mused of ancient battles. Tears in their eyes; braggart oaths; the lust to smite. They called on the soul of Brian O'Boru, and lifted their arms in war. This was betwixt the dark and the dawn, and the full moon shone.

All would have been well, but Constable Burke, neighbor to the Gradys, intruded in the private family fight. He was ill-advised. His head was caught beneath two splintering bottles. He went down beneath a stamping of feet.—So he was no more.

With Dinnis McGinty, a neighbor lad, wanted for theft, Tim Grady crept from County Cork, from Ireland, like a red-headed, towering shadow. Arms coiled about his head, he ran. Horror lay on him; he blubbered in straw-ricks in the day, whined as he trotted down ghostly roads in the night. Dead men swung from nocturnal trees; demons were in the continents of the moon.

West with the sun, west with the bloody moon, Dinnis McGinty and he stowed away for America. Ah, long ago it was—forty years. Between lay the long procession of days. Yes, many a star and many a crimson moon had grown and blown since then. . . .

To Tim Grady, riches and power. All which money buys he had, much that his heart desired. He had bought love. He had effaced his enemies. Yet there was an oblivion which could not be bought, a memory which could not be effaced! Often in the night (often through those forty years of it) came to Tim Grady ghostly vision of Constable Burke. In the night, the dead! On the sod floor lying, while the bleak bloody moon sketched devils on his face. Between the dead man's staring eyes a worried frown, as though not beyond the ultimate veil could he be entirely freed from the economic worriment over his wife and childer. His nose broken by a boot. Blood frothy on his lips.

It is surprising, perhaps, that Tim Grady had not done other murders.

Here stands Timothy Grady! Loud, ignorant, lecherous, jovial, superstitious, wrathy, conceited, generous, quick-witted, arrogant. A tall, strong man near to sixty years, the life so thick in his veins it is purple. His hands are huge, they could batter down a door. Or so they once could. But now the old heart is not so steady. Is not so steady.

No braver man ever rushed with bull roars into a fight. No greater skulking coward ever howled at a mouse's patter in the dark.

And now about him, life at apogee. . . . His marriage night, whereby man cheats mortality. . . . His guests move about with the humming of flies. . . . Violins pin-pank! as musicians strum them for the next dance. . . . Brazen lights of ten thousand candles shine. . . . Laughter rises, shrill as crickets beating in sudden song. . . . Old Tim Grady is drinking yet. He is a little unsteady.

Drinking yet. To the last he will be drunk. Washael! That is a good way to go out into the much traversed dark!

XIII. CLAY GRIPS THE KNIFE

THE hour was half between midnight and morn. That withering moon fled down the froth of the stars. It grew redder with its setting.

The jazz orchestra, rumbling of the jungle, made whirring notes like the rapid drumming of a love-sick grouse's wing, an aphrodisiacal song. Tim Grady, pacing uneasily from ballroom to library, upstairs and down, stopped now again to watch the dancing.

Why, he himself had never yet embraced Rose so close, so sweet; had never drunk the glances of her marvelous blue eyes with such intensity of desire. Had he married her that Arsen, Schermerhorn, van Chuch, Higgleson Todd, and the rest of the pack of fools should pass her around like a common thing, her bosom never cooling from their embraces? It was his wife, it was his liquor, which lent joy to their feet.

He was rubbed raw with suspicions bitterer than salt. Tim cursed the world, cursed women, cursed his bride, with the curse of Cromwell. He left the ballroom, stalking with his bodyguards to his own rooms in the front of the house. This house was new. Old ghosts live in old houses, but they are too old to prowl abroad.

Tom Jefferson examined the west window fastenings at Tim Grady's command. Beneath those windows was the carriage entrance; the porte-cochere roof served for balcony. Night seemed pale beside Tom's countenance as he drew aside the shade and peered out. Superstitions older than man's oldest wisdom played in the corners of his eyes.

Old Tim hung over a table to pour seltzer and rye. Carafe and siphon were ornaments missing in few rooms of Dawnrose. His hands were none too steady, for he had done this thing this night before. He lifted his glass.

To him, ere drink had touched his lips, came by some quirk of mind horrible remembrance of Constable Burke. White that worried face, yet duller than clay. Words of the dead rang in Tim Grady's ears.

While Grady was in the grip of this dismal recollection, old Thornwood Clay, who had been drowsing and awaiting Grady in a huge fireside wing-chair, arose and came up behind. Tim saw him in a mirror. No ghost, but Thornwood Clay, though his face was livid as a tombstone. In the mirror Tim's stultified eyes beheld close at his shoulder the face of Clay, white and damned.

For a space Grady remained rock still, his heart swelling and dying. The horror of dead ghosts was on him. He had not thought before that Clay's face was so like the constable's. Probably it was not like, but memory had faded. To old Tim they were one and the same. In his madness he thought that dismal face was borne upon no shoulders, but upon blank pillows of air, being the dissevered head of that long dead policeman come back to gibber him to insanity. The illusions of existence passed from old Timothy Grady. He knew that time and space are nothing, and that he dwelt in Hell.

He did not know that he opened his lips, but he roared, and roared again, with bellows which shook his guests from their smooth priapean dances.

Old Tim, seizing hard on the table's edge, came back to his senses. It had been but a flash of the "trembling delirium." Those staring eyes were alive, the brain behind had sense. It was nothing more than Thornwood Clay. The room was alive with pulsing hearts.

"Is that you, Thorn Clay?" Grady's voice was a hoarse whisper. "Is that yourself, yourself?"

"I'm sorry I startled you, Grady. Your man at the door told me to come up here. I must have fallen asleep."

Old Clay jerked at the lapels of his morning coat, and waited an invitation to sit down. Grady rapped his knuckles on the table, shivering. "Uh! Uh!" He was still frightened.

Thornwood Clay sat down without invitation, crossing his legs elegantly, pressing his palms together beneath chin. He and Grady had once been partners in business ventures which always miserably failed, and the superiority he had assumed at that time towards Grady had never left Clay. Of Grady's later riches he was contemptuous. Grady's charity he hated while he took it.

"What do you mean by prowling around my house like a leprechaun?" yelled old Tim, furiously angry, master of himself again. "Do ye think I am a babe in ar-rms to be frightened by your creepy ways?"

"Great Judas, Grady! I had no intention of scaring you."

Old Tim foamed and snarled to quell the fright yet bubbling in his heart. "What have ye sn'aked in to stale from me on Christmas Ave, on me wedding night?" he cried, in brogue almost unintelligible.

An ill thing for anyone to frighten Tim Grady. An ill time for old Thornwood Clay to intrude with his beggar's whine.

"I insist I had no intention of startling you, Mr. Grady. I merely dropped in to see—to see—" Clay hemmed and paused.

"S-spit it out! Don't mumble and grumble to me!"

"Well, what the devil, Grady!" Clay had a flash of anger, but it faded.

Tim stood over him, glaring so malignantly down on Clay's thin gray hairs it might well seem he had a special murderous hatred of each thin gray hair. "What the divil yourself?" Tim growled.

"My money has gone, Mr. Grady, I don't know where. I find myself in very sorry financial straits. I must have money. It is imperative that I have money!"

"Imperative, is it?" Tim drawled, narrowing his eyes. "Didn't ye get your graft today from Todd? Where's all the money I've handed out to ye, eight thousand dollars a year?"

Thornwood Clay did not care to dwell on the matter. Since he and Grady had been partners in business which swallowed all Clay's fortune, he considered that half of Grady's later wealth was justly his. But he knew Grady might look upon it differently.

"I don't wish to emphasize my personal difficulties," Clay said wearily. "But a demand has been put on me which must be met. Met, I say, at once!"

"I hear ye."

"Dollar for dollar, it must be met!"

"Well?"

"That's all. It's plain. A gentleman must have money, and I haven't a cent. That's true, Grady. Doesn't it sound absurd? I haven't got a nickel; I couldn't buy a newspaper." Clay tried to smile buoyantly; he waved his hand as if he told a witty jest. "It's amusing. Of course a gentleman must have money. You can understand that, Grady. It isn't reasonable to expect a gentleman to live without money."

"I've been without it, many the day and night," Tim said, with quiet pride. "Up and down I've walked the streets. I've gone to the garbage cans. I've thanked God for a crust of bread and a rotten turnip."

"O, of course, you—" Clay shrugged.

"Why don't ye git to war-rk, Clay?"

"This is no time for silliness. My honor hangs on it. I must have funds!"

Must was a word Tim Grady did not like. His eyes grew small. In him was an imp of perversity which brooked no command of any sort.

"I will be satisfied with twenty-two hundred tonight," said Clay.

"You'd be satisfied, would you?"

Grady's thunderous sneer could not be mistaken. Clay was aroused. He arose slowly, adjusting his glasses to stare at Grady, clasping his hands behind him. "Well, it's my money," he said.

"Your money! Getting pretty uppish, ain't ye, Thorn? Do ye mean to say this is all ye sn'aked into my house for, to rile me with your begging yap!" Tim nursed himself into a fury. "Your money! I'll say this is pretty! You crazy old loon! Ye don't own the shir-rt to your back!"

Such familiarities were vile to old Clay, coming from lips so lacking in blue blood. He had always known Tim Grady as jovial and generous, even obsequious. Clay's brittle, foolish old pride could tolerate no word of contempt, no lessening of his own vast self-esteem.

"O, don't grow indecent, Grady! Is it necessary to speak plain facts, to name you a thief in your own home?"

"What's this? What's this?"

"Let me recall several matters. Weren't we partners in the Florida Oil affair, and in the camera patents? How does it happen then that you are rich, while I've lost every cent I have?—"

"You old bucket-shop plunger!"

"I'm a patient man, Grady, and no yelping Jew. But I've got to a desperate pass. I'm desperate, I say!"

Clay rapped his frail fist on the table. Though Tim Grady was bellowing and stamping, his high-pitched precise utterance could not be drowned out. It was like a violin's note in drumming.

"Speaking plain facts, such as one gentleman never needs do to another, you know you took my money from me. You've been trying to salve your conscience with this beggarly pittance Todd doles out to me. Eight thousand a year! A common dirty mechanic would starve on that! Wait! You can't yell me down, Sir! If you forget your position as host, I may ignore mine as guest. You stole my money from me. You know it, Tim Grady!"

Tim choked. He was almost bursting. Facing him, shaking, yet dreadfully set of purpose, old Thornwood Clay seemed dry and crumbly as a stick of dust. Pouf! A breath of wind, and he'd be gone.

"I stole—stole—stole your money! If I did, I got it. And you won't get it! You lizard! You louse! You toad! You jackal! You dodo!"

Tim had a spasm. He waved his fists at Clay's nose. Of faces in the doorway, of whispering voices, mocking eyes, Tim was only distantly aware. He did not care if the whole world stared. He hated the whole world. It is an Irish trick.

"Out—out—get out o' me house! If it hadn't been for ye and your Florida Oil, I'd been a millionaire tin years before. What's this? What's this? If ye didn't wear glasses, I'd kick your pants! Out! Get out! Out of me sight, Thorn Clay, ye and your family and the name and the smell of ye! Arrah! I'll lose holt of meself and forgit you're wearing glasses."

"I'm an old man, Grady, past the seventies," Clay whispered, striving to hold fast to his dignity. "But, by God, Sir, I never thought to live to hear a man speak this way to me!"

"Get out!"

"Do you know I am Thornwood Clay, born of the Clays? Do you remember you are addressing a gentleman? I came here with a reasonable demand—"

"Ye'll make no demands of me! Get out! Out, ye auld gray fool!"

"I'm a gentleman, Sir! You *will* listen to me. I came from the Clays, a line of gentlemen who were never either beggars or fools. I am a Clay, Sir, of the Clays! My father was—"

"I heard ye the first time!" old Grady screeched. "Your father was a Clay, and your grandfather was a Clay, and—God! God help us, Clay!"

Thornwood Clay stood rigid, formal as a hollyhock. People were watching, sneering, listening, he knew; but to him, as to Grady, they were a blur.

"The Clays, Sir, as you may have had the honor of being informed—The Clays, Sir, pay their debts—The Clays, Sir, as the whole world knows—"

"If ye didn't wear glasses I'd cut off your ears!" Tim howled.

"The Clays, Sir, don't cheat, and they don't shout, and they don't wave their fists like ruffians—"

"Who's shouting now?" Grady bellowed. "Who's waving their fists?" He shook his freckled paws. "Who's cheating? Who's a liar—who's a dog—who's a crook—who's a dirty, black-tailed scalawag?"

"Speak for yourself, Sir. The Clays, Sir, have always been gentlemen."

"Gintlemen! Gintlemen! To the hogs with all your gintlemen! Ye bet I'll speak for meself, and so rapid you won't know what hit ye! If ye didn't wear glasses, ye lousy-headed runt—I know how to talk like a gintleman, ye swine! Get out! Gintlemen! Gintlemen! O, the dirty Clays! *Get out!* What's the Gradys been, if they ain't been gintlemen, with me ancistor, Terence Rory Grady, lord mayor of Bally by Donegal Water?"

Solemn Ike Duval wrapped his arms about his stomach to hold his laughter down. In black Tom's eyes burned an entrancing light, the beacon blood of war.

Far away the orchestra still tootled the Indigestion Blues, with a weariness supernal, with discord never faltering. But the dancing had stopped. Curious and frightened by the uproar coming from Tim's room, guests were scurrying on with their wraps and to the outer door. There they waited for their cars, cocking ears to the tumult from above with as much gawping curiosity as though they were a dirty little gang of muckers, and not the cream of society.

Several people were pressing into the entrance of Grady's room—Todd, Spencer, Bellbender, Arsen, such as by professional position felt themselves entitled to witness family fights. They delicately scuffled, drawing back, each one of the four learned professions striving to enter not first. Over their heads Maveen Grady peered, biting her lips; in tow she had a momentary cavalier, Captain van Chuch. Dr. Spencer felt he ought to caution Grady about exciting that fierce old heart; but Grady's patronage was worth twenty thousand a year, and he had a son in Harvard, a wife with a passion for diamonds. No one spoke.

"What ha' the Gradys been, if they ain't been gintlemen?" howled Tim again, pushing his hand against old Clay's breast. "If ye wasn't wearing glasses, I'd skin ye!"

Stony white was Clay's face. Illimitable pride was his, the vastest pride in the whole universe, and the silliest, his honor in the deathly dead. The very ancient and honorable Clays raised not one of them a bony hand to aid him, though he looked to them for strength. Bah! They could not break a cricket's leg, the whole ghostly pack of 'em.

"Out! Out ye go! The Gradys ain't gintlemen, ain't they? You pig—you swine—you gray old hog! I'll gintleman you! I'll show ye what a gintleman is! If ye wasn't wearing glasses—"

Deliberately little old Clay removed his gold-rimmed glasses. He danced about, his arms waving like a spider's before him. Crack! His thin, brittle fist pushed out, hitting Tim square on his hooked nose. Blood spurted. Tim's shirt was polka-dotted with red.

"You march right in there and stop Grady up quick!" Mrs. Higgs, in the doorway, commanded Rose. "Slap his face for him. Start him right. He's making a arful fool o' hisself."

Rose Dawn was dizzy; the world swam around her; she felt in presentiment Tim's big red hands striking her face.

With her elbows Higgs forced entrance to the room between Spencer and Bellbender. "I'll learn him!" she said. "I ain't afraid o' him."

All bloody of face, old Tim Grady seized Clay by the throat. His hands dug in. He grunted and roared. Clay, older and vastly less powerful than Grady, gagged, fighting outward with useless hands. Blue veins swelled on his livid forehead. He swept his arms outward, as does a swimmer who is drowning.

Grady's fury had stirred a like passion in Maveen, mad hatred of the insanity which was her heritage. Stamping her foot, jerking her head, she watched her father shake and throttle Clay, forcing him back towards a window. "Isn't he a fool?" Maveen asked herself over and over, twisting her fingers for the shame of it. "Isn't he a fool, an utter fool?"

With horror she realized she had spoken aloud, as though another tongue had seized the thought in her brain, clamoring it. Peter van Chuch leaned over her elbow agreeably: "Pardon me—Yes, isn't he?" Van Chuch was pleased to have been taken into Maveen's confidence.

"You fool!" Maveen flung back at him, injuring his good Dutch soul.

She was furious with him, furious with herself, furious with the great universe and the God who laid the madness on the Gradys. Van Chuch looked like a spanked pug-dog. In his dour memory van Chuch put Maveen down for a black mark. The fury of van Chuch is cold, but burns forever.

"Get off! Get away! Get out!" Tim screeched, sniffing the blood which streamed from his nose, pushing old Clay towards the windows.

Mrs. Higgs grasped Tim by the collar band. She tried to shake that big bull. "You're making a monkey of yourself, Timothy Grady! Behave yourself! People is looking at you. Behave yourself!"

"Get out!"

That howl bowled over nine men like nine-pins. Tim Grady threw a look so fierce, so threatening, malignant, on the crowded faces in the doorway that each little face thought itself singled out for injury, and folded up in its own shell.

Now what scuffling, as Law, Theology, Medicine, Journalism, crawl crab-wise back through the door! What kicked shins! What trodden corns! What stomachs dented by what elbows! No hesitation now at which should be first, for all would be first.

Mrs. Higgs tightened her hold in Tim's collar. "Don't you think you're going to bully me!" cried she. "Not in my own home. Behave yourself!"

Tim bent, dragging Higgs from the floor. He swung her off his shoulder. His elbow caught the lady beneath the chin. And her legs went up and her head went down. And she cracked to the floor with a howl.

Ike Duval, sworn to uphold the law as interpreted by clients of the Argus Agency, did not raise one finger as Clay was shaken and choked like a dead cat. Wigley Arsen, who made it his boast he knew all the great, who had in more prosperous days bowed and smirked to Thornwood Clay's proud back, now had the decency, as he watched from the safety of the hall, to grimace with disgust.

"Ga! Ga!" Clay groaned.

And whether he was trying to call to God, or merely wishing for more breath, was not plain. Blood from Tim's flowing nose speckled his thin hair.

Stumbling backward, from a table his insensate fingers picked up a weapon. His fingers closed; they held. Feebly fighting, he lifted up a knife. The knife Tim Grady bought from Bliss's pawnshop for eighteen bargained dollars; the knife Lopez stole from John Dawn; the weapon of the dead! Its gold-green serpent bit the pads of old Clay's grasping hand.

Up, flashing, at Tim Grady's breast the heavy blade pointed.

A blow from Grady on Clay's arm. The knife went spinning from Clay's lax fingers. High, in an arc. With a hoarse grunt, Ike Duval dropped to the floor. The serpent knife flashed over his head. Point first it drove into the floor.

Roaring mad, Tim pushed old Clay against a window. The window hangings fell in a cascade. The window's shade buckled and tore, jerked from its roller. The window pane caved outward with a boom, followed by a tinkle of showered glass shards. The window alarm broke out in fierce jangling, sending warnings sharp as arrows forth against the stars.

"Get out!" Tim screeched triumphantly.

And Clay was out. He'd been pushed clear through. Down the sloping porte-cochere roof he slid, clawing like a cat. Departing guests, awaiting their cars below, loosened a hubbub of chilly murmurs at that slipping, slithering, clawing sound. The wild Irish was off again. No one knew what might come of it.

"There!" Grady stuck his head through the broken window, shaking a fist as Clay sprawled down. "Bide there till great earth rots!"

Out alone in the crackling frost, the merciless night, the exceeding great cold of Christmas morning. Thrown like a beggar from a gentleman's house, to share the night with the rats and the bats.

The full blown moon shone carmine. Over the hills, over the river, shone the full blown moon, a frozen peony in the fields of the west.

"And ye, damn ye!" Grady shrieked, at the moon, or chaos, or Divinity, or at some ghost which fluttered in the night and was seen to his eyes alone. "I'm not afraid of ye!"

Something unseen struck Tim Grady in his oathing and his strength. He collapsed over the window-ledge, groaning. His face was white, and blood dripped from his nose as from a leaky faucet.

"That old heart will crack on him some day," Dr. Spencer muttered to Higgleson Todd.

"Anything serious? No danger of his dying?"

"He's got a chance to outlive his wife, and you, and me," said Spencer. "But he may not do it."

The square-faced lawyer bent his brows. He seemed about to say something, but refrained. Black Tom lifted up his master, carrying him to bed. Once or twice Tim Grady groaned, but it didn't do him any good.

So passed the night and morning of his wedding night. Mrs. Higgs slept with Rose.

XIV. INTO THE DARK

AS on a greased chute Thornwood Clay slid down the porte-cochere roof. His neat feet dangled over the edge. For an instant he hung back from the drop, feebly striving to dig his fingers into the tiles. His shoulders followed his feet, and he took the sharp drop to the ground.

"Dollar for dollar," he mumbled dizzily, feeling his forehead, trying to locate the cord of his lost eyeglasses. "The Clays, Sir, have always been gentlemen. . . . You insufferable, insufferable bounder. . . . I demand my money!"

His hand came away red from his forehead; raw cuts of the window-glass burned with cold. He sat down, on the ground, in the snow.

Ike Duval, fearing murder, crawled out on the roof, peering over. Clay sat with his back against a pillar of the porte-cochere. His shoulders sagged; his head lay on one side. He was dreadfully weary.

"Ahoy below! All right?"

From Clay's closed lips came no answer to the hired guard of Tim Grady save the supreme answer, the final boast of the proud—silence.

Loud through the night, sharp as the crack of the stars, Saltpeter called motor-cars up to the entrance. "Mister-r Bon-nell! Mister-r Todd-d! Miss-ess Wi-hi-hi-higgs!"

The guests, eager to be gone, flowed out through the doorway. No one spoke a word to old Thornwood Clay, who had fallen so abruptly raindroppishly into view and now sat with back to them. Distinguished in his day he had been, his very engraved card an honor on any silver tray. But the days go by—his day was done. And they were children of the

In the door or on the steps silk hats shining; coats of ermine and sable; scarves, blue, pink, or gold chiffon over carefully molded coiffures; red rubbed eyes; flash of walking sticks; a lady in hysterics; a lady in intoxication; frosty breath puffing out like engine exhausts; Buddy Schermerhorn, one owl eye cocked, towering up like a flagpole; bumbling buzz of voices; great grewsome yawns; cheeks pink and nippy beneath powder.

Mrs. Tiffany Bonnell murmured to many sympathetic ears that, by the soul and honor of that great cousin-in-law's husband who was a Sir, she'd never set foot in such an ill-bred house again. Mrs. Wiggs intermittently tossed out her scrawny neck, lifted up her beady eyes, like a chicken sipping water; it expressed her highest disdain. "Where do we go from here?" Schermerhorn gagged. And that *was* a question.

Dozing chauffeurs scrambled from the servants' entrance one by one, wrapping coats about their ears for fear of the almighty frost. They fell into their cars, and, spinning their engines with pumping thumps, tornadoed up to the porte-cochere.

Dr. Bellbender, delayed inside by aiding old Tim to bed, left last. He was a kindly man, well-meaning. Crossing the drive, he bent down to old Clay with a gentle tap on the shoulder. He cleared his throat for speech. Bellbender recalled days when most hallowed in the sight of Heaven was that church from whose pews the Clays spoke with God.

"Can't my driver take you home, Mr. Clay?"

Old Clay looked dizzily about him, blind without glasses, wiping his forehead again. The cuts on his face had frozen to black drops. Stupidly he peered at his palm. "Leave me alone, please."

And fell into taciturnity so bleak, so profound and blank, that Bellbender felt himself insulted, and turned away with a snuff.

Proud were the Clays, sire and son, proud with their pride in the dead. Old Governor Clay, old Speaker Clay, old Ambassador Clay, old Thornwood Clay, had held themselves in their esteem above the kings of earth. Yet in the days of their utmost grandeur was none of them more filled with pride than old Thornwood Clay, sitting silently in the snow at the threshold of his enemy. Hollow, leer, bubble pride, as empty as an old tin can.

Saltpeter warily watched the old man. Once or twice he thought of calling for Ike; but old Clay apparently meant no harm. He sat motionless while full a quarter hour passed, looking at shadows in the sky, thinking thoughts long as space and multitudinous as the stars.

Ike Duval slipped on black derby and belted green overcoat, emerging for a breath of air. His jowls were set and lowering. He paused to borrow a cigaret from Saltpeter, giving Clay a wise glance.

"Pretty cold night, brother."

"It ain't so much the cold as it's the chilliness," Saltpeter replied.

Ike gave him a sharp look, painfully pondering this word of wisdom. "I seen a lot colder nights that wasn't so cold," he said grimly.

"And I seen a lot of nights that wasn't so cold that was colder," Saltpeter insisted. "Say, I seen some fellow hiding out in front. I'd like to go out and hand him a good swift kick, only I belong inside the house."

"Scared, are you?"

"Scared! Who's scared? You're scared."

"I'll go out and look him over, Fish-face," said Solemn Ike. "I don't want you to tremble yourself to death on your feet."

"It's the cold," said Saltpeter. "And the chilliness."

Hunching his shoulders, Ike Duval strode bravely forth. Always brave. As in a dark vision Saltpeter saw the unknown watcher emerge from shadows of bushes—saw Ike running forward, fierce as leaping cougar, his hand reaching towards his hip—saw them meet, saw them merge in shadows. Umbers of gaunt winter-withered trees wrapped them round.

Thereafter no word, no sound. Only the shadow.

And the butler watched for long. But Ike Duval did not come back into the light again, not he, nor his black derby, nor his solemn green overcoat brightening the midnight. The hour grew late, the shadows blacker.

"Guess he knows his business," Saltpeter thought. "It ain't none o' *my* business." His knees shook, for far away he heard a dog howling.

He made ready to bar the door. "Good-night to you, Sir!" he called to Thornwood Clay. No word answered him, but only the supernal arrogance of indifference. Clay stumbled to his feet and silently crept over the snow, tracing a dizzy arc. Saltpeter muttered something about the proud as he locked and double-locked the door.

XV. MORNING MIST

AND the night lies. Old Tim groans all night long. Shadows pass about his home. Dreams come. Rose Dawn sleeps alone.

And the night passes. This is Christmas morning.

A newspaper is a mighty thing. Nothing greater except, perhaps, the dinosaur, and it's dead.

In the *Morning Mist* the whole world comes neatly wrapped. For two cents you can have floods, politics, Russian wars, Irish jubilations, strikes, scandals of the always delightfully scandalous rich, want ads, obituaries, tooth-paste advertisements, empires and republics swiftly nethergoing, the dubious destinies of God. For two cents—*He* knows what you'd get for a nickel.

The tune the corner newsies wearily chaunted, in everlasting paean, in universal Christmas carol, was that news which, above all other in this fierce and teeming world, they thought would most satisfactorily palsy the great heart of humanity—

"Fight in a millionaire's home! Read about Tim Grady, the movie magnate!"

Sleet snow howling down from iron skies. No sun was given, and hardly light. A rather tough day for Santa Claus and poor little children forced by artists to stare at bake-shop windows, but pleasant enough for those whom business did not call abroad. The cyclone that blood-red moon forespoke was risen.

Newsboys crouched in subway entrances, whence arose a steam of melting snow and the odious odor of wet woolens. Few walked abroad at Christmas noon; fewer bought newspapers; the newsboys' mythical annual Christmas dinner was aided by no funds.

On the *Morning Mist's* society page a column and a half about the Grady-Dawn wedding, with names of all who were there and of many who weren't. The clothes described were more than the ladies wore.

In the automobile-for-sale columns, notification that Gay Deleon, of Park Avenue, would be willing to dispose of his custom-built French car. That meant the God of Dice was looking illy at Deleon.

Covering half a page was an advertisement of Rose Dawn in the latest Grady super-picture, "Sin," first metropolitan production at the Alhambra Palace. Right across from it another, smaller advertisement of a cut-rate department store, offering for ninety-eight cents, reduced from five dollars, "My Hero Husband: Life of John Dawn; by Rose Dawn." The ninety-eight cent copies, it was explained, were slightly soiled.

And much robbery; hold-ups; shooting of husbands, lovers, and such; old-fashioned murders done with an ax. Notable account of the arrest of one Lopez, alias Greasy Pete, alias the Sieur Nuit, for practicing clair-voyance without contributing to the police fund, and for stealing a widow's pearls.

Account also of an attempted hold-up of Dr. Russel Spencer, of East Fifty-Ninth, on his way back from the Grady-Dawn wedding, by one Dinnis McGinty. The doctor had cracked the aspiring robber over the head with his automobile fire-extinguisher and taken him to the police station, offering in case of cerebral complications developing to trephine without fee.

John Dawn Post 3 of the American Legion gives a Christmas dinner to cinema actors out of work. Anthony Anthony, head of the Argus Agency, has been spoken of as chief of the Federal Treasury secret service. Dr. Bellbender, of St. Cecil's All Souls, will follow his annual custom and preach a sermon to the poor. Colder tomorrow. . . .

Out of Times Square subway exit came three citizens. They paused to catch their breath before the blizzard, glancing over the newspaper head-lines. "Paper?" a boy asked. "Two cents. All about the fight in a rich man's home!"

"BRIDE SEES GRADY WAR!"

This the unintelligible heading, epic in its brevity and nonsense.

"Clay Ousted from Grady Home while Society Looks On!"

Wigley Arsen had been inspired to humor.

". . . Grady, known familiarly as 'Auld Tim' to the Hodcarriers' Union, remembered the days when he used to shovel cement, and shoveled Clay out the window. 'Next!' he yelled, looking for his wife, Rose Dawn. But she wasn't ready to go just yet. Grady's mother-in-law, Mrs. Higgs of Kansas and Illinois, joined gayly in the affray.

"It is rumored offers will be made to Mr. Grady to put the act in vaude-ville. . . ."

The three citizens bent their heads and plowed down Broadway.

"I wouldn't be that fellow Grady for ten million dollars!" said Citizen A. "I always held myself a gentleman. If I'd been that there Clay, I'd sloughed Grady in the puss." Citizen A was a little man, given to rickets.

"It'll cost him all of ten million to support Rose Dawn," said Citizen B, a very hideous man. "*I* wouldn't 'a' married her. No, Sir! Them sort of women come high. They say she uses powdered pearls to take her bath in. They say—"

Citizen B, who was a married man, a gentleman, and a Christian, gur-gled over scandals so vile they should have rotted out his clacking tongue.

"I don't believe a word of it!" said Citizen C, who had quarrel-some eyebrows.

"They're all alike, these movie people," affirmed A. "I've got a cousin who knows a fellow whose aunt married a man who's a photographer—"

"She'd better not try any of her vamping on *me*," said hideous B. "Not if she gave me ten billion dollars," agreed rickety A.

"I don't believe a word of it!" snarled quarrelsome C.

Then they, this being Christmas Day, plunged their way into the pack standing in the Alhambra Palace foyer, there to wait two hours like stifling cattle just to see Rose Dawn in "Sin."

XVI. DICTATION!

HIGGLESON TODD was in a fury, and his stenographer was aware of it. He stretched right fist forth as far as it would go, pounding his glass-topped desk. His big bald head shone with indignant sweat.

"What the devil do you know about this!" The poor stenographer, whose frail head was filled with thoughts of toddles, vampires, jazz, and fellas, knew nothing; nor was she the devil. "You know that lousy, rum-soaked old Irishman who's been coming in here the last five years for Grady's money?"

"Mr. McGinty, Mr. Todd?"

"*Mister* McGinty, *Miss* Dubby. I mean *McGinty.* Din—Din— Dinnis McGinty. That beet-faced beetle! That loafing blackmailer! That snorty old scalawag—McGinty! Do you know whom I mean?"

"Yes, Sir," said Miss Dubby, slowly, as great light dawned on her. "You mean McGinty!"

"You are right. I mean McGinty. He tried to hold up Dr. Spencer Christmas morning near Dawnrose, and the good old doc smashed him flat."

"Smashed Mr. McGinty?"

"Smashed McGinty! And now what do you think he's done?"

"What has he done?" breathed Miss Dubby.

"What do you *think* he's done?" roared Todd, who delighted to entice forth the frail little opinions of his stenographer and pounce on them like a cat on a pink babe mouse. "What do you *think* he's done?"

"I don't think," Miss Dubby gasped.

"*Verbum sapientis. Verbum* IN*sapientis,*" Todd chuckled.

"Sir?"

"I say you're a sap." He was in better humor; a pun always makes a man feel good. "When the doc had him locked up in some country hoosegow out near Grady's place, he said he was a friend of mine, and that Todd, Todd, Todd, and Todd would be his counsel. Damn his lying hide!"

"I beg pardon?"

"You don't need to. I say, damn his lying hide! He had letters from *me;* he had a check from *me;* he had my card. So they released him on *my* cognizance, on the cognizance of Todd, Todd, Todd, and Todd." (Higgleson spoke the words as reverently as though they were initialed with a G). "And now they tell me they want *me* to produce him for trial."

"Yes, Sir."

"What?"

"No, Sir."

"Of course he's skipped out. But I'm going to comb this universe for him. I'll set the dogs on him! And when I catch him, he'll hang, if there's a law in New York State!"

"Yes, Sir." Miss Dubby patted her back hair, not vastly concerned how many old men hanged.

"Dictation! 'To Colonel Stoughton Dawn, Biscayne, Florida. Dear and so forth. *In re* your inquiry of recent date concerning royalties accruing to the estate of your son, John Dawn—' "

Miss Dubby was fluttering for notebook and pencil. The one she located on her lap, the other behind her ear. "The address, please, again?"

"What address?"

"Captain Stoughton's address."

"Colonel—Dawn! Colonel like in nut."

"Dawn like in sky. 'Dear and so forth—' "

Higgleson Todd prayed.

" 'Dear nut,' " fluttered Miss Dubby, in a profusion of apology.

Todd laid his bald head on his tired hands. "Whom do the Giants play today, Miss Dubby?"

"Why, no one, Sir. It's December."

"Are you sure?"

"Yes, Sir, I think I'm sure."

"You think?"

"Yes, Sir. I think I think."

"Good!" Todd grinned like a tiger. "Great!" He clapped his hands. "Splendid! Now you chase out and see if you know a pen when you see one. Bring it to me. I want to write a letter!"

This was not a good time for old Thornwood Clay to enter the Toddian presence. He came softly in, shivering a little, coughing, bent of shoulder. There was (out, damned spot!) a smut on his collar.

Higgleson Todd looked gravely up. Todd's air differed subtly from that cheerful cordiality he was wont to show to old Thornwood Clay. He was not so certain now that the Clays were quite as good as the Todds. The Clays had been kicked out. Todd drew circles with his thumbnail on his desk.

"I want to speak to you, Mr. Todd."

"I see."

"I've been here before."

"I know."

Old Clay drew up straightly. He didn't like to glance at his pants, which were uncreased. "It's a very cold day," he said.

"Mr. Clay," boomed the lawyer, placing his forearms on his desk and gripping his hands, "there's nothing I can do for you." Old Clay bowed. "Mr. Grady has been so sick I haven't been able to see him, not even about the matter of a new will, which is important. He hasn't instructed me, consequently, to discontinue the—ump—remittances to you. If he does *not* so instruct, I'll have your quarterly check for you April first."

"April first?"

"That's the date."

Clay coughed. He sat down, though not invited. His hands fumbled restlessly over his thin old knees. Todd had never seen him before without a walking stick. Todd's impression was that Clay had suffered amputation of a limb.

"It's a very cold day," Clay muttered.

"But Mr. Clay," Todd continued firmly, squeezing his interlaced fingers, "I witnessed the altercation—ump—between yourself and Mr. Grady Christmas Eve. Am I wrong in assuming he does not feel kindly towards you?"

Old Clay pulled his knees. "Great ghosts!" he whispered. "I never thought I'd come back like a kicked dog to beg his charity!"

"Then why do you?" Todd asked with a kind smile.

Thornwood Clay plucked at his lapels. "It's a cold—"

"Indeed, the weather *is* quite brisk and seasonal," broke in the lawyer, with voice brisk and seasonal. "I don't need to tell you, Mr. Clay, that Mr. Grady is a very set man. If he takes a disliking to anyone, he never changes. Never! In your place, Mr. Clay, I'd rely on other resources."

Old Clay muttered. "Other resources?"

"Yes. Your revenues; your invested funds. What every man has."

Long silence. "I will speak plainly to you, Mr. Todd," Clay said at last. "(It's hard to speak plain facts!) I've thrown away everything. I have nothing. I haven't a nickel!" Clay gasped. Likely if he'd been inured to poverty all his life he wouldn't mind it now, at seventy years old; might likely enjoy it; might chuckle over it in some old man's home with a chew of charity tobacco. "I haven't even enough money to wire my son for funds. I haven't got—you understand?—a cent!"

Todd wove his fingers in and out. He had not thought Clay's affairs quite so bad as that. "Well—the banks. Borrow?"

"I owe thirteen thousand dollars," said Clay quietly, "including debts of honor, which must be paid, dollar for dollar! Dollar for dollar!" Again on his supercilious old face hardened that dreadful murderous look. "I have no one to go to. That's why I come to you."

Todd mumbled and withdrew his face. "I'm sorry Mr. Grady—"

"I come to you as a friend, not as to Grady's lawyer."

"Tied up," said Todd steadily. "First of the year. I'm sewed up tight. You know how it is."

"I see," said old Clay, stiffly arising. "Yes, I know how it is. Of course. It's hard to speak plain facts—"

"It is," said Todd with vast frankness.

"I've been staying in a rooming-house—I'm going to speak plain facts—a rooming-house, you understand!"

"I understand, a rooming-house."

"I am a Clay," the old man gasped.

"Yes, I know. You are a Clay."

Todd's soothing words did not soothe Clay; they seemed rather to irritate. He raised his fist and shouted. "A dirty, filthy rooming-house! With truck-drivers, and—and a fellow who sells something—and workingmen, and—and—"

He ended in a feeble swallow. His knowledge of workers did not permit him to catalog any more classes.

"And chauffeurs," Todd helped out, though his knowledge, also, of workers was limited.

"And chauffeurs! But I have no money, not a cent! And they've turned me out!"

"They'll do that," said Todd. "They've got the law on their side."

"My creditors have taken all I possess. I haven't got, Sir—I haven't got another shirt!"

"Well, well," said Todd. "But you can only wear one at a time."

"It's hard to speak plain facts," Clay said again. Yet it was easier than it had ever been before; a couple of days on an empty belly make facts exceeding plain. "But I haven't got a place to sleep! I haven't got—"

Todd sorted over some papers. "O, Miss Dubby!" he called over his shoulder. Miss Dubby slicked in. "Dictation!" Todd said in parenthesis. "As soon as Mr. Clay—O, yes; what were you saying, Mr. Clay?"

Clay spoke bravely out; strange words these, not known to the proud lexicon of the Clays. "I'd be obliged for a small personal loan, Mr. Todd. The Clays are good for any amount. Dollar for dollar, we pay our debts!—"

He waited, bowing slightly. Save for the shadow of his outward pride, he was no more the Thornwood Clay of a week before than he was the ghost of G. J. Caesar.

Higgleson Todd thought of the honor of the Clays, and he thought of old favors accepted, and of old friendship. And he thought of his own bank balance. Clay fees had made the legal Todds; the first Todd had been pantry-boy to old Ambassador Clay; out of the scullery he'd been taken up to honor the heights of the law. Todd thought of old friendship, and of old favors accepted, and of the honor of the Clays. He grew ashamed. His eyes faltered. Sweat was on his bald head. But he remembered his own bank balance.

"See if you can get that letter to Colonel Dawn straight now!" the lawyer snarled at Miss Dubby. "O, Clay. I'm damned sorry, Clay—"

The old man gripped his hat. "I'm not a beggar, Sir!" he said.

And turned, and strode forth from out that place.

Something magnificent in that exit; something Roman and heroic. He was a Clay, and old Speaker Clay, old Senator Clay, old Ambassador Clay would not have been shamed of him. No, nor the devils of Hell, who plot murder.

"Dictation! Dictation!" Todd called, to yell down his own shame.

"Maybe he's not a beggar now," Todd thought, "but he will be. He's too easily got rid of. I'd have given him a hundred if he'd squawked a little more!"

He turned to Miss Dubby, who waited with pencil poised.

"Was I a little abrupt with you a while ago, Mary?" he asked gently.

The visit of Clay had put him in good humor. He reached forth a square right hand and patted her on the knee. The girl clutched her note-book to her breast. In his eyes she saw that light more terrible than all his wrath!

XVII. THE RICH UNCLE

OLD Clay stumbled steadily from Trinity up Broadway. Miles of pavement, cold and stone. He did not know where he went. Winter night dropped on him near Times Square. His knees shook; he felt that he was sawed in two. The odors of a bakery-restaurant made him sick to vomiting.

Down Broadway came three citizens. "Old gent's drunk," said Citizen A.—"Awash to the scuppers," said Citizen B, who had been a yeoman in the Navy and was saltier than the ocean.—"I don't believe a word of it!" C scowled, snarling his straight black brows.

They stopped to watch old Clay feeling his way down a curbing. They nudged elbows and winked. In one half minute, a hundred gapers gathered about, all staring at whatever it was at which the three citizens were staring. A traffic officer moved over, patting his stomach.

"Wha's matter, Mister?" asked Citizen C. He sniffed, turning in argumentative triumph to his two confreres. "He ain't drunk; what'd I

"Young man!" Clay gasped. ("Yes, Sir!" said C, all attention.) "It's a very silly thing—" ("Well, Sir?" said C.) "But to speak plain facts, which are very hard to speak—" ("Indeed they are, Sir!" said C, while A and B nodded.) "To speak plain facts, I'm hungry!"

C scratched his head. The others looked surprised. "Why don't you get some chow?" he asked.

"I beg your pardon?"

"Why don't you feed your face?"—"Why don't you grub?" A explained, anxious, like all puny men, to be heard.

Clay heard a terrible laugh, but he did not know it came from his own lips. He was quite sure now he was not Thornwood Clay. Why, Thornwood Clay would no more have stopped to pour his troubles in the ears of three common fellows than he would have—than he would have starved. He wondered where Thornwood Clay had gone, and looked around in the wall of faces for the proud countenance of Thornwood Clay.

"Young men, I haven't got a nickel!"

"Gee, that's tough!" said A.

"Pretty rotten. Out of luck. Up the creek," said B.

"I don't believe a word of it!" said C. "Why don't you hock some of your jewelry? That ring and that watch and Lord knows what-all cigaret cases and cigar-clippers and solid gold note-books you've got would give you a good stake."

"He's right, old fellow," said A. "Go to your rich uncle."

Old Clay heard ringing in his ears. "My rich uncle!—You mean the Senator? Why, he's been dead forty years; and all his money went on the races."

"Cuckoo!" said A, tapping his feeble skull.

"I don't believe a word of it!" said C. "Here you, old guy. You've never been up against it before, I'll bet. Your rich uncle's a pawn-broker—see? You just go to him, any place on Seventh or Eighth Avenues, and pass over your jewelry for some jack. He'll fix you up."

The crowd pressed densely around, a wall of open mouths. Many bright ladies' faces were in it, cunning, beautiful, and bold. "The old guy's broke, Dot," said one fair girl. "No place for us," said Dot. "We're off." They shoved their way out of the crowds, Dot's red curls nodding with anger that she had been so long delayed, her stumpy legs looking absolutely bare in their fawn lace stockings.

A fat man called: "Who's killed? Is he dead? Does he want a drink?" A silver flask was proffered above the heads of the crowd.

The policeman sauntered up and began to shoulder people out of the way. "Cut out this here blocking of traffic. What's the matter? Move on, you. Move on! Get out of the way!"

Thornwood Clay, thus directed to a last recourse of which he had never thought, found on Eighth Avenue the shop of A. Bliss. Inside was a demi-professional actress, haggling for three more dollars on a diamond bar-pin, undoubtedly genuine. Twice Clay walked furtively up and down before those straight-barred windows, before the array of guns, mandolins, and brassy toilet-sets. He called up courage; hunger gnawed him. He had now forgotten quite the very ancient honor of the Clays, forgotten even that he was Thornwood Clay. He entered beneath that three-balled sign into the doors without hope.

"Fifty dollars," Gus Bliss offered for the trinkets on the counter. "I'm not buying 'em. Pay interest, and you get 'em back. It's more than I ought to allow, but you look honest."

Thornwood Clay did not know he was highly complimented. To Gus Bliss, against whom all men set their hands, who set his hands against all men, few were those who looked honest. Clay had a faint idea the initial cost of his trinkets was well more than a thousand dollars. He bowed, not squabbling.

"O, Miss Bliss!" howled Gus.—"Yes, Mr. Bliss!" a female voice howled back. A girl with high yellow hair and jutting nose appeared from a back room. She was sharp and shrewd and cursed the world with her nose. "Give the gent fifty dollars, Miss Bliss."—"Certainly, Mr. Bliss." As she passed Gus, she muttered: "Wha' jew gi'm so much for?"—"Mind your own business!" advised Gus, instantly on the defense. "Ain't I got a right to be a gent once in a while?"

"But wait!" whispered Clay, not counting the dirty fives. His face was working. "I want to get a revolver."

"Got your permit?" Clay did not understand. "Got to have a permit."

"O, Mr. Bliss!" Sadie howled, her voice like the amorous cry of a howling female monkey when love time falls on the forests. "Go ahead and trust him." She poked out her elbow. "He ain't no cop. They's a real pretty gun you could sell him for forty— forty-five dollars and not lose money on it, Mr. Bliss."

She laid out a little tin and mother-of-pearl weapon worth about twelve dollars, pawned for two. "I think you ought to oblige the gent, Mr. Bliss," she said, aggrieved. "He's a nice looking old gent, Mr. Bliss."

"Forty dollars, Miss Bliss! Why, that there gun didn't cost—"

Thornwood Clay paid down the money. "Is that right?" he asked.

In his coat pocket he thrust the gun, and his unaccustomed fingers curled round its cold stock. It hardened his heart. He thought for a little while he had killed a man, and that man was Thornwood Clay.

"Dollar for dollar!" he muttered crazily. "The Clays, Sir, pay their debts."

As he passed again the corner of 42nd and Broadway, on his way to register at the Hotel Babylon, he saw the crowd still shoving and gawping. "Don't push me," Citizen A crossly admonished Clay, not recognizing him. "Some guy's been hurt here."—"Some guy's killed," said B. C snarled that he did not believe a word of it. But all three remained watching, victims of the curiosity they had incited.

The girl in fawn colored stockings bare as flesh hurried by, drawing her plush imitation sable coat about her naked breast bone. "The old guy again," said she. "He's bust. I'd like to make a touch from Deleon."

"Try it," said her friend, laughing harshly. "He'd give you a kick, Dot."

"O, God! O, God!" whimpered Dot, as they scurried on. "And all the things he promised me. I loved him so!"

Her friend laughed, for she was a friend.

XVIII. THE BLACK CAT

IKE DUVAL, grim and relentless, found Dinnis McGinty, for whom the police were looking. He brought him to the Argus headquarters, into the office of Anthony Anthony down by the Battery. McGinty foul with dirt, as if just pulled from an ash-barrel; unhealthily fat, as if he'd just swilled on garbage. From his coat pocket a thin, weazened black kitten stuck its face, dolorously whining. McGinty truculently pulled up his pants, to show his independence.

"Picked him up on Tenth Ave.," said Ike Duval. "Thought I might as well haul him and let Argus get the credit. Stand up for Mr. Anthony, McGinty!"

"Give him a chance, Ike."

"I'm not afraid of ye!" said McGinty to Ike, with jerk of his head. "I'm not afraid of ye!" to Anthony, with another jerk. He reached down one of his great red fists and closed it about the kitten's neck, softly stroking that scrawny little black imp till it bubbled and boiled with purrs.

"Ye know," said McGinty to Anthony, surveying him close. "Ye have a face that I have seen befar-r." ("You've been against the law before," grunted Ike Duval.) "I like yer face, Mister-r Anthony. 'Tis a keen and fri'ndly one. Ye are a man that feels deep in the heart. And ye have the devil-may-drink- wit'-us look about ye that belongs to the fighting men of Car-rk o' Car-rk!"

"Go an and git off and away wid yer blarney!" said Anthony, laughing suddenly. "What are you trying to get from me, McGinty?"

"I mane it. 'Tis no blarney. And 'tis nothing I'm after-r being after-r."

The black kitten had wriggled out of McGinty's pocket. From table to chair to floor it bounded in little parabolas. It strutted with waving tail. In its promenade it paused beneath a picture of Roosevelt, staring up. It sharpened its claws on the floor; it arched its back; it spat, striking out unsheathed claws like a boxer. Roosevelt glared down. " 'Tis a good Dimmycrat!" said McGinty with pride. The kitten turned tail, and scampered, and leaped to a window ledge, still spitting.

McGinty grew grim and serious. His bloated, red face wore that expression of comical intensity seen often on the faces of ludicrously fat people. "I have something I want to say to ye, Mister-r Anthony!"

Solemn Ike Duval moved over, standing by the door. "My duty to warn you that anything you say may be used—" Anthony began.

" 'Tis not o' me. 'Tis of auld Tim Grady. Know ye him? Yer men have guarded him. Listen to me, Mister-r Anthony Anthony! I have a word to tell ye about that rum-soaked auld hog!"

Anthony's deep brown eyes half closed. He picked at his cuff.

"Hark ye! He's kicked me from his house—I'll tell the tale of it. And make of it what ye may! 'Tis known to no man bar-rn but me, Dinnis McGinty! 'Twas far-rty years ago, in Car-rk o' Car-rk..... Tim cracked him wit' a bottle on the head. . . . And Scotland Yar-rd itself is after-r being after-r him! Tim Grady is a murder!"

Anthony opened his eyes sleepily.

"He'll tr-ry to ditch his auld fri'nd, will he? He'll l'ave Din McGinty to star-rve—kick me out in the snow—have his doctor slam me on the nut when I ask him for some money—make his ly'er sic the cops on me!" Dinnis was working himself into a fury against old Tim, in which his animosities against Spencer and Todd had equal weight. "No man knows of it but you and me. He's a murder!—Ye hear-r me, Mister-r Anthony?"

Anthony shook his head. "Easy! Go easy, Dinnis McGinty."

"Where's me black kitty?" roared McGinty, in a childish passion. Tears of rage started from his watery red eyes. "I'll take him and go. I though ye were me fri'nd. Are ye tr-rying to stale me black pussy-cat from me, Mister-r Anthony? I'll git auld Tim for all o' ye! Where's me cat?"

"What did you say, McGinty?"

"Ay, but ye heard me! Ye heard me! Are ye hired by auld Tim, too? I'll write this to the newspapers! I'll sprid it broadcast o'er the land!"

"He's crawled out the window," Ike said sourly, coming up.

"Ye lie!"

"What did you say to me?"

"I said ye lie; and lie ye do. Put not your fists on me; I come from Car-rk o' Car-rk! Ye lie! He's not a he—he's a she! Give me me cat!"

The south window was six inches ajar, and the black kitten had crawled through. Anthony threw the window open. On an icy ledge not a foot wide the kitten clung, whining and waving its tail. Anthony tried to reach it with his arm, but it was too far.

"Me black kitty!" cried McGinty, strangely tender, strangely maternal. "Me black Shamrock! O, me poor little star-rving pussy-cat!"

"Take a good look at it, brother," said Ike Duval. "It'll be a grease spot on the Battery in about seven seconds."

"By God!" said Anthony, looking at the cat's scared, piteous blue eyes. "I don't like to see a living thing die alone!"

He did not smile, but he did not hesitate. He threw himself over the window ledge, his feet dangling into sheer space ten stories deep, and began to edge his way towards the cat. Sleet on the stone, slick as glass. The air which stirred his cropped black hair was keen and thin.

"I'd not do that for living man!" whispered Solemn Ike, his throat dry. "Not for my brother. Watch out, watch out, Chief! You're slipping!" Ike leaned forth to grasp Anthony's arm, but Anthony was out of reach. Far, deep below roared the street, with voice like Niagara's caverns.

Space was blue below, hazy and unreal. Cruel snow lay over Battery Park. Beyond the park the scummy gray waters of North River, where river and tide fled out to sea. Tug-boats whistling, sail-boats drifting, great ocean liners sliding forth to brave death beyond the outermost horizons.

Blue and cold and clear it was. The gray surge ran upon the bay. "Come out, come out with us to death!" the passing boats saluted.

Down in the streets hurrying noontide crowds halt. They gather in knots, staring up a hundred feet at the man alone upon the narrow icy ledge. Stolidly they wait, impassively hoping for catastrophe.

"The human fly!" says Citizen A, straightening his feeble shoulders. "I always felt I'd like to try that myself."—"Bet he's doing it for the movies," says Citizen B. "It's all a fake."—"Ha, ha! What's the matter with you lunatics!" Citizen C jeers. "It's only a dummy."

Police Lieutenant MacErcher grasped the arm of his brother, editor of the *Morning Mist.* "It's Anthony!" he shouted. "That crazy fool!"

"What Anthony?"

"That crazy fool! Runs a detective agency just to look for trouble. Always in it. Watch him! What's he after! Out of the way! He's falling! Run from under, you fools!"

A groan of horror swelled from the crowd as the little man far up swayed over. Men hit and kicked to get out of the way, their eyes crazy with terror.

But Anthony did not fall. He picked up the cat by its scruff. Carefully he edged his way back towards the window, holding hard to the treacherous ledge. Ike and McGinty grabbed his shoulders. They pulled him back to safety.

"For a black cat!"

Ike Duval's solemn face was working; his hands trembled. Horribly he began to swear. "That was a fool thing, Chief!"

Anthony wiped drops of snow from his face. "It has such pretty blue eyes, Ike."

"The damned blue-eyed jinx! It has a look like the woman Grady married."

Dinnis McGinty clasped the kitten in his fat arms, rocking it, crooning over it. "I don't mind telling ye, Mister-r Anthony, ye're a brave man. A br-rave man! Here's the hand of Dinnis McGinty. Ye did it for me!"

"I'd do the same thing for nothing," Anthony said coldly. "I'm not afraid to die."

"I'll take no back denial! Ye did it for me! The hand of Dinnis McGinty! 'Twas niver clasped by coward. We're fri'nds! Remimber it, if ye ha' need of me. 'Tis Dinnis McGinty who has clasped yer hand!"

Dinnis reared back, infinitely proud. It is a lie that the Irish are not true. They abide by an oath. They are lealest of the leal. Infinitely and tragically they are sincere.

Anthony was inclined to laugh. He was a poseur and afraid of posing. A solitary and egocentric man, he distrusted friendship, all sworn vows of faith. But the clasp of Dinnis was warm with earth and a quick pulse. Anthony felt himself smiling. Misanthropy is not justified.

"Well, shall I turn this fellow over to MacErcher?" growled Solemn Ike.

"That wouldn't be friendly, would it?" Anthony asked, with a gesture.

XIX. CUP OF DEATH

THOUGH old Tim lay upstairs in a darkened chamber, dismally ill, New Year's Day was not unhappy in his home. New homes, new laughter. New brides, new mothers-in-law.

The indomitable spirit of always loquacious Mr. Higgs, merry as a buzzard, kept things up. It was her home now. She was established as firmly as Gibraltar on the pillars of the deep. She ran things much as she had run the Harvey eating house in Moline, much as she ran all things which came beneath her claws, including her daughter. She swayed importantly on her hips, with a slow and easy motion.

"Precious fish! My eye!" muttered Buddy Schermerhorn. "Will Rose be like that when she grows up?"

Higgleson Todd, to whom Squirmy spoke, looked from Squirmy's feet up full eighty inches of length, and back again. Todd's square face was angry. Not less than sacrilege to compare Rose Dawn to her mother! Slowly Todd turned his back, giving Squirmy view of his bald occiput, which was shiny as his face and much like it, only it had no nose.

A dinner party was assembled with the intention (as Ma Higgs put it) of disgusting the turkey. Higgs was very simple, holding simplicity the essence of true breeding.

In spite of all the reasons she had for pride—her daughter, son-in-law, and herself—she did not believe in assuming airs. All these here people who purr so soft, who sniff, and shudder, and slide around like as if they didn't have no bones—in short, the gentry—are only pretending. Mrs. Higgs believed in being plain-spoken and natchel.

They dined. Todd, Schermerhorn, van Chuch were there; van Chuch was always there with food. Dr. Spencer had come accompanied with his son Laurence, and his wife. Mrs. Spencer had a wonderfully arched nose, silver hair, and many glittering diamonds; even in her sleep she could not forget she had been a Sears, of Boston, and consequently wore a nightcap. Laurence Spencer was a big, broad young fellow, with pink skin about which women raved, and innocuous blue eyes. Ten years before, football helmets had made him nearly bald. His left arm was stiff as a bough, no flexion in the elbow; that was a memento of the glory of war.

To complete the party—Rose and Maveen Grady; a Boosten Claude from Biscayne, Florida, knife-faced and small, but with a bush of hair big as a lion's; a bobbed-haired girl of forty who went in for art; and the usual thirsty young female shifters.

Talk paused. Higgs led all in discoursing the entrails of oysters.

"Are these things poisonous, Doctor?" asked the girl with bobbed hair, who here (because her name is famous) will be known as the Arty Girl.

"Not necessarily." Spencer dug his fork tines into the squirmy animals. "Sometimes, though." He caught the eye of Todd, who sat on the other side of the Arty Girl. "I was thinking of the case of Mrs. Mallow, Todd."

The Arty Girl giggled. "Mallow! What a silly name! Marsh- mallow?"

"I think her first husband's name was Marsh," said Spencer.

"Married twice? Don't you think marriage is silly?" asked the Arty Girl.

Spencer was not to be drawn into such a sweet discussion. "The first husband died of drinking arsenic," he puttered.

"What a very dreadful habit!" The Arty Girl half swallowed her napkin. "I've tried perfume, but not that. Isn't prohibition frightful? I know a man who never touched a drop before in his life, and now he's acquired the most consuming thirst for Worcestershire sauce. He mixes it with—"

"But I was speaking of oysters," Spencer said loudly, waving an impatient hand. "Mallow, the second, died from eating oysters."

Todd tapped his fork. "I'd not say that, Spencer," he advised, leaning around the Arty Girl. "You testified that at the trial. But it wasn't proved."

Spencer pulled his sandy beard. "You handled Mrs. Mallow's case excellently, Todd. The odds were all against you."

"I will always fight for justice!" Todd said loudly.

"An excellent defense," Spencer insisted. *"Entre nous,* Todd, wasn't she guilty?"

Todd wiped his mouth. He sipped water. "She was acquitted."

"Why was she tried if her husband ate oysters?" the Arty Girl demanded indignantly. "You talk about equal laws! You men have it so fixed that we women are simply your slaves if we marry you."

"I diagnosed rat poison with the oysters," Spencer said drily. "Rat poison contains phosphorus, arsenic, and other indigestible things. Though my friend Todd thought differently. She was a good-looking woman."

Other conversation had died. The table listened.

"You say she *poisoned* him?" Maveen Grady called across, fixing her glances, not on Spencer, but on Rose Dawn's beautiful blue eyes. "How could she do that!"

"Why, with poison!"

Boosten Claude yapped sharply. "That woman is in Biscayne now."

"They's plenty o' men," said Mrs. Higgs, "I wouldn't mind poisoning."

"Isn't that just too true!" cried the Arty Girl.

Spencer looked over to where his son sat beside Maveen. He would have been very pleased for Laurence to develop interest in Maveen; not that he believed in fortune hunting. That brought up thought of marriage.

"Mrs. Mallow wouldn't be such a bad match for you, Todd," he said with an ironical flicker. "She was something of a looker once."

"Thanks, Spencer. I prefer my relations with her to be legal."

"But marriage is so disgustingly legal!" chirped the Arty Girl. "Are you a confirmed bachelor, Mr. Todd? You know, I think that marriage—"

Arty Girls of forty years don't get much attention. They may know as much as pouting little seventeen-yearers, but it doesn't seem plausible.

"I mean I prefer to be her counsel," Todd explained irritably. "If I ever marry, it won't be to a woman twice a widow."

From the windows of his round spectacles Spencer looked at Rose Dawn, who was lightly chatting with young Squirmy, snaring his poor pickled heart. Already once a widow—Todd followed Spencer's glance and thought. He broke off abruptly.

Laurence Spencer, who was on vacation from Harvard Medical, talked quietly to Maveen of Harvard. "My brother Padriac went to Yale," Maveen said. Young Spencer nodded with quiet condescension. "O, yes, a goodish school," he said.

Mrs. Higgs's blue eyes were closing. She awoke to her social duties with a little grunt. "You say she used rat poison?" Higgs demanded, though the conversation had drifted ten minutes beyond Mrs. Mallow.

Boosten Claude drank steadily, quietly, as becomes a gentleman from the South. "She's trying to get married again. Ten men she's after in Biscayne call themselves the Suicide Club."

That brought laughter.

They were in the salad. Squirmy, not to put too fine point on it, was in a stew. He pulled his budding moustache, sprawled back in his chair, and surveyed Spencer thickly. "How's our Harp host, Doctor?"

Spencer did not like the tall young man. He raised his eyebrows.

"Yes, Dr. Spencer; how *is* Mr. Grady?" asked a proper flapper, recalling that she should have asked before.

"Just a little fluttering of the heart. I'll keep him quiet for a while," Spencer said. "In a month or so, I'll send him South."

"The *Thorn's* ready," said Captain van Chuch.

Talk ran on ships, wintering resorts, golf, women, the new books, and suchlike oddities. They were in the demi-tasses.

"Did I tell you, Doctor?" asked Rose, leaning over with limpid eyes. "Mother had me send up some light wine for Tim. He is so restless. She thought it would be all right with you."

"O, yes, perfectly all right." But Spencer was fidgeting nervously in his seat. Throwing down his napkin, he arose; and his chair toppled back. "That reminds me I ought to see him. I'm going to be rude and break away."

"Be as rude as you please," said Mrs. Higgs graciously.

Slowly from the dining room the physician walked, hands clasped behind, staring at the carpet. Once around the turn of the door, out of sight, he dug in his toes and hurried. He leaped up the stairs, pattering without dignity into Tim Grady's chamber.

"Don't let him touch it!" he gasped. Then: "How much has he taken?"

The night nurse, a plump girl with yellow hair and broad, clean forehead, arose softly, covering a letter she'd been writing. "What's that, Dr. Spencer?"

"Didn't Mrs. Grady send up some wine, Miss MacErcher?"

"O, yes." She smiled. "Of course I didn't think of giving it to him without your orders, Doctor. I simply thanked her."

"Well, that's good! Of course you wouldn't. Excuse me, Miss MacErcher."

Jennie MacErcher brought forth a bottle of muscatel. "I tasted it," she confessed. "And it was bitter."

"Bitter? Like what?"

"O, just bitter."

"All liquor is bitter," said Spencer, curiously agitated.

Jennie MacErcher looked at him understandingly, reading the perturbation he endeavored to hide. She drew her own conclusions.

"Well, well! I'll take it along, and analyze it. Might be boot-legged stuff. Might be—You understand a wife is apt to want to provide little delicacies for her husband," Spencer explained lamely, wiping his glasses. "It is your place to prevent them."

"I think I know my duty."

"Of course, of course." Spencer clapped his hands and turned to Tom Jefferson, who sat silently, at the bed's foot. "No need of your staying here, ah—Doctor—ah—" could find no suitable form of address, and for the rest of their intercourse would address Tom as You. "I don't think I'll need to call *you* into consultation," he finished.

"He likes to have someone to curse at when he wakes up," growled Tom. He arose, and his great bulk filled the shadowy room, his eyes were dangerous with light. "It makes him happier."

"And he can't curse at Miss MacErcher," Spencer smiled.

"O, can't he!" Jennie MacErcher cried.

"Well, it's his way. You mustn't mind, Miss MacErcher. Ten dollars a day, instead of six. That's something."

"And eat alone, or with the servants!"

"Do you prefer to dine with Mrs. Higgs?"

Jennie laughed. "I wasn't brought up with the pigs," said she.

Tim Grady groaned in his sleep. His wild eyes opened, staring without sight, or with sights too horrible for most eyes. He muttered: " 'Tis a bloody, bloody moon! I feared for it!"

"He's always moaning that," Jennie explained.

"Mr. Grady's looked on the liquor when it was red," Spencer smiled. "And you won't forget, Miss MacErcher? Not a thing, except under my orders!"

"What do you take me for!" Jennie cried, forgetting professional dignity.

"A credit to your profession, I'm sure," the physician said, patting her arm. "Of course. But keep watch!"

Jennie MacErcher suspected dangerous things. She set her broad mouth.

Dr. Spencer wrapped the bottle and put it in his overcoat pocket. But that night, after he'd driven Buddy Schermerhorn and the Arty Girl to their homes, he looked for it, and it was missing.

XX. MURDER IN THE STARS

PETE LOPEZ crept through Deleon's door like a shadow, stood with his back to it, listening for sounds beyond. "Look, Gay!" he whispered, drawing Deleon over to a window. "I'm being spotted!"

Deleon looked. Eighty feet down, on the far side of Park Avenue, Ike Duval stood. Hands in overcoat pockets, unwinkingly he watched the apartment house entrance, as though if he but blinked his solemn eyes it would dry up like a bubble and blow away.

Deleon sneered. "Not the first time you've been shadowed, Pete. What are you blubbering about? No one thinks any more of you than I do. You're worth ten thousand in cold cash bail to me."

"It's a private dick from the Argus Agency. Old lady Schermerhorn's sworn to get me. What's wrong with the painted old fool? She got back her pearls."

"Tell her the stars say pearls are unlucky."

"She doesn't believe in the stars any more."

"Does old Tim Grady still believe in the full moon?" Deleon asked. He sat down, picked up a pack of cards and swiftly ruffled them. "You went out to Dawnrose and saw him?" The crisp pasteboards snapped.

"I went out. He's still laid up. Sleeps most all day. He's raving mad because Spencer won't let him have liquor."

"And Rose?"

"So far as I know, he hasn't seen her since the wedding night."

Deleon shuffled the cards, and smiled. As by magic, from the top of the deck he dealt four aces.

"That's the kind of card reading I believe in," Pete admired. Deleon made an impatient gesture. "Old Grady had mentioned my name in his ravings, so I got into the house easy enough. Old Higgs hates me, and Rose—Well, Rose kind of looks down on me, though she was always soft as a kitten, and tender hearted. You see, she thinks I was friend to Johnny Dawn."

"You did me a good turn there, Pete," Deleon admitted.

"I didn't have much chance to throw a bluff into old Grady," Pete said. "The nurse was a superior blond thing who had to listen in to everything."

Deleon laid down his cards. "Pretty?" he asked, with tongue on his lips. He brushed his sleek black hair.

"Can't you think of anything else?" the Sieur Nuit asked with a smirk. "She's husky enough to crack you on the jaw and lay you by the ears. Old Spencer'd given orders Grady mustn't be excited, and every time I opened my trap she put her fingers on her lips and shushed me. And then that ugly black ape of Grady's was watching. He hates me. I'll get him yet, the growling nigger!"

"You'll get hanged yet, too."

"So I couldn't get a private word in edgewise. Did you ever see that nigger's arms? They're like an elephant's hooves."

"But you spoke to old Tim?" Deleon said impatiently.

"Yes. Not sure if he knew who I was, or even heard me. He only gave signs of life when he opened his trap and groaned for whisky. But I fed him a little of the old bunk. Scared him about the full moon. Told him he was a fool to marry Rose. Put the fear of Hell in him. Hinted he'd do well by his soul to give her a divorce, with a fat dowry to keep her in chinchillas."

"You didn't need to be so plain, Pete."

"I thought I might as well go the limit. Tom, this big smoke, must have heard me—he's got ears like a cat's. Before I knew it I was down the stairs and out the door." Greasy Pete felt his brown neck. "Had a chance to palm a souvenir at that," he laughed. "I picked up, from a table in his room—this!"

"Can't keep your hands off, can you Pete?"

In Pete's thin, sensitive fingers shone the broad-bladed serpent knife. Sharply he whirled it, admiring it with glances fierce and ecstatic. No better hands had ever been fashioned for the knife, no better knife for those hands.

"Look, Gay!"

Lopez flicked his wrist. He cast the knife, spinning, tumbling, over the room. It struck against a pillow, its sharp point shearing silk.

"Johnny Dawn used this in 'Hearts Afire,' " Pete said. "I stole it—"

"You stole another thing, too, Pete, from old John Dawn—"

"But I stole this. I loved it. Had to hock it. Queer it should have come to Grady eh?"

"Queer," said Gay Deleon. He shook and cast a pair of dice, rattling them over the table. "Snake-eyes!" Pete cried with a hiss. He retrieved the serpent knife, soft a lover fondling its carven hilt.

"You're wondering, Pete, why I wanted you to give a scare to old Grady."

Lopez's brown face wrinkled. "Not wondering so much, Gay. Maybe Rose Dawn with a couple of millions alimony would be more worth marrying than Rose Dawn without a cent."

Deleon rolled the dice again. They turned up seven. "I win, Pete."

"Not so soon, Gay! You haven't a chance with Rose, rich or poor. I know her! In her heart, I'll swear, she's still dopey about John Dawn."

"I know her better," Gay Deleon said softly, wisely.

Lopez, small as a monkey, smaller than Deleon, who was undersize, drew up his heels on his chair, clasping his knees. "I'll lay you a thousand, no."

"You haven't a thousand, Pete, and I haven't. Don't be a fool!"

"Well, I like to gamble."

"So do I. And I may win."

Deleon's Chinaman opened to a knocking at the door. Ike Duval thrust in his head, fixing Pete with his solemn, steady eyes. His right overcoat pocket sagged with the weight of something iron. "Does Mr. Smith live here?" he asked for exit cue, satisfied at seeing Lopez not escaped him.

"Yes, I'm Smith," Pete jeered. "Want to see me?"

"I mean Mr. Jones," Ike muttered, taken off guard. "Where can I find Mr. Jones?"

"Lots of him in Hell," Pete said.

Deleon watched at the window till Ike emerged from the apartment house entrance and took up his stand again. Deleon thrust his hands in his pockets, scowling at Pete.

"A fine stink you've got yourself into, Pete! And fine for me! Do you realize your bail has tied me up for ten thousand, every cent of cash I had or could raise?"

"It's gone. Let it go. God bless it!" Pete yawned.

"What do you mean?"

"I'm skipping out, Gay. Heading for happier climes. Vamoosing South."

"You mean you're jumping bail on me?"

"That's the English of it, Gay. Old lawyer Wiggs himself couldn't get me off this time; and he's saved me a thousand years up the river. They've got me dead, and old Lady Schermerhorn's fixing to nail me. I hauled up the ghost of her husband in a séance once, and she's never forgiven me for it. If I stick around, I'll get twenty years."

"Listen, Pete," said Deleon coldly, walking up and standing over Lopez. "This is nothing funny. We all know you're witty as a fool. I tell you that ten thousand dollars is everything I have. My God, I can't even stake my table!"

"Take a chance, and run it without a bank."

"And find myself blown full of holes if some fellow makes a winning! You know what happens if I can't pay."

"We all take a chance, Gay." Lopez was very lighthearted.

"You've taken one too many! Do you know I've had to put up my car for sale? I need money to pay my rent. Clay (damn him!) never paid up twenty-two hundred he owes, though I tweaked and cursed him till I thought he'd go out and rob the mails to come clean with me. His damned old honor!"

"He's good. He'll pay some time."

"When Hell shows dew! I'd counted on him. You see what a mess your foolishness has got me in, Pete. You've tied me up, Pete. You can't jump bail!"

"Well, I hope I can, 'cause I'm going to."

"Listen to me, Pete!" Deleon tapped his finger on Pete's sleeve. "Now, wait! Suppose—suppose I say you shall not go?"

"Suppose you do?"

"Suppose I say a word to him," Deleon whispered, brushing his arm in the direction of the window. "Suppose I call in my bail and surrender you?"

Lightly Lopez brought out a cigaret. "Suppose," he said, between puffs. "Suppose I say a word" (puff) "about a man named Weinvoll in Milwaukee" (puff, puff) "or about a man" (puff, puff, puff; Pete's brown face was merry) "named Dusty Hoag, of Waco, or about—"

"Damn it! You won't!" Deleon crashed the table. "You'll hang!"

Pete puffed like a locomotive. He squinted through blue. "Gay, my friend, we'll hang together," he said gently.

Deleon brushed his sleek black hair. His hand jammed in his right coat pocket. His black eyes grew narrow.

"Pete," he labored, "I'm speaking to you as a friend and I tell you you can't skip out! I need that ten thousand. It means too much right now."

"Your ten thousand, or my twenty years, Gay, old-timer?"

"I said—that you—won't go!"

"Stop!"

"You heard me!"

Pete leaped from his huddle in the chair quick as a rattler strikes from coil. A sharp point bit into Deleon's ribs.

"Drop that gun in your pocket, Gay! Give it here! Not that way, you fool! Butt first!" Pete was still laughing. "This knife, a gift from the Gradys." He pocketed Deleon's gun. "Sharp! Feel it!"

"It is sharp," whispered Deleon, swallowing.

Pete sat down again. He scratched his head. "Listen here, Gay. No sense in your getting excited about your ten thousand. I'm worth more money than that to you. I'll make a strike again, and you'll get it. Damn it, you'll get it, as you always do! I'll toss it over the table on your loaded dice or your educated cards!" Pete smiled his dark smile. "We don't want to break the old friendship for ten thousand. I helped you with Rose Dawn once; I can do it again!"

"You mistook me, old Pete," Deleon said thickly. "You were too quick."

"Quick enough."

"Now give me that knife."

"Some day," said Pete, suddenly sober, "perhaps, my friend!"

XXI. PADRIAC GRADY WALKS ALONE

WIGLEY ARSEN, always well-dressed, always an agreeable mixture of confidence, equality, and obsequity, beat his way down Broadway in the evening throngs. This was a night of blizzard.

He blew snow from his brown moustache. Vaguely he wondered how in the name of the Demons of Frost the red-lipped women stood it, with melting snow on their deep bare breasts and freezing snow on their cob-web stockings. They were sylphs of snow, they were living icicles, garbed in wraithy star-strewn gowns of mist. Now night and snow fell about them, and they were shadows.

Their gaudy ways were not for Wigley Arsen. He drank like a bounder, and he talked too much, and he was a good bit of a snob and rather an ass, but he was decent. And, remember, he was no fool.

A taxi crawled through the misty snow. Arsen peeked inside (he peeked at everything) and saw Gay Deleon, sleeky, cheeky, fur-coated, with a woman. She was a bobbed-haired personage of very great name, the Arty Girl. She hung on Deleon's glances as though for kisses, while he sat back with, hands on cane, confident, too confident, arrogant, with an arrogance assumed to combat scorn. He removed his silk topper to sleek his shiny black hair.

Arsen was amused. Women loved Deleon; why, women know. But the Arty Girl should not have permitted herself thus to be seen abroad. She had something of a face to sustain, though it was not beautiful. Deleon went with women whose men-folks would not have named him with a worm. Arsen remembered when Broadway scandal had linked Deleon's name with Rose Dawn, even before John Dawn died.

Smashing head-on into a man, Arsen mumbled apology in contemptu-ous tone, feeling he owed it to himself, if not to the man he'd bumped. Silently the man bent to pick up his hat, which had rolled to the snow. His bared dark red hair, curiously rich in color, showed a broad forelock strand of hair white as the snow. It was a brand unmistakable.

"Hello, hello, Padriac Grady!" Arsen cried, scrambling to retrieve the hat. "Haven't seen you in seven thousand years. Why weren't you at your father's wedding? My good friend, old Bellbender, was in top form. I wish they'd kept the jolly old custom of kissing the bride. Rose looked stun-ning."

"Rose?" Padriac repeated dully. "You call her Rose?"

Without being actually much smaller, Padriac had the appearance of being but half his father's bulk. Old Tim surged through life with a roar like storm. Men knew when he was coming, knew when he had passed. Padriac went like a shadow, attracting no one's notice. He might walk away down the street, and it could not be told just when he ceased to be visible. And he went alone.

"Of course I call her Rose," said Arsen. "Know her well. In love with her myself, old lad. My word on it. How's it seem to have her as mother?"

"I don't know her," said Padriac Grady, looking at the snow.

A monosyllabic man. By his red hair Padriac may have been born with as much inclination to loquacity as his father; but it had been knocked out of him. Padriac Grady seemed to have forbidden himself laughter, or expression of other emotion. His eyes were gravely gray, and so looked at life.

"Don't know her, Paddy! Great Lord, where've you been?"

"I've been in Chicago," Padriac said literally, "since before the wedding. And I live alone in town."

"But not to know your own step-mother!" Arsen paused. "Not to know Rose Dawn! Why I—I know her well!" he said, as though that settled something.

"She's been doing pictures for us ever since John Dawn went to war," said Padriac, feeling explanation was due this strange young man who knew his family so very well. "I've seen her in pictures."

"Then you know she's a damned fine-looking woman!"

"So I've heard."

"Why, any man could fall in love with her from her pictures!"

Young Grady made as though to push on. Arsen was conscious that Padriac, who had been a contemporary at college, did not know him from a jumping kangaroo. But that didn't worry Arsen, he was so sure of himself.

"Where can we go for a drink?" he demanded, grasping Padriac's arm.

"I don't, thanks."

Arsen stuttered, thinking of old Tim. "You don't at all?"

"Milk," Padriac said, without trace of humor. "Coffee, sometimes."

"Well, I say," Arsen jested, "I'll bet you don't even know my name."

Padriac coldly admitted ignorance. He did not know there were a thousand men Arsen called by first name who did not know Arsen's, first or last.

"I'm Wigley Arsen," the journalist said, with the simplicity of the great. "I was three years behind you at New Haven."

"I see."

"But we must celebrate! I'm just on my way to see Anthony Anthony. You know the famous Anthony Anthony, head of the Argus Agency?"

"I think I've heard of him. He's a detective?"

"One of my most intimate friends. A famous person. I know him well."

"I see," Padriac said once more. Conversation lapsed.

"You and he and I might go out for a blow," Arsen volunteered, "to celebrate your father's wedding, or your return from Chicago, or anything else you want to celebrate. Tony'd be glad to meet such a famous man as yourself, Paddy," Arsen added with a half laugh, showing trace of that servility, or power-worship, of which he himself was unconscious.

"I'm going to a movie," Padriac stated. "I'm going alone!"

Arsen was not rebuffed. "Well, cheerio. See you the club."

He watched young Grady drift down the street till snow covered his retreat. "A movie for a spree!" he thought with contempt. "Heir to twenty million, if it's a dollar. And old Tim makes him work harder than I do for a living." That was a pleasing thought. "A movie! And he doesn't smoke, drink, or go with the girls! He doesn't know how to laugh. Wait till old Tim dies, and he comes into his money. He'll blow up!"

Dot, of the street, stumped along, her imitation sable coat flung open from her breast. She did not even see Padriac Grady; she was looking for someone with money. But his quiet gray glances marked her out.

Arsen scudded from the thick of the crowd into the entrance of the great Hotel Babylon. The Babylon had once been very fine, though like all fine things it was now decayed. It was a bit flashy, and demi-famous. The new Tenderloin had grown up about it. Actors frequented it, and actresses with gentlemen friends.

On a tapestried lobby chair Arsen spotted old Thornwood Clay, sitting with bent shoulders. Clay did not stir; it seemed he had not stirred for hours. Arsen hurried around another way, for various mixed reasons of shame and snobbery not liking to greet old Clay. He needed not worry; Clay did not know him.

Anthony Anthony had his rooms in the Babylon. He had an arrangement with the Babylon's proprietor, Tiffany Bonnell, by which his men policed the hotel.

A queer sort of place for a detective to live, Arsen thought, in a theatrical hotel. Yet it seems reasonable detectives should do all things in a queer manner. Thinking it over, Arsen decided the Babylon was not an improper place, for he was conscious of a certain theatrical air in Anthony.

Anthony being out, Arsen wandered about the lobby looking for him. Tiffany Bonnell, a small-round-fat man, quite as bald as though his cousin had never married a Sir, was talking to Ike Duval. "Hello, Ike," said Arsen, breezing up and bursting in as he always breezed and burst. " 'Evening, Mr. Bonnell."

Ike had his hands jammed in the pockets of his belted green overcoat. His derby was over his eyes, showing he was watching someone. That derby served Ike as a sand-hole serves the ostrich. Suspiciously he stared at old Thornwood Clay, sitting motionless in his tapestry throne. Solemn Ike and Bonnell were talking Clay over.

Ike nodded a surly greeting to Arsen, and turned back to the hotel manager. His glance lingered just long enough to say: "This man's a crook!"

Bonnell was more affable. Arsen's face was unknown to him, but the reporter's bearing was magnificent. He bowed. "Good evening, Sir." Bonnell's hands were behind his back, but his voice rubbed them; his voice salaamed; his voice intoned: "O, what a wonderful fellow you are, Sir! I'm glad you are stopping at my hotel!"

"How fares my old friend, Mrs. Bonnell, Bonnell?" Arsen asked, pulling a handkerchief from his sleeve.

"Very well, Sir. Thank you."

"And my good friend, your cousin Janice, who married the Baronet of Chomdeley?"

"A little domestic trouble," Bonnell admitted, with a worried air. "The English allow wife-beating, you know. Other than that, she's very well."

"A bounder, that Chomdeley!" said Arsen, wiping his hands. "I'd cut him dead on the street." Arsen had never seen the English Sir. "I know him well. One of my most intimate— enemies." Arsen had almost slipped.

"Neatly said, Sir," Bonnell applauded with wan laughter. " 'Intimate enemy!' Ha, ha! Mine, too. You have perhaps visited him in England?"

"I'd cut him dead on the street!" Arsen repeated. "Beating his wife! That's no laughing matter. Why doesn't she shoot him?"

Bonnell rubbed his head. "I don't know she ever thought of it," he said.

"And Janice was one of my dearest friends," Arsen mourned. "For a whole season I was passionately fond of her, took her every place, danced with her once at the Schermerhorns. To think that beatings should bring tears to her bright blue eyes!"

"Janice has brown eyes, Sir," Tiffany Bonnell corrected, smiling archly.

"Her bright brown eyes, confound it! I'll bet I have in my collar-box yet a lock of her bright brown hair."

"Janice's hair is yellow," Bonnell said a bit stiffly. He no longer smiled archly. "A peculiar combination—brown eyes and yellow hair."

"Damned peculiar! I've been thinking all along of your cousin Maudine."

"I have no cousin Maudine, Sir."

"Of your wife's cousin Maudine."

"My wife has no cousin," said Bonnell, with narrow-glance. "Consequently she has no cousin Maudine." Arsen bowed to this clearly stated logic. "I know of no Maudine. I never heard of the name Maudine."

"Well, she's one of my most intimate friends!" Arsen cried in a fluster. "I know her well."

Bonnell turned away, his fat little stomach fluttering. "Who is this fellow, Ike?" he whispered audibly.

"No guest here," said Ike gruffly.

Bonnell turned his back completely to Arsen, seeming to kick out his heels behind him.

"Well, Ike, still watching Mr. Grady?" Arsen asked loudly, not wishing to beat shameful retreat. "Last time I saw you, you were sticking to him like a louse."

Ike did not care to think of himself as a louse. He heeled and faced Arsen squarely. "Mr. Anthony called me off the Grady case," he said sharply.

"Indeed, and why did my friend Tony do that? Of course you weren't doing any good there, but my intimate friend Mr. Grady seemed to think—"

"Mr. Bonnell and me are talking," said Ike surlily.

"Yes," said Arsen, in shrill, hysterical tones. "Yes, I see." He rose on his heels. "As my friend Mr. Bryan says, talking is good for the digestion—"

Ike Duval and Mr. Bonnell marched a few steps away. Arsen wandered off, somewhat discomfited, and wrung the hand of a total stranger whom he mistook for the French Ambassador. The Ambassador was a dark, graceful, greasy sort of fellow, answering to the name of Greasy Pete Lopez, and at present out on bail from the calaboose. He returned Arsen's salutation, looking all the time somewhat inauspiciously at the Arsenic watch.

"That fellow bears watching!" grummered Ike, flicking his thumb at Arsen.

"You don't say?" cried Bonnell, aghast. "What's he done?"

"It ain't so much what he's done, as what he might do," said Solemn Ike ominously. "He's never been caught yet. But I'd not be a bit surprised if he was implicated in *that* affair—You know."

"It couldn't be possible!" Mr. Bonnell was terrified to think he harbored such people in the lobby of his nice hotel. "You mean *that* affair—?"

He waited on his toes. Ike nodded heavily, affirming the worst.

"But what affair?" demanded Bonnell, after a pause.

Solemn Ike scratched his head. "Any affair," he explained.

Arsen's Serbian Ambassador (Arsen had decided Pete came from there now) shook hands again. He slapped Arsen on the back, thus entering Arsen's large, but select, circle of intimate friends. "Say, old-timer, lend me ten dollars till tomorrow, will you?" he asked in the voice of a brother. Arsen coldly glanced at his Turkish Ambassador. "I haven't got it," said he. So their brief brotherhood ended.

Ike Duval and the Babylon's manager turned their attention to old Thornwood Clay again. He sat silent as stone, staring at the floor's carpeted flags.

"He didn't bring any baggage with him," said Bonnell, "and he's stopped tipping the waiters. I caught him today fumbling for the price of a newspaper at the stand. Signs! He's broke."

"Make out his bill," Ike suggested. "If he doesn't settle, I'll give him the bum's rush to the street."

"Thornwood Clay, of the Clays!" Bonnell cried. "He's a gentleman!"

"He's broke, so he can't be a gentleman. Remember the first night he came here he sent a collect telegram to some joint in Florida? I got copies from the telegraph files. Clay wired—" Ike pulled tissue slips from his pocket. "He wired: 'Thornwood. Am short of cash. Can you send me funds?' And here's the answer came back tonight: 'Thornwood is away from Biscayne at present. He needs all his money. Mrs. Mallow.' So that's all."

"Well, well!" said Tiffany Bonnell. "That must be little Junior Clay."

"When a fellow like that," said Ike, jerking his head, "says he's short of funds, it means he's broke harder than gravel. With five dollars in his pockets, your gentleman struts into your hotel lobby and damns you out of it, so almighty proud is he. Thornwood Clay is done."

"It doesn't seem possible," Bonnell mused sadly. "The Clays have always been gentlemen."

"You ain't running an old man's home, Mr. Bonnell."

"It was in a Clay home that Chomdeley met my cousin Janice. . . A Clay once kicked a Vanderbilt down the steps in '43. . . ." Bonnell mused slowly. "When the Prince of Wales, God bless him!" Bonnell ducked his fat little body, "Edward the Seventh of sainted memory, visited the States with Newcastle in '60, he dined at the Clay mansion. And my grandfather, Ike, my own grandfather, was proud to be head butler. Proud to serve soup to the Clays!"

"He's in the soup now," said Ike Duval, having no reverence for kings or Clays. "It's his turn to be kicked down the steps."

"It's heart-breaking," said Bonnell, turning away his face. "Heart-breaking."

"If Grady could kick him out, I guess I'm good enough to do it."

But when Ike Duval approached old Clay, he was afraid of the old man's face of stone, afraid of the withered right hand which lay so steadily in his pocket. Afraid was Ike Duval of old Clay's eyes, in which burned the dreadful dreams of him who thinks of murder!

XXII. "HEARTS AFIRE" WITH ROSE DAWN

PADRIAC GRADY, walking alone, did not turn into one of the cinema palaces with sixty-piece orchestras. He passed the Alhambra Palace, flaunting Rose Dawn in "Sin," with eyes on the street. South on Broadway past Herald Square he walked alone. He found the place he had been seeking, a second-rate little theater, admissions seventeen and twenty-eight cents; children, eleven cents. A revival was advertised of the old Dawn thriller, "Hearts Afire."

It was not a success. No one with more than seventeen cents to spend cared to see the Rose Dawn of eight years before. And John Dawn was a dead one, forgotten by the New York which once panted at his name. Old things pass (and eventually new things). In eight more years, lovely Rose Dawn in "Sin" would be as forgot as now in "Hearts Afire."

Padriac stumbled to a seat beside a solitary man. Not more than two dozen spectators were in the house. The theater's lessee, Augustus Bliss, stood at the back biting his fingernails. An evil fairy had counseled him to try and gamble in the movies. Better the safe thirty per cent of the pawn shop.

"O, Miss Bliss!"—"Yes, Mr. Bliss!"—"I never ought to have took a chance in Art, Miss Bliss."—"I think you are a sucker," said Sadie Bliss.—"Ain't I got a right to be a gent once in a while?" asked Gus Bliss.

It was Anthony Anthony beside whom Padriac sat down. Only one glance he gave to Padriac Grady, whom he did not know. But that glance served him to remember young Grady at a later time.

"Hearts Afire" was gun-and-thunder Western stuff, in the good old style. Revolvers big as machine guns flashed in every scene. Indians charged around on truck-horses. The villain had black mustachios. Dead men died, and breathed on the ground, and raised up their heads slyly to see what was going on.

Rose Dawn, not starred yet, crude and artless, but the loveliest of golden-curled children, played leading ingénue to John Dawn's hero. A wildly laughing, acting, skipping creature with fleeting dimples and sudden eye-flashes. Nothing evident at seventeen of cold Rose Dawn, smooth in her perfections, the queen of art and hearts.

Where are gone those dimples now, Rose Dawn? Where are gone those sparkling eyes, richly promising true love? You may be artist now, Rose Dawn; and men may love your sculptured grace, Rose Dawn; and you may ravish the flat-chested clerks with the fury of your "Sin," Rose Dawn; and you may be an old man's love, beautiful Rose Dawn. But there are men with hearts afire for you, Rose Dawn, as you were in the old time, with golden curls down your back, joyous with artless love, your speaking eyes upon your hero who was your lover and your God!

How the flame dies. How the flame is gone. How the ash is bitter.

An old man, the ingénue's father, with floury hair and penciled wrinkles, passed away. He sat up in bed, tossed wide his arms, and toppled backward with a flop, to show he had passed away. Then the villain entered with a mortgage on the old cow ranch, and insulted Rose Dawn with an offer of marriage.

"O, Mr. Bliss! That there villain's the same gent pawned the Schermerhorn lady's stolen pearls, or my name ain't Sadie Blumkuss!"—"It's Mr. Lopez himself," Gus admitted gloomily. "You bet he's a villain!"

Debonair and dashing, brave John Dawn heroed it through flashing reels. He wore sombrero on black hair long as Buffalo Bill's, white silk chaps, and two guns; he rode like a Cossack. Now he galloped in billows of dust straight into the midst of Greasy Pete's Apache band; and snatched Rose from the burning stake; and shot ten men, biff-bang-boom! and galloped away again.

"O, Mr. Bliss! What are you staring at?"—"It seems funny to watch a dead man on the screen that way."—"I don't see anything funny, Mr. Bliss. I wish he was deader than he is, Mr. Bliss."—"He couldn't be no deader than he is, Miss Bliss. They's only twenty-three ladies and gents here to see him, and a Chinaman."

And now the squeaky piano begins tinkling music. Slapping sombrero to pony's sweaty flanks, John Dawn gallops straight for a cliff, Greasy Pete's howling Apaches behind him. Up to the brink, up to the brink, and over! Horse and man, over the cliff's lip, taking the hundred-foot drop to the river! The pony drops more swiftly. In two spouting towers, a big one and a smaller, the river water rises. John Dawn emerges, swimming in dizzy circles. The pony does not come up again. . . .

Anthony's eyes glistened. He took deep breaths, as does a man who smells the open wind. He struck his knee with clenched fists in a kind of tune,

And now in the last fade-out John Dawn and Rose Dawn, those two true hearts, vanish away, kissing languorously, black curls and golden curls entwined, swearing the forevers and the forevers. And the moon drops beyond the seas of Lower California. And that is the end of "Hearts Afire."

Dead, dead in the darkness. "Good-night!" on a colored plate. The piano stilled. Quick as a cat Padriac Grady went out, the cat which walked by himself. Anthony stopped a moment, speaking hesitatingly to Gus Bliss.

"You don't seem to be drawing very large audiences," he said in low tones. "What sort of an offer would you consider to kill that picture?"

"What's the matter with that picture?"

Anthony hesitated again. "Say, if you want, that I don't like John Dawn's face."

Sadie Bliss laughed shrilly. "O, Mr. Bliss!"—"Yes, Miss Bliss?" —"Tell the gent if he wore his hair long and had a moustache, his own face'd look pretty much like John Dawn's face."— "Maybe that's the reason he don't like it, Miss Bliss," Gus grinned. "But, say, ain't it the truth?"

XXIII. TIM GRADY'S WIFE

OLD Tim Grady moaning all the night.

"Who tied me down? . . . Get up, get out, get away! . . . O, the curse of Cromwell! . . . Rose! Rose! . . . Out ye go, Thorn Clay! . . . What's this on my head? Ice, ice! 'Tis winter cold. Tom! Tom Jifferson! Do ye hear me, black man? . . . Am I dead? Who killed me? . . . Killed! Killed! O, God, I didn't mane to do it! Burke! Wake up, Burke. 'Tis your childer crying after-r ye. . . Man—God! 'Tis blood upon his face! I didn't mane to do it! . . . Hark! 'Tis a bloody, bloody moon! I feared for it! . . . Ah, God have mercy on my soul! But ye, Rose Dawn. . . . The bloody moon! Pull down the shade! Tom, Tom, Tom! Where have ye gone?"

Dreams conscious and unconscious. A crazy-quilt of visions. Silken rags of splendor, bits of witless gathered wool, bloody tatters. Old men have old bad dreams! Tim Grady turned and twisted hugely on his bed. An ominous clock drew near to midnight.

Lights through Dawnrose were mostly darkened. Mrs. Higgs had gone to bed at nine. Maveen was out with Laurence Spencer, sowing her wild rye. Rose sat alone in her own chamber, before a little fire, far enough away from old Tim that his cries were not audible. Jennie MacErcher straightened Tim's coverings, but repeatedly old Grady tossed them off. His voice swelled and whispered alternately, like a rocky brook. One small light burned in a corner.

Giant Tom sat at the bed foot, great arms crossed, shaven, head on slowly heaving breast, waking to doze again, and breathing by starts. Long night vigils had carved in his cheeks, put a gray unhealthy pallor on their burnished black. His huge bulk, unsteadily visible in the murk, was awful and cloud- cloaked as any chimera of the Caves of Smoke. Glimpsing that terrible figure in his waking fits, deliriously dreaming, old Grady thought he beheld the devil. He slept again. His visions were kisses of the daughters of despair.

In her room alone, by the hearth-fire's whispering shadows, sits Rose Dawn. Late, but she does not go to bed. Sleep does not come well these days. And what sleep comes is dismal with dreams. The small fire fails. The long hour passes. Through a door ajar sounds Mrs. Higgs' snuffling breathing.

In the hearth of winter man's deepest verities are to seen. What dreams to Rose Dawn as she watches the frail flame, what memories of burnt out days? It may be none. Her blond head is beautiful, but not necessarily ponderous.

Dullness of midnight about. None here to pay her homage for her beauty's sake, for her honor as a rich man's wife. Her bearing grows a little wilted, her loveliness stale. Unknown to herself, perhaps Rose Dawn has grown to need adulation. It is a soothing morphia.

No lie abides in the light of fire. In that hour alone could Rose Dawn help but see her bridegroom for himself, an old man, vicious, foul-hearted, wilted with hours of joy known long ago, miry with the earth? Is that worth ten million dollars?

Rose heard her mother turn in sleep, and shuddered. Yet she thought she loved her mother. And knew God meant her to love her mother.

If Rose repented of the bargain her mother had forced upon her, she said no word. Some women have repented who bargained no worse than she. And some have said no word; but some have shot with a shotgun in the night, and some have taken gas.

Youth is precious, young love dear. But so is wealth. For Rose remained the future. Tim Grady was a rich old man, and he would not live long.

Mrs. Higgs snored heavily, muttered, slapped her pillows, and rolled off again into wheezing dreams. Rose's fingernails bit into her palms.

And in old Tim's chamber—"Is that yourself, yourself?" Tim groaned, leaning up his sick neck and surveying Tom, "What sor-rt of a worrisome funny-diddle is this, I want to know!" Tim struggled. Grim, silent, efficient, dangerously strong, the black man bent over him.

"I want my wife!" muttered old Tim Grady. "My wife!"

Spencer had predicted a month of convalescence, and Grady had not been ten days abed. He was strong; he was of the old race of giants. Writhing, threshing, kicking out, he threw coverings from him. Vainly Miss MacErcher strove to quiet him. Tom kept himself sullenly aloof. The girl had reprimanded Tom once before for what she considered a familiarity. And Tom did not forget.

"Lie down!" Jennie cried to Tim Grady. "Behave yourself. You must rest a long time yet, so you will be well and strong. Close your eyes and go to sleep."

"Sleep!" old Tim jeered, sitting up. "I've slept all night. Talk to me like a babe in ar-rms, will ye? Who are ye?" He was not unappreciative of her looks, for she was a woman. "What time is it? 'T must be nearly Christmas mar-rning.—Lay but your hands on me, Tom Jifferson, and ye'll rue it!"

He threw his feet over the bed's edge, swaying a little. He rubbed his face, which had grown grayer, less red, and scratched his rumpled red-gray hair. Now he began to curse, with a strength and fluency he had not excelled in the prime and heat of youth.

"Arrah, ye black nigger! Want to tell me what's good for me, do ye? Giving me some of your iducation? I'll tell ye when I'm after-r wanting your advice. I know what's good for Mister Grady!"

"I'll telephone Dr. Spencer this instant," Jennie threatened, "if you don't lie down like he's ordered."

Old Tim jeered. "Where's the whisky? I mind me I've asked for it be-far-r, and got some o' your sour looks. Who are ye, Susie? So I've been sick? Ye'll tilephone Spincer, you will! I pay Spincer! Fetch some whisky, Tom!"

Staggering, he rose, drawing a brocaded robe over his shoulders. "Fetch me some whisky!" he howled. "Am I going to wait all night?"

Jennie MacErcher fluttered about him like a chicken about a bull. "If you dare to touch a single drop of anything, Mr. Grady, I'll most certainly—I'll—telephone Dr. Spencer! It will kill you!"

The girl was nearly crying. Tim patted her cheek with great familiarity and pinched her chin. "Spincer thinks the liquor'll kill me? Whisky niver killed me yet, Susie. Saltpeter! Saltpeter!" He pulled a bell-cord madly, and fell down into a chair. "Where's my wife?" he demanded again.

Saltpeter came, buttoning himself into respectability. And went again; and returned with carafe and tumblers.

Tim's hand was shaky. Tom made no effort to help or hinder. Grady performed the sacerdotal rite of pouring liquor. He stood up to drink. The ichor of the gods raced in his veins. "Ah-h!" he sighed, cocking an eye.

His face grew redder. He slapped his chest. He poured the rye once more. "Ah-h!" He rubbed his stomach. His complexion grew boiling red. His shoulders squared. Again. At third quaffing of that usquebaugh on which infancy had been nursed, old Timothy Grady was himself again.

"Ay, that's the stuff! Puts some fire in ye. Help yourself, Saltpeter, Tom Jifferson, and ye, Susie, if ye've a mind to it. Ye've watched o'er me like sojers," he said. "I'm beginning to get recolliction. What day is it?"

Tim paraded out the door, flowery as a mandarin in his robe. He tapped on his wife's door, whispering impatiently: "Let me in!" No answer coming, old Tim Grady turned the knob and entered.

Rose was crouching by the fire, stirring it till it hissed with the fury of snakes. She shivered, though she was heated to red heat. With brass tongs she traced a design in the glowing coals. She had not heard Tim enter. She did not look up.

Old Tim paused to gloat over her. That joy had never died. His breath strove. Gray and yellow shadows passed across Rose's face. Her dimples were pits of black.

You know the trick of firelight: it may enhance ugliness, but never beauty. Firelight is a demon painter. By some subtle alchemy of shadow, Rose Dawn's lovely face was rendered peaked and grim, face of a witch before a cauldron. No more than a shadow is the change from beauty to foulness. A dullness fell on old Tim Grady, on the edge of his desire.

Rose Dawn listened, not hearing him. She thought she'd heard a whisper at her windows. And still she listened.

A stir, a tinkle; such sound as the wind, or an owl's passing, or the shattering of ice by reason of great frost, or a bat's whirring wing. Only that little single whisper in the confounding silence of night. But she felt cold, and did not look at the window.

Again she roiled the logs with tongs. Blue flames shot up. Rose squatted close to the woven fender, still shivering. The fire might be a semblance of a face. Her hand pressed her yet virginal breast. The face within the coals' glow was as of one burning in everlasting fire.

As she stood up the ugly shadows fled from her countenance, and it was mysteriously fair. Grady saw the tears upon her cheeks, and they were salt to the thirst of desire. He started towards her, not able to speak.

For an instant Rose saw him only as a dream. His rumpled gray hair was a halo. His brocaded robe looked like a carnival costume. She cowered behind the divan, gasping with excitement, involuntarily raising the fire tongs she held.

"It's me, Rosie. It's Tim!" Those languorous, crooning notes!

"Who let you up?" she asked in unsteady whispers. "You shouldn't be up! What are you doing in here!"

"Don't be frightened, Rosie, colleen! Who has better right, Rose Dawn?"

Rose Dawn—he used that name! Once her blue eyes winked. She paced back from him, curiously gasping, shuddering at sight of him, sick to her marrow. The fire-tongs pressed against Grady's breast. He reached for her, but she eluded him, keeping the divan between them.

"Dr. Spencer said—" Rose gasped.

"O, the whiskered old fool!"

Tim paused. He fell down on the divan and tried to grasp her gown. He was weaker than he thought. "Come, come to me, Rosie!"

Rose could hardly speak. "Mr. Grady—Tim! Go away! Please! I had a dream—" ("Yes," growled old Tim Grady.) "I dreamed, Tim—I dreamed—"

"What's all this acting, Rose? Haven't I seen you in the movies?"

"Tim, *I dreamed last night John Dawn is still alive!*"

Grady dropped his hands flat. Desire was greater than fear, desire of the living greater than fear of the dead; as always will it be.

"Ye're r-raving!" he snarled. "Ye're after tr-rying a trick on me! Ye and your old woman! What's this for—for that gutter-snipe Deleon? What's the game? Don't tr-ry to put your play-acting over me, Rose Dawn!—Rose Grady!" he roared. "Rose Grady! That's your name! Ye are my wife!"

"No, no, no! Can't you understand, Tim?"

"I understand a lot! I wasn't bar-rn so 'arly in the mar-rning!" Grady shouted the louder as fear grew heavier. "Don't look so scary just to fool me, colleen! I don't believe it! I'm too smar-rt for ye! He's dead!" cried old Tim Grady. "John Dawn's dead! He's deeper than Davvy Jones! He's drowned in wan water!"

Rose was crying. "I had a dream—I saw him—"

"Are ye tr-rying to scare me with your spooky flibberty-gibbets? Am I a babe in ar-rms to be afraid o' the dark? John Dawn, he's fallen in the war-r!"

"That's what we know—But he was wild and fierce. And he loved me once, before—If any do come back—"

"Do ye belave this, Rosie; or are ye tr-rying to make a fool of Timothy Grady? Don't fool me, girl! Ye'll rue the day ye married me!"

Ah, she was beautiful in the midnight there! In noon or midnight beautiful.

"You're mine, Rosie Grady! To put it plain, I've bought ye. None o' your acting tricks on me!" He went along the divan on his knees, reaching out to take her. "Damned to the damned or living who come between! You're my wife! If Bellbender knows his letters, you're my wife! By the law of God, you're my wife!"

"The law of God!"

"Ay, law of man or the devil. You're married to me! No ghost will come between us!"

"Don't—don't—don't, Tim! Don't put your hands on me!"

The door from the next room opened. The face of Mrs. Higgs, surrounded by a halo of steel curlers, and plastered with wrinkle-patches, poked through. She came shuffling through in mules. Her teeth seemed fewer than of usual.

"Wart's the matter?" she demanded. "Wart's all the rumpus and the to-do and the rough-house? Clear out!" She snatched the fire-tongs from Rose's hand. "Clear out, you condensible old man! You Iberian! Wart do you mean disturbing an honest widow-woman's sleep in her own house, in her own bed, at the hour and night and time when all decent, law-abiding people are asleep?"

"Shut up!" Tim yelled. "Close your tr-rap!"

Higgs swung the fire-tongs in a circle, and Grady stumbled back. "I'll trap you!" said she. "I'll shut you up! I'll jaw you! Did we marry you to have you make a roaring, cussing, broiling saloon-joint out of us? Take that!"

Tim did not take what she offered, for it was a deathly swing. He backed out through the door, shielding his face, muttering queer quips in Gaelic.

"Do you know what I did to Higgs for cussing that-a-way?" Ma Higgs screeched. "I jus' natchelly hit him a good swift—"

Slam! She locked the door.

Dr. Spencer, summoned by Miss MacErcher, came to Dawnrose an hour later. He found old Tim foaming up and down the corridors, roaring and blind and stepping on his own feet. "I'm all right!" Tim howled. "If ye say I'm not—"

"Better than you ever were in your life, Grady," said the physician, smiling oddly behind his round glasses. "But be careful of the liquor!"

XXIV. THE LAW ON HANGING

"DICTATION, Miss Dubby!" said Higgleson Todd.

Lawyer Wiggs, a man with very thick lips and wonderful receding chin, pulled the lobes of his long ears. Wiggs was the greatest—if not the greatest, the shrewdest—trial criminal lawyer in all the world outside Chicago. His greatest distinction in his wife's eyes, much as district attorneys feared him, judges hated him, and juries wept for him, was that he had married a woman whose grandfather was a gentleman.

"Yes, Sir," Miss Dubby fluttered, poising her pencil.

"Dictation! To Miss Mary Dubby. Dear and so forth. Replying to your kind regard of instant date—"

"The address, please?"

"The wastebasket," said Todd softly.

"To Miss Mary Dubby, the Wastebasket. Dear and so forth!" cried Miss Dubby, all distracted. "What city?"

"New York," Todd groaned. "State?—New York, Country?—America. Planet?—The earth. Constellation?—The solar system. Universe?—God's."

"To Miss Mary Dubby! The Wastebasket! New York, New York! U.S.A.! The earth! Dear God!" screeched poor Miss Dubby, her raveled brains flapping.

"No! No! No! No!" wept Mr. Todd. "No! Dear Miss Dubby. Replying to your kind regard of instant date, I beg to advise that you retreat into your favorite den of insanity—"

"How do you spell insanity, Mr. Todd?" fluttered Miss Dubby.

"L-O-V-E. L as in women. O as in rye. V as in stenographers. E as in fish," explained Mr. Todd, gently patting her knee.

That made Miss Dubby more excited than ever. "But wait a moment, Mr. Todd, please. How do you spell favorite?"

"F-A-U-V-O-R-I-T-E," Todd sadly intoned.

"F-A-V-O-R-U-I-T-E, Todd," Wiggs corrected, in sonorous sobbing tones.

"Leave out the favorite! I beg to advise that you retreat into your den of insanity—"

"O, I've got all that hours ago," Miss Dubby said confidently.

"Your den of insanity, and leave Mr. Wiggs and myself to discuss a private matter—"

"How do you spell Mr. Wiggs?"

"Two Gs," rolled Mr. Wiggs.

"W-O-double G-S?"

"Two I's. No, I mean one I. Two Gs. One S. No O. A W." Wiggs spoke patiently, for his stenographer also was of the quick-witted sex.

"But that doesn't make sense!" cried Miss Dubby, greatly good-natured at his stupidity.

"My name doesn't?"

"Mr. Two-eyes. G. S. O. A W," read Miss Dubby triumphantly. "G. P. O. means General Post Office; and G. O. P. means Grand Army of the Republic; and G. O. S. means Go Out Side. But G. S. O. doesn't mean a single solitary thing! And what's A. W.? That spells Aw!"

"Leave out the single, solitary thing!" prayed Todd. "Dictation! Are you ready?"

"I am always ready, Sir," chirruped Miss Dubby.

"Dictation! Dear Miss Dubby. Beat it!"

"O, I have everything," said Miss Dubby. She folded her knees.

"All right, Sir. Next?"

"That's all."

"Yes, Sir." Miss Dubby thrust her pencil into yellow locks. Languidly she fished therein for her chewing gum. She yawned like a lady and scratched her knee. "You want me to get this out tonight?"

"If you please."

Miss Dubby picked up Blackstone "On Torts," and began to read. She had always been curious to know what was a tort. She imagined they were something like pretzels, only you ate them with champagne instead of beer.

"Will you please read that over, Miss Dubby?" asked Todd despairingly.

"Why, Sir, it says here: 'If a man cuts his neighbor's throat, whether or not they have existed theretofore in a great mutual state of harmony and concord, it shall be a *male fide* done, and the heirs of the injured man shall have just cause to sue by the ancient law of England—' "

"A sepulcher for the ancient law of England!" Todd yelled. "An upper on the slow local through Hell for it! I want you—to read—those notes!"

"What notes?"

"The stenographic—notes—of the letter—I just dictated to you!"

"May I fetch you a glass of water, Sir?" asked Wiggs thunderously.

"Yes, Sir. Why didn't you say that at first!" Miss Dubby brightly fluttered the leaves of her notebook. She sucked the end of her pencil, and slowly mumbled. "Wait a minute." She erased several lines. "Here it is." She scrawled the figure of a cat devouring its own tail. She blew her breath on the notebook. "Are you ready?"

"Quite ready," whispered Todd, after several feeble passes.

"Here it is. Are you ready?" Todd nodded, unable to speak. Miss Dubby sucked her pencil again. She rapidly read her notes—

"To Mister Sarah Hubble Wastebasket. The Earth. Dear Universe. Replying to you in an instant, I peg—" ("Beg," said Todd.) "You upset me," said Miss Dubby. "Where was I?"

"Begin again."

"Replying to you in an instant, I beg to advise that you repeat into your favorite—Favorite's crossed out," said Miss Dubby efficiently. "Repeat into your favorite—crossed out— den of love, women, rye, stenographers, fish, and leave Mr. Woggs, two-eyes, G.S.O., aw, and my help to cuss a private batter.—Shall I sign this for you?" Miss Dubby asked brightly.

Higgleson Todd clawed forth his strong right hand and tore her notebook away. He ripped it to pieces, slammed it to the floor, and stamped on it, growling.

"What is your religion, Miss Dubby?" ("Sir?" asked Miss Dubby.) "I say, where do you pray? What is your church?"

"O, I am a free thinker."

"I thought it! In the name of all great free thinkers and of the ghost of Robert Ingersoll, listen to me! One word!" Todd raised his forefinger. "Skip!"

"Sir?" ("Skip!" Todd gasped.) "You mean to depart?" Miss Dubby asked.

"That's the word! Depart! Do you understand me?"

"Yes, Sir."

"All right."

"All right, Sir. You mean now?"

Higgleson lifted up Blackstone "On Torts." Miss Dubby's frail blond head drifted grandly out the door.

"You've got a pretty good stenographer, Todd," said Wiggs.

Higgleson Todd wiped his forehead. "She's above the average," he said, "and smart as they make 'em."

"A good girl," Wiggs said, in his cavernous way.

"Too good," said Todd. "I wanted her to go to Montreal with me last week-end, and—what do you think? Do you know, she turned me down!"

"She's very foolish," said Wiggs. "Montreal is wet."

"She's been very snippy and independent since then," Todd growled, souring. "A wise little kid! Damn it, Wiggs!" he cried sharply, gripping Wiggs's knee. His arm shook. "I've got a passion—a passion for blondes!"

Wiggs wiped his glasses. Rose Grady was a blonde, he knew well. Wiggs put that away in his cunning old brain for future reference.

"But now." Todd tiptoed softly over and closed the door. "Now your business!"

Wiggs stroked his dubious chin. His ways were ordinarily circumambient, and he paced like a leopard round about before he leaped and struck. But he dealt now with Todd, who could be just as dilatory, and could be just as direct.

"Todd, I'm representing a fellow named Dinnis McGinty. Big, fat, lousy old bum. You know him. He's got something on Tim Grady. He wants money."

"He won't get it!"

"No-o? Well, well! Think it over. Let Grady think it over. Are you up in the English law of hanging?"

"They hang 'em for murder," said Todd.

"Well, well! Think it over."

"I've thought it over."

"And your thoughts?"

"I'll give you five hundred to turn that bum over to the police."

"That's neither here nor there, Todd. Got something personal against him, have you? I'm not one to stand in the way of a fellow member of the bar," Wiggs rolled reverently. "And later, of course. Later, no doubt, if you still want him. He tried to hold up Spencer, didn't he?"

"Yes, and used my name! He hasn't got a nickel."

"I know it," Wiggs admitted. "I got his last. By the way, it was a check of yours, drawn for the account of friend Grady."

"What are you messing with a pauper for, Wiggs?"

"Because," said Wiggs. "Because," he said more loudly. He straightened up and banged his chair arms. "Because!" he roared. "Because poor McGinty is an honest man!"

"Put-and-take, Wiggs," scoffed Todd. "Double-jointed peanuts. Shinny on your own side."

Wiggs collapsed. "Because he wants money. *We* want money. And I think we'll get it."

"Think again. You won't get it."

Wiggs slapped his knees and arose. "I believe in plain talking. All in good fellowship, Todd. We'll be playing golf in three months. Think of it! The lush little grass, tender as a woman's cheek, is already pushing forth its little sprouts from its little seeds beneath this blanket of snow. I think I can give you a handicap of three and beat you seven-up next spring, Todd."

Todd grunted. "Never saw a woman's cheek green as grass."

"And the lambs will gambol on the green grass," said Wiggs, undisturbed. "By the way, heard the latest about old Thornwood Clay?"

"No," said Todd, tapping a pencil. "What is it?"

"I've forgotten," said Wiggs absently. "*What* did you say is the punishment for murder?"

"They hang 'em," said Todd.

"That is certainly unpleasant, certainly unpleasant."

"And I don't give a damn if they do!" roared Todd.

Wiggs stroked his hat. He understood. "She'll make a lovely widow," he said.

Todd stood up. "What's that?"

"I say Mrs. Higgs is a lovely woman. I hate the winter. No golf. Br-r-r! Br-r-r!"

"Br-r-r!" Todd echoed nastily. He felt like making a face.

He walked up and down with his hands in his pockets for a long time. Something in the crafty old eyes of Wiggs had made him afraid.

And Wiggs stuck his head in again, as though just outside the door he'd been watching and waiting. "Thinking of Grady's will—I suppose you'll be having a new one drawn, Todd?"

"What of it?"

"O, ask Bellbender."

"What's this? What business is it of yours?" Todd snarled. And was sorry of it.

XXV. OVER THE HILLS AND AWAY

GREASY PETE LOPEZ sat alone in the grill of the Hotel Babylon, watching the supper dancing. At the door Ike Duval was also watching him, as Pete was well aware. Laurence Spencer and Maveen Brady sat two or three tables away.

Into the grill, dodging round and about among tables and dancers, his dress collar jerked awry, came running Gay Deleon, terrified and panting with horror of murder! He tried to seize self-possession when he was aware of eyes on him. Here he was well known, as on all Broadway. Nonchalantly he made pretense of straightening his collar. He curled his dagger moustaches. Gay Deleon would do that on the scaffold, if a bright jade were glancing at him.

He sauntered. But he could not keep from turning about him uneasily, for death dogged his steps!

The sight of Pete Lopez gave heart to him. Pete was bravest of the brave. Poor little Gay Deleon, so strong and cavemanlike with women, as wilted as a yellow cankered rose at sight of cold blue steel!

"Pete, Pete!" he gasped, sliding into a seat across the table. "Anyone behind me? See a little man with a great big bush of hair. Look, Pete! Don't laugh! He'll have a gun—"

"If I see him, I'll tell him not to shoot; you'll marry the girl," Pete yawned. "What have you been messing up in now, Gay?"

"O, damn you! Tried to run my wheel without a cent of bank. A damned gun-toting Southerner named Claude made a killing! A killing! By God, he'll kill me! He's hot as Hell after me! Pete!"

"I'm here. Don't bleat my name. People are looking at you—women. I've got troubles too, Gay. Old Solemn Ike Duval's going to put the irons on me tonight; I feel it in my blood. What got on your hip? Look around easy. Play the game. You're a gambler, better gambler with the cards than I."

"I wish I had your nerve, Pete."

"All right, all right. Go easy. We hang together." Pete laughed again at his grim jest. "We'll make a break of it; see? Got your car? Good. Nothing built on wheels can beat it. Now play the game easy. Last night in New York—maybe last one under Heaven. Play the game easy. Take a drink of this. Pete Lopez's not finished yet!"

Gay Deleon became heartened, became boldened. Pete Lopez was all carelessness and light. But that was for the watchful eyes of Ike Duval. In his heart the little Mexican was nervous; it showed in the steady liquor he drank, against his custom. He sat on needles.

"See that big young fellow over there?" Pete asked. "And that girl in green with him? See, she's lighting a cigaret now."

Deleon nodded, his fright forgotten at the sight of a new face. "Not a bad looker, though I never was keen for red hair." He slicked back his own hair.

"Doc Spencer's son; a young college smarty. But the girl with him is Maveen Grady, old Tim's only daughter."

"Rather neat," Deleon decided, insolently surveying Maveen. "Looks like a devilish hot temper. She'll be worth marrying some day."

"Yes," Pete said, exhaling smoke. "Old Grady'll leave some rich women."

Deleon tapped the table. When Laurence and Maveen arose to dance, he followed, and after one turn of the floor cut in with soft apology. Laurence relinquished Maveen ungraciously, looking unpleasantly at Deleon. He did not know the gambler, but he did not like him.

Gay whispered his stock nonsensicalities into Maveen's ear. He praised her dancing, her hair, her gown. He swore, in such brief time as was his, a measured eternity of devotion. He'd spill his soul thus for any new woman.

Maveen did not recognize him, perhaps understood she had never met him. But the new society, that of the Gradys, the Bonnells, the Wiggses, and the like, takes a good deal for granted; it has to. And even the old society, of the Spencers, the Schermerhorns, the Clays, and the like, follows suit; *it* has to. Maveen felt quite able to take care of herself, since she was a millionaire's daughter and smoked cigarets.

And Deleon, in his black fashion, was handsome. He had a way with women

Laurence wandered about uneasily. He spoke to the maitre-d'hotel. "I say, Mr. Dubby, do you happen to know who is that chap dancing with Miss Grady?"

Mr. Dubby, a man with frail blond hair and enormous domelike head, did know. "That's Mr. Gay Deleon, Sir. One of the best known men on Broadway."

"Well, *I* don't know him," young Spencer muttered. "Never saw him at Cambridge in my life. Nor New Haven either." That quite settled Deleon.

Laurence wandered farther, and found Mr. Tiffany Bonnell. Mr. Bonnell also knew Mr. Deleon. He had lost a good deal of money to Mr. Deleon, trying a roulette system which didn't system.

"Yes, Sir; he's a professional gambler, Sir. And a beggar of the first water," said the Babylon's owner. "What is our society coming to? My grandfather, who in '60 had dinner with the Prince of Wales, God bless him!—Edward the Seventh of sainted memory, would not have permitted that fellow to pour the second wine."

Laurence was coldly angry. He surmised that Deleon did not know Maveen. Even in Boston, among the gods, such liberties are not taken. When Deleon, slowly bobbing up and down in the tangled, unhappy mob, pushed Maveen round again, Laurence intruded. "I'm sorry!" he ordered, his good right hand on Deleon's shoulder.

Deleon did not care to relinquish Maveen. He kept his arm about her, shaking his head. "I said I'm sorry," Laurence repeated, in tones far from sorry. His fingers dug into Deleon's shoulder bone, and he pulled him away by sheer hard force. "I'm sorry," he stated for a third time, grimly smiling as Deleon stumbled away, muttering and threatening.

"What was wrong?" Maveen demanded, her temper flaming.

"You won't dance with that bounder again," Laurence told her.

"Who said I won't?" Maveen was angry; no man had ever been born to give commands to a Grady. "I'll dance with whom I please!"

"Not while you're with me, Maveen," said Laurence.

Abruptly she left him and sought out Buddy Schermerhorn. She scowled as she passed by the table where Laurence sat alone, to show him she was good as he. Deleon also danced past. He had borrowed the Arty Girl from young Urban Wiggs, a fat dull fool. "Yes, a most infernal fortune hunter!" Deleon said loudly as he got within Laurence's hearing. Laurence clenched his hands.

Maveen by now had found another cavalier, and another. At midnight Laurence left her and went home alone.

At midnight Pete Lopez directed Deleon. "Out by that door. The police aren't after you yet. Meet me at the west entrance with your car."

Ike Duval trailed Lopez, walking closer than he had done before. Pete's keen desert nose scented the imminence of arrest. Up and down the lobbies of the Babylon he saw a fierce little man pacing, with grim thin lips and great mane of hair flying out. When the Prince Albert coat of Mr. Boosten Claude blew open, it gave view of a heavy leather gun-belt dragging at the hips. Keenly right and left Claude glanced, turning sharply, staring menacingly at all men who looked like Deleon. Lopez could understand why Gay had been afraid.

Lopez approached Claude. "There's a fellow I'm looking for I'd like to get! Name o' Deleon. Know him? The son-of-a-dog!"

"Are you looking for him too?" asked Boosten Claude. "Stranger, I never liked to play the hog. But I got first rights!" He hitched his belt. "I'll tend to him myself! But if there is anything I can do for you, friend," Claude added, "I'd be pleased to do it!"

Solemn Ike Duval had his suspicious eyes on Boosten Claude as well as Pete Lopez now, watching for a gun to be passed. He sauntered up.

"See this fellow?" Pete whispered. *"He* knows where Deleon is. He's hiding him. But he won't tell where."

"O, he's hard, is he?" Claude cried, looking unfavorably at Pete and then at Ike Duval. He put his hands on his hips and stepped over to Ike, thrusting his fierce mane of hair beneath Ike's chin; Claude was about five feet high. "What've you done with Deleon?" he demanded of Ike. "Hand him over!"

"Shoo, fly!" growled Ike. "Where'd you buzz from? You're buzzing into trouble!"

"I know you New York slickers!" Boosten Claude snapped his fingers beneath Ike's nose. "You work in cahoots! Hand Deleon over, before I grow nasty!"

Ike Duval gripped Claude's wrists. "Friend of Greasy Pete's? Huh!" His expert fingers ran over Claude's clothing. "Got your battery with you, I see." He held the squirming grape-fruit farmer, slipping from hip-holsters two enormous shiny forty-fives.

Little Boosten Claude fought and bit like a weasel. He threshed and wiggled, now sideways, now upside down, held inescapably in Ike's strong arms.

"I'm a Southern gentleman!" he yelled, in a booming voice larger than himself. "Don't you dare lay your hands on me!"

"Boy, I was brought up on Southern gentlemen. I eat three fried every day for breakfast. Hey! Hey! Where's Greasy Pete?"

Ike pounded through the revolving doors and out to the pavement. Deleon's long blue racer, with little Pete Lopez like a monkey at the wheel, was roaring south down the lefthand side of the street, daring head-on collision, cramming cars to the gutters, riding over shouting policemen.

Ike Duval got to a telephone, sending warnings over the city. "Watch the south ferries and the Brooklyn bridges! Greasy Pete Lopez has broken away for the south!"

Police boxes flashing red! Whistles blowing! Motorcycle men roaring down the avenues. Fat sergeants, two by two, squeezed into little tin runabouts, skipping over the city. Plainclothes men at the Jersey ferries. Traffic men at the bridges. Horse and foot, wheel and gasoline, eleven thousand police looking for Greasy Pete Lopez, who's stolen Mrs. Schermerhorn's pearls!

Before the night is over, one hundred and forty-two assorted Sicilians, Lithuanian Jews, Catalonians, Chihuahuans, Gypsies, Croats, and mulattoes have been hauled into precinct houses. Even one American, but in New York he is a foreigner.

Up along the Hudson's shore, shadows flying in the night. A whistling wind. Cold clouds across the moon.

Deleon and Pete drive hard in the long blue racer. Seventy miles an hour. The cold road flies. Lopez stares straight ahead of him. His quick little brown eyes seem dreamy, but Gay Deleon is afraid of them.

Into Riverview with a roar. Through a flimsy barricade. The blue racer trembles. "Stop, stop, stop! In the name o' the law!" a man is shouting. His cries are a mile behind in forty seconds. The blue racer does not even hear the report of the following shotgun.

And then a red light in the midst of the road, mounted on a pile of stones. Lopez drives straight up, squeaking on the brakes when he sees he can't go over. He throws gears into reverse, cursing the tribe of road-menders. "What are you doing?" Gay Deleon yells, seeing a man behind the light.

"S-stop in yer tr-racks!"

Pete's eyes shine; and something shines in the right hand of the hulky man who cautiously approaches. "Up wi' yer hands!" roars a deep brogue command. Dinnis McGinty tiptoes cannily towards Deleon, whose arms are stretched stiff. "Hand o'er yer pr-retties!" His right hand menaces with the weapon. "I mane business!"

"What's your graft?" Deleon mutters. "I'm Gay Deleon. You can't do anything to me. I stand in with all the boys."

"No back-talk!" whooped McGinty, waggling his weapon. "Absolute silence is me watchwar-rd. Niver talk, but act! I mane business! I ain't going to say it again. I mane—"

Lopez laughed. "Put down your monkey-wrench! I guess we're all in the same boat," he said to the foolish McGinty. "Want to come off with us? We're heading south."

"Why didn't you toss a knife, and slice this wind-bag through the heart?" spat Deleon.

"Might have," said Pete. "But Anthony's men frisked my knife from me. And now I think Anthony will give it back to Grady."

Half a mile up the road lay Dawnrose, somber as a mausoleum in the darkness of white wind and blue snow. Deleon swerved his car toward the drive entrance. "We might pick up a stake here," he growled.

"I know what you want to pick up," said Pete wisely. "Shove on! She's not for you, you fool. Don't be crazy."

That, to be sure, is excellent advice.

So north they went, the three of them, Gay, Dinnis, and Pete. At Tarrytown they ferried over to the Jersey shore. Then south they went, the three of them, Lopez, McGinty and Deleon.

XXVI. LOVE HEAT

MISS MARY DUBBY, Higgleson Todd's secretary, patted her pale hair and scratched her scalp with a pencil. She surveyed Padriac Grady, who waited in Todd's anteroom. Todd was closeted with Mrs. Higgs and Rose Dawn. Miss Dubby thought young Grady dull as an owl. And who gives a hoot about an owl?

In Todd's inner office Todd was smiling at Rose while his square fat hand strove continually to part hair on a head where there were not two hairs to part. His heavy heart was all on fire. Or perhaps it was indigestion which gave him that hot internal burning.

Of course Higgs was talking. "You see, if we're leaving for the South, and Grady sick and dilapidated and liable to die, and like the first thing I told Higgs when I married him—"

"Natural for you to want your affairs in order, Mrs. Higgs," the lawyer soothed. "Mr. Grady has made no new will since his marriage, and as things stand, all your daughter would receive is her dower rights."

"Did we throw away our youth and beauty for some dar rights?" screamed Mrs. Higgs. "Did we—"

Desperately Todd waved her short. "I've drawn up a will already to protect you, and Mr. Grady will sign it today! I am also going to urge on him incorporation of the family. It saves a lot of taxes. Anything to help Mrs. Grady." Languorously his fat eyes dwelt on Rose.

She stood up. "I had no idea what Ma wanted of me," she said, a trifle bitterly. "I want no claim on Tim Grady. I want to be free of him!"

"And you shall be free."

"Sit down! Sit down!" Mrs. Higgs harshly commanded.

"You mean annulment is possible?" Rose whispered.

"I mean—ump—We might as well speak plainly. Ump! Mr. Grady won't live forever. You'll still be young."

"I want no thing of old Tim Grady's!" Rose cried, growing hysterical. "I'm not married to him! I know—"

"Sit down! Behave! Close your mouth!" ordered Higgs. "Well, I never saw the like of it! You never were so impydent before. What's got in you?"

Neither Todd nor Higgs could hold her. Sobbing throatily, her handkerchief to her mouth, Rose Dawn went out the door. They followed her.

"I'll protect your interests above all else!" Todd said loudly, drowning out Mrs. Higgs's exasperated vocalizations. "I'll see that *you*—Why, hello, Mr. Grady! Hello, Mr. Grady! Hello, hello! I never expected to see you here. Hello, hello, hello!"

For the first time Padriac saw Rose Dawn face to face. He was standing unsteadily, his hand on his chair-back. He would have liked to say gay, gallant words, but no words came; his throat was dry; he could not even look at her. Todd stuck his hands in his pockets and jangled keys indefinitely. The droning of Miss Dubby's typewriter was a sound of flies.

Stifling her tears, not giving him a glance, Rose passed out the door.

"Well, Sir, I'd not have kept you waiting if I'd known," said Todd, when Mrs. Higgs had followed her daughter forth. "Miss Dubby, why did you make Mr. Grady wait?" Todd was excited, and he sensed excitement in Padriac.

"I told him he could go if he wanted to," Miss Dubby fluttered.

"You did! You—You—What was it, Sir? How can I serve you?"

"I've forgotten," said Padriac, staring at Todd's waistcoat buttons.

"Why, Sir!" cried Todd. "What are you doing to your glove?"

Padriac Grady, with strong, steady fingers, had torn it clear across the thumb. That hushed excitement in the air! Todd wiped his head.

"How's business, Mr. Grady?" he asked. "Understand you've been West."

Padriac did not answer. Still his gray eyes looked dazed. He muttered silently. Suddenly he smashed his great right fist against his breast. "Business! You think that's all I'm good for! By God, I'm young! I've got money! I'll show you fellows! Think I'm a dumb-bell!"

He struck his breast again. And walked out.

"Dictation!" roared Todd. "What's got into young Grady?"

And that night Padriac Grady went forth on Broadway, walking alone, but with intent not to walk alone all night. Came walking toward him Dot, of the street, with little Boosten Claude hanging to her arm.

What had got into Padriac Grady? What furnace fires burned behind the iron door of his face? He scooped Dot in his arms, pressed her tightly, kissed her on her painted lips.

Dot slapped his face. A crowd gathered in an impassable wall. Padriac turned to run, but he could not escape. He was taken with panic fury.

The crowd stood on its mutual feet. "What's the matter?" everyone asked, turning and peering into everyone's face, for your true crowd-man considers everyone else an oracle. "He ought 'o be lynched," said everyone, since lynching is a way out of all difficulties.

Dot's hennaed hair was dry and crackly as straws. Her plush coat was opened, showing much of the stuff of which woman is made. "Lis'n to me, Mr. Cop!" she shrilled. "I was walking down the street, with my ge'man friend, not doing anything but minding my own bus'ness—"

"What is your business?" growled the officer.

Dot looked about her for Boosten Claude, her ge'man friend. That gun-toting gentleman had wiggled away beneath the crowd's elbows, departing from Dot's life as informally as he had entered it.

"I never saw *this* guy before in all my life! Did I?"

Some female from the crowd, evidently addressed, shrieked back: "Never before in all your life, Dot!"

"You hear what m' friend says, Mr. Cop!" cried Dot in triumph.

"All right, all right! Clear out of the way wi' you! You I mean, you with the fly-trap mouth!" (This to Citizen A.) "Girl, you come along to the station-house and make your complaint."

"I never saw him before—"

"Tell it to the lieutenant."

Dot turned to more sympathetic ears. Fifty mouths were opened fishily. A hundred eyes gazed at her fishily. A hundred ears appeared to flap with a slow and fishy motion.

"This guy I never saw before kissed me!" Dot stated angrily to a citizen.

"What do you know about that?" cried puny Citizen A. "I got a notion to bust him in the jaw!"

"And him with a mug like that!" said B, shuddering over all his hideous face.

"I wish you'd crack him!" Dot said viciously. "Insulting a lady!"

"You tell 'em, lady!" said A.—"Don't let 'im get away with it, lady!" said B.—"Anybody can see I'm a lady," said Dot.

"I don't believe a word of it!" said C quarrelsomely. "Get off my feet, you kike!"

"O, Miss Bliss!" cried the plump gentleman standing on C's feet. "Was this gent talking to me, Miss Bliss?"

"If he was talking to you he ain't no gent," said Sadie Bliss.

Fury of fear came to Padriac Grady, ringed by those peering, unknown faces. He knew terror of the law. "Let me out of here!" He fought. He used his great fist. A policeman went down beneath a blow like a hammer. Men swarmed over him like worms over dead carrion. Still he fought on, standing tall above the street. "Let me go! I'll hurt some of you!"

Strong, that silent young man! He had beef in him; he, too, was of the race of kings; he, too, could kill a man with a blow. He was near to murder. "I'll hurt you!" He struggled hugely, seeming to grow broader, taller, to be as great a giant as old Tim Grady. He let loose a formless roar he had not known his lips contained. The world dipped, whirled, rocketed around him. It was a bedlam of mad lights and crazy sounds. They were leading him to prison!

His hands were bound so he could not move without pain. "So you're a scrapper, are you?"—"Pretty tough fellow, are you?"—"We'll show you, battling buck!" A blow upon his head. He heard the clang of a patrol wagon. Darkness lay on him while he was jolted over streets.

Hands hauled him from the wagon at the precinct house. "Want to fight some more?"—"Guess he's got it most out of him."—"Remember that face, boys! He's a bad un,"—"Going to walk in nice, or d' you want to be carried in on a stretcher?"

Padriac faced the desk-lieutenant steadily. "Name's John Doe," he said.

Lieutenant MacErcher smiled. He knew who Padriac was well enough. He recalled a time he'd commented to Ike Duval on Padriac's quietness, and wondered what had brought this change about. MacErcher laughed, wrinkled with fat and much good nature.

"John Doe, I'm glad to meet you."

"He butted in on my ge'man friend!" screamed Dot. "He kissed me. He asked me where he could find some excitement. I never saw him in my life before. I wasn't doing nothing but minding my own business—"

"What have you to say, Mr. Doe?"

Padriac mouthed silently before he could speak. "Up and down the street I see them walking," he whispered tensely. "Every man has a girl!" He grasped the railing in front of him. "How do you get women? I never had a woman. I've never done a thing but work. Work as a boy! Work in college! Work myself to death now! Is it right? They think I'm a crab. They think I don't feel. There's something wild inside here! I like to live!"

MacErcher rubbed his jowl. "You ought to be ashamed, a quiet, decent, respectable young fellow like you!" His glance twinkled.

In Padriac's still gray eyes smoldered passions fierce and hot as those of old Tim. Only smoldered yet. But they'd break into flame!

"It's not right," he muttered, with lips scarcely moving. "I work like a dog. I've got to live! We go this way only once. I've got a right to live!"

"Well, son, who's stopping you?"

"I've got a right to live as much as any man! I'm no stick of wood! I'm going to show 'em! I'm going to get drunk! I'm going to tear loose—"

Police Lieutenant MacErcher rubbed his chin for a long time, while Padriac's long-pent words exploded. MacErcher was not in doubt for long. It would not be wise to bring notoriety and disgrace on a Grady. That was not good public policy. The newspapers played it up too much. It was bad example for the middle classes.

MacErcher slapped his palms on his desk. "Charge dismissed! Only before you leave, Mr.—Doe, I want to say a word to you about the police. It's funny to laugh at them. I like the comic paper jokes myself. But remember, they guard your property for you, and they guard your life for you. They'd have got you just the same tonight if you'd been a two-gun gangster. Remember the pension fund for the widows of men who died under fire, Mr. Grady!"

Padriac was dazed at his freedom, at the lieutenant's knowledge of his name. He stumbled forth, trying to look small.

MacErcher laughed. "Feel better about him now," he thought. "He'll go the pace like a rich man's son ought to. I thought there was something queer in all his quietness. He might have done one of these nasty silent murders!"

XXVII. THE FACE IN THE RED DAWN

OVER the frozen hills and the river dull bells ring in the seventh hour of morning. Stars tinkle crispily.

Holy hour; moon at nadir; sun at Capricorn; earth at perihelion. The Hudson crackles and grumbles beneath its thin black ice. Frozen mists mount heavily, chained spirits lifting to the resurrection dawn.

Dreadfully dolorous a wolf-dog howls, "Yow . . .r-r-r . . . yow!" Wolf dirge to the dead. "Yow . . . r-r-r . . . yow!" Dirge to the dead, the wolf-dog howls.

Old Tim stirred and awakened, calling to black Tom. "What's that!"

"A dog, Sir. It sounds like a dog."

" 'Tis a foul-mouthed dog! What's that? I thought I heard sound below!"

Tom bent his flat, keen ears. Each sound rippling through the air was audible to him, but now there was no sound. Yet the silence had become audible.

"Some soul has passed tonight," said Tom. "That's why the dog's howling. I've heard it often. It's something they don't teach in colleges; but *we*—we know it's so! My grandmammy came from the Carib isles—"

A brave man was Tim Grady before men, in the thick of the fight, swinging with club or fist, roaring oaths of war; but a truest coward before the austere visage of the invisible. He sat up in bed, drawing blankets about him.

Black Tom, rolling his fierce eyes, told stories of the dead. He knew them all, witch stories of the Sudanese, of the White Nile, of the Carib voodoo men, of the sorcerers of the savannahs. He forgot he was an educated man, whispering lore the learned do not know. About the Woman with the Moon in her navel. About the Goat without Horns. His thick fingers wove symbols in the air. His guttural voice was like the witch-chant of the black magicians.

"Shut up, ye nigger!" screamed Grady. "Shut up! Shut up! Shut up! Are ye after-r tr-rying to scare me like a babe in ar-rms? Hark! Cease your moaning! 'Tis someone at the dar-r! 'Tis someone wanting in!"

Again Tom listened. Again the silence. "When they come that way, don't you open!" whispered Tom. The dog had ceased its sorrowful lament. No doubt some righteous boot had kicked it to its kennel or the Hell of hounds.

"Why don't they ring the bell?" Tim gasped. "Where's Saltpeter? Who is 't?"

Since neither he nor Tom could be sure it was anything, no answer came.

"Who is 't? May a galloping goblin eat their mother's bones! The curse o' Cromwell on 'em! On 'em and their childer's childer, on their roofs and their pigs and their prayers and their graves!" Thus fortified by prayer, old Tim climbed out of bed and into his mandarin dressing gown. "See who 'tis, Tom!"

Too great a coward to face the dark alone, too great a coward to show himself the coward before another, old Grady shoved Tom before him. Mumbling murderous threats, he shuffled downstairs to the front door. Tom Jefferson flashed on lights before them, till stairs and all the rooms were yellow.

Sharply the Negro listened at the door, his barbarian ears flat to the glass. His straight nostrils did not seem to breathe. He crouched, his muscles hardened. He shook his head at the absence of all sound, and opened.

The night had lighted to ghostly gray. Tim stretched his scaly neck out over the giant Negro's shoulder. Nothing happened.

Down the walk, in the shadow of trees, Tom thought he heard the faint pattering of some creature hastening away, a sound no louder than a chipmunk's feet. Night is always replete with such tricky ghosts of sound. If Tom's ears were true, they were sharper than old Tim's, who heard nothing.

Becoming emboldened, Grady roared out: "Who's there?"

No answer. The air was shivering.

"Who's there? Damn ye, stand far-rth and show your face!"

The sky visibly lightened. It seemed the false dawn, yet behind thick winter fog the sun was already risen. A chill of impending rain or snow was in what feeble wind there blew. At a word from his master Tom stalked fiercely forth, his eyes glaring about him, his hands softly swinging. He went across a gray salt scum of snow.

As minutes passed, old Tim also went out. He stood at the head of the porch steps, roaring to right and left, promising death to the shadows. Huddled behind the opened door he saw a man crouching, a gun within his hand.

It was old Thornwood Clay, sitting there against the marble house with infinite patience. His thin white countenance was dreary and sardonic. No threat he made with his feeble little bauble gun. No word or sign he gave to old Tim Grady; but waited as calmly as though he owned this big new mansion, as though he owned the moon and wind and world quite as much as Timothy Grady. For what he waited God, He knows.

Old Tim, dreadfully afraid, whispered: "Is that ye, Thorn Clay?"

Tom had turned and came back across the snow; Grady grew braver. "So ye didn't get your bellyful on Christmas Ave? What are ye back far-r? Answer me!"

Clay made no answer, insolent or meek. But his very silence was insolence insufferable. Tim made threatening gestures, clutched Clay's shoulders, shook him. Ah, many a cup of his forbidden wine would not drown the memory of that insolence!

"Stand up like a man! Don't sneer at me! Who gave ye the right to prowl about my own front dar-r so 'arly in the mar-rning?"

The sky was light enough; it held no terrors; there seemed nothing to make old Tim fear. Blood rose in his glance. He shook that frail figure till it sagged and wilted in his grasp, till it was upheld only by his own two angry hands, till it was a bag of rags, dragging in limp folds. Thornwood Clay's head fell over. And still he said no word.

Now the sun came forth from cloud, but no larger than the littlest of moons. It was small and bitter, and red with a dull haze. Upon a chain of mist its crimson lamp swung through the east, sweeping clear of black storm welkin. From a pinhook of the fading morning star it hung its ruddy light. The gray snow was incarmined.

The sky to the west burned back like a mirror the refulgence of that false red moon.

Old Grady's hands seemed red, but not the face of Clay. It was white as mist. It was cold as snow.

"God! My God! Who did this thing? Why, look at him—he doesn't say a war-rd!"

XXVIII. SHIPS PUT OUT TO SEA

"BODY OF RAGGED STRANGER FOUND NEAR HOME OF MOVIE MAG-NATE!"

So ran great black letters in the *Morning Mist*.

". . . Discovered yesterday morning on the road in front of Dawnrose, after Mr. Grady and his family had left to board the *Thorn*, the palatial Grady yacht, for an extended cruise. . . . Revolver in his hand. . . . Papers indicate the body may be that of Thornwood Clay. . . . Mr. Grady, on board the *Thorn*, which sails today, has denied himself to all interviewers. . . ."

Not Thornwood Clay's importance justified the news, but Grady's. How that must have frozen his lone soul upon the winds!

Wigley Arsen had written those sentences. It was his epitaph on one whom in more prosperous days he had presumptuously called his intimate friend. For a long time after writing them, Wigley Arsen sat silent, to the amusement of city room copy boys. He had a dim vision of the futility of greatness, knowing all things end, even the pride of the Clays.

Beneath a ruled line followed a paragraph from the *Morning Mist* "morgue," prepared long years before for this grand climax in the life of Thornwood Clay. Your name may be there too, reader; and we some day will read it.

"Thornwood Clay, of the Massachusetts Clays, was born in 1851, the eldest son of Caspar Clay, once Ambassador to the Court of Prussia. . . . Graduating from Harvard in 1871 . . . became associated with Fiske and Gould. . . Famous market plunger, 'Lose-a-Million Clay.' . . . Older New Yorkers remember him as leader of social ten. . . . Famous old Clay mansion on East Twelfth visited by the late King Edward. . . . In partnership for years with Timothy Grady. . . . One son survives. . . ."

Dust and grass roots and old dead bones! Thus ended the honor of the very ancient Clays. More ancient yet will they be, but never more honorable.

Anthony read this on a somber day. Old Clay was nothing to him, yet like Arsen he felt frustration. If pride can perish, then so can strength, courage, and cunning. Anthony had for years never doubted that love fails. Chill assailed him which did not come from the cold windows facing the bay.

"So Grady's shipping out," remarked Lieutenant MacErcher, watching Anthony's troubled face. "A honeymoon trip for his bride, I suppose."

Ike Duval came growling in. Ike had taken bitter liquor, and was beset with ponderous black demons. He gave no greeting to Anthony. Shoving his hat on the back of his head, he spat at Anthony's foot.

"Lopez and Deleon ha' beat it," he said. "Blame it on me if you want to, but by God—"

Anthony tossed a letter across his desk. "Why did you write that, Duval?"

Gloomily, wiggling his derby on his perplexed head, Ike Duval read. The letter was curt, threatening, and obscene; and Duval's name was signed to it.

"What the devil makes you think I wrote that?" he growled, smarting under premonition of a rebuke in front of MacErcher. "I'll tell anybody anything I got to say to his jaw. I ain't afraid."

"It's your name," said Anthony grimly. "Suppose you say now what you said in the letter."

"I'll say what I want to say," said Ike, looking away, twisting his mouth in ferocious self-confidence.

Lieutenant MacErcher took the letter. "Excuse me," he said. "I'll bet I know who wrote this. I'll bet Pete Lopez wrote it. He'd do anything to get a man in trouble."

"He uses a pen?" asked Anthony.

"Copy work," said MacErcher. "And see that quirk in the A? Lopez never could make a straight A in his life. That little thing has kept him from becoming a high-class grafter. Sort of a shame."

Ike was sullen, feeling he had been humiliated before MacErcher. "Any fool'd know I didn't write that," he said gloomily. "If I want to say anything, I say it. I'd just as lief say it to your jaw. Ain't that right, MacErcher?"

MacErcher maintained diplomatic silence. Anthony's lips twitched.

"And let me tell you," said Ike more loudly, "that there ain't anything Lopez would write I'd not say. Take that, if you want to!"

"If I don't want to take it?" suggested Anthony.

"I'll give it to you."

Anthony was up. MacErcher also jumped up, and Ike Duval walked backward slowly, doubling his fists and growling.

"You're a faker!" said Ike. "A faker!" Then he went speedily out the door.

Anthony sat down again. For a long while with angry eyes he looked out at the stormy waters of the bay.

"Tired of the life?" asked MacErcher. "You got the rover's eye, Mr. Anthony. Often I've wondered why you stay so long."

Down the river, out the bay, ships floated, great and small. Moaning whistles crying for the sea again, dirty sails flapping for the sea again; old weathered planks of steel and oak straining for the sea again! The storm flag flies. The black gull dips. The north wind blows. The tide slides down in long and frothy waves. Liner and fisherboat, tug and tramp, drift off into the deep.

And one proud little white steam yacht heading out. Her paint shines in the mist. Ensign and pennon fly. Smoke riffles from her stack. She shears the gurly water. Sirening the shore in long farewell, mincing daintily past the great dirty tramps, with sturdy van Chuch on deck, the *Thorn* puts out to sea, bearing Rose Dawn, loveliest of women.

Hurricane will beat upon her, death hunger at her board, men die, and women be in terror, before she cuts these waters coming from the sea again.

She takes the deep sea to her breast. She disappears in gray haze.

"You're right," said Anthony, "I've stayed too long. Something has seemed to hold me to this damned city. You know—something holds a man at times where he doesn't want to be. God knows, though, where I'd go."

"You'll go where the thing has gone that'd held you here," said MacErcher.

When MacErcher had left, Anthony searched patiently in a dusty packet for a certain letter. He found it. Though it was signed with the name of Rose Dawn, he examined it carefully all afternoon, looking for trace of that peculiar crooked A which was the sign-mark of Pete Lopez.

XXIX. LIGHTS GO OUT

DOWN past Florida keys ripples the white yacht, the *Thorn.* To tramps bearing up from the Caribbees she is a lovely lady, disdainful in her slim virgin white. To lighthouses along the hidden coast she is a crown of jewels as, blazing from stem to stern, she crawls down on the waters of the night. To those aboard, from old Grady to black Tom, she is roof overhead and floor beneath foot, safe enough and sure enough in whatever winds there blow.

Black sky lies breast flat on black ocean, winking and coruscating with huge tropic stars like tears. Dreams walk the deep.

"When do we meet—when do we meet—when do we meet again, my lover?" cries the endless wind.

In the little bijou gold-and-white saloon sat Rose, Maveen, and van Chuch. Tim Grady was in his cabin. Van Chuch was much about the women these days.

Maveen Grady sulked. She knew herself the daughter of a man who had "raised himself by one suspender," and was afraid of her young step-mother's poised, gracious ways. Maveen liked to do things with a bang to show herself as good as anyone else. Reasonably, she blamed her unreason on her father. Furiously she smoked cigaret after cigaret.

"Start the gramophone, Pete," she ordered Captain van Chuch, who didn't know whether the salutation was cordial or contemptuous.

"O Lord, for some excitement! Say something, Rose! Isn't it dead?"

Our land is filled with such boisterous daughters of the recent rich. Newport, Hot Springs, the East Coast, the West Coast, know their loud and confident voices, know their dazzling garments, know their floss, their froth, their drivel, and their sweet seduction. That's the worst of it. They screech about in scarlet cars. They wear cloth of gold, but little of it. They are snorty and loud, full of noise, liquor, and cigarets. They have the itch. It is not wantonness nor pride that their fair legs are always displayed in filigreed lace, but remembrance that their mothers wore no stockings at all when they went out to feed the slops to the pigs.

Copper bobbed locks close to golden curls, Rose and Maveen played with an ouija board. For three or four minutes, dragging like ages, they asked silent questions of the Dark. Lights in the saloon were none too bright. Mysteriously, nothing happened.

"I know these things can work!" Maveen said viciously. "I'll make it work."

Peter van Chuch, gold-braided, sleek, and a little fat, was uneasy with the nearness of these two young women, either of whom considered herself as far above him as the cold north star, growing farther the more directly the mariner steers to it. And he had not forgiven Maveen for once calling him a fool. Now he was on his own ship, and he was master here. The ocean makes brave hearts, even in van Chuchs. It abides no rabbit feet pacing its valiant ships!

"The spirits may be on strike," van Chuch joked heavily. "Or maybe they belong to the class of undeserving poor who can't go South for the winter."

Baal's proud priests thus once mocked the prophet sacrificant. Were the Almighty what it was of old, undoubtedly van Chuch would have been struck down immediately with battle-ax of lightning. But his only doom was a kind smile from Rose, who pitied him, and a toss of the head from Maveen.

Muttering loudly, old Tim reeled into the saloon, the heaviness of anger and usquebaugh on him. He was thinner than he had been, but large and powerful for all his deliriums. He flipped a letter beneath Rose's eyes, roaring loud enough to awaken sleeping Mrs. Higgs, if not the dead.

"What's this letter about Gay Deleon doing in your cabin?"

Rose Dawn stood up, sick and frightened. Van Chuch stepped away on his short legs, bumbling like a bee some apology. But Maveen came to the attack against her father. His anger against anyone never failed to rouse Maveen to a furious defense. Rose was incapable of speech, of fighting Tim's fierce anger in his own way.

"What business have *you* reading someone else's letter?" Maveen asked.

"What business have you as-king me what business I have?" Tim shrieked at his daughter, forgetting his anger against Rose.

Maveen snatched the letter. "Here, Rose—your property!"

"Well, what—Well, what!" Tim howled. "I'll strap ye well, ye impudent girl! I'll slap your face! I'll learn ye manners!"

Rose Dawn found her tongue. "This is the last letter John Dawn wrote to me," she whispered. "Do you object if I keep it?"

Clumsily old Tim bent over her. He had had two wives before; he was afraid of tears. Passion came on him. He pressed his lips to her neck. Rose shivered; her shoulders lifted. Young flesh and old moist lips! The one will burn, the other rot.

In decent fashion van Chuch had turned his back, staring at the gold and white wall-panels. His square Dutch jaws gritted. Mirrors were set between the panels; in one he watched Rose. Seafaring men, it's said, have an eye for women. Van Chuch's fists tightened. Now the *Thorn* fell in the trough of a roller. Van Chuch teetered and sprawled unseamanly.

"There, there," old Tim said gruffly, feeling her shrink, and a little ashamed in his own lecherous heart. He picked up the ouija board. "What's this? Fit for fools and idiots! I'll make the damned thing jiggle!" (To Maveen) "Come on! Sit down! I'll show ye how."

"You'll have to keep still," Maveen told him.

"Keep still! Who's shooting off their mouth? I can keep still."

"Then keep still for only five minutes."

"I'll keep still for five hundred minutes! I'll keep still far-rever! Keep still yourself!"

"Can you keep still?"

"Yes! Yes! Yes!" Tim barked. "I can keep still as long as I got the notion for it. I've got self-control; shut your mouth! Keep still!"

"Then, if you can, keep still!"

"I'm doing it! 'Tis ye not keeping still! Keep still!"

So they sat and barked commands, their hands on the triangular planchette, ferociously glaring at each other. The ouija board was much more calm than they. That convenient wooden oracle, whereby spirits of the disembodied damned are summoned from their great thrones in the outermost Hells, maintained miraculous silence.

Old Tim assumed scornful levity, but that passed after minutes of silence. The board throbbed, for the whole ship throbbed with engine pulsings. The saloon's shadowy lights worked heavily on Tim's spirit as they shifted like gray ghosts in the corners. The *Thorn's* monotonous surging was as solemn music.

Maveen had closed her green eyes, shivering. "Have you asked your question yet? Think it; don't say it."

"Ah, ye spoke fir-rst!" Tim crowed.

"Well, keep still now!"

"Who's opening up their jaw?"

"For God's sake!" cried Maveen, half crazy. "Will you shut up! Something's trying to move this board!"

In old Tim were deeps of faith unplumbed, the eternal credulity of the Celt. It may be faith transcending truth. The Celt does mighty things, wields powers not known to reason. He harks to unseen voices.

The souls of the darkness and the silence gripped the soul of old Tim Grady. Maveen opened startled eyes as the board trembled and slipped three inches. Old Tim Grady stared; his face was moist as a dewy rose. The helm of the *Thorn* had taken a slight turn. Only the weight of mountainous waters clutching at her keel caused that board to tremble. Nothing more.

The fear gripped old Tim Grady. His lips moved in a silent question, mute and afraid. Tim Grady asked question of the Dark. On the sea, in the dark of middle night, old Tim Grady addressed to the invisible world that interrogation whose answer lies closest to all men's hearts, however great their faith or small.

"How long am I going to live? Answer me that!" Answer him that, vast Dark!

From out the restless Atlantic rollicked up a wave, smiting a buffet on the *Thorn's* ribs. The board stirred; no doubt of it! With popping eyes Tim read.

"C! 'Tis a C, Maveen! O!—N!—S!—What is't? What is't?"

"Keep still, for Heaven's sake!"

"I'm keeping still. Girl, look at it! *Look at it!*"

C-O-N-S-T-A-B-L-E B-U-R-K-E T-O G-R-A-D-Y

"God! God!"

"Keep still!"

G-R-E-E-T-I-N-G-S F-R-O-M T-H-E D-A-M-N-E-D, Y-O-U-N-G G-R-A-D-Y—

Tim's face was gray. Maveen spelled out the letters, sharply excited. The old man's heavy fingers shook, and he gulped wind.

" 'Tis a lie!" he muttered with palsied tongue. " 'Tis a tr-rick! I don't belave it!"

The board faltered, as though giant spirits wrestled for it, as though in that chaos which knows not space nor bounds king devils uprooted sod of stars in furious battle for it!

T-H-O-R-N-W-O-O-D C-L-A-Y T-O O-L-D T-I-M G-R-A-D-Y—

Tim's fierce red glances were nests of venomous spiders. He wallowed in oaths, indifferent alike to the ladylike living and the gentlemanly dead. A horror of silence lay on the little gold-and-white saloon.

C-O-L-D H-E-R-E—R-E-M-E-M-B-E-R—A B-L-O-O-D-Y M-O-O-N —I F-E-A-R F-O-R I-T—D-I-E, D-I-E, T-I-M G-R-A-D-Y, W-H-E-N B-L-O-O-D I-S O-N T-H-E M-O-O-N—

The quivering board hesitated at the last N. Strength went from the wood as old Tim's arms crashed at his sides. From foolish X to Q the pointer rambled on spindly legs. No more sense was in it than in the dead. Its message dwindled off to drivelings and wool.

Thus for the warning. Say that truth spoke from the wood. Or say old Tim's delirious fears sent himself that message. No law forbids either belief.

Grady strangled to breathe, as though ghostly hands had him already by the windpipe. He threw back his head. He ripped forth oaths. He cursed God, and he cursed Satan by the name of God. He cursed himself, and all souls living. Cursed Burke and Clay, and all souls dead.

He cursed God by the name of God! And then he spoke of Cromwell.

Smash! He brought down his fist. From crescent moon to star the board split wide. Yes and No were broken off clean, like the answers of the doubtful Delphic oracle. The split board seemed to grin.

Tim's rust-shot eyes were wild and rolling, but his voice showed small diminution of its accustomed strength. It was harsh and furious. With his roars he would have filled up the wastes of the void, though likely in the void they sounded thin and small.

"That for the damned thing! 'Tis a tr-rick in it! I don't belave—I don't belave it! Could a soul come sailing back from—O, Cromwell's curses—"

The *Thorn* listed heavily in the valley of a ground swell. Here, for an instant, sight of Rose Dawn sitting silently, van Chuch weaving his hands, Maveen nervously lighting a cigaret, old Tim lifting his fists and shouting. Then the dark, swallowing all. Over the *Thorn* the dark. Red and green and dazzling white, running, masthead, starboard, larboard, bow and quarter, through all her sparkling length her lights went sharply out.

Confused shouts came from the deck. Running naked feet pattered. Past the windows drifted wan shapes of sailormen. "Put her sharp around, helmsman!" van Chuch roared out the window.

"Sharp to port!"—"Ay, ay!"—"Hard over with 'er, Red! Hundred and eighty, set your course!"—"Haul on this here wheel, Tom. Beef in it, smoke! Down!"—"Who set us straight on the keys?" van Chuch boomed.—"Not I, Sir. All clear ahead."

Old Tim Grady howled, precipitated into that sudden dreadful dark. He fought with blind fists at chimeras invisible. The blackness of the air had serpent coils; the night's breath panted. Treacherous the arms and breath of the night! The night sucked old Grady's soul from out his lips like a demon woman with love on fire.

Loudly a table overset, bearing down an avalanche of porcelain. Something was rolling, pitching on the floor, creeping under Tim's feet, snatching at his ankles. Old Tim panted as he swung his fist in front of him. It struck against something hard. A sharp thing, tooth, or knife, or pin, bit in his arm.

Muffled, harsh-breathed oaths. . . . A faint, deep cry. . . . Dim sailormen rushing down the deck. . . . Continually the ocean, solemn and dolorous, its brass drums beating on far shores. . . .

Piercing above all for one sharp note was a cry of hysteria, the sound of mirthless laughter. The laughter rose. It became a scream, and passed out to silence on a high note, superaudibly vibrant.

"Whisky, Tom!" Tim Grady was croaking. "God—! your hands! Get off my throat! Help! Rose! Rosie!"

Sounds of ripping, staggering wrestling. From afar did Tim Grady hear the muttering of van Chuch, the growling of Tom Jefferson, as he strangled in the blackness of the night?

"Fetch—light! I got it!"

Ay, he had got it.

XXX. THE QUEEN OF SPADES

IT happened that on a night there gathered in the Royal Poinsettia hotel, Biscayne, Florida, five men. They were gathered with the purpose of combining and conspiring in the commission of a crime against the laws of the sovereign State of Florida and the Methodist Church, viz., to play poker.

Three of the men had more money than they would spend, and the other two had never earned a dollar in all their parasitical lives. But here they were, in one of the most perfect tropic nights which ever lay on shore and bar and ocean, trying to capture pasteboard cards with certain markings on them, and so take each other's money.

Of those five men, one was young Laurence Spencer, sent to Biscayne by his genial physician father in order to greet the Grady yacht when it arrived, and with the delusion that Laurence's interest in Maveen Grady might develop into something more fruitful than an occasional infecund embrace during dancing. Not, to be sure, that Dr. Russel Spencer believed in fortune hunting; but he did believe that any young lady desirous of attaining to the legitimate marital love of Laurence, scion of the Spencers and the Bostonese Searses, should be willing to pay for it.

A second man was Boosten Claude, the fighting little grapefruit farmer who had run foul of Deleon in New York. Returned now to his native grapefruitage, he had abandoned his determination to shoot Gay Deleon. Across the table from Deleon he sat, his long, stiff bristles of hair rising in an angry tower, his narrowed eyes looking hotly at Deleon.

The other two men were Thornwood Clay, son of that old man who died at Dawnrose's doors, and Colonel Stoughton Dawn, father of John Dawn. The last of the Clays was a smooth-faced man, well barbered and massaged, with gray moustache and hair. Though his cheeks held blood, they too seemed gray—a man of mist, a shadowy man, a locust-shell of dead delights and a husk of gentility.

Old Stoughton Dawn was an old man, withered and parched with heat. His hair was of the whitest white, blue white, a tinge of whiteness more intense than the rainbow whiteness of snow or the gray whiteness of milk. Yet his brows were astonishingly heavy and black, shielding black eyes of a quite youthful fierceness.

Deleon threw down cards, and with clutching, snapping fingers tore the whole pack to bits and flung it to the floor. "Lousy, bastard luck!" he gasped, using adjectives oftener heard than seen.

Two of those four men who played with him were deathly inimical. Boosten Claude hated him for his own sake, and Thornwood Clay for his father's. It may be that they had previously agreed to break Deleon, playing the game together against him. The younger Clay held little respect for the honor of the Clays; he had lived his life for cards and women, and they were more to him than a hypothetical question of fair play. And Boosten Claude, like some others of the rich new gentry of Florida, came from the lowest Georgia cracker stock, and held anything honest which did not land him in jail.

Beyond half-shaded windows a filling moon ripe as an orange swam up from the ocean, sailing over tall palms. A week, and it would reach its round red fullness. It tinted the waters of Bay Mimayne, tinted the bowl of ink which was the sky. Faint green phosphorescence shone on bay and ocean, separated each from each by the narrow tongue of Key Mimayne. But no light shone in Black River, flowing past the hotel from marshlands down to the bay.

Night grew later. Deleon tried to summon up an assured defiance of damnation, the gambler's boast and confidence. But his hands trembled, and his eyes were dull.

"I've won your car, Deleon," barked Boosten Claude. "Now do you want to play your pants?"

Clay passed chips to Deleon. "Last of my father's debt," he said. "The Clays pay, dollar for dollar!"

The knob of the unlocked door rattled. Boosten Claude threw a newspaper over the gaming table. Colonel Clay picked up a hotel Bible, assiduously reading that Enoch begat Gog. Silently the five men sat, pleasantly aware that they were criminals, and that the laws of all nations were set against them.

A woman of middle-age thrust her face in, prettily pouting, smiling with small, hard eyes When young she had been told those simperings were ingenuous, but in her ripe years they gave her the appearance of a surprised cow. She was inconspicuously clad in negligee.

"Mrs. Mallow," old Dawn whispered to Laurence. "You'll have to be initiated into the Suicide Club now. Claude is president."

" 'Xcuse me," said the famous Mrs. Mallow. "Didn't expect to find anyone else with you, Thorn. How do, Colonel. And Mr. Claude!"

Bobbling forward, with a swaying, knee-dragging motion, she extended her fingers. She was especially pleased with Laurence's looks, who, in spite of his bald head, looked pink and young; and at him she directed sly, amorous glances.

"Are you wicked, wicked men playing poker?" she asked. "Ten dollars for this little chip!" She squealed. Deleon snatched from her hand the chip she had taken up.

"Aren't you afraid of the police?" she roguishly asked old Dawn, who was chief of police in Biscayne.

Then she pranced around the table, stepping like a high-school horse. "Can't I give somebody luck?" she screamed in high tones. "Won't somebody let me give him luck? I want to give somebody luck!"

Deleon had planted his elbows on his chair arms, frustrating Mrs. Mallow's attempts to perch there. No perch was available on which such a plump last spring's chicken might roost. She drew up a chair between Clay and Deleon, tripling the folds of her chin as she rested it on her knuckles.

Deleon surveyed her cunningly, with that thirsty insolence of look best known in hotel lobbies. His eyes had acquired a certain brightness. He breathed more quickly. He sleeked back his shiny hair. A smile caused his moustache to ripple. Lucky at love—!

The game was breaking up. All men but Deleon had risen, receiving money from old Dawn in exchange for chips. Mrs. Mallow saw her group of admirers disintegrating.

"Have you heard that rich Mr. Tim Grady is coming to Biscayne?" she asked. "I want you to introduce me, Mr. Claude."

"O, we'll initiate him into the Suicide Club," said Boosten Claude.

"What club is that?" asked Mrs. Mallow. "What a dreadful name!"

"It's named for the queen of spades," said Claude maliciously. "A club for the queen of spades, the lowest card in the deck."

"Tim Grady," Deleon repeated, looking cunningly downward.

"Married a show girl," said old Dawn.

Deleon sat up, kicking the table leg. "A show girl!" he said contemptuously. "He married Rose Dawn, that's whom he married!" He looked up at old Stoughton Dawn, and for the first time the significance of the old man's name came to him. "Were you related to John Dawn?"

"I was his father."

"Then you know Rose?"

Old Dawn shook his head. "I never met her," he said.

"I knew Dawn," said Deleon, frowning, thinking uneasy thoughts.

"Two hundred years the Dawns have lived here," said the old Colonel. "Came with the Spanish. We used to be Dons. Two hundred years! But *he* was wild, and ran away. Married a foreign woman out in California."

Deleon was smiling at Mrs. Mallow. She interested him, for she had been a beauty, and she was yet a woman. Though the affairs of that woman with the late Marsh and Mallow were ten years old, Gay Deleon knew all affairs of the devil for the past ten thousand years, which is as long as women have used paint.

Out the door they had gone, Colonel Dawn, and Boosten Claude, and Deleon. Mrs. Mallow took the uneasy arm of Laurence Spencer before he could withdraw. As Clay opened the door for them, switching off the lights, Mrs. Mallow turned back toward the darkness and Laurence with a hushed giggle.

"Do you dare to kiss me?" she asked, putting up her face.

Laurence stammered. Her moist lips were on his, like to the touch of a sponge. When he could, Laurence furtively wiped his lips. Thornwood Clay stood by with a weary smile, saying nothing, and possibly thinking nothing.

In the darkened room a slim sliver of reflected moonlight was shining. The moon had passed the zenith and gone west; this was but the silver mirage of stars far waning past the Everglades. Mrs. Mallow's eyes were moonstruck. Clay's eyes, too, filled with a wan fire.

Far away on the shining ocean, past bay, past key, a lean white ship was limned. She lay in at the entrance to Bay Mimayne, just beyond the narrow cut which sliced through the coral rock of Key Mimayne. Laurence excused himself, and went forth. But Mrs. Mallow and the son of old Thorn Clay stayed, watching long and silently that lean white ship, that floating palace of wealth and power, that little white chip on the ocean.

"I wonder if that's Grady's ship?" said Clay.

The ship lay still as a ship of the dead. No motion rocked her. Her white strakes were dead men's bones.

XXXI. SORROW OF THE DOG-FACED SPHINX

ANTHONY was packing his bags. He answered the insistent questions of Arsen by saying that he was going South.

"To New Orleans, after rum-runners," he said, in answer to Arsen's demands. "I'm taking the Gold Express tonight."

"Bacardi rum," muttered Arsen, thinking of New Orleans. "Dark-eyed senoritas. . . . Mardi Gras. . . .Creole guitars. . . . O, Hell!"

"I'm not going to play," said Anthony.

"A good story just came up from Jacksonville over the A.P. wire," said Arsen with a fleet grin. "About old Tim Grady. He's down off the keys now. A fight took place on board the *Thorn* the other night. Someone came mighty near being killed."

Anthony folded shirts and stowed them in a bag.

"A fisherman passing in hailing distance of the yacht got the story," Arsen explained, "and told it in Palm Beach when he came to shore."

Anthony turned. His countenance was tense. "What's the story?"

"You don't need to bark at me that way," said Arsen sulkily. "Nothing for you to be interested in. *I* might be worried. *I* know Rose Dawn. Know her well," said Arsen complacently, straightening his cravat. "Well, it seems old Grady got drunk the other night, as usual, and somehow or other something happened on the *Thorn*—lights went bad, I understand—and old Tim got scared of the dark, and threshed around trying to kill everybody he could lay his hands on. He tussled with van Chuch—"

"I thought something had happened," said Anthony, his glance dreadful.

"Old Tim must have been half crazy," said Arsen, "(though of course we haven't got the whole story straight yet), and van Chuch had to put him in his cabin. They had it hot and heavy. Grady claimed van Chuch tried to kill him, but I guess it was the other way around. You know the law of the sea—the captain is king. That elephant coon, Tom, sided with Tim, and the whole crew had to hammer him quiet with belaying pins. I'll bet old Grady's mad as a blue baboon. And scared! He seems to think someone is trying to murder him."

"I'd not be surprised," said Anthony.

Arsen's restless glance had fallen to the rug and its woven dog-faced Sphinx. "You never told me what that means," he complained. "Is it a river or a snake? The Sphinx looks sad tonight. Is there anything symbolized in the whole mess?"

"Then you don't see it?"

"I suppose it's a symbol of fatality," said Arsen. "Wise old Babylonian stuff. But I don't believe in fate."

"I was thinking about Grady," said Anthony. "You don't believe in foreordination?"

"O, of course not," said Arsen, but doubtfully. "What do you take me for? Nobody believes in fate now. I'm no fool." He cocked his ear; Anthony did not confirm Arsen's statement. "Squirmy Schermerhorn doesn't," Arsen said defiantly, "and he's smart as anything. A fortune-teller once said he was fated to fall in love with a black-haired girl. But it happens the only girls he loves are Rose Dawn, who's blond, and Maveen Grady, who's Titian, and the Arty Girl, who's chestnut brown this season; not counting the girls he takes out on parties, who are generally mud-colored. *That* shows you what fate amounts to!"

"Some things are fate," said Anthony after a pause, speaking softly and with intense bitterness. "If you die, it's fated you'll be forgotten. If you hand over your soul to a woman, she'll use it to light a cigaret, and throw it in the ash-tray with other burned-out flames. And if you try to die for a woman, you'll live on like damned Ahasuerus!"

Sorrowfully the dog-faced Sphinx looked up at Anthony with motionless woven immortality.

Arsen said: "The dog's got the blues tonight, though it's pink and purple." He was restless, and kicked his feet. "If there is fate—" he began argumentatively—"well, if there is fate—Take Tim Grady, for instance, who's afraid someone will kill him. Why, I believe you said something about him once before," said Arsen with some excitement—"something about fate!"

Anthony closed his lips. "I talk too much," said he.

"So do I," Arsen admitted frankly. "What makes men do it?"

"Nemesis —the Avenging God."

Arsen was thinking. "A mighty interesting thing to figure *there*, if it's ordained—"

"I never predicted the old man's death," said Anthony clearly.

"I thought you did."

"Great Lord!" said Anthony. "You might kill him yourself."

Arsen drew in his breath, laughing faintly. "I?"

"Certainly," said Anthony. "His daughter might fall in love with you—since all women are fools—and to get her father out of the way, stuff his mouth with bed pillows till he choked."

"Maveen Grady, for me!" cried Arsen, aghast and delighted.

"Not likely, but not impossible," said Anthony. "Playing in Lower California once, I knew a woman went mad over a Yaqui Indian. Dirtiest animal you ever saw. But she loved this blasted cannibal so much that one night she took his tomahawk, and when he was sleeping with his squaw—"

"You're making fun of me," said Arsen angrily.

"Murder is fun, the greatest nonsense possible. Except love. The two go together."

"Tim Grady's likely to live longer than you or I," said Arsen, "and lay Rose Dawn beside his other wives. What could happen to him?"

"What's written is written," said Anthony. "Though I don't know what's written."

Arsen did not know whether to laugh or be grave. He had great faith in all his great friends, and their opinions were his own. "My friend, Dr. Bellbender, says this is an age of free will," said Arsen.

Anthony pulled out a watch, and held it in his palm. Click-click! panted the seconds, endeavoring to overtake the hour forever gone, forever ahead of them. They rustled with the trickling whisper of falling water.

Shadows and points of light lay on the watch crystal. Anthony's eyes were dark. Wigley Arsen felt small.

"Here's the hour hand," said Anthony, "and the minute hand. They go their own ways. But you and I know that some instant they will come together. That hour is twelve. It's the ending of the day. The ending of the day—call it the instant of accomplished destiny."

"Every day ends some time or another, Tony."

"Each ends at twelve, at the hour appointed."

Wigley Arsen was not shrewd enough to disclose the fallacy in Anthony's analogy, its specious but reasonable-appearing sophistry.

"Just as sure as time, Wigley Arsen, Tim Grady's hour draws on him!"

"And your hour on you, and mine on me," said Arsen.

XXXII. DAWN SUN

IN the dusk of earliest morning the *Thorn* stands off Key Mimayne. Up and down van Chuch paces, dourly grim. His round, itching nose promises heat this day. Red the Sailor, chewing tobacco, holds the wheel. Signals have gone shoreward for a pilot to take the *Thorn* through the gut of the key and into the bay.

"Remember, all you fellows are to tell the Federal officers that Mr. Grady assaulted me without reason!" van Chuch warns Red the Sailor. "He's crazy!"

"Year the Capting," says Red.

"Rouse out that coon Tom. Set him to swabbing down decks."

"Ay, ay!" Red spits. Charmed, I'm sure! (thinks he).

Against the western black of sky ripple dawn winds. On the shore they toss crested palms, awake the peony, hibiscus, orchid, hyacinth, and many another gay and gaudy flower with names like the angels of Heaven. Dark rivers from the marshes lap their fenny banks. The sea grows lavender and violet.

The *Thorn* tosses her white flanks in rainbow waters. The dawn winds blow the stars from out the sky. The east is shaken with the thunder of the sun!

Crimson and purple is the rising dawn, an emperor of Araby or Cathay, wrapped in twelve glorious mantles. Passion and tremendous fire, heart of the earth, the tropic dawn! Peacock clouds, fluttering with a cry. The tiger sun, lashing, feral, leaping on their trail. "Behold!" cry the rejoicing winds. "God is arisen!"

As Rose leaned over the railing and looked far over coloring waters at the sun, a hint of the hushed sea was in her blue eyes. Like the sea they took color and a fire. She breathed deeply, shaking her golden curls.

Van Chuch stood beside her, resting his knuckles on his hip. "Going to be a hot day," he said. She did not answer. Van Chuch thought he had never seen her look more beautiful, never quite so alive. "I hope you'll stand with me, Mrs. Grady. I'm going to carry this through against Mr. Grady!"

"That is between you and him," Rose said. "You are captain at sea;" (van Chuch was surprised at her tone of passion) "he's master on shore!"

"Who's master, dearie?" Mrs. Higgs gawped, coming from her cabin. She patted her mouth delicately, flashing rings to the sun. "When are you letting Grady out of his cabin, Capting? If you was me you'd just natchelly send him to jail for attacking and assaulting and hitting you. *I* got a word to

say to him myself. He kept me awake all night last night with his cussing—"

With muffled engines the *Thorn* rumbled through the cut of Key Mimayne, sandy dikes pressing her close on either hand. Her slicing sides
sucked water underneath. The pale waters of Bay Mimayne, shut off from
ocean by the coral keys, took the *Thorn* gently. South-west she plowed
across the bay. A dory carrying newspaper men tried to hail her, but van
Chuch waved them off. A steam dredge shrilled blasted greeting. A sea-
plane, dipping and skimming, bustled out with thunderous buzzing. On
one wing it whirled about the *Thorn,* and little Boosten Claude leaned out
to wave.

Maveen smoked cigarets and ate chocolates as they made across shallow waters to the main shore. She devoured a novel redder than her hair,
all about life in the small towns, dutifully thanking God she was not born
in the Midwest.

The crew of the *Thorn,* in dirty brown uniforms blue-trimmed, bellowed
nautical blasphemies at one another. Red the Sailor stood guard over black
Tom, who on hands and knees holystoned the fore-deck. Red supplied
many exhortations, as: "Dig into it, black boy!—Hey, youse! Put more
beef in it! Year not massaging year grandmother's back. Wipe it with year
nose, smoke!" Tom worked silently. Now and again he lifted his head,
sniffing the warm air.

An old song of the sea arose. Far and mightily had the singers ventured,
and now they cast moorings on the magic isles. Briny their words, deep-
seawise, pelagic of ocean weed, as they roared and laughed at each other.
The *Thorn* neared the palmy mouth of Black River.

Rose thought, listening to the men, that they were right brave fellows,
after all, and heroic. Vaguely she remembered Ulysses, the Phoenicians
and the triremed Saracens, the old Norse sea-kings. Vaguely, for she was
not classical. Her golden head (it seems unlikely) was less ponderous than
many a bald one.

It may be in the ditty sailor fellows really stirred, as Rose thought, vague
memories of heroic ages, only half dissolved in death's forgetting.
Memories of Red Eric and Lief Erickson sweeping forth to lay the tropics
at their feet, twenty ships of loud-lunged warriors roaring down the sea
lanes together! Of storms flailed beneath iron-shod prows. Of men "the sea
lay in whose hands."

But not likely they had such memories. The sailors labored for their pay
and chow; men do the same ashore. They dreamed, as do all men who go
down to the sea in ships, of liquor and ready women. They were glad of the
land.

Rose walked slowly towards Maveen, head back, drinking deep the
sultry morning. Her lips were apart, as though the wind were a lover.
Maveen had never seen such vivid emotion in her young stepmother's
face.

"You look wild this morning, Rose. Ready to do anything once."

Into Black River the *Thorn's* bow cut. Ripples stirred. Trees nodded. Something unseen plumped into the water with a splash. Above palms loomed the Royal Poinsettia hotel, a great yellow wooden elephant big as two castles. The *Thorn* headed for the hotel's quay. The river banks, overblown with rioting grass, pressed so close it seemed they could be touched with hands.

"First time I've ever been so far south," said Maveen. "Everything looks green and sticky. It makes me feel lazy." She stretched her silk hose. "It was some place around here that old Spaniard found his fountain of eternal youth."

Van Chuch overheard. "Of eternal death you mean, Miss Grady."

"O, Pete, Pete, Pete! You are so sweet!" Maveen sang derisively, giving him a wicked glance.

They cast off lines, making them fast to chock and pile on the quay. The ungeared engines died. Van Chuch ordered out a gangplank from the bow. He had headed the *Thorn* down river. A dozen or more winter idlers, reporters, roustabouts, and curious coons were waiting on the dock.

"What's this story about Mr. Grady?" a journalist bawled.

Black Tom Jefferson was jigging on the forward deck. A half dozen white men squatted about him, laughing and beating the deck. Some of the Negroes on the quay imitated Tom. The Negro swung his gorilla shoulders loosely, slack as a doll on a wire. His shuffling shoes never missed a beat. He cracked his fingers. The sailors laughed; and Tom laughed back, shaking his shaved head. "Go it, Tom!"—"African shimmy!"—"Ow-wow!"—"Shake a leg, black boy!"—"Getting hot!"

Tom sang a song he improvised, rhymeless, yet musical and harmonious. "I'm coming home!" he sang throatily. "I'm coming home!"

"I'm coming home, I'm coming home!
Smell those palm trees; hear them singing.
No more cold, and no more snow;
No more work for Uncle Joe. . . ."

Tom swung his mighty arms more furiously, slumping them against his ribs, infuriating himself. His beating shoes were drums, sounding monotonous as the ocean. His eyes rolled. Perspiration streamed. It was a war dance now he did, and his eyes grew fierce. War-light of the kings of the jungle!

Midst of the dance heat he stopped, suddenly aware of himself. Scowling, silent, looking at no one, he stamped away.

"What's the matter, smoke?" asked Red. "Give us some more!"

Tom grumbled. "Trying to make a fool of me. I—why I, damn it! I'm educated!"

"Year in fer trouble, smoke!" warned Red. "We'll take no belly-wash from coons. We'll swab out year mouth with soap and water."

Van Chuch, coming forward, drove them away.

Late in the morning Tim Grady awoke and pressed his face to his stateroom window. The windows, wide and clear, were nailed down from outside, and the door was locked. Tim stuck his mouth close to a small porthole, and screamed.

"So we're here, are we? Van Chuch! Van Chuch, Chuch, Chuch, Chuch! O, damn ye, Dutchman, where are ye? Ye'll hang for this! And the rest o' ye—iver last one o' ye—ye bums —the curse of Cromwell on ye—ye're fired! Git off my ship!" He saw Tom. "Let me out of here, ye nigger, and help me kick the gang of them from off my ship!"

Since Grady had spent most of the past two days in suchlike howlings, no one paid him much attention.

XXXTII. WIGLEY ARSEN AT LARGE

"MR. PADRIAC GRADY—where is he?" Arsen demanded. He surveyed the club attendant. "I say, you, aren't you the fellow used to buttle at Dawnrose?"

Saltpeter, that button-faced man, bowed smugly. "Here temporarily during Mr. Grady's absence South, Mr. Arsen," he explained. Arsen was pleased at being remembered by name; he cast a side glance at Schermerhorn to see if Schermerhorn had noticed. "Mr. Padriac's not in town, Sir. He took the Gold Express last night."

Squirmy had led Arsen into his club. He draped himself through the air like the Washington monument, feebly clawing at his moustache. "What's all the frenzied row about Grady, Arsen?"

Arsen had no particular reason to see Padriac; but he liked to mention well-known men. It made him known. "A big story," he said mysteriously.

Schermerhorn, who didn't give a hoot about all the famous people Arsen knew, was much impressed by Arsen's air of mystery. Journalism seemed to him quite as grand a thing as society seemed to Arsen. "I wish I were a jolly old reporter," he said discontentedly. "All the wise eggs I know are reporters."

Saltpeter asked Mr. Arsen if there was anything else.

"Everyone knows me," Arsen said to Schermerhorn, "even the butlers. I can't go any place, Squirmy, that some confounded fellow doesn't pop up and call me by name."

"Rotten! I hate it, too," said Squirmy, instead of betraying jealousy.

Urban Wiggs, that fat dull fool, wandered up to Schermerhorn; newspaper in hand, fat cigar drooping from fat lips. The fat man typical to all good clubs, less dispensable than leather lounge chairs, card-room, or stone fireplace. Urban groaned; apparently he always groaned. He whiffled; apparently he always whiffled. Schermerhorn introduced him to Arsen.

Arsen was delighted, though Wiggs only grunted. "Not the famous Urban Wiggs?" Urban groaned, to show he was not famous.

"I know your father, the famous lawyer, well; and your mother is a very close friend!" cried Arsen.

Wiggs groaned again. He loathed his father, his mother, he hated. He did not respond cordially to Arsen's cordiality, having no means of knowing Arsen's great-grandfather had been a gentleman. In fact, he quite ignored Arsen. Twining arms with Squirmy, who he knew was all right, he walked into the bar, letting Arsen trail behind like a chattering little dog. Arsen talked about Urban's mother's grandfather, who everyone knew had been a gentleman. It was not quite clear whether this personage had been one of Arsen's close friends.

Squirmy spoke to the bartender who poured prohibition pilsner and sad ginger cocktails. A locker was opened. They glanced about them. Tumblers appeared. Then they were off.

Wiggs brightened as drinks departed. He began to look at Arsen as though at something human. Arsen listened for some sapient word he could later retail.

"To crime!" toasted Squirmy, after his formula, proud of being a wit. "Did you read in the *Morning Mist* about the rumpus on the Grady yacht, Urb? Everybody's laughing about it."

Urban groaned. "No. Grady is an old fool. Never ought to have got married."

"I'd ha' married her myself," said Squirmy. "Always was hellishly passionate about her."

"I'd marry her now, with Grady's money," Urban conceded. He sagged and wheezed like a circus elephant sitting on a tub. "Stinking place, the South!" he groaned. "Got letter from Larry Spencer. Fellow tried to knife Larry other night. Larry busted left arm fighting war, but made whooping scrap of it. Caught the fellow. Little greaser name o' Lopez. Trying to hold him up after poker game. *I* don't want to get knifed." Urban groaned. "*I* don't want to get knifed," he insisted.

"Larry Spencer—I know him well!" said Arsen, feeling ignored.

"Fool to get married," groaned Urban, speaking of Tim Grady. "Fool to go South. *He'll* be knifed, too; if he doesn't get yellow fever."

Arsen thought of what Anthony had said the night before. "What makes you think that?" Urban ignored Arsen. Schermerhorn repeated the question.

"Whole town knows she tried to poison him, Squirm," young Wiggs grunted, startling both Squirmy and Arsen. "Maybe not whole town. Got it fr'm m' old man."

"Sacred blasphemy, dear old fool!" squeaked Schermerhorn.

"M' old man got it fr' police l'tenant, name o' MacErcher," said Urban, almost too weary for speech. "Don' know where M'ercher got 't. Um-hum! Hell'sh liquor. Secret stuff. No' wor' 'bout 't."

"Not a word!" promised Squirmy, quite startled out of his wit.

Afternoon passed to night, and much of Squirmy's liquor to destruction. The world had become a blur. Arsen sat dizzily thinking.

That evening he wandered into the *Mist's* city room with mazy motion. Sailed his hat over a dozen clacking typewriters. Draped his coat on the floor. Tucked his neat black tie behind his ear. "Ge' Tim Grady's life from morgue!" he thickly commanded a rudderless copy boy. "Wha's news from South wire? I say—I say somebody's going to be murdered!"

The city editor did not look up. "Which one of your intimate friends gave you the hooch, Wig'?" he asked wearily. He didn't think the news was worth an extra.

XXXIV. THE GOLD EXPRESS

OVER the Gold Express, stammering southward, comes midnight and dawn and noon. Through Baltimore tunnels in frosty gray light; through Washington tunnel and over the river; into Richmond and out again before noon is high. Dim hills far away walk south with it. Mellow melting snows patch the earth.

Anthony, sitting in the observation car, looked up to meet Padriac Grady's stare. Anthony did not know his vis-à-vis's name, but remembered well enough having seen him once in a little movie theater on lower Broadway. Padriac looked him over in the way they have at old Yale; not with personal malice, but with the normal hostile insolence which is the prerogative of all men who ride the Gold Express.

Padriac strolled to the rear platform, his clothes flapping thin dusty vortexes about a frame which showed itself strong and tall. Carefully he lit a cigar, smoked it from the tip, exhaling in quick disgusted puffs. After an instant he threw the weed away, rocking dizzily with the motion of the train. He leaned over the brass railing, his head in his hands.

Anthony, having some curiosity and no scruples, arose and examined Padriac's unclasped bag. No passengers were in the car. Sprawled full length in a chair, the porter snored through his official cap. Reading Padriac's name brought a train of thoughts to Anthony. He had surmised the son of old Tim Grady would be a different sort of man.

Nothing untoward appeared when he opened the bag, not even the customary green bottle. On top was a photograph of Rose Dawn, proudly staring from her perch on a pair of socks. Rose Dawn at the period of her greatest fame, not more than a year before; Rose Dawn of "Sin," far more polished and confident than she had ever seemed in times when hearts were afire. Anthony made a bitter mouth. Certainly she was beautiful.

He was afraid young Grady might have seen his liberty. Anthony pretended to have lost his ticket. The porter startled from dreams, diligently crawling about on the aisle, till Anthony made play of finding the ticket in wallet.

But not before a bald, square-faced, square-headed man, lurching from the dining car with a frail blond specimen of girlhood trailing him, had endeavored to help Anthony. That necessitated introductions; and Anthony gave a card indicating he was "A. B. See, Toilet Goods, Atlanta"; receiving in exchange the card of Higgleson Todd, of Todd, Todd, Todd, and Todd, attorneys and counsellors at law.

Mr. Todd drew himself in when he found Anthony was nothing more than Toilet Goods. He turned to his companion without more words. "O, Miss Dubby!"

Mary Dubby fluttered feebly. She appeared to search for a pencil in her hair.

Padriac Grady lurched in from the platform. Todd popped from his seat, seeing him with red dismay. He had no time to flee. "Mr. Grady, how are you! Surprised to see you here! *Surprised!*" Todd didn't look like he was lying. His forehead glistened. He released Grady's unenthusiastic hand to mop his brow clear back to his neck.

"Going to Daytona. Just a little business, a little business. Surprised! Whew! Hot weather! And you, Mr. Grady?"

"To Jacksonville," Padriac said drily. He looked curiously at Miss Dubby, whom he did not recognize; and she gazed haughtily back from beneath pale arched brows. "I've heard Jacksonville is lively," said Padriac, striving to speak nonchalantly. His eyes drifted to Miss Dubby again.

"Too lively for you; ha, ha!" Mr. Todd was near to hysterics. He wished his beloved Miss Dubby at the bottom of the deep. He wished her frail blond head back in the moon whence it came. In the affairs of other men his mind was legal, cold, and precise; but in his own affairs he was panicky. Seeing Padriac's interest in Mary, Todd glubbed unintelligibly: "My wife, Mr. Grady!"

Padriac did not know Todd was a bachelor. He was not interested in Miss Dubby, and forgot the introduction an hour afterward. But Anthony remembered. And so, you may lay odds, did Miss Dubby. The cat that ate cream was never half so sweet.

"So you think Jacksonville's all right for a little fun?" Padriac asked.

"Ha, ha! I guess you'd be all right any place, Padriac Grady."

Padriac did not take pleasantly this compliment, though it should have cheered any nice young man. Later that day, Todd caught him staring long at his face in a smoking-room mirror. Padriac scowled, pretended to hunt for a wen. He would not let Todd know he had been looking to see what his face lacked which makes women passionately love a man's face at first sight. Perhaps he didn't use the right sort of soap.

But now Todd and his lady friend laid low. Mary Dubby was not nearly so flustered as her employer, or, whatever you want to call him. Secretly Miss Dubby debated if she should address him as Higg. Possibly she was not quite as much of a sap as Todd had once called her.

Padriac paced up and down in front of Anthony several times, speaking at last. "I'm sorry. But aren't you an actor?"

Anthony looked up, startled; he gripped his knees.

"Actors I've known were always pretty good men for living well," Padriac stammered. "I'm asking you frankly—How would a man that's never done it start out to have a good time?"

A difficult question, of course. Anthony slid out by the easiest way. "I'm A.B. See, Toilet Goods," he said brusquely. "You've made a mistake."

"I beg your pardon, Mr. Goods," Padriac retreated.

That ended conversation. Anthony's manner was repellent. All through that day, as they thundered and rocked southward through nearing summers, Anthony was aware the man across the aisle was still looking at him. Vague premonition rose that sometime they might exchange looks with less unconcern.

Next morning the Gold Express reached Jacksonville. Anthony left, feeling eyes watching him all the way down the platform. He turned and saw young Grady slowly walking after him, amber glasses on his eyes, as though this Southern sun was too hot for him.

Anthony hurried into a waiting room. The Gold Express lingered twenty minutes, and went on south to Biscayne.

XXXV. DAY OF DOOM: DIM MORNING: MAN HUNT

THEY'VE arrested Greasy Pete Lopez for attempted banditry on young Laurence Spencer; and they've put police to guard him. But he's a snake that can wriggle free; and he's a rat that can run away. He's broken clean from Hell-hot Biscayne jail! The nets are set for him. He creeps along the dawn.

Near the railroad, in the town's center, a mile from the bay and all cool breezes, is a mean little wooden house flaunting like an old drab: "For Rent." A narrow corner of attic crammed beneath the roof, well suited to soak up all the heat of tropic days, is Gay Deleon's lodging.

Deleon sleeps on a cot. Quite different this from Park Avenue, with birds and icemen whistling in the dawn. Even in sleep his hair is slick like a wet cat, his insolent moustaches are waxed. He wears heliotrope silk pajamas.

On the golden oak bureau are a torn cracker box, opened tins of stale cottonseed-oil sardines, numerous bills, three white poker chips, a wilted rose-bud, a small drugstore phial of some colorless fluid, and a purse, quite flat.

Deleon's fat chin sags. He tosses, pursued by devil dreams. High sun streaks in his window, burning his hairy chest, focusing on his eyelids. He awakes, mouthing disgust. Shivering, scratching his eyes, he creeps to the bureau, looking for a watch long since in hock. The mess of food and trash nauseates him. With an oath he sweeps that to the floor, catching up the phial.

The colorless fluid in the phial may be Canadian gin, and it may be carbolic. Improbably it is water. Deleon removes the cork, sniffing it. For a moment he appears to debate. To be or not to be! But one answer.

Of course it wasn't gin, for Deleon threw the stuff viciously out the window. Glass tinkled below. Deleon wondered in what spirit of courage he could have bought it. Thinking more fully of that hateful stuff, he gagged. He fell back on a chair, lowly muttering the first name of God.

The door-hinges creaked. The doorknob softly began to turn. Deleon watched in fascination and fear. "Don't say anything! Awake, Gay?" Cunning and brown and quick of eye, but panting deep, Pete Lopez crept in.

"Where did you come from?"

"From Heaven, like the angels. Not so loud, Gay! I'll be on my way soon. They're after me. They're hot around me, old Dawn's men! I'll try to make for Malimus. Wait; listen. It's funny! Two fat cops guarding me in the calaboose!"—Pete bowed with silent laughter. "I lifted a gun from one of 'em, held 'em up, and breezed away, leaving 'em locked with their feet in the air. Spike and Stubb—If you ever get to jail, give them my compliments."

Gay paced up and down on the edges of his bare feet. "They'll be looking for you here first of all! You crazy fool, beat it!"

"I'm going to. To Malimus tonight. McGinty has the boat."

"Well, beat it! I haven't got any money for you. I'm cleaned. You know how luck's been running against me. Sometimes I think of killing myself."

Pete chuckled. "Don't fool yourself. You'd sooner see the whole world die."

"Do you know what's happened? I've lost my car to this gun-toting assassin, this magneto-mouthed Boosten Claude. You bet I didn't give it to him! I turned it over to McGinty; he'll give me half of what he gets from hocking it. But no money's in from that. Think of me turned to that for money to live!"

"It's a good graft. If my mother hadn't raised me honest, I'd ha' turned out a chauffeur," said Pete.

"And Claude's after me! I can't give him a cent. I'm desperate, Pete. I don't know which way to turn. If had that ten thousand—"

"How about old Grady, Gay? Some sort of blackmail over Rose?"

"Not a thing there. Not a chance! What could I bring up?"

"I signed her name once to a letter for John Dawn," Pete said coolly. "I can sign her name now to a letter for you, or me, or Larry Spencer. She'd pay high to get it back. Or old Grady would."

"You dirty dog! I'm fond of her!"

Pete laughed at that.

Someone was coming up the stairs, trampling higher, flight by flight. Pete squirmed beneath the cot; and Deleon lay down, pretending sleep. He called: "Come in!" at a knock.

Two officers, in faded blue coats and dusty gray helmets, entered uneasily. They spoke by turns, taking words from each other's mouth, nudging each other on. "Mr. Deleon, your friend Lopez—" "Has give the slip to Spike and me—" "And Stubb and me wanted to see—"

Spike was evidently he with narrow head surmounted by stiff brown bristles. Stubb was a butter-ball, broad as he was long, coming to Spike's top button. They were both embarrassed, no doubt at Deleon's silk pajamas.

"I know nothing!" Deleon said loudly. "If you find him, tell me."

"We'll do that, Sir—" "With pleasure." They cast their eyes about in perfunctory search; and clumped down the stairs, glad to be gone.

Pete crawled out. "I'll dust away tonight," he whispered, not smiling now. "I'll stick close here today, Gay."

Deleon did not fancy that. "You'll drag me into your messes! You'll put the jinx on me! Old Dawn hates me—he'd not mind shoving *me* behind bars!"

"That'd be tough," Pete jeered. "I've swilled enough jail grub for things you did or wanted done. You can do the same for me. I've put my neck in the noose for you—you'll stand by me now!"

"O, easy, easy, I'm not going to turn you over to Dawn."

"No," said Pete softly, with glittering eyes. "You'd better not! Suppose I let slip a word to Mrs. Weinvoll about—"

"All right! All right! In the name of death!"

Walls were thin between the attic rooms. Deleon thought he heard someone stirring.

XXXVI. DAY OF DOOM: FAIR MORNING: SAND FRINGES

GAUDY as a rainbow were sand and sea, bright spots of color speckling them, green, yellow, crimson. Below, frothy wavelets washed the sand; the stark noon sun above. Under striped and checkered awnings awfully beautiful girls lolled, or sprawled, or flopped, or burrowed in the sand. Their bathing- caps were candle flames. Their bathing-suits scorned the scorching morning and blushed the day to shame.

Peter van Chuch, strutting on short bowlegs and puffing out his chest, paraded on the beach, conscious that old Tim Grady was furiously surveying him. Van Chuch was followed by his own admiring flock. Van Chuch was not particularly lovely, and he had a paunch; but in Biscayne young men are rare. Old Grady watched beneath a marquee, his hands folded on his stomach. At periods he grunted. "Chuch, Chuch, Chuch! The Dutchman!"

"That's the man locked Grady in his own cabin," said Mrs. Weinvoll, of Milwaukee, Wis. "They say he's sweet on the Grady girl."

"My hotel room looks out on the river," said Mrs. Dusty Hoag, of Waco, Tex. "I heard Grady yelling and singing on the *Thorn* till all hours of morning."

"High jinks!" said Mrs. Weinvoll, nodding shrewdly. "His wife wasn't around, I'll bet. I hear she's going to leave him and take rooms in the hotel, like the Grady girl has went and done."

"Do you know what he's done? He's fired all his crew; and he's got only one big black nigger left to wait on him. It'll give his wife a good chance to learn to cook."

Mrs. Weinvoll laughed heartily, causing Mrs. Hoag to flush.

"I've done my own cooking," Mrs. Hoag said honestly. "And so've you, I bet."

"My dear! My dear!" shrilled Mrs. Weinvoll, throwing up her arms as she'd often seen Rose Dawn do in the movies. "Don't speak of it!"

Mrs. Weinvoll was in swimming suit of lavender and pink. She was a lady small above, but very large below; something like a kangaroo. Mrs. Hoag wore solemn black skirts reaching nearly to her ankles. The Texan lady was tall, and mostly joints and angles. She was dark of skin and hair, very serious and Methodistic. Like Mrs. Weinvoll, she found it not too easy to begin being frivolous at fifty years.

In the water Bunnie Hoag, a dark chit of seventeen, sported with Larry Spencer. Mrs. Hoag eyed her tenderly. All the dreams of her ugly grim years, all her joyless youth, found new life in her daughter. She would have plucked forth her eyes for Bunnie to shoot at marbles. Though she was gawky, and bony, and hideously dressed, in that moment there was nothing lovelier on the beach, than Mrs. Dusty Hoag, of Waco, Texas.

Mrs. Weinvoll watched her own daughter with not such great satisfaction. Arethusa was kneeling on the sand, happily endeavoring to bury Gay Deleon alive. Mrs. Weinvoll did not like Gay's dapper black hair, his sleek ways, the fat he wore amidships. She suspected he was more interested in the very certain Weinvoll fortune than in the less certain beauty of her daughter, charming though Arethusa was when garbed for the amorous sea.

She called: "Come here a minute, Thusy! Thus-ee!" But Arethusa continued her maidenly mirth, paying no attention.

"I don't trust that feller Deleon," Mrs. Weinvoll complained. "Though he seems to know everybody and stand right up to the best. He even knows Rose Dawn."

Mrs. Hoag assented. "He looks to me like a man out in Texas who cheated Dusty out o' everything we had. Dearie me! It was dreadful hard."

Mrs. Weinvoll twitched. "Why, they was a feller looked like that used to know Weinvoll! It was before Weinvoll—" The fate of Mr. Weinvoll must not be mentioned. "It was before we had our trouble. Listen! Was a little foreign-looking feller with him, dark-complected like, with mean eyes?"

"Greasy Pete!" Mrs. Hoag gasped. "Could it be the same, y' s'pose?"

Mrs. Weinvoll looked at Deleon, shaking her head. Much as she disliked him, she was secretly proud her Arethusa knew a Deleon who knew the Gradys. "It couldn't be," she said. "He knows the Gradys. He's way up in New York society. Why, I've saw him myself dancing with Rose Dawn."

Bonnie Hoag was all in scarlet. She was vivacious, quick, and much attracted to Laurence. On the water and in the sand she splashed about, looking like a little boiled lobster or a red devilfish. Patiently Laurence tried to teach her to swim. He wore a kind smile, and she—she wore her little scarlet suit. Sundry impertinent waves interrupted the swimming lesson, rushing up and throwing Bonnie into his arms. She clung about his neck, squealing. Deeper and deeper they went out, she luring him on to scarlet destruction.

Cigaret smoke drifted. Women dried their hair with slow, shimmering arms. Occasionally one of the bright beach throng, more hardy or more restless than most, darted up and sprang, or bounded, or waddled down to the indigo waters. Then over the miraculous blue of sea was a bright cap floating, or a dipping bobble of hair, and an arm far out again and again reaching forth to strike the languid ocean. Farthest of all swam Rose Dawn, out so far her blue cap could not be seen.

Boosten Claude stood on his hands for the squealing admiration of a female audience. "O, dear Mr. Claude! *Do* do that again!" urged Mrs. Mallow, pouting. "How strong you are!" And little Claude, who was five feet and one inch, stuck out his chest till it nearly exploded.

"Thusy! O, Thus-ee!"

Arethusa did not give even a flip of her tongue at her mother. Milk white her arms and neck. In her boy's bathing-suit the size of a dish-rag she lay down, letting Deleon heap sand on her. She wiggled her freckled little nose, closed her freckled little eyes. Deleon looked at her with silent ardor, his glances speaking a language known as well to Milwaukee as Biscayne, perhaps to Heaven. Many a wiser girl than Thusy had felt her pulses tremble at those black eyes!

In pink sweater-coat and pale green skirt Maveen Grady sat on a beach chair, digging a bright green parasol in the sand. Like all women illy dressed, she was angry. Van Chuch stalked up and down before her, chest thrown out, arms folded, uncertain if to speak. She paid no attention to him. Furiously she watched Laurence and Bunnie Hoag.

A huge billow, the ninth wave, rolled inward, sending both of those swimmers down to weedy depths. Bunnie opened her mouth to shriek, and swallowed the whole ocean. She began to swim valiantly. Surprised at this show of skill, Laurence stared at her. Laughing, he trotted out of the water and up the shore. Bunnie he abandoned to the unkind ocean and a fate no doubt horrific.

Maveen summoned him imperiously, greeting him with sulks.

"That girl in red must be very interesting," she snapped. "That young Hoag person, I mean." Viciously she jabbed at a tiny sand-chigoe, whose life by a hair escaped untimely fate.

Maveen's garments of pink and pale green made Laurence shudder. "What's the matter with *you?*" he asked. On a pretext, he removed the pink silk coat.

"The matter is father!" Maveen was not less pretty than she was angry. Her green eyes were hazy, like the sky before storm. "He ought to know he can't drink in the South like he can in New York. I'm tired of having to apologize for him!"

Laurence did not know what to say. He murmured something. He was uncomfortable as though Maveen had begun publicly to undress.

"And chasing around after that Mallow woman! If I were Rose, I'd not stand for it. I would *not!* You know what she is!"

Laurence couldn't think of the right answer. To say no would brand him a fool. To say yes would make Maveen jealous. He said nothing.

"He had a party for her on the *Thorn* last night," Maveen said lowly. "A lot of men who call themselves the Suicide Club—Colonel Dawn, and that Mr. Claude you met at Dawnrose once; and *her.* There's no crew on now, you know, but Tom. Lucky Rose and her mother weren't there. And *I* wouldn't stay. I left and got a room at the Poinsettia. That Mallow woman was probably on the *Thorn* all night. You can guess the rest."

The modern young woman's frankness confounds nice young men. Laurence squirmed his toes. Laurence had an idea Rose Dawn was with Gay Deleon the night before. He tried to cough easily.

Maveen lit a cigaret. Her lustrous hair was like impossibly fine copper filaments, quivering magnetically in the heat waves of the sun.

"Where is your father?" Laurence asked, to turn her aside.

Old Grady sat beneath his striped marquee not many yards distant, scowlingly watching his daughter. His hands twitched; so did his nose. His huge bulk was sunk low in his chair. Grady was suffering from an ingrowing disposition. He was ready to curse God and die, if that be possible.

"Why do you ask *me* where he is?" Maveen retorted to Laurence. "*I* only see him when he's drunk. Don't look at me so—so sacredly. I haven't any filial respect. *He's* always telling me to honor his gray hairs." Maveen sniffed.

The hopping sand-chigoe skipped up, unwarned by its previous short escape from death. Bright murder was in Maveen's eyes. Warily she raised her green parasol and stabbed the little insect. Vain its silent screams, vain the supplication in its eyes, vain the hopeful skipping on its giddy little legs! The parasol point squashed it. Its life pulsed out. Its *manes* passed to its ancestors, to the vast hordes of slaughtered insects which lie beyond the Styx. It would hop no more.

"Thus-ee! Thus-ee!" Shouting noisily, Mrs. Weinvoll went down the beach like a kangaroo, and extracted the milk-white Arethusa from Deleon. She was a little proud at being seen near Deleon, who knew the Gradys. "I want you to come and meet my friend Mis' Hoag, Thusy."

Deleon walked saucily over to Maveen, smoothing his slick hair. No one could think he had the same morning contemplated suicide. He looked proud as a skunk. Maveen was very pleasant, though Laurence looked away. Few were the women who did not admire Deleon. Remembering Laurence had once forbidden her to dance with Gay, Maveen took pains to be particularly nice to the gambler.

"I'm planning a supper-dance some evening, Gay Deleon. You must come. You know I like to dance with you."

Deleon pressed her elbow. Laurence went down to the sea.

Swimming far out, Rose Dawn struck for shore. She splashed out of the shallow shore ripples, shaking water from her shoulders, slapping her thigh with her bathing cap. Her damp gold hair was in curly knots.

Bathers arose from the sand and followed her slowly. "That Rose Dawn?"—"Surely. It's Rose Dawn herself."—"Well, by George! Rose Dawn!"—"Yes, indeed. Rose Dawn." So the elegant people stared her over, parading behind her. Maybe they thought she was going to sprout wings. Maybe that she would explode. "I've seen her lots of times in the movies. Do you think she looks like herself?"—"Well, *some*thing like herself."—"I've heard—"

Mrs. Dusty Hoag watched her with yearning. "Such a pretty, pretty thing! Never a sorrow or care in her life, I'll bet. It must be wonderful to be like that."

"I've been told I looked like that when I was a girl," said Mrs. Weinvoll. "Look at her, Thusy! Ain't she sweet? You know, I've heard—" The whispers! Mrs. Weinvoll leaned over to impart matters not meant for

Arethusa's ears, but which Arethusa could probably understand better than she.

Old Dawn arose from the sand, dusting himself off. "She's like her picture," he said to Boosten Claude. "Never thought girls were so pretty in the No'th. I don't blame the man who would love her!"

"Something's changed in her," said Claude. "When I met her in New York she looked like a human icicle. Different now."

Deleon leaped up, calling: "Rose! O, Rose!"

She looked at him over her shoulder. Deleon left Maveen without courtesy. Rose smiled at him tolerantly, as a mother smiles at a child with well-known weaknesses. "I saw you with that little girl from Milwaukee, Gay. Still the same gay Gay, flying about and sucking honey!"

Deleon grasped her arm, putting his face close to hers. It was a meaningless gesture, unless something was meant. The mirthless, unaffectionate smile faded from Rose's lips. Her eyes grew wide. She whispered with terror.

"Let go of me! Tim is watching! He's coming this way!"

Old Tim heaved his way towards his wife. His face was purple. He walked as thunder walks on the sea. Half the gala beach watched him, but he did not care. He stepped on stomachs. He tripped over knobby knees.

"Dileon, you bla'guard! What do ye mane making play with my wife?"

Deleon had been insulted many times before; he had learned to bear contumely. "My dear Mr. Grady—" he began, in his soft tones.

"Dear—ye buck! Are ye after-r making fun o' me? Shut up your mouth! I'm plain Tim Grady; but that's better than ye are, hoof or hide or hair! I'll whack ye in the jaw if ye dear me, ye lavender-scented pup! Get out! Get out!"

"The law gives me as much right here as you," said Deleon.

He spoke unwisely. Nothing exasperates a good Irishman more than reference to the law. Old Tim bellowed oath to Sathanas or other tribal god. He knotted his fists, and Deleon went back.

"Ye'll call my wife by her first name, with all the war-rld to hear! The law gives ye a right—I know the law gives ye a right—ye can't tell me the law gives ye a right! The law gives ye a right to breathe, but if I hear breath out of ye, I'll choke your breath up short! I'll break ye in my fists! I'll wr-ring your neck! I'll smash your bones and feed 'em to my dog, if his belly doesn't tar-rn! Run, run, ye sharping swine! Ye scurvy dog!"

Here indeed was sport for the gods, a rich man's family squabble. Mrs. Weinvoll nearly choked with giggles and titters. Hoag shook her head and smiled. Van Chuch puffed out his cheeks. Boosten Claude laughed outright. A hundred faces pressed in close circle, as intent as though it were a dog fight on the street.

Beneath the eyes of the watching world Deleon heard a rain of insults more fierce and loathsome than he had ever known before. He lost his temper; for an instant he was braver than he had ever been. "To Hell with you!" he invited.

Tim's face was veined with cords of purple. Deleon pushed quickly away.

"What a vulgar exhibition!" said Mrs. Weinvoll, lifting her eyebrows till her face looked like a puckered persimmon. "That's New York society for you."

"It just goes to show all people are alike," said Mrs. Hoag.

"They say he used to work for his living," said Mrs. Weinvoll. "You might know it!"

Tim turned to his wife. "Don't you give me any of your nasty looks!"

All that training, all that pride may give was in the face of Rose Dawn, forced to be silent witness, as she had been innocent cause, of this scene. All that the scornful may know of scorn, all that the stage may know of art. The English scorn— scorn of Rollo the Norman, Canute the Dane, Hengist the Saxon! Quite a mongrel scorn. But how the Irish hate it no tongue, not even that of an Irishman, may utter! It is a torch, it is blood, it is black murder.

Old Grady roared. "I'll tend to ye! Don't look at me that way!"

He grew afraid of his own murderous temper, ashamed of the crowds. "This is no place for a gintleman!" he howled, striding away.

Maveen followed as his long legs carried him down the shore. She was furious. She caught up to him and grasped his elbow, unable to voice her indignation. "You!—you—" Grady shook her off, advising her to keep her mouth shut. She wanted to cry. Her green eyes were luminous with strangled anger.

The shore was strewn with gray kelp, with rotten coconuts and fronds of the coconut palm. Grady stumbled over some flotsam barrel staves, cursing as they tangled about his legs. His heart was sore.

A hundred yards ahead a man and woman were sitting in the sand. As Tim and Maveen approached, the man arose and passed them. It was the younger Thornwood Clay. Old Grady did not know him, but he cursed, for the woman Clay had been sitting with was Mrs. Mallow.

Alone she sat, waiting for him. Maveen halted, angrier than ever. Mrs. Mallow looked up with a pout. Her face was stupid; but her full ripe lips might compensate to some men for the smallness of her eyes.

Old Grady bowed ludicrously. "Nancy! All mar-rning have been looking for ye. Sure 'tis the kind fairies have led me to ye!"

Mrs. Mallow lisped. "O, your dreadful, dreadful blarney, Tim, boy!"

A flame shone in her cheek, but it was rouge. A flame in her little eyes, but no flame of the soul.

Maveen stared at them contemptuously, and yet with certain curiosity. Grady's anger was gone; he caught at the air with silly gestures. Mrs. Mallow lilted and pouted and squealed. Most stern of judgments was Maveen's as she watched them, the judgment of child on parent. That ye be not judged, says the wise man, ye must not—bear offspring!

Rose shook off the curious throngs, hurrying down again into the water. Boosten Claude went with her. His thick mane looked like a prickly sea-urchin floating on the waves.

"If Grady shouts at you like that again, call on me!" said Claude grimly. "I'll not stand for it. We know how to treat that sort of thing in the South."

Her shoulders shuddered. It may have been the sudden water. She breasted an easy roller, trying to swim away from him.

"Mrs. Mallow didn't stand it," said Claude. "And a jury acquitted her."

A high wave dived beneath them, filling Claude's mouth with salt, tossing Rose boisterously. She shook her head free from the spume. "I'm going to swim out beyond the life-lines," she said. "I love deep water!"

She went where Claude could not follow. He spluttered about in the shallows, watching her sky-blue cap bobbing far out till it was lost.

XXXVII. DAY OF DOOM: HIGH MORNING: MAN WITH GLASSES

THE Gold Express has left Jacksonville hours behind it. It has passed Daytona, thundering down beside the cloudless tropic sea. Shrilly its whistles echo before it. Anthony's two hands of the water are coming together!

Dinnis McGinty has Deleon's big blue racer parked by the railroad station. He dozes in the warm sun. His round pug nose glistens with pits. Folds of fat lie over his belt, for which a rope-length serves.

Boosten Claude, clad in much rumpled white linen, strode up and shook McGinty's arm. His bush of hair was damp with sweat. "Hey, wake up!" he shouted in his loud voice. "Isn't this my car? Isn't this Deleon's car?"

McGinty glowered sleepily. "Git out wi' ye!" he invited. "Go stick yer eye wit' a pin. This is me car-r. What do ye mane wi' ye, yerself?"

"I see his initials here. This belongs to me!" Claude hammered the panels. "Get out!" He placed his hands on his hips. "Get out, you bum!"

McGinty unlimbered. In towering rage he clambered over the door. "Are ye after-r tr-rying to pick a fight with a peaceful man? Are ye wanting to ir-r-ritate me? Stand up! Stand up, small potaties! I want to knock ye down!"

He threw his coat to the ground and squared away, milling his fists. McGinty seemed happy. "Whoop! Who's looking far-r a fight?" Boosten Claude, muttering ferocious threats, backed; and turned away. For a pace McGinty pursued him, yelling for a fight. Not satisfied, he went back to his car, and slept.

Rumbling and roaring shook the bright steel tracks. Dogs barked. Coachmen and chauffeurs began to stir. In squeak of steaming wheels the Gold Express ground in, puffing like a runner.

McGinty awaked and started his motor racing. With shouts and waving arms he tried to attract a fare from the outpouring hundreds of passengers. One man came towards him, hesitatingly, looking at McGinty curiously through deep amber glasses. He wore a hat pulled far down over reddish hair, whose dry lusterlessness made it seem false.

"Here ye are, Doctor! R'yal Poinsettia? Two dollars to take ye there."

The man with amber glasses tossed his bags into the blue car's tonneau. He sat down where he could study McGinty. "You spotted me," he said drily. "Trust a chauffeur."

"I always know what a man is," McGinty boasted. "Niver made a mistake in me life. And I always remimber them. I got a head for faces."

"You've got a good head for your own face," said the man with amber glasses. "Not the Poinsettia. Take me to some quiet boarding-house. Steady!"

"Now, ye have the app'arance o' a man I might ha' known," said McGinty. "Ye were on the Far-rce? Belike we had a drap o' the stuff togither in New York?"

The man with glasses didn't think so. He seemed uneasy. McGinty raced his car furiously through the most crowded part of town for, though the boarding-house he had in mind lay close to the railroad, he wanted to earn his two dollars. The divinity of drink alone kept him from collision.

"Whose car is this?" the man with glasses asked. "I see the initials G. D. on the door. Now, that might be Grady-Dawn."

"Ah, ye know old Tim Grady?"

"Everyone's heard of Mr. Grady," said the man with glasses.

"The curse o' Hell upon 'im! I know him well."

"So it seems."

"Listen, ye Doctor!" McGinty cut across traffic and halted at a curbing. They were on Biscayne's largest avenue. Dinnis drew out a flat bottle, uncorking it with his teeth. "I know a thing! I could tell ye—Hark! 'Niver to soul befar-r have I br'athed it! In Car-rk these far-rty years ago—hark ye!"

"Drive on!" said the man impatiently, uneasy at the crowds.

"Ah, but me fri'nd!" McGinty twisted around and strove to grasp the man's lapels. He tendered the bottle. "Take a swig to auld Tim Grady—may he be damned! 'Tis Bimini liquor, Doctor, and 'twill set well wi' ye!"

But the man with amber glasses refused. McGinty drove him around by the bay, and back to that little frame house near the railroad where Deleon had quarters. Dinnis introduced him to the landlady, a frayed, discouraged spirit.

" 'Tis me gr-reat fri'nd, the Doctor. Doctor—?"

"Dr. Dichter."

" 'Tis me fri'nd, the Dichter Doctor. Trate him well!"

The man with amber glasses took an attic room next to Gay Deleon.

Rose and Maveen had been on the street when Dinnis McGinty halted with his invitation to drink. Only a glance the two women had; crowds and moving vehicles came between.

"That looked a little like Padriac!" Maveen said.

Rose was tottering. Maveen led her into a drugstore, forcing her to a seat. "Rose! Rose! Your hands are so hot! So hot! O, you've got the fever, Rose!" Rose Dawn shivered in an ague, her hands before her eyes.

"It's this hot sun," Maveen said nervously. "I ought to get hold of father. But I don't know where to find him. He's probably with Mrs. Mallow."

XXXVIII. DAY OF DOOM: FULL NOON: GHOST OF JOHN DAWN

LAURENCE watched from the golf-club veranda Maveen alone on the last green. Sandy level links they were, free of all natural hazards save the ocean. On one side Bay Mimayne, pale lilac; on the other side sea, blue and purple.

Mrs. Weinvoll sat at a far end of the veranda, Bunnie Hoag with her. Bunnie kicked her little heels against her chair-rungs, desperately wishing Larry would notice her. Mrs. Weinvoll read "Society Scandals," looking for her name. Her name was not there, since she was unfortunately neither in society nor scandalous. Maveen waved greeting to Laurence. Her bright hair flamed against a background of green. The air dozed; the ocean was still.

Thornwood Clay dropped to a squeaky rocker beside Laurence.

"Not a bad looking girl," he said. "I noticed her on the beach this morning."

Maveen jiggled the ball into the cup. Madly as she had pursued it over dusty fields, she was now indifferent to its fate. She left it to sprout or rot. Laurence introduced the daughter of Tim Grady to the son of Thornwood Clay.

Maveen did not associate him with that old man she had seen her father kick out of Dawnrose. "Rather fast looking, Larry," Maveen said, when Clay murmured a banality and left. She puffed a cigaret. "He might be amusing. I like the older men."

"O, Clay's been around," Laurence said sulkily. "We've all been around."

"You haven't any business making friends with the fast crowd," Maveen said sharply. "You're not that sort."

Her tone was proprietary. Laurence was satisfied; he was not a man to hate petticoat strings. Men who do hate them, the Deleons, Urban Wiggses, Higgleson Todds, Anthonys, walk with spiked heels on women's hearts. Soft tears are set to snare them, unavailingly. Laurence was satisfied.

He caught her hand. "I'm really not so wild, Maveen," he said; a truth quite apparent. Mrs. Weinvoll watched with a knowing smile. Youth will be served, and also unserved. Little Bunnie Hoag kicked her chair-rungs.

"O, Spencer! A word with you, please, Spencer!" Gay Deleon was calling. He stood a rod away, motioning. "It's important, Spencer!"

Deleon appeared unhappy. That was strange, since he was handsome enough in his soft fashion, since he was young, and since (if his sporting toggery was evidence) he enjoyed vast wealth. What more does anyone need to be happy?

Laurence met Deleon impatiently; for a thousand reasons, he disliked the gambler. Deleon led him out of Maveen's hearing, scrutinizing him keenly, reading him well. Laurence suspected something connected with Maveen.

"Spencer," said Deleon, not letting his eyes drop from Laurence's candid face. "I was to receive a check for a thousand this morning." He paused.

"You can spend it very quickly in Biscayne."

"But it didn't come. It will surely be here tomorrow morning."

"Quite nice," murmured Laurence, blinking his blue eyes. He wondered if Deleon was contemplating buying him off from Maveen, and pondered just where he could hit Deleon with a blow which would stun and not kill.

"Well, Spencer," Deleon said uneasily. "I'm just a little cramped for cash." Laurence nodded. "Cramped as the devil for ready cash! For dinner this evening, you know." Laurence nodded again. "And the evening paper, and so on."

Laurence was puzzled. "I read the papers, too," said he.

Deleon hadn't eaten anything but sardines for a week. He was hardly in control of himself. But still the gallant front, the poker face! "I'd like to borrow some money!" he said at last, seeing Laurence still didn't understand.

"Surely! Glad! Got all that filthy stuff I won in Clay's room. How's a hundred?" Laurence tumbled over himself in eagerness. He was as embarrassed as if *he* were the beggar; he tried to cover up the transaction from Maveen. "Anything I've got. It must be like the devil to have to ask for money."

"O, I don't mind," said Deleon truthfully. Thought of money was wine in his blood. "I got into a game the other night, Spencer; and I swear to you on my word and honor I dropped over two thousand!" Laurence nodded, not caring for Deleon's word or honor.

"That's why I'm cramped. I'm no child with the cards, Spencer. My luck has got to turn. It will turn! I'll pay you in the morning, Spencer, without fail, so help me—"

Laurence didn't want any man to perjure his soul for a hundred dollars. "You've given your word. It's between gentlemen," he said. Deleon's insistence had brought up doubts. But he was generous, with youth's indifference. Deleon pocketed the bills.

"A word of advice, Deleon. May I?"

"Glad to hear it, Mr. Spencer." Deleon would take advice with money.

"It may be worth more than that hundred: Marry that little Weinvoll girl, or marry a lamp-post if it's got a million!" Laurence grew ashamed as soon as the words were out. "You called me a fortune hunter once," he said.

He was afraid Deleon would throw the money back in his face. But he didn't know his Deleon. "Thanks, Spencer! Thanks! I'll think it over."

Deleon shook Laurence's limp hand. Laurence walked away, feeling dirty.

McGinty drove Deleon back to his hot little attic room. Pete Lopez, cowering in a closet, knew Deleon brought good news when he heard Deleon running up the stairs. He crawled out like a snake, his bright eyes glittering.

"I'm flush, Pete! I fished for a sucker, and caught that half-witted Spencer. Here's your half. I hope to Hell you clear out now!"

"Not so loud, Gay. These walls are thin. Someone will hear."

Pete was not so carefree and merry as usual. His brown face was strained; his uncombed moustache draggled over lips that quivered. Six hours in Deleon's hot attic, behind the bureau or beneath the cot, had dulled all sparkle in him. And he loathed sardines. He yapped disagreeably, nerves on edge.

"What's the matter, Pete? Afraid of ghosts?"

Pete muttered, puckering his nose.

"I got this, when all you got was jail!" Deleon jeered. "You didn't know how to go about holding Spencer up. When are you going to clear out?"

"Sick of seeing me around, are you?"

"I've got troubles enough of my own."

"This old Dawn isn't like any hick cop I ever ran into before," Lopez muttered. "You'd know he was Johnny Dawn's old man, a fierce fighter and a good hater. Damn the pack of 'em! He's got eyes everywhere. McGinty has a boat to take me to Malimus Isle; but how can I break clear? Not so loud, Gay! I hope some day they hunt you, and you'll think of me, Gay Deleon!"

"All right, all right, Pete! Shoot off your mouth some other time. What are you going to do now?"

"I'm going to lie low till old Dawn forgets me. Why don't you do something yourself? Why don't you get money from old Grady on what McGinty says?"

Deleon shivered. "He'd strangle me, even if it's the truth."

"More likely than ever if it is the truth," said Lopez, cheering. "Go at it through Rose. She always had a tender heart. Bleed her. Bleed him. Tell her Scotland Yard is after him. She doesn't love the old man, but it wouldn't be nice to watch him hang!"

"Get money from him yourself. He always carries a few loose hundreds."

Pete bit his fingernails. "Would you marry Rose, Gay," he asked slowly, "if you could?"

Deleon walked up and down. "I'd ha' done it when we got John Dawn out of the way," he muttered, "since I couldn't have her any other way. But what chance had I? You know, Pete, that fool girl is still crazy about John Dawn!"

Up and down Deleon walked. He came to a halt by the little attic window. Resting his elbows on the ledge, he stared out at the sky.

Pete was still buried in gloomy thought. He started up with a groan. "Be still, Gay!" Yet Deleon had said nothing. "Be still!"

Between Deleon's room and the next was a wall of pinewood no thicker than paper. Beyond it someone was walking up and down.

"What's wrong with you, Pete? No one's listening to us."

"Listen to that step, Gay!"

"I hear it."

"Before my God! *It's the step of John Dawn!*"

XXXIX. DAY OF DOOM: SIESTA HOUR: DEAD DREAMS

IN his wide cabin facing the *Thorn's* afterdeck old Tim Grady is taking afternoon siesta. The door is locked from within. The two plate-glass windows are still nailed down, as van Chuch had them nailed down, for old Tim's confinement on the high seas. One round porthole above old Tim Grady's face lets in a shaft of light no bigger than a man's right arm.

He sleeps. And sleeping, come dreams to old Tim Grady.

He lies on his back. He gasps like a whale. His limbs are sprawled out wide, one hand dangling to the floor. His mottled gray hair is rumpled to a peak. His blue and white flannels smell of spilled sherry. His red face glistens with oil and heat.

A lazy summering fly hums through the porthole. As other insects to brighter flames, it is drawn irresistibly towards old Grady's lambent nose. There it squats. There it thinks. There it surveys the world calmly, waving its wings in thin song, looking for other worlds to conquer. Hopping on six prickly legs, it washes its little face. Philosophically it ponders on the mystery of the opened mouth beneath. Grady sneezes. The fly is blasted away.

With a fling of his arm old Tim struck outward. He dreamed that a galloping goblin with six pink eyes was munching on his nose. His out-flying arm struck a shelf above his head, knocking down a skelter of books and writing things. Fell a flutter of paper; Tim dreamed he lay in the woods while robins covered him with leaves. Fell pens, pencils, scissors and a blotter; Tim dreamed he was the circus lady at whom the wild-man throws knives. Fell the dictionary; old Tim knew that he was dead.

Fell a bottle of ink. Half-arousing, old Tim wiped the iron- smelling stuff from his face. He sneezed, and fell back again. He was heavy with sleep and drink. He dreamed of the drowning seas.

Sleeping, thus came the dead dreams to old Tim Grady!—

He is in a dark room smelling of sod. He drinks potato whisky. Come foul faces. Comes a cry. A dead man lies upon the earth with the red moon in his eyes. And even now, as Grady watches, the dead man stands and speaks (as no dead man ever did). " 'Tis a bloody, bloody moon!" the dead man cries. "I feared for it!"

Thus this dream passes. Old Grady whispers.

And old Thornwood Clay stands before him, saying: "Ye are no gintleman!" "Ye lie! Ye lie!" cries old Tim Grady in his dream. But his voice is empty as the wind, and old Clay mocks him with low faces. He grapples breast to breast with old Thornwood Clay, striving to cast him down a cliff. "L'ave me alone!" cries Thornwood Clay. "Far-r I am dead, am dead!"

Thus this dream passes.

And Rose Dawn lies on a bed of gold, weaving and winding her hair. Above her head flashes a sign, now white, now dark: "Sin" in ten thousand lights. A wavering host of men kneel about her, whose faces change even as shadows. Deleon, Todd, Arsen, Spencer, Ike—they pass. One dreadful shape has come to take their place. O, shape of death! A man who sits upon a horse, with hat far back on long black hair, with fierce eyes shining. "Ye stole her from me, old Tim Grady! Ye stole her from the dead!" Rose Dawn vanishes, and a death-white witch lies in her place, drowsing on bed of gold. A skeleton presses kisses to her death-white lips, and his bones are wet with the sea.

Thus this dream passes. Old Tim Grady whispers.

And Tom Jefferson kneels while Grady whips the lash. "Take that! And that, ye dog! For I am Imperor, and I have bought ye!"

But Tom leaps up, smothering him in python coils, and high above the ocean hangs his soul. "O, ye! Ye loud ignorant white man! Ye fool, to death! I am the black king!" Through swart abysses falls his soul, and goblins scream at him.

Thus this dream passes.

And comes a blood red moon with but a single eye. It walks, and Grady screams, for not before has man or ghost seen a single eye which walks! " 'Tis a bloody, bloody moon! I fear for it!" Again he screams. Again.

And screaming, thus passed the dreams from old Tim Grady. He awoke.

Maveen was sitting on the *Thorn's* deck. She hammered on her father's door at sound of that hoarse, bellowing cry. Black Tom came leaping down the decks. He shook the door-frame with shoulder blows.

Old Tim fumbled at the lock and sprawled forth, blinking at the high sunlight, tasting vinegar in his mouth. "What are ye after-r prowling about my door?" he gasped to Tom. "Where is it? Where is't?"

"Where is what?" Maveen asked indignantly.

"The moon! The bloody moon!"

"Great Heavens!" mocked Maveen. "Are you asking for an orange?"

Old Tim was coming to himself. He blinked about. Waves danced merrily around the *Thorn.* Palms rippled on the shore. Hot and fragrant rose the odor of drowsy flowers. Voices of laughter sounded far away.

"A fine girl ye are," he snarled, "ye colleen bawn! No rispict for your father's gray hairs. What do *ye* care if I'm murdered in my sleep? Didn't ye hear-r me call?"

"Not a sound," sneered Maveen. "Who murdered you?"

"None o' your lip! Shut your mouth when I'm talking! I was lying on my bed—I couldn't lift a hand—I couldn't yell—"

"Of course not. Couldn't even whisper!"

Old Tim would have liked to smite her dead with his fist. But he didn't touch her. He was a gentleman, and a gentleman never smacks a lady unless he is drunk.

"I dreamed—"

"Are you an old woman, Tim Grady, to have hysteria over a dream?"

Tom Jefferson entered his master's stateroom to set back the fallen books and scattered writing things. Mrs. Higgs, sans lipstick, rouge, eyebrow-pencil, whitewash, face cement, and all things which make women what they are, stuck her head from her door and scowled.

But Rose Dawn, drowsing in blue silk, a creature of pink and gold, beautiful as the Shulamite, did not once awaken from deep sleep.

XL. DAY OF DOOM: DEPARTING SUN: MRS. MALLOW'S HATE

OLD Timothy Grady was in furious anger with all which is. He stamped around the four-square veranda of the Royal Poinsettia, growling and shaking his shoulders. He passed the chair of Maveen with a louder growl and more vicious shake. A man with amber spectacles nearly bumped into him at the turn of a corner.

"What do ye mane by slamming into me?" old Tim yelled. "Haven't ye got eyes? Get out o' my way!"

The man was smaller than old Grady, hence arose Grady's courage. He had never seen a man so big as himself except black Tom. The man passed silently on.

"That's right! That's right! Ye'd better!" Tim growled after him. He continued grumbling and threatening for half an hour. Mrs. Hoag was terrified to hear him mutter as he passed, striking out at the air: "Don't you bump me, four-eyes! I'll learn ye to be a gintleman!" Mrs. Hoag shivered. "I'll learn ye to be a gintleman!" promised old Grady, striding on.

Maveen watched Laurence playing tennis with little Bunnie Hoag on courts in front of the veranda. Little Bunnie was all in crimson. "O, Larry!" Maveen cried. Laurence turned, and a hard driven ball plunked into his stomach. He waved his racket, and resumed his game with a stifled curse. Petticoat rule galls at times even the pinkest-cheeked of men.

Out of a long blue racer hopped Mrs. Mallow. "O, dearie me!" she gasped prettily. "I've lost my change. Wait for me, will you please, McGinty?" She puckered her small eyes and made a sweet mouth at him. McGinty spat.

Mrs. Mallow tripped merrily up the steps to the veranda, her rounded shape seemingly filled with gas bags which ballooned her. With a dainty smile she nodded to Maveen, who completely ignored her. Green frost was in Maveen's glance, and she puffed nastily on a cigaret. Mrs. Mallow was not disconcerted. She drew a chair up close to Maveen and plumped down in it. In crocodile calm she waited for something to drift along in which to close her teeth. She basked and sunned. Her small eyes closed.

"Have you seen any of my dear boys?" No answer from Maveen. "Dear old Colonel Dawn is quite heartbroken. He says your father has cut him out with me." No answer. "And Mr. Boosten Claude swears he'll shoot himself with one of those dreadful, dreadful guns he carries." No answer. "He calls them gats. Isn't that just too perfectly droll?" No answer.

Mrs. Mallow began to lisp. "That young Spencer boy is rather nice, isn't he? He's raving crazy in love with me. Why, do you know, my dear, that the very first night I met him—up in Thorn Clay's room it was, before you came to Biscayne—he fell down on his knees and actually *wept* as he begged me to marry him."

No answer from Maveen. She tore a cigaret to shreds.

"But I don't suppose I ought to feel pleased, even if he did take me home that night and stay to a dreadful, dreadful hour. He's such a flirt. He's told me that any girl would fall in love with him. That's the reason I wouldn't marry him."

Mrs. Mallow paused. "Shut your mouth!" said Maveen. Mrs. Mallow did.

Old Tim, pacing round the veranda, saw his wife coming towards him, Boosten Claude with her. Mr. Claude was not so tall as Rose, even including his bushy hair, and he walked along on tiptoes, smiling up. His white crash suit was fearfully wrinkled; one trouser leg had caught and was bunched about his knee, disclosing a somewhat soiled white sock and a purple garter. Rose was in gingham pink as her name.

"I'm going to organize a Suicide Club for you, Rose Dawn," said Boosten Claude, with true Southern gallantry.

Rose liked admiration, but Boosten Claude wearied her. He was so dreadfully conscious that he must be gallant, had the traditions of the South on his thin shoulders. He took love seriously, as he took liquor.

"Go as far as you like," she said.

Mr. Claude was muffed. He did not know whether she had given him permission to form his club, or to suicide.

The light of battle shone before old Tim Grady as he advanced. His nostrils sniffed war. He snarled and foamed and chewed the cud of his anger. He would have preferred to lash into Deleon, but Boosten Claude would do. Mad men cannot always choose.

"What are you doing with my wife!" he howled.

The two were first aware of him with these words. Claude stood with his hands on his hips, rocking up and down. His brows met. He thrust out his neck.

"I'm *talking* with your wife!" he howled, just as loudly.

Old Tim made unintelligible passes. He had expected Claude to turn tail and run, for Claude was about the smallest man he had ever seen. Boosten Claude stepped forward three inches.

"And I'm *walking* with your wife!" he howled. He stepped forward another three inches. "What are you going to do about it!"

He was now treading on Grady's toes. His chin rested on Grady's bosom. His hair brushed Grady's nose.

Tim drew back. Claude's hands were on hips, and those hips bulged. "You ought to be shot!" yelped Claude. "If I were your wife I'd shoot you! Clear out of here before I remember I'm a Southerner! Pardon me, Mrs. Grady, this is my affair. Now, I'm tired of hearing you yell around here, Grady! I'm on to you! Just you dare to hit me! Just you dare—you dare!"

Grady did not dare. Boosten Claude took another step, and Grady was forced back. Cursing Cromwell and the English, Tim turned and stamped away. He tried to break the planks of the veranda; his soles ached, so heavily he stamped.

Claude turned to Rose. "Do you like kumquats?" he asked, in a soft, beseeching voice.

Rose could think of nothing to say. "Your garter is showing," she told him.

Grady thundered around the corner of the veranda. He saw Maveen sitting with Mrs. Mallow. Laurence Spencer was wandering up, wiping his forehead.

Grady thrust the big young man out of the way. He was blind with passion, and took no notice of Mrs. Mallow's simpering greeting. "Have you been talking to this woman?" he asked Maveen directly.

As he had hoped, Maveen was at once as furiously angry. "Who are you talking to?"

"I'm talking to you! I want to know if you have been associating with this woman!" He waved his hand at Mrs. Mallow, a gesture which only escaped being a slap. "It *is* my business. You shut up when I'm talking. She isn't fit for you to associate with. Do you hear me?"

"Dear Tim!" cried Mrs. Mallow.

"Now, you listen to me!" said Grady, waving his finger at Maveen. "I won't stand for you making a show of yourself with any female like this. You're making yourself disriputable—"

"I'm of age," snapped Maveen. "I do as I please. My affairs are my own."

Old Tim panted for words. He wanted a fight. "All right, all right!" he yelled, unable to think of anything more witty. "Your affair-rs are your own. But your money ain't."

Maveen walked away with Laurence. Tim was partially satisfied in having the last word. "Don't let me see you making a disgrace of yourself again!" he bellowed.

Maveen was shaking with passion. "This is the last time," she said ominously, as Spencer led her away. "I've sworn it. I'm not going to be disgraced again like this."

"What do you propose doing?" asked Laurence.

It was ungallant. Worse, it was unwise. Wise men do not consult oracles, look for a reason in the thunderclouds, nor ask purposes of an angry woman.

"Don't worry about me. I can look out for myself, Mr. Spencer."

Coldly she spoke. Laurence realized he had missed an incomparable opportunity of proffering his life and devotion. Perhaps he had not wished to. If he had, there would be other opportunities. Maveen would see to that. Missing incomparable opportunities is a prerogative of young men.

Mrs. Mallow had dropped her simpering mask. Her small eyes were hard, and she puffed. "What is the matter with you, Tim Grady?" she asked, without trace of coquetry. "Are you looking for trouble?"

"Maybe ye think ye can supply it for me?"

"If that's what you're after, I can, and a plenty! So you're tired of me, are you? Been making fun of me, have you? Think you can call me names to all the world, do you? You're sick of me, are you?"

"I was sick of ye the first time I iver laid eyes on ye!" screeched Tim. "For God's sake, hide that face!"

Mrs. Mallow drew in her shoulders. "I'll pay you back for this, you dirty old mick!" she hissed, as no lady should.

Quivering till her bustle shook, darting poisoned glances about her, squinting her beady eyes, Mrs. Mallow sailed down the steps and across the sward. Watching her as she flounced into a blue car, old Tim was stricken with a sickly fear. Ah, they were bad dreams he had these latter days! The chauffeur of the blue car was Dinnis McGinty.

Grady cursed. He shook his head, but could not shake away the vision. Fear, with wretched, wretched fingers, cowered up to stifle him!

XLI. DAY OF DOOM: SEVEN THAT NIGHT:
NAME OF THE DEAD!

"I FOUGHT the fish five hours," narrated old Colonel Dawn. "Seven feet from spike to tail. The biggest sailfish that ever sailed the Gulf Stream! Now—"

"My gr-reat grandfather, Terence Rory Grady, who was lord mayor of Bally by Donegal Water," old Tim Grady broke in, "hooked a squid once weighed far-rteen stone."

All other voices hushed when Grady roared. Not much else they could do. And then Grady was a very rich man, and his words on anything were important.

A dozen or more men sat in the Deepsea Club of Biscayne. The room was foggy with smoke; old Tim was foggy with drink. He had swilled largely that day, for liquor fortifies the heart. Liquor is Æolian, bringing soft winds or storms. Yet beneath all that loud blustering induced by drink, Tim Grady was afraid. His heart rattled. He wanted the companionship of many men. A dozen men, a dozen living hearts about him. Nothing could harm him here!

Old Tim was at his best. Not better had he ever seemed in life. Not better would he seem again. O, drunken hour!

He was the strong man now, his tones like clashing swords. He was the merry man now, laughing boisterously. He was the boon man now, slapping the knees of his neighbors. He was the judicious man now, narrating the oracles.

His reddish face, his hooked nose, his strong jaws, appeared softened in the hazy smoke. More cherubically pink his visage now than satanically red. His hair seemed darker. He sucked a cigar, and roared.

His glances fell upon the old Colonel, upon Boosten Claude Laurence Spencer, even Deleon, Thornwood Clay, whom he did not know, with equal favor. He did not mind the presence of Peter van Chuch who sat, his hard jaws working, out there near the shadows. In the utmost shadows was a man with amber glasses. No one could tell at whom he looked. Tim Grady passed his glance over the man with amber glasses. His face brought up neither memories nor fears. No vision surely, as the shadows deepened, of the bitter face of fate!

"One thing," said old Tim Grady. He proceeded to tell a dozen things, each one of which was a lie. He was not contradicted. Mighty in the mouth are the words of a rich man when he talks of anything, and many are they who hearken.

Grady talked. He touched on everything from politics to poetry. He waved his cigar. He handled a glass. He talked of all things with vehemence and wit, for he was an Irishman, to whom all things are vehement and witty.

Old Professor Schermerhorn, a retired college president with six hairs on his chin, listened reverently to Grady's exposition of international politics; although old Schermerhorn had spent fifty years of his life on that one subject, and come to the conclusion that no one knew anything about it. He did not so much as bat an eye, if professors are ever addicted to that vice. Grady talked of art, and a painter hearkened. He talked of college; Laurence Spencer hearkened. He talked of the sea; van Chuch hearkened. He talked of war, and a soldier hearkened.

"I'm for prohibition, gintlemen!" shouted old Tim Grady, banging down his glass. "I'd like to have you gintlemen come to my ship sometime," he added parenthetically. "I'll show ye hosth-pitality."

Grady told of good men ruined by beer. . . .He swore it was the working man's destruction; although a small amount of whisky, before or after dinner, never harmed a gentleman. His audience approved with murmurs. Old Schermerhorn thrust out his scraggly beard with the suggestion that college students might be added to working men in the ranks of those whom drink had ruined. Having piped, he settled back with many knowing little nods.

"R-right ye are!" boomed old Tim. "Ye can bet I niver let my boy Paddy take a drop. And a soberer, harder working boy ye couldn't find in a month o' Sundays! Niver got in a scr-rape of any kind. Niver turned a card, niver was mixed up wi' a woman, niver smoked, niver—"

"What does he do for a living?" asked the old Colonel.

"Speaking of prohibition, gintlemen, reminds me of the women," said old Grady.

Then he was off. He was on sure ground here, with a subject which always interested him. There was a nodding of heads when old Tim said women are a great deal less intelligent than men; the same assent when old Tim said they are a great deal more intelligent than men. It is a poor Irishman who can't argue both sides of a question, and both wrong. No one denied him either proposition, which irritated old Tim. After usquebaugh, and after women, he most dearly loved a fight.

"Ah," said he, growing reminiscent. "I knew a girl, as honest a looking girl as ye might care to wed—" He drank, wiping his lips. "Gintlemen, that girl comes from the very highest society in New Yor-rk city, and I will not say her name, but she goes in much for ar-rt. They call her the Ar-rty Girl. Ye'd niver guess—"

Many men smirked, Deleon most dazzlingly of all. Old Grady recounted things which some men keep dark. It was only the dangerous eyes of Boosten Claude, I think, which kept him from speaking of his wife. It would not have shamed him. Ribald laughter struck Grady's ears pleasantly. Old Professor Schermerhorn, like a shrill piccolo in an orchestra, piped his senile cackles.

Argument feeds on opposition, wit on concord. Grady grew intimate, almost affectionate. He chewed his cigar and flung it to the floor. His arms waved out. He tapped Colonel Dawn intimately on the knee.

Many men were stirred by that intimacy with a rich man, many men perhaps as rich as old Tim Grady. The riches of another man seem more powerful than our own. At the end, when life's good things are weighed, the blessings counted, the honors polished, it may be not the least of them will be to say, in the Wigley Arsen manner: "As my intimate friend Tim Grady once remarked, while we were chatting together—"

"Ah, but speaking of women, there's Nancy Mallow," said old Tim Grady. "Did ye iver hear, gintleman, about her and Higgleson Todd? Wait. 'Twas this way. No one knows the straight o' it but me. Todd de-finded her, ye know, at the trial. 'Twas Wiggs should have done it. He ate—ha, ha!—he ate an oyster—ha, ha!—"

Old Tim Grady was roaring with such laughter he could not go on. He had never been so happy. He drank and sputtered, still laughing.

Thornwood Clay arose. Colonel Dawn called to him: "This promises to be good. Something for the Suicide Club. Wait a moment, Thornwood Clay!"

Old Tim gagged. He wilted. His hazy eyes stared about him in the smoke. *"What did you say?"* he screamed.

"Told Thornwood Clay to wait a moment."

"O, God! O, God!" Tim Grady gasped. And dropped to the floor.

XLII. DAY OF DOOM: NINE THAT NIGHT:
THE WHISPERED WORD

TIM GRADY was drunk, still drunk. Perhaps drunker. The dancers, dancing to barbaric music in the ballroom and on the verandas of the Royal Poinsettia, laughed at him. The Irish bull is a goat when drunk.

Hopping about, shaking his arms, he grabbed one partner and then another, in the fashion of a barn dance. He danced with Mrs. Weinvoll (an epochal day in the annals of Milwaukee!); grabbed up from a chair Mrs. Dusty Hoag, who did not dance, and whirled her; took Arethusa from the arms of Deleon, Bunnie from the arms of Laurence Spencer; offered to dance with Mrs. Higgs; tried to dance with his own wife, though that is always bad form.

He tripped over Boosten Claude, knocking him down and kicking him. Then he apologized. In his right mind Tim Grady would have apologized to no man.

Out on the veranda, morose and alone, sat Mrs. Mallow, mad as a slavering dog. Near her sat a man with amber glasses. Clay bent over Mrs. Mallow and whispered. She nodded. Clay walked around the veranda.

Rose Grady watched her husband continually as she danced with Laurence Spencer. She was not amused by Laurence's formal Harvard airs, and the awkwardness of his stiff left arm was a continual irritation to her. "You're too much like your father," she said. "Medical men are stupid. Take me back to the *Thorn.* I'm tired of this."

Deleon was looking at her over the head of little Arethusa Weinvoll. He stumbled, and missed for a moment the amorous nothings he whispered into Arethusa's all too attentive ears. Her freckled little nose was uptilted; her milk-white arms clung very closely to his dapper sleeve. Deleon's tongue was always deft with women, and Arethusa was unskilled. He pressed her white and silver bodice, felt the beating of her heart.

Rose moved towards the door, dragging Laurence with her out of the swirl of the dance. Mrs. Higgs, who had been putting on exorbitant airs to awe Mrs. Hoag, saw Rose's movement, and followed. Not one man, blind besotted with drink, with age, or with satiety though he might be, but watched Rose with both his eyes. No one but Tim Grady, who was casting his unholy eyes upon little Bunnie Hoag.

"I'm tired of it all, Laurence," Rose said. "O, I'm sick of all the light, and the stares, and Tim's noise. Take me home!"

Her blue eyes, clear and deceitfully shallow as the deepest tropic waters, looked up at him. A faint weariness and unutterable wisdom were in that look. Laurence Spencer was reminded, seeing her golden curls, of fierce sunlight on blue sea. For the time he lost all thought of childish little Bunnie Hoag and foolish Maveen Grady.

The music ceased. The verberant drums rolled away. The violins were on the wind. The dancers broke up and drifted away, and many a heart was parted. It seemed that music ceased because Rose Dawn had left them.

Thornwood Clay walked slowly around the great veranda, looking down at the bushes. He came to a place where motorcars were parked. Dim headlights gleamed in a mist of frustrate tears.

For a few moments, leaning over the veranda railing, Clay watched a man below him. Glumly squatted on his haunches, this fellow groaned and wheezed as he tossed a knife. From his knees, from his ears, from the top of his head he drove it blade deep into the turf.

"Playing mumbly-peg with yourself, McGinty?"

McGinty fell on all fours, startled by the sudden voice. With a grunt he climbed to his feet, putting the knife in his pocket. "Mumbly-peg," he said. "Just a few old tricks."

"Sharp tricks," said Clay. "Knives cut. Like women. I'll want you to-night, McGinty."

"All r-right. I'm here."

Clay had whispered. But the man with amber glasses, following him around the veranda smoking a pipe, happened to overhear.

XLIII. DAY OF DOOM: ELEVEN THAT NIGHT: SCOTLAND YARD

DOWN into the patio grill-room of the Royal Poinsettia old Grady stumbled. Even here the flags of glazed bricks were scuffled by dancing feet. Restlessly, restlessly moved the dancers; or stood in a spot and jiggled up and down again. Soon the heavy trampling of dancing in the ballroom above ceased, and orchestra and dancers came down.

A fountain flickered in the center of the patio. Heavy baskets of ferns hung about. Out the windows stretched mysterious gardens and groves of palms. Groves of palms and gardens clear down to the river where lay the *Thorn*. Old Tim glanced out and saw the *Thorn's* red port light like the red star Mars.

Caged birds sang. The night was heavy and hot as steam. The musicians sweated and toiled. The faces of young girls dancing were glistening, their hair in damp strings. But still they toddled on and back and forth, as though they had sworn a vow to Vesta or Priapus to dance the planets under.

Bunnie Hoag hummed a song into the ears of Laurence Spencer, or as near as she could get to his lofty ears. More exactly, she hummed it into the second button of his shirt. Laurence felt dimly that she would fit very nicely into his coat pocket, with just her dark curls hanging out.

"Don't you just love Spanish music?" demanded Bunnie, tapping his back to the time of the dance.

"Love what?"—"Spanish music."—"Yes, indeed!" said Laurence, scenting the fragrance of her curls.

Old Tim had reserved the largest table in the grill. He had planned a supper in honor of Mrs. Mallow; but Mrs. Mallow's love for him had gone, as such loves do. Now he sat almost alone, and with a maudlin voice invited whomever passed to come and bide a wee.

Birds of various feathers assembled to his invitation. It is an honor to sup with a millionaire, even for a millionaire. Old Professor Schermerhorn, squeaking and pulling the six hairs of his beard, sipped a weak highball delicately. Mrs. Weinvoll occupied the honored place at Tim's right hand. No one had invited her; but no one had restrained her. Exuberant pride had colored her face a brick red. She had never hoped that God would be so good as to let her eat shrimps with a Grady.

An exceedingly tall and thin young man stumbled down the grill steps and took Maveen from Deleon. Before the red-haired girl had time to look up at his face she knew who it was. With his first step he walked all over her shins.

"Got to Biscayne at ten," said young Schermerhorn, dangling about in a mosquito dance. "Got you at eleven. Going to get drunk at twelve."

He dragged her over to her father's table, where Maveen unwillingly sat down. Squirmy slapped old Professor Schermerhorn on the back till the professorial teeth rattled and almost spilled out.

"Greetings, honored relative! How are the jolly old bones?" Old Schermerhorn looked unpleasantly at his brother's son, whom he held in senile contempt. Squirmy greeted Tim. "I see you're drinking, Mr. Grady. I'll sit down." He made his words good, taking a bottle from Tim.

Grady turned from jovial sottishness to quarrelsome sottishness as the hour grew longer and the drinks shorter. The looks he began to cast on Mrs. Weinvoll reminded that lady she was neither beautiful nor young, though undoubtedly heavy and unfortunately virtuous. Old Tim lost his alcoholic wit. He had mixed his drinks. He began to gloom. Some who sat at his table observed the change in him. Having eaten enough and drunk enough, they left him with scanty thanks, or none.

The grill was startled by seeing old Colonel Dawn enter, obviously on official business. Two uniformed police were at his back.

"Stand by the door, Spike, Stubb," said the Colonel. His withered body was bent. His thick black eyebrows were one line. Grimly he advanced on a table where Deleon sat with Arethusa Weinvoll.

"Where is Lopez, Mr. Deleon?" he said, with an apology to the girl.

Deleon betrayed vast surprise. He smoothed his hair. He twirled his sharp moustaches. "I understand he broke out of jail, Colonel. Is that so?"

"Word came indirectly," said the Colonel quietly, "that you were concealing him in your room, Mr. Deleon."

The fire left Deleon's eyes. He drank ice water. And pulled a handkerchief out of his sleeve, and drank ice water again.

"We searched for him, Mr. Deleon. Turned everything out. *Now I want to know where he is!*"

"Good God!" said Deleon, startled white. "He wasn't there?"

The old Colonel nodded. "So you don't know. Never mind. We'll get him before morning. Mr. Deleon, do you know what can be done to a man who harbors a jail-breaker?"

"I've heard," said Deleon thickly.

"It constitutes complicity after the fact."

"Yes, Sir."

"We've got a good jail."

"You wouldn't put me in jail," cried Deleon, in a hoarse whisper. "If I ever see him again, Colonel, I swear I'll wring his neck! I'll bring him straight to you. I don't know anything about him."

"Excuse me, Ma'am," said the Colonel to Arethusa, stalking away.

"What a hideous old man!" whispered Arethusa, touching Deleon's sleeve. Though for the truth of it, the old Colonel was quite pleasant.

"Let's go," said Deleon heavily, putting his empty glass to his lips.

They went out. Mrs. Weinvoll was so interested in her famous Mr. Grady that she did not see. Through the gardens, through the groves of palms, all through Biscayne the search went on that night for Greasy Pete.

Black memories had come again to old Tim Grady. He thought of his dreams of the afternoon. With a sharp movement he snatched Mrs. Weinvoll's wrist, fixing her with his red eyes. "Hark ye!" he said, drawing her closer to him.

Mrs. Weinvoll gasped. What terrible iniquities he was about to speak she did not dare guess. She fluttered. "No, no, no," she said to herself. "I am a lady." Terrified, yet hoping to be tempted.

" 'Twas murder!" hoarsely said old Tim Grady. He turned his eyes around, from young Schermerhorn to old Schermerhorn, to all who heard. " 'Twas murder in its eyes, gintlemen. Will ye stand for that?"

Uprose no man who would not stand for it. All understood old Tim Grady was soused.

Grady was angry at the lack of attention. "I won't stand for it!" he shouted. "Something will be done about it!"

Maveen arose in a flurry, seeing the storm lowering. Old Grady reached forth before she could escape, clutching a fistful of her gown. She drew back, but he held her fast.

"That's right. Ye know it. Don't ye run! Ye heard me calling!"

Old Tim was roaring like a bull. Maveen thought the eyes of the whole world were on her. She would like to have the flags of the floor open up and drop her down to the pit. Hatefully she wondered if all her life she would have to know these fits.

She heard laughter, saw the swimming, grinning faces. It is amusing to see pride humbled, to see a red-haired girl in a passion. Maveen grew more furious as she tried to be calm.

Old Tim pointed his free hand directly to old Schermerhorn. The professor wabbled his mouth. "I had the dream that I was mur-rdered!" he shouted. "How do ye like that?" Professor Schermerhorn gasped.

Squirmy winked his far eye and reached for the liquor bottle. Mrs. Weinvoll wrung her hands. Mrs. Dusty Hoag began hysterical giggling. She looked, in the ill-fitting black gown which draped her bony frame, like a disgraceful skeleton.

Maveen ripped away her dress. "I like it fine!" she said. She slapped him ringingly on the face. "Be respectable!" she said, and tried to slap him again.

For a long, long time old Tim Grady sat at table. Silently his guests left him, Squirmy emptying the dregs of the bottle as a parting shot. The music died. The dancers went away. Lights were flicked out in the grill, and the caged birds tucked their heads in sleep. A solitary waiter hovered about. The fountain flashed no more.

The stupefaction of sitting at the right hand of Timothy Grady had quite stultified Mrs. Weinvoll. At last she became conscious of the increasing chilliness, the darkness, and her position. She remembered her matronly dignity and the strict standards of Milwaukee. Gathering up her skirts, she hopped away like a kangaroo. Uncertainly at the exit she paused. She dropped a curtsey.

Old Tim Grady saw one last man sitting at a table not far away. Through amber glasses this man read a newspaper, though the lights were dim and low.

Grady remembered that this fellow had tried to bump him on the veranda of the Poinsettia. No one else was visible with whom he might stage a battle. He imagined the man with amber glasses stared at him too indecently. Tossing down a glass, old Tim stared back. The man paid no attention. Tim snarled. He banged fists on his table.

Holding heavily to chairs, reeling a little, Grady stepped over to the stranger. "Well, what do ye intind doing about it?" he demanded.

The man surveyed him coldly. "Ye don't need to stare at me like a monkey!" old Tim yelled. He paused. "I'm as good a man as ye are!" he said brightly.

The taciturnity of the man with amber glasses oppressed old Tim. The eyes behind those glasses were dark and fierce, and old Tim Grady deemed that in a nightmare or foul weather he had seen those eyes before. He leaned over the napery, striking down his fists.

"Get out!" he shouted.

The man did not get out. With a frown he returned to the reading of his newspaper. "Get out," Tim said less certainly. The man turned his paper with much fluttering of leaves. He filled a pipe and smoked it. "I don't like your impudence," said Tim. "I won't abide it! Get out!"

The man with amber glasses stroked his temples. His lean fingers stole up beneath his dry red hair, seeming to walk like a spider's feet.

"Who are ye!" yelled old Tim, working himself into passion. "Where do ye come from? Why don't ye an-swer-r me?"

"I come from Scotland Yard," said the man with amber glasses.

Old Tim Grady fell back, whimpering. He began to choke. Lights shone on those amber glasses. They crimsoned. They were twin round moons.

XLIV. DAY OF DOOM: ONE THAT NIGHT: THE BLACK KING

ROSE DAWN shivered beneath awnings on the afterdeck long hours after Laurence brought her to the *Thorn*. She pressed her knees. Hoarse drum and viols drifted through the even groves of palms. So they dance. So they dance.

"O, God!" she thought. "I used to dance like that."

Voices of laughter. Music of love. Soft words too sweet to last in this hot land. A girl softly crying some place near the river: "O, Gay! O, Gay!" Wind rustling tall crests of palms. Lights went out. And all sounds perished.

Rose heard some place behind her black Tom stirring about. He had never walked so softly; she could almost see his velvet fingers. His breath was hushed. What a great panther was he! The fear she had known when Tim Grady first brought Tom to her had never left Rose Dawn. Once she had seen his eyes fully on her. Remembering that glance, she drew a wrap about her shoulders and shivered.

Her mother was snoring. Unevenly droned that sawing sound. With a snortle and a gasp Mrs. Higgs turned on her bed. She breathed more evenly.

Only the three of them on that ghostly white yacht, she, her mother, and Tom. When Tim came home, that would be four.

"Are you there, dearie?" called Mrs. Higgs. "What's that big fat black nigger doing, sniffing and prowling and sneaking and snooping around in Tim's cabin? Is he—" Ma Higgs drifted off to nightmares, still talking.

"Tom!" Rose called softly. "Tom, what are you doing?"

Her only answer was a grummer. Tom was in his ancestral tropics. He did not speak meekly these days. His mumbling might be interpreted as an opinion that Tom was no Georgia ace of spades, but a freeborn Virginian colored gentleman, and as good as anyone else. More softly he stirred. She heard a cupboard open.

Rose's beautiful eyes reflected back the misty little stars. No moon had yet arisen. The stars fainted with heat. Now a still wind came up, more cooling. The river rippled. In refracted streams the lights of the *Thorn* cut the water like swords.

A heavy tread struck on the wooden quay. Rose turned to go into her stateroom, thinking it was Tim. She did not care to see him.

"Ahoy!" cried a voice she knew as van Chuch's. "Who's watching on the *Thorn?*"

The woman walked along the decks to the gangplank, meeting him before he came aboard. "What do you want, Mr. van Chuch?"

Staring uncertainly in the darkness, van Chuch doffed his hat.

"Good evening. Is Mr. Grady aboard?" He received her denial.

"Well," he said more loudly, advancing a step up the plank, his hands sliding back and forth on the railings. "I wish you'd tell him I've got a temporary injunction issued against him, forbidding him to sail out of Biscayne port."

"I think he has no such intention, Mr. van Chuch."

Van Chuch was sullenly angry that she didn't address him as Captain. "It's a good thing," he snapped. "I've got his crew that he signed up for the full voyage, and I'll see that they have their rights. And I've got my rights, too, Mrs. Grady. He can't think he'll dismiss us this way without legal measures. There's a law on the deep water, Mrs. Grady!"

"All right," said Rose, dismissing him. "This is hardly the time, though, to argue about it."

She turned her back. After some hesitation van Chuch walked away.

Mrs. Higgs stuck her spiked curls out of her door as Rose went back. Dolefully she rubbed her sleepy eyes. "Ain't Grady back yet, dearie? For Heaven's sake, what is that nigger Tom up and doing? He's opy'ing and closing all sorts and kinds of cubberds. I've been listening to him for the last fifty million hours. He's just natchelly got into Grady's liquor, that's what he has. I'll stop him!"

Rose made an impatient motion. "Why should I worry about Tim's rye?"

Perhaps she cared little about anything which belonged to Tim Grady. Mrs. Higgs caught that thought. "We should worry," she said. Nevertheless, being a born trouble-maker, she shuffled out and opened Grady's stateroom door.

"You, Tom Jefferson! What are you sneaking and snooping about for in there? Come out here! Come out at once, Sir!'

Ma Higgs never used the designation of Sir except to dogs. It is likely she confused it with cur. "Stand up and beg, Fido! Stand up, Sir!" was a favorite command of hers.

Now her tone bore all that contempt. "Answer me, Sir!" she cried, advancing into the cabin. Rose stood nervously at the doorway. "Answer me, Sir! I'll—Wee!" She squealed.

Giant Tom pushed her away contemptuously. His terrible eyes rolled in the darkness. His breath was thick with drink. Mrs. Higgs squealed again, terrified out of her tongue. She tumbled down on Tim's bed.

Out of the cabin Tom came striding, stalking. Straight at Rose he stared. O, horrible were his glances! She could not move, could not move even when she felt his hand feeling its way up her arm.

"Pretty girl!" he purred. His voice was guttural, never so thick before. Gone were the polished sentences, the Northern tones. "Don't you be afraid, " he whispered. "I'm a man," he whispered. "A man!" He struck his chest.

Fiercely passionate the purple tropic night. His shaven head was terrible to see. His eyes were foamy as storm waves.

"He'll whip me, the roaring dog!" (His hands were on her upper arms.) "He'll God-damn me, will he!" (His hands were on her shoulders.) "Me!" (His hands pressed her cheeks.) "I am a king!" the giant roared. "I am a king! This great heart—" (He drew her pinched face towards him.) His straight nostrils were quivering. He crooned. "O, woman—"

Rose screamed. Again she screamed as his mighty arms went around her.

Steps thundered. A shout: "What's that?" From the dock a man leaped clear two yards of black water, caught the *Thorn's* stern railing, and toppled over it. It was van Chuch.

The Negro dropped Rose. She fell against the cabin-house, tearing at her cheeks. With his hands jammed in his coat pockets, van Chuch advanced. His short, sturdy little bow legs never faltered. His square head was drawn between his shoulders.

Tom drew up to his full height, swinging his arms gently. Van Chuch thrust his face close up to Tom. He had been master of men, and in this moment it counted.

Easily could Tom have throttled him, as easily as a cat. Van Chuch drew himself up directly, glaring long at the Negro. Tom's eyes dropped. Van Chuch's hand came out of his pocket. Flatly he slapped the Negro.

"March!" he commanded loudly.

He pointed to the gangplank. Hunching his shoulders, the great Negro marched. Van Chuch followed him toe to heel. Down the plank, along the dock. Into the groves of palms. Into the night.

Rose, fallen in a chair, heard van Chuch shouting.

"Halt!" He shouted again, and started running. But Tom Jefferson, fleet as jungle beast, sped away in the black wind. The shadows wrapped about him. He was gone.

XLV. DAY OF DOOM: THREE THAT NIGHT:
O, BLOODY MOON!

PALE shone the stars, and white with tears. The light they cast was less a light than a dull argent shadow. Dark roses blew within the gardens of the Royal Poinsettia. The smooth palms, sleek and bare, towered to high Heaven and the spangled night. They tossed the stars in their topmost crests. Their fronds caught hold of chaos.

Deleon walked nervously through the shadows. He saw the red light of the *Thorn* gleaming by the river, answering fire to the light of his cigaret. A tenebrous rose-tree struck his cheek, and he startled. He was afraid.

O, something walked abroad that night! Something hissed within the dark! The palms were gibbets on which dead goblins swung.

The wind sang small. An old tune it sang. Smaller than the wind was the soul of Gay Deleon. He whimpered mutely, afraid of the great dark.

A hand lay on his shoulder. Deleon sagged from the knees. Screams would not come. In terror he clasped a rose branch, crushing its spikes into his palm.

"Don't bleat, Gay! It's Pete. They searched your room, I know. I heard them coming, and got away in time. What's the matter, Gay?"

"My heart."

"Your heart!" Pete's laughter rattled like dried peas. His mirth was brief. "Gay?"

"What the devil do you want with me now? Do you know I'm near in jail for your sake?"

"Sweet of you," whispered Pete. "Listen, Gay. Old Grady's still up at the Poinsettia. He had some sort of fit, and young Spencer has been working on him. He won't be back to the *Thorn* for a long time yet. Now's the time!"

"For what?"

"To tell Rose he's wanted in Ireland. McGinty may have lied, but she'll believe it. Wring her!" Pete made a motion with his hands.

"No!"

"O, sure, Gay."

Deleon thought. He looked at the white and red lights of the *Thorn.* They aroused some courage, they were so brave and bright. A shadow stirred. He startled. "What was that?"— "Nothing, Gay. Only the wind." Deleon thought further. If not for the sake of money, for her own sake it might be worthwhile to share a secret with Rose Grady.

"Grady might find us, Pete."

"You've got the soul of a rabbit," Pete spat. "I'll take care of Grady!"

At the edge of the quay Pete stopped. "I'll wait here," he said. "Rose loves me like poison. *You* know, Gay."

Deleon hesitated. He saw something stir on the *Thorn's* stern, and clasped Pete's arm. He was terrified to think old Tim Grady might have flown, like some foul witch on broomstick steed, from the Poinsettia to the *Thorn;* might be waiting for him now. Deleon did not care to meet the old man's wrath, drunk or sober, righteous or wrongful, day or night.

Pete laughed silently again.

"It's Rose. See the shadow of her head against the sky? No one else aboard but the old lady and the nigger. *He's* another good reason I don't care to go aboard."

Deleon crept silently up the plank, and aft down the decks. Rose had slipped down in her deck-chair, half asleep. Deleon saw tears cold on her cheeks. Alone, unguarded, the sleeping beauty! Would a kiss awaken her?

Rose opened her eyes as Deleon slipped to a seat beside her. "I thought it was—" she murmured. "Gay, what are you doing here?"

"Didn't *he* leave me in charge of you?" Deleon asked, with tongue always ready for women. "I saw your bright eyes, Rose, and wanted a moment of talk. Nothing like you, Rose," he said more confidently, "to make the night seem lovely."

Rose looked at him sadly. "Tim may be down any moment now, Gay. What can I tell him when he finds you here? I wonder, do you ever think of other people?" ("Always think of you," Gay muttered.) "You know what he is when he's angry, like some strange wild beast. I'm afraid of him, Gay!"

"Tim won't be down. He had a dose of the D.T.'s—passed out cold."

"He was with that Mallow woman?" Rose shuddered.

Deleon shrugged; he offered a cigaret. "No? You don't need to be afraid he'll find me here. Longer you're married to him, less you'll see him. When you've been married a year, any one of a thousand women will know his face better than you." That wasn't the right way to begin; he was talking of women; he should talk of McGinty.

"No danger of his finding me here," he said.

"So you're not being brave for my sake, Gay?" she mocked.

Rose fell back in her chair, looking wearily away from him. Her knees were doubled under her. She fidgeted and played with her curls. Her bosom was turned to Gay Deleon. It was lustrous as satin. Deleon's heart grew hot.

With a hushed gasp he looked at her night-enhanced beauty. Never had she seemed so lovely. Gay Deleon, whom many women had loved, who had never loved a single woman, felt as much love for Rose Dawn as he could ever know.

He wondered if he had not been a fool for letting her go when he might have had her. He was doubtful if he might ever have had her. What had he been to her? It was not true, as he had complacently dreamed, she could have been his when John Dawn died. Never! One woman to whom he was as dust.

Nervously Deleon brushed his glossy hair. Rose gazed at the river with sad musings. Her hand, bent like a weary lily, touched her breast. The desire for her was like ten-day hunger in the desert, like a thirst unquenched.

"Rose!" he whispered. She turned. Deleon faltered, "Tim Grady—"

She looked at him curiously over her shoulder. Deleon stared down at her face from above. Sweet was the curve of her cheek, and dimples held pockets of darkness.

"Rose, Tim Grady—"

"Tell me, Gay! Is he ill? He *isn't*—"

"He's a murderer!" Deleon hissed. "He's been wanted forty years in Ireland by the police!"

"What on earth, Gay!"

"I know it's so!"

Rose looked out at the dark river. "Some one has been trying to make fun of you; or you are trying to make fun of me. It's not possible," she said.

"It is true!" Deleon spoke with conviction.

Rose started up, becoming more excited. "But you say he is still wanted, after all these years? Why, if that's so, he—he—"

"He'll hang!"

Rose relaxed. This was too new and terrible to be grasped. It must be thought over a long time before she could understand it. Once or twice she shook her lovely curls. Deleon stared up at her, his eyes dilated, his soft hands trembling with the passion of his thoughts.

"Rose! Rose!"

"I don't see why you tell me this," she whispered, "even if this is true. It can't concern me. I don't want to know it!"

"Well," said Gay. He swallowed: "Well!" He could think of nothing more.

Rose jumped to her feet and leaned over the stern rails, gripping hard to the brass. She stared intently down the dark dock. Dull steps rumbled on the wooden planking. "It's Tim! He's almost on the gangplank!"

Deleon looked right and left with rapid glances, a scorpion in a ring of fire. No way out! The silky river rippled against the *Thorn,* its infuscate waters hid horrors beyond thought. He bit the back of his hand, suppressing the desire to shriek.

Old Tim Grady's voice now sounded as he stumbled on the gangplank, repeatedly trying to feel his way up. He staggered back, and again lurched forward to ascend. "Damn ye! Damn ye!" he roared. "Who's moving this plank!"

Deleon was not stirred with fear of disgrace for Rose. He cared not what happened to her now. Terror possessed him. He knew the wildest and littlest fear the heart may know, the fear of death.

"He'll kill me! What can I do against a great big drunken brute like that?"

He, the great gambler, was a poor sort to gamble with death. Though she herself was frightened, Rose spared him a glance of contempt. "Still the same old Gay. You never forget yourself."

"Why didn't Pete stop him?" Deleon whispered in panting gasps. "He swore he'd do it. Hasn't he a knife?"

Old Grady was wavering on the quay. He grasped the gangplank railing and inched his way up. "Who's there?" he cried. "Who is 't with ye, Rose?"

"No one," said Rose in her terror, knowing full well what would happen to her if Grady found Deleon. "I'm all alone."

Old Tim growled. "I see some one! I see him! Don't ye lie to me!"

"No one!" Rose cried again. To Deleon she whispered, "Not there. The next door!"

Deleon had been trying to enter old Tim's cabin. His stultified hands obeyed Rose's directions, opening her cabin door. He slipped through.

Grady swayed down the deck, feeling his way with hands on the cabin-house. He lurched to the stern-deck and grasped for a chair. Rattling it steadily, he glared at Rose, who tried to meet him calmly. Old Tim gave her owlish looks. His eyes rolled upward; his throat moved convulsively. He threw out his arm, losing his balance and his hold of the chair. He sat down heavily on deck. Grasping the rail, he painfully hauled himself upright again.

"Where is he?" he muttered. Growing angrier at sound of his own angry voice. "Where is he?" he roared. "But let me put my hands on him!" He wallowed in oaths unintelligible even to the devils he named. "I know of your doings, ye white witch! Where is your lover-r? Where're ye hiding him? *O, ye damned whore!*"

That was enough, I think, to kill old Tim Grady.

He slammed open the door of his cabin, cunningly alert to surprise some lurker within. "I've got ye!" he yelled, kicking about the floor insanely. "There! Take that!" He snarled like a dog worrying a bone. "Arrah! Out with ye!" Less certainly, as he found no one, "I've got ye! Where the Hell are ye!"

Deleon, cowering on the other side of thin walls, in Rose's cabin, felt like a grass snake whom the great king snake is hunting. He knew the sharp anguish of dissolution.

"He's in there, ye common wench!" Old Grady rushed towards Rose's door after lurching from his own. "How many lover-rs are ye hiding?"

The night was dark. Now all the stars had fallen, and on the horizon the new full moon was gathering strength to soar.

Death-white, death-sick, death-terrified, Rose Dawn stood with her back to the door. No acting now in the shivering terror of her face as her arms spread like a cross. It was the pose of the Grady super-drama "Sin." Yes, the last reel.

"Get out o' the way!" Grady roared, giving her a heavy push.

She cowered, but did not move. "So he's in there! Ay, I'll kill 'im with my hands! Out o' my way! Ye are my wife. This is my ship. I go where I damned please!"

"Take your hands off," Rose whispered. "Take—them—off."

"No cur-r will hide behind your skirts, ye Molly McBride! Out o' my way before I smash ye down! I'll strangle the two of ye togither! I'll knot ye in a gunny-sack and cast ye deep into the sea!"

Rose stood aside.

"Go on in," she whispered.

Deleon saw, as he cowered behind a trunk, in one yellow flash all the days of his life like a pack of cards that is spilled. In mad terror he caught up a pair of shears, holding them like a dirk.

Grady halted, his hand on the latch. "Ye say for me to go on in?"

"If you want to." Rose was sobbing. "But it will be the last!"

"The last! What do ye mane?" His roaring soul was shaken. Through the door's opening crack blew a dismal draft. "What do ye mane by saying that to me?" He paused, still fumbling at the latch.

"Is he in here?" he demanded, his voice wavering.

"Do you doubt my word?" whispered Rose, who had given no word.

"Ye're a divil! He is in there! I'll tear-r him out! I'll r-rip—"

"Look, Tim!" whispered Rose. "O, look at that!"

The moon rose late that night. But now it was arisen.

On the horizon it lay as a long oval, full, red, unwinking. Over the sea it lay, over bay and bar. It gathered, upward, and stood as a full round circle. Round, round, red as eternity.

"O, bloody moon!" screamed a voice from shore. *"O, bloody moon!"*

Old Tim Grady yelled. With eyes upon that dreadful light, he backed to his own door. He stumbled through. He turned the lock. He howled again. For a little while light shone from his cabin. Then darkness and silence.

XLVI. DAY OF DOOM: HOUR OF FATE

PALMS waving on the shore in sorcery. Ripples on the river. Gay Deleon creeps from the *Thorn* and goes to join Pete. The light which flashed for an instant in old Tim Grady's cabin has gone out. Gay Deleon darkens into the night. Like a cricket he is gone.

The wind which rises in the nether void, beyond the grave, beyond the night of nights, blows unremittingly, calling wearily, running desolately over unsure waters. All night through it blows.

Hark to the voices of the unhappy dead! Of the unshriven, of the unforgiven, of them cut off by murderous hands. Now hold your heart, now close your eyes, for ghosts glide on the lances of the crimson moon!

The *Thorn,* pale as mist, rocks heavily, for a horror of deep silent waters sucks her keel. Thin vapor wraiths upon Black River. Upon the pressing shore vain waverings of trees, vain apparitions, vain memories. Vainest of ghosts are memories. And with them all Terror, first born and mightiest of passions of the soul, stalking with gryfon hands through the dark.

The morning and the evening were your first day, Lord Adonoi; as they may be your last. But to what devils mad and howling have you given up the night!

A cry arises from the waters, the voice of some supernal watchman watching out the stars: "And all is well!"

Trees monstrous as mountains stir in the crying of the wind. They bend, they dance, they cower, hiding within themselves for dread of their own unholy countenances. Shadows flitting on the shore are tenuous as air, black as dead hope, foul as swamp water. Yet strength is in them, in those shadows, a murderous power, to claw the heart out of the breast, strangling the breath.

Red and green lights quiver and shake on the river tides; shake and coruscate and fade away, drowned in deep blankets of water. Green for the fecund earth, red for fire, dark waters for the night which endly covers all.

Faint and far away beats heavily the washing of the waters of Bay Mimayne. Fainter yet, beyond the coral shoals, the harsh booming of the mighty sea, rolling past chaos and the formless deeps!

"All is well-ll!" rolls forth that cry across the waters.

Dear hour of sleep and dreams which soar to Heaven! If ever all be well, surely it should be now, within the silver silence. For the frustrate, great deeds. For the overthrown, victory. For the lover, love too frail and dear to be remembered. For the weary and the wise man and the drunkard, oblivion, which surpasses all desires.

Cold blows the tropic wind. Cold blows the wind until the dawning. On old Tim Grady, on his bed, shines through a little porthole one red strale of the moon. But that light passes, and there is no more light at all. The moon goes under.

What dreams come to Rose Dawn, sleeping in silken beauty bathed by the cold moon fires—what dreams to Deleon, tossed by his own private devils—what dreams to black Tom, fugitive within the slimy swamps— what dreams to Maveen, Clay, Mrs. Mallow, Anthony, and the rest of this pulsing world, no man may say. Least of all the dreamers, for dreams are a mystery past reckoning.

Some damned night bird, beset with devils, screams with a deadly cry. The moon is gone.

No dreams to old Tim Grady. He lies on his bed, staring with wide eyes past roof and night and stars above him, his hands gripped tight on air and shadows, the haft of the driven serpent knife rising like a cross from his breast!

XLVII. FAITHFUL TO THEE, CYNARA!

LAURENCE SPENCER caught Maveen on the beach in the morning. "I've got something for you, Maveen," he blushed.

They sat down cross-legged in the sand. Maveen adjusted her green bathing cap. "What on earth—going to read me something? O, hello! There's Mr. Clay just coming out of that blue racer. Doesn't he look cynical?"

Thornwood Clay came towards them. Dark half-moons were beneath his eyes. He sat down with them. "Don't mind, do you?" Maveen took one of his cigarets.

"You look like a night of it," said Laurence. "Didn't see you last night."

"O," said Clay lazily. "What's this—a poem?"

Laurence blushed again. "It is an—ah—"

Maveen bent and took a light from Clay, their noses almost touching. "Little Boy Blue's going to read to me," she said, looking long into Clay's eyes with siren glances.

"It's a poem," muttered Laurence, swallowing. ("How nice!" yawned Maveen.) "It's called: 'How Wise You Are!' " Laurence ventured further.

Clay smiled. Laurence felt his pink cheeks burning clear up to his bald scalp. "How nice!" said Maveen, with more gusto.

Laurence began reading in a rapid mumble. "It's called: 'How Wise You Are!' O, I told you that. It's a poem. I wrote it last night. It's like this—

"We walked beneath the moon
Wherein this burning winter melts like June.
O, lovely, lovely are your emerald eyes
Which quiver, dusk, and lighten to the tune
Of viol and violin in melodies!
Now will a song arise.

"Low heard I that sweet song
Striking an interlude. 'O, silence long
And vain forgetting! Will our love afar
After the years be drowned as that sweet song?'
Then rose your clear voice, tinkling like a star:
'O, lad, how wise you are!' "

Silence dropped. "Neat," said Clay at last. Laurence fumbled the leaves.

"What does it mean?" Maveen asked impatiently. "I'm sure I never said any such silly things at all. Goodness, Mr. Clay!" She turned to him, lifting up her eyelids so Clay could see clearly. "Are my eyes emerald?"

"So the poet says," Clay laughed.

"It doesn't seem to make much sense," said Maveen frankly. "Let's go in swimming."

Grimly Laurence started to tear the leaves to tatters. But he bethought himself. No occasion for committing infanticide. He folded the poem and thrust it in the pockets of his bathing-trunks. Disillusioned, he looked at Maveen.

Noon passed. Laurence bought sandwiches from the beach restaurant and ate them in his dripping bathing-suit. Little Arethusa Weinvoll came hopping up on all fours over the sand. She closed her pretty little freckled eyes, wiggled her pretty little freckled nose, and Laurence fed her puppy-dog bites of sandwich. In her innocence she made much play of her milk-white limbs, which shone to great advantage in her little boy's bathing-suit.

"Where's your sweetie, Deleon?" Laurence asked, immediately sorry.

"Don't speak his name to me!" cried Arethusa, crouching down on the sand. "Just you don't dare!"

"I'm sorry," Laurence stumbled. "I thought I saw you at supper with him last night." He pulled out a sodden handkerchief and wiped her nose.

Mrs. Weinvoll, skipping grimly over the sands like a kangaroo, called sharply to her daughter. Mrs. Dusty Hoag was with her, in her long black bathing-suit looming ominously against the horizons of sea blues and greens.

"Thusy," said Mrs. Weinvoll, giving that young lady a searching look as she gamboled up. "Where were you last night?"

"Good Heavens, mamma! In bed, of course."

Mrs. Weinvoll nodded at Mrs. Hoag in satisfaction. "I told you so!"

"I didn't want you to mention it!" cried Mrs. Hoag in distress. Her dark, work-sodden face flushed. "I didn't suspect Arethusa for the world!"

"We heard, Thusy," Mrs. Weinvoll explained, "that a young girl no more 'n your own age was seen last night in a very disrep'table place with Deleon."

"O, mamma!"

"Of course, of course, honey. Don't you cry."

"O, mamma, he told me—"

"See what you've done!" Mrs. Weinvoll cried to Mrs. Hoag, roused to ferocity at sight of her daughter's tears. Mrs. Hoag waited with arms crossed in grim Methodistic silence. "See how you've hurt the feelings of this poor little lamb!"

"Mamma, I didn't mean—"

"Don't you cry any more, honey! There, there, mamma knows. Mamma trusts her little girl. *You'd* better keep an eye on your own!" she angrily advised Mrs. Hoag. "Instead of casting aspersions on those who are above aspersions. You'd better think a thought! What *are* you crying for, Thusy? Mamma doesn't believe a word of it."

Mrs. Hoag stood in uncertainty, tugging at the blouse of her suit.

"I don't want to have you think, Mis' Weinvoll—"

"There's only one thing I want to say to you!" shouted Mrs. Weinvoll, though she had a hundred things she wanted to say, after the manner of women. "And that is watch out for your own, Mrs. Hoag! That's all I have to say!"

And, after the manner of women, she proceeded to say a hundred things.

"It couldn't be Bunnie!" Mrs. Hoag gasped.

"O, and it couldn't, could it! But it could be Arethusa! With your little Bunnie so sly and double-faced, deceiving you all the time. *I* know that sort. They don't fool *me!* She wears scarlet clothes, doesn't she? And she was dancing with Mr. Grady last night, wasn't she? Your child! She's a grown woman!"

Mrs. Hoag's face was sternly righteous. "Bunnie!" she cried, as the thought came home to her. "It was Bunnie with that Deleon! O, I could—I—"

"Of course it was Bunnie," Mrs. Weinvoll said furiously. "There, there, Thusy, honey! Mamma believes you. Don't you cry any more!"

Boosten Claude had brought Rose Dawn to the beach. Van Chuch saw her and came up with a greeting. "The Negro got away from me last night," he said. "But Colonel Dawn has his men out hunting. And others are hunting," he added grimly. "It's goodbye to Tom when they catch him!"

Rose shuddered. She did not care for van Chuch, but she felt great gratitude towards him for his sturdy help the night before. And she was always gentle-hearted. She let him fall into step beside her, while Boosten Claude glared furiously around the satin of her shoulders. They went down to the sea.

"I'm sorry I troubled you about that injunction last night," van Chuch said. "I was angry. How is Mr. Grady this morning?"

"He was still in his room when I left the *Thorn*," Rose whispered.

She left the two men at the shore, striking out for the horizon.

Laurence Spencer caught sight of little Bunnie Hoag's dark curls and scarlet gown. He threw his sandwiches to the chigoes and pursued her.

"I've got something for you, Bunnie," he said shyly.

She closed her eyes. "Good to eat?"

He dragged her to the sand. Frothy wavelets lapped their feet.

"It's a poem," he blushed. "I made it up myself. It's to you."

"O, how lovely!" she squealed, clapping her little hands. "I just adore poetry!" She laid her head on his shoulder and closed her eyes again. "For me! Read it me softly and slowly, Larry. It makes me shiver when you moan."

"It's called: *'Memini mihi!'*" he faltered.

"Um-m. Isn't that thrilling!"

"It's Latin. It means: remember me!"

"Yes," said Bunnie wisely. "Of course."

And wondered how he ever knew so dreadfully much. He must think such deep thoughts, about immortality, and Latin, and medicine. Laurence in his turn was afraid he had got the Latin wrong. Bunnie seemed to know so much about it. He dug a mess of clammy paper from his trunks.

"It's a little torn," he apologized. "And the water's blurred it."

He unfolded it. The paper was a sticky wad, of the color and consistency of a hornet nest. "Never mind. I remember it."

"Speak it slowly, Larry. I love to hear poetry roll."

"We walked beneath the moon," Laurence moaned. He did not permit himself to be hastened now, for Bunnie had her eyes closed and her head on his shoulder. Laurence moaned the N's and M's.

"We walked beneath the moon, wherein this Floridian winter melts like June. O, lovely, lovely were your emerald—shadowy!" he shouted, making Bunnie jump. "Lovely were your *shadowy* eyes—"

"Shadowy eyes," she repeated. "Don't you just adore that!"

"Indeed I do," said Laurence, looking into her shadowy eyes. "I might as well begin again. 'We walked beneath the moon—' "

For several minutes after he had ended Bunnie lay on his shoulder with eyes closed. The sun was warm, the crooning of the sea a slumber melody. Laurence had an unjust suspicion she was asleep. Unjust, even if she was.

XLVIII. MORROW'S MORROW

THE WINDOWS were nailed. The door was locked. Papers, pencils, a dictionary, a "History of the Irish Kings," lay scattered over his breast, where some hand had knocked them. A dribble of ink from an overturned bottle had mingled with his red-gray hair.

They peered into the windows of the cabin when morning of the second day had dawned. They broke open the door. Thus they found Tim Grady. Strangely, on one arm had fallen a "Journal of the Days." Strangely, for his days were done.

The gold-green serpent winked its emerald eyes from the haft of the knife within his breast. Ah, it was a lovely thing! And sharp.

Above his head swung and batted a porthole no bigger than a man's right arm. He did not heed the entering shaft of light, for he slept quite tranquilly.

No such excitement in the state of Florida since the great freeze of '96. No, nor such excitement in New York since the last election.

"Tim Grady, the movie magnate! Worth ten million dollars!"—You can read it in the newspapers.

Ten men may perish in one flash of death, in mine, in shipwreck, or the roar of war, without one line to mention it, unless it be of a dull Monday morning. Ten murdered millions are worth front-page columns. That is immortality.

Bulletins, specials, and what-not flashed on the wires north and west. The nation woke. It was interested. New York devoured the Grady mystery with its luncheon chops, San Francisco with its breakfast bacon.

"It's here," said Arsen, in the offices of the *Morning Mist.* "What did I say?"

"You said a lot," replied the city editor wearily. "You always do."

"My intimate friend, Tony Anthony, said—"

Colonel Dawn took charge. Mrs. Higgs wanted to tell him many things, but he staved her off. Still she talked on and on, endlessly, senselessly, with many knowing references to what-might-be-expected, and any-body-might-have-known, and cause-enough-Heaven-knows, and poor-old-man-he'll- sleep-in-peace, and may-his-sins-be-forgiven-him.

And all the rest of the clatter which female Higgses are fond of saying in disaster. The old crow, the old buzzard, couldn't keep her beak shut.

Ominously Stubb and Spike shook their heads, ominously wagged them back and forth, after the immemorial manner of police at a mystery. They were like jays on a fence-rail. Spike, who had a bristly mustache, twirled it often; Stubb wished he had one to twirl. They stuck their thumbs in the armpits of their vests, showing their badges.

Five dozen amateur sleuths arose as one man in Biscayne, and wandered around as five hundred. After a struggle, the old Colonel found he could not keep them from the *Thorn*. It was remarkable what detecting talents lay buried in hitherto seemly appearing citizens. Boosten Claude, it developed, had a scent like a bloodhound. Anyway, he said he had, and he sniffed around, sometime on all fours, sometime hopping along on his haunches.

Van Chuch trusted rather to his eagle eye. He stalked around with hands behind back, fixing everything with that eagle eye. Laurence Spencer only brought suspicion on himself by refusing, although a medical student, to analyze some cigar ashes found on the *Thorn's* deck. All criminals, practically, are traced by cigar ashes, as any child knows. Even young Schermerhorn poked about, doubling his tall neck to enter doors, tugging at his frail mustache.

"I've seen that knife before," he said sagely, surveying the heavy-bladed weapon. "Though where I saw the jolly old thing I can't just think."

The knife went from hand to hand. Each man ran his fingers along the butcher's blade. Each weighed it in his palm. Each turned it upside down, over, and round about. Each squinted at it thoughtfully, using first one eye and then the other. Each pinked his thumb with the point. Each nodded deeply, as though saying: "I thought so!" Each one said nothing. Each one thought nothing.

If that winking serpent handle had been stained with criminal prints, they were confounded with the fingerprints of all the detectives in Florida. If the deck had shown footprints, they were confounded with the footprints of all the detectives in Florida.

Spike raised and lowered the window shades. Stubb tried the nails of the windows. Spike flapped the porthole cover for half an hour. Stubb worked the door on its hinges. Crawling under the bed from the foot, Spike met Stubb crawling under from the head. Commotion ensued, and both scuttled backward out.

"Shoe, Spike?"—"S'me. Shoe?"—"S'me. You scairt me"— "Me, too."

"No need fiddling with those windows," said van Chuch. "You can't get the nails out from inside. But here." He gave a twist, pulling out the spikes. The window opened. "I fixed them that way," van Chuch said.

Painfully Spike and Stubb measured the dimensions of the stateroom, the height of the door, the width of the bed. Took names of manufacturers of the furnishings, the engines, and the ship. Counted the boards in the floor and the cracks between. Finding one less crack than boards, however they counted from east to west or back again, excitement arose; till the old Colonel came and shooed them away.

The officers rested from the methods of the great Holmes. The amateur sleuths stood about disconsolately. Squirmy went on the prowl for the Grady private stock. Men walked around the little gold-and-white saloon, talking in low voices about baseball, politics, and women. They plucked moist cigars from Grady's humidors, clipped them with his clippers, lighted them with his matches. There was much fumbling of hands in pockets, much jerking of lapels. Every man seemed impelled to straighten his tie. They looked at their cigar points often. Van Chuch began to assume a more commanding air as the day advanced. He was Captain. This was his ship. Though it was old Tim Grady's funeral.

A sort of holiday. As Mrs. Higgs truly said, a man is not murdered every day; meaning, of course, that it's not every day a man is murdered. Everything except the post-office closed in Biscayne. The old dog that had slept for seventeen years in Confederate Park arose, turned round, and slept again.

Late in the day Gay Deleon dared to come down to the *Thorn.*

"Get off!" old Dawn shouted to him, meeting him on the plank. "Don't show your face around here!" And Deleon turned, and walked away.

Mrs. Higgs consoled Rose Dawn in her new widowhood. Other consolers did not lack. The *Thorn* rocked emptily her snowy breast. A last year's chrysalis. The butterfly was departed.

XLIX. NIGHT WHISPERS

"I'VE called you in, Captain van Chuch," said old Dawn, "because you seem a pretty sensible man." Van Chuch clicked his jaws and bowed. "And because yon were a friend, I think, to Mr. Grady." Van Chuch knit his hands. "And because you are a friend to Mrs. Grady. She needs friends now."

Van Chuch wiped his forehead. He pulled out his spare handkerchief, for he would need to wipe his forehead again.

"Well, Sir," said old Dawn, rubbing his hands and casting oblique glances at van Chuch, "I want to give you a general survey of what we're doing, since you represent the family till Mr. Padriac Grady arrives."

"Young Grady is coming?"

"I kept the wires hot. Located him at last, through New York information, in Jacksonville. He'll be down in a few hours—may be in town now. What sort of man is he?"

"To tell the truth, I never saw him," van Chuch blurted.

"He wires me to use every means I can to get this thing cleared up. Here's his wire—'Have Anthony, Argus Agency, New York, take charge of case. No expense spared.' So that's that. If Anthony takes the case, it will be laid bare. To the last! No one spared, however high he is—or she. You've heard of Anthony?"

"Yes," nodded van Chuch, keeping his handkerchief to his forehead.

"He never misses!" Old Dawn's eyes were sharp.

"So I've heard."

"He won't this time. The thing's too plain."

"Who killed him, Colonel?" van Chuch muttered.

"Well, we'll see. I found a will on the *Thorn*. Some people may be surprised by it. Certainly surprised."

"Yes?" Van Chuch was curious.

"I'll have to keep that for the Grady lawyers. I've also located Mr. Higgleson Todd in Daytona. I'll give the will to him."

"Anything else?"

"Nothing much, Captain. I've found Mr. Grady's cabin was robbed of a considerable sum of money—"

"By the man who killed him!"

The Colonel shrugged.

"We'll say that. I'm looking for Pete Lopez. I've wired Jacksonville and Key West. We'll get him!" Dawn drummed his fingers. "It was clever of you, being on the *Thorn* that night in time to get Tom!"

Van Chuch wiped away the sweat. "What do you mean?"

"We're looking for Tom, too. We've got out rewards for the nigger, dead or alive. And God help him when he's caught!"

Van Chuch went out, still mopping his forehead. He felt limp. Birds singing in Confederate Park stirred no joy in him. He knew that he'd been sweated.

"Father knew it was coming!" Maveen whispered to Laurence. "He knew! ''

Her glances were superstitious. Unsteadily she held her cigaret. They sat on the Royal Poinsettia veranda, staring out at the *Thorn.* The day was clear and blue; but the superstitions of the Celt flourish in even the bluest paradises.

"What could you have done, Maveen? What's fated is fated, and nothing is going to stop it," said Laurence.

Anything else but fate, said other people in Biscayne. Eyes lingered on diverse suspected people. Heads nodded. Thicker than wedding rice were the whispers.

"I do not say it," declared Mrs. Higgs. "No, not I! But if you want *my* opinion and idea and suspicion breathed strictly in privacy and secrecy, I'll say the Weinvoll woman did it!"

Mrs. Weinvoll was not libeled by that. The curving finger of question beckoned to many greater than she. Old Dawn's eyes were sharp. His black brows bent together above fierce frowns.

"That red-headed Grady girl told him in my own hearing she hoped he'd be murdered!" said Mrs. Weinvoll. "And if 'twasn't her, 'twas that Deleon. There, there, Thusy! Don't you cry, honey."

"It was that Mallow creature," spoke Mrs. Hoag grimly, drawing her arms about her like a starved black vulture. She inhaled sharply. Her lips were bloodless. "That my daughter should be like her!"

"It must be nice to be Rose Dawn," said Arethusa. "The widow of a man with ten millions!"

"I wonder whom she'll marry now?" thought little Bunnie Hoag. She had no one to say it to, for her mother had locked her in her room.

Could suspicion rest on the weeping head of beautiful Rose Dawn? Ask one of her dozen volunteer consolers, and meet his fists! Impossible eyes so blue could nourish murder. And if she did it, Sir, it was well done, Sir, by God! She was justified!

"A man did it," said Boosten Claude. "A woman would have shot him down at noon on the open street, trusting to God and an honest Southern jury. I'd ha' shot him down myself," said Boosten Claude.

Gay Deleon had never seemed so sleek and polished. He walked alone, like a cat. He seemed to lick his moustaches, like a cat. He went on padded paws, like a cat. He was fat, like a cat.

But where he walked, or where he supped, where he gambled, loved, or slept, always happened to bump into him Spike or Stubb. And the eyes of

Colonel Dawn were growing blacker. Now dreadfully he scowled. The nets were closing in on Gay Deleon!

"Tim Grady got what was coming to him," Deleon babbled to everyone. He itched to talk about the thing. "I tell you, Thornwood Clay, Tim Grady got what was coming to him!" And he did not mind the look of hate in Clay's eyes.

True. All men get what's coming to them. If they don't get it, it wasn't coming to them.

Coming from the Biscayne Club, where roulette is played, late that night, Deleon bumped into Laurence Spencer. "O, I say, Spencer!" Laurence slowed his walk, scowling. "Here's that hundred I owe you, Spencer. My luck has turned at last!"

Laurence refused the money. His look was suspicious. Broadly he looked down at the sleek, smooth gambler. The two of them were almost of an age; but in some ways Deleon, for all his cunning, seemed a foolish babbling child. Laurence felt that puerility now. He hardened his face.

"Ever hear the story of the dog which barked too much, Deleon?" he asked. Deleon shook his head. "You see, Deleon, it barked too much!"

"Well, what's the story? What's the end of it?"

"The dog was shot. That was the end of it."

Deleon drew back. "What's the point?"

"No point at all," said Laurence. "But people are wondering who was the dog that killed Tim Grady for the money in his cabin."

"I don't follow, Spencer. First you talk of a howling dog. And then of old Tim Grady, who every one knows was killed by his nigger Tom."

"This dog was killed because it barked too much, I say!"

"That's a black word, Spencer!"

"A black dog killed Tim Grady. Take that, or leave it!" He turned, but Deleon still held forth the bills. Laurence lost control.

"Your dirty money would rot my fingers off!" he said.

Deleon took care to pocket the money. "I'll pay you back for that some day, old timer!"

"I'll be on the look-out."

Laurence strode off in a passion. He had not gone three steps but he was sorry he had spoken. Time would be when he would be sorrier yet.

And Deleon vanished out in the dark. Spike and Stubb hurried after him, but for a while they lost the track.

In the shadows of palms by Black River banks murmurs are rising. Dark words. Whispers in the night. "If you don't stick by me, Deleon!—" "Be still, be still!"—"But if you think to do me dirt, Gay Deleon!"—"In the name of death!"—"I'll tell old Dawn a story about Johnny Dawn that'll make him shoot you through the heart!"—

"Be still! We hang together."

Spike and Stubb rushed through the palms. All they found was Gay Deleon alone, nervously lighting a cigaret.

L. QUAGMIRE DEEPS

TEN miles south of Biscayne, ten miles west, lie the Everglades. Closer even than that, reaching with grassy quagmires to the very outskirts of the town. There hid black Tom. There, in the morasses.

Into his shoes oozed up sludgy mud, spreading out his toes, chafing the skin ragged raw. His belly was filled with cypress moss, peat, sticks, and mud. A purse (old Grady's) with nearly a thousand dollars did not satisfy his hunger.

Savannah and morass, coiling creek and scummy pool, hummock and bubbling bottomless quickmire, false trails upon the drowning mud. Palm and pine rioting for life, strangling like wrestlers, gripped to the death. Fern and marsh grass wallowing in the muck, blossoming quickly, rotting to quick decay. Black Tom stepped into a slough, grass-covered, and felt the universe turn mud about him.

Vines choked the cypress trees. Thicker they than a woman's fingers, stronger than her arms. Softly, lethally, they kissed the branches of stagnant oaks. They clasped throttling arms about the palms. They sucked life from the gray cypresses.

These are the cypress swamps. Above, thatched branches blotting out all light. About, ominous shadows. Beneath, cabbage palm and the sinking muck, stirred by the still slush! slush! of the things which crawl in it. The cardinal flits through those dreadful solitudes, on vans which are flashes of scarlet. To few men, and but dimly to those few, are known the narrow trails which lead from isle to isle. Yet the copperhead and the moccasin find those dank depths grateful.

These are the cypress swamps. Half a million years from now they will be peat and coal, crimson fires to warm men's hearts. Mountains will be piled on them. But now they are the watery and the dissoluble, that chaos, that very undivided deep from which the lands are risen. Creation in too fecund travail. Not more than this were once the tallest hills. Not more will they be again.

Now Tom walks softly, and now he turns around, for death stalks him. He sinks. He groans. He clutches hard to ropy vines and hauls himself from sucking pools. Well for those mighty arms of his!

A white stone road ran down between sea and swamp, not many hundred yards away. Rock upon coral rock was massed beneath it; it was solid as the mountains. Thundered along it roaring cars. Sound-ed the whining dogs. And men walked up and down, and talked. Tom could hear their laughter.

That causeway, that white stone road, man had hurled across the Cambrian bogs to show that he is man. To me (who am no engineer) it is a slap upon Creation's face. A shouting oath: "I, Man, thus smite you on the face, Creation! I build my roads across your muck, Creation! I go where I damned please!"

Arrogant, to be sure. Blasphemous, to be sure. And blindly hardy. All of that was Lucifer. He was no stinking angel.

All day the soggy rain fell, less pouring than hanging in the air. The southeast wind was hot from ocean. Raveled edges of a cloud blanket clung to the cypress tops. Nothing so wet, not even the utter sea, as tropic rain in winter. Its sad caresses (pale, odious lips of clinging love!) rot the flesh. Tom felt his feet. They were like the rotten grasses.

A cardinal bird twittered dreamily beneath a roof of leaves. An old sot he, with draggled crest and drunken eye, yet gay and valiant heart. He cocked his eye and looked below with a trilling note of fear. The slimy things within the deep crawled loathsomely, bending the marsh grass. Their unseen ripples writhed. This was their day of ecstasy.

Seventh day of black Tom's hunger; second day of rain. He stumbled on a mango tree and tore at its rotten fruit, cramming it two-fisted into his maw. "To eat! To eat!" sang the cardinal bird. Tom cursed it, throwing a stick toward the mocking cry.

The cloud broke. Water crashed in tons. A splattering pool dripped constantly with the vile unweariness of water. Grasses rustled with sinuous voyagings. The blanket of cloud dropped down like a deflated balloon. Still the pool dripped unwearily.

Near to him the firm stone road. Yet Tom did not venture forth. He heard the voices of men who walked up and down, and far away the yap-yapping of lolling-tongued hounds. He cowered beneath a matted tree. Above him whined an airplane. It turned on drooping wing, steady as a swallow, and with loud roaring swept over him once again. Now in the distance it died away, with a noise like gnats.

There in the cypress swamp hid black Tom. Tom Jefferson, M.D.: Doctor Thomas Jefferson! Ah, the beast lies in us all, learned Doctors!

A thin streak of blue sky broke in the east, wonderfully clear as the eyes of Rose Dawn. As Tom watched, it took the shape of a knife.

LI. IKE DUVAL'S TERRIBLE IDEA

"SO, YOU'RE back?" Arsen asked Anthony. "You didn't stay long in New Orleans?" Anthony shook his head. "What happened, Tony?"

"Nothing," said Anthony darkly. "Tim Grady's dead!"

"Great Greece! I read the newspapers. I'll bet I was talking about that with Lieutenant MacErcher a day before you knew about it. You made a lucky guess, Tony, when you said the old man would be killed."

"Not too lucky," said Anthony softly. "But you can call it that."

"Hear Padriac Grady's asked you to go down. *He's* doing all he can."

"They've wired me," Anthony said after a pause. "It's hardly worth it." He tied his shoe. "Queer they should call on me. Yes," he said, "it's queer!"

Arsen knelt on the rug, stroking the dog face of the Sphinx with such soft purrings as: "Nice doggie! Down, Tige!" Such mannerisms he had picked up from Buddy Schermerhorn. They marked one for a wit in any assemblage. Wit or nut.

"How are things in Orleans?" Arsen demanded. "Happen to meet my intimate friend—O—Can't think who. But I've got a lot of important friends there."

"I met Monsieur Vent-a-ventre," said Anthony.

"Ah, there's one! I'll bet he remembered me, huh? The devil! I can't think just who he is."

"He's a coon," said Anthony, with a mocking glance.

Arsen stamped up and down in a rage, casting wrothy glances at Anthony. He could not endure scorn. Anthony was indifferent to Arsen's rage. The reporter sulked, straightening his tie.

"Where's your specimen of the wild Grünwald praline?" Arsen went on, when he'd walked his anger away. "Where is the man-eating Sajerac cocktail, domesticated in New Orleans alone?" He spoke brightly, in the best Schermerhorn manner. "Of course you met the inebriated Southern gentleman who falls on the necks of perfect strangers, begging them not to call him names because he is a Southern gentleman. One once accosted me in the Babylon, and pursued me up and down elevators, weeping: 'Don't dare to call me a son-of-a-female- hound, because I'm a Southern gentleman.' Old Tiff Bonnell was going to have Ike throw him out. But I discovered the Southern gentleman was Boosten Claude, a friend of my friends, the Gradys. So he's one of *my* intimate friends now."

Arsen was better pleased with himself. "When do you leave for Biscayne, Tony?"

"I'm not going!" Anthony said harshly. "I don't care whom they hang for killing old Tim Grady!"

Arsen narrowed his eyes. "I'll bet I can tell you right this minute who killed the old man," he said. "I've put my intelligence on this."

"'Never saw a reporter yet who didn't think he could do anything better than any other man," Anthony growled. "You're always telling *us* how to do it."

"You can hear it from Lieutenant MacErcher and Urban Wiggs that Rose Dawn tried to poison him once. The whole world knows about it—"

"You lie, you fool!" Anthony shouted, springing up.

For an, instant Arsen could not make sound, Anthony's wrath was so unexpected. "Give me the lie, will you!" Arsen stuttered, hating Anthony more for calling him a fool than he could hate him for any other cause. "By God! You'll not give me the lie! I'll show you something!"

Anthony swayed forward. *"Who touches the name of Rose Dawn touches death!"*

Wigley Arsen walked out of Anthony's door hurriedly, cursing his intimate friend, the devil.

Down town the *Morning Mist* building was a tower of lights. Great presses snarled and roared. Slushing through the snow from the Babylon Hotel, all the blood of his body wrathily rushing to his head, Arsen's feet got cold. He began to sneeze. "Hoo-ch! Hoo-ch!"

Entering the *Mist* offices, he sent out a copy boy with one of Dr. Spencer's prescriptions to be filled. "Hoo-ch! Hoo-ch! Maig id snabby!" Arsen commanded. The copy boy returned with a bottle of malted milk tablets.

"Dis is a fide dig!" cried Arsen, disgustedly looking at the bottle. "A fide dig for idibate fred to gib be!" He meant to say it was a fine thing for an intimate friend to give him. He hurled the bottle to the floor.

A large-headed young fellow came in and began hammering a typewriter. "What'sa matter, Wig—scooped again?" he asked kindly. On top of his big head was a tiny green hat, which he scratched as though it were a disease. "Here y' are, Bill," he said to the weary city editor, unrolling a sheet from his typewriter. "Another girl gone and drowned herself."

Bill nodded. "All right, Dubby." He went on reading copy.

"Sgoobed!" Arsen repeated angrily. He scorned Dubby, whose father was no more than a head-waiter and whose sister worked for her living. "You gub!"

"Fine thing to call a white man!" said Dubby indignantly. "Don't speak Yiddish to me." The hands of Dubby, of one of the proletaire, of a fellow not Arsen's intimate friend, pulled the Arsenic hair. "That's good for gubs," said Dubby. "Hab you gaught a gold?"

A boy with pimpled face and gangling legs came hopping out of the managing editor's office. From hair to shoes he was one long, unillumined smear of ink. A grin shone forth in the midst of the inky pimples.

"Out, damned spot!" shrieked Dubby.

"Mac wants to see you, Wig," said the pimples impudently.

"You get the pink slip, Wig," Dubby rejoiced. "The razzoo!"

"The bum's rush," said the animated ink. "Mac's got his shoes all polished up for you."

"Get oud!" Arsen commanded sourly. "You ibudet biece ob butty!"

Editor MacErcher was always formal to Arsen. "Close the door please, Mr. Arsen. I want to speak to you in confidence." Arsen shut out the clack of the city room, the sight of Bill and Dubby. "I'm going to send you to Biscayne, Mr. Arsen. We believe big news is just about ready to break in the Tim Grady matter."

Arsen stroked his moustache, nodding and blowing his nose.

"We've got word confidentially—O, I got it from my brother, Lieutenant MacErcher, and he got it from my niece Jennie—Women *will* talk—We've got word interesting things may be turned up about Rose Dawn. We'll play it big!"

"Whole world dows she dried to boisod Tib Grady," said Arsen.

"All right, Mr. Arsen," said MacErcher grimly. "Go to it!"

As Arsen returned to the city room, Bill was reading the paragraph Dubby had handed him. Bill's weary face was deeply lined. He jabbed a pencil at his desk. Again and again, till the pencil point broke.

"What's the matter, Bill?" asked Dubby, pushing back his little green hat. "Ain't it right? I say, ain't it right?"

Nothing much of news in that paragraph. Only a sentence or so telling how a girl had been found in East River. Dark red curls; age about twenty; stocky build; she had been dressed in yellow frock, fawn stockings, and plush imitation sable coat. In her pocket had been found a note addressed to Gay Deleon, Park Avenue, the contents of which the police had not divulged. The girl's last name was unknown; the street knew her as Dot. Plain suicide.

Bill jabbed down his broken pencil. "I had a sister," he said in strained whisperings. "I had a sister Dorothy. If ever—If ever —By my God! If ever I meet Gay Deleon—" He gasped, snapping his pencil in two. "At night, or in the morning, if I meet Gay Deleon—!" Bill sprang up, banging his desk. "Alone, or with a dozen men about him!—if I meet Gay Deleon, though I have but my hands!—if I meet up with Deleon!—I will—I shall—I ought to—It would be a good thing if I—"

He sat down. Dubby and Arsen watched him curiously. "I've broken my pencil," muttered Bill, and picked up another. He poked at his desk again, as though he knew no more heroic action.

"I got a sister," said Dubby. "But Mary tends to her own business, and I tend to mine. If she gets in trouble, she'll get out. Ain't that right?"

"That's right," whispered Bill.

"No," said Dubby. "I mean the story I wrote about that Dot. Ain't that right?"

"It's right," whispered Bill.

When Arsen bought his railroad reservations for Biscayne, a man stood behind him in line whom he recognized. The stern jowls, the black derby, the belted green overcoat marked Solemn Ike Duval. Arsen would have turned without recognition, but Ike tapped him on the sleeve.

"Mr. Arsen," commanded Ike. Ike didn't like the loquacious reporter. He liked few men. But he had learned by devious ways that Arsen had quarreled with Anthony. "Mr. Arsen, I'm going to Biscayne, too. On my own. I'm not with the Argus people any more. Didn't like their way o' doing business."

"Come along," said Arsen. "I've heard poor old Tim Grady speak highly of you, Ike."

That night on the Gold Express, Ike Duval emerged from long taciturnity. "Mr. Arsen, Anthony didn't go to New Orleans!"

"Why, he told me so himself—"

"He lied! I've traced him to Jacksonville, where he disappeared. But a man with amber glasses got off the Gold Express at Biscayne!"

"I don't follow," said Arsen.

"Anthony is nervy," said Ike. "Nervy as they make 'em."

"My intimate friend says—"Arsen stammered, knowing not to what intimate friend he referred, or what the intimate friend had said.

"What do you think?" he cried. "What's your idea, Ike?"

Ike closed his stone jowls. "I don't think till I know," he said. And after further silence. "But I do know one thing, Mr. Arsen."

"What's that?"

"Anthony popped up out of nowhere two years ago. No one had ever heard of him before. Just like that, out of nowhere. That's queer enough to think about! Anthony made a name for himself by taking chances on anything. No man will say he's not brave. I've seen him walk square up to two armed yeggs, and knock 'em cold with his fists. Afraid of him. You don't know what he'd do. Where did Anthony come from? Who is he? It's not natural a man comes that way out of nowhere, Arsen. *Who was Anthony Anthony before?"*

"That's so," Arsen mused. "I met him first at the Astors'—No. Let's see. My friend—No. It was old Tiff Bonnell introduced us, one night in the Babylon. I (I think) was drunk," said Arsen. "But ever since he's been one of my intimate friends. That is, till lately," added Arsen.

"And I know another thing, Mr. Arsen," said Ike Duval, after a long period of pondering. He ground his teeth. "Not that I hold grudge against Anthony, you understand, for kicking me out of the Argus Agency, you understand! But I want to see justice. And I have my own thoughts!"

"What do you know, Ike?" Arsen asked, shivering inside himself.

"Anthony Anthony was watching Dawnrose the night Tim Grady was married. Called me off the watch himself. Told me to go on home, there was nothing to worry about."

"I remember," Arsen whispered. "I remember! Mrs. Higgs gave a cry when Rose Dawn was being married. She looked at the window, and she saw—"

"What did she see?"

"Nothing," said Arsen stupidly.

And the Gold Express roared on. He watched the face of Ike Duval in the half lights of the smoking car grow stony cold.

LII. TIM GRADY'S MONEY

BY the edge of Confederate Park stands Biscayne jail, a battlement of porous gray stone. Not much sun shines here, though a great deal of heat. Old Colonel Dawn's offices are in the upper story.

Spike and Stubb sit on a bench at the jail entrance, whittling. They have, at one time or another, whittled almost all the bench away. What remains is only a narrow plank of initials superimposed on carved hearts, of carved ladies dressed in stockings and hats, of arrows, ships, unsymmetrical horses enormously haunched, palm trees, and various vulgar symbols. In labor consumed that bench has cost Biscayne taxpayers about seven thousand dollars. As art it is not worth it.

But it is dear to Spike and Stubb. Eft and anon they spit.

"They's something going on in the Colonel's office," says Spike.—"With that lawyer Higgleson Todd," Stubb continues. —"Higgleson Todd is a queer sort of cuss," says Spike. "Seen that blond stenographer of his?"—"Stenographer, my foot!" Stubb says.—"My neck!" says Spike.

"I wisht they'd catch Lopez or the nigger," says Stubb.—"Ain't seen a lynching since I was a pup," says Spike.

Stubb stretches out his thick arms in a yawn, swelling his barrel chest. Spike fishes for a toothpick, tosses it in the air, catches it between his teeth. Slowly he chews it. His bristled scalp moves back and forth. His saw-tooth moustache moves sideways.

Old Colonel Dawn had summoned Padriac Grady, Higgleson Todd, and Rose to his office. Padriac was silent, twining his white forelock nervously, glancing beneath his hand at his father's widow. Higgleson Todd, wiping his glasses, wiping his big bald head, stared at her also.

"I found this lying beside Mr. Grady," said old Dawn, handing over a sheet of paper. "It's for you to read, Mr. Todd."

Gravely Higgleson Todd adjusted his glasses. "Well!" he stammered dully. Quickly his glance ran down the page. "It's a joke!" he said. "You don't take this seriously, Colonel—Your name, Sir? Colonel Dawn!"

Rose startled, looking at the old man. She had never known his name before. With widening glance she beheld his black brows, his lean face, the determined droop his mouth. A resemblance, dreadful as though the desert had suddenly grown old, but breathed!

"Who are you!" whispered Rose involuntarily.

"I'm head of the police, ma'am," said old Dawn ominously.

"That damned Wiggs!" Todd snarled, shaking the paper. "This is his dirty work! I drew up a will; Grady signed it. It'll stand in any court. It's sound enough. But this thing! I'll finish it—"

"It's the last testament of Timothy Grady, Mr. Todd! I'd not advise you to tear it up," said the Colonel.

"No. Didn't intend to. You're right."

The last will of old Tim Grady. The last joke of the dead. A typewritten sheet, drawn up secretly by cunning old Wiggs, its signature scratched off in haste by old Tim Grady in his last moment, with the red moon beaming through the porthole, with the heavy knife poised above his heart! Sharp and soon had struck that knife. The signature was hardly finished.

Words from the shadows. Terrified chaffering of a lost soul to buy fare back from the road of the damned. The very authentic words of old Tim Grady, as he had dictated them to Wiggs with the fear of death upon him, fear of old Thornwood Clay upon him, fear of the red moon upon him, while the *Thorn* lay ready for the sea.

"I, Timothy Grady, of New York—"

Of where, Tim Grady, when Higgleson Todd read those words to your young wife?

"I found it on his bed beneath a mess of papers and books," said old Dawn. "Looks like he had that ready, and signed it at the last moment because of something which had just happened. Why should he sign this will, Mrs. Grady? Who tried to stop his hand?"

He bent his black brows at her. Rose Dawn twisted a handkerchief.

Todd, calm as a square granite block, but with teeth which clicked and ground, read the paper through—"Being in sound mind and body, do hereby will, devise, and bequeath—" ("The hand of Wiggs!" Todd muttered.)—"to my son Padriac all my interests in Grady Pictures, my home Dawnrose, my liquors—" ("The voice of Wiggs!" Todd snarled.)—"To Maveen, nothing but the good sense I gave her, having supplied her liberally in life—" ("The wit of Wiggs!" Todd frothed.)—"To Rose Dawn Grady, nothing but her dower interest in my real estate—"

Todd slammed the will on Dawn's desk.

"O, that damned Wiggs!" he shouted. "Everything else goes to Bellbender for St. Cecil's Church!"

"What does it mean?" asked Padriac Grady.

"It means nothing! Your father was *non compos mentis!* He was crazy as a loon! I'll smash *this* flat! (That Wiggs!) And here's a lot more about 'atonement and forgiveness'; about 'the gates of Hell shall not prevail'; about 'pray for my soul'; about 'chimes'; about 'merciful forgiving God.' Wiggs' smooth words! Those are hellish fine things to put in a legal will! Bellbender and Wiggs! St. Cecil's! Bellbender'll throw Tim Grady's money away on charity! I wrote out a will that would give everything to Rose Dawn!"

"Well, there it stands!" said old Dawn grimly. "You're the lawyer. But *that*—" he shook his finger at the will—*"that's* the law! Guard it!"

"O, sure!" said Todd savagely. "A fine thing you've stirred up! Wiggs will fight me if I ever try to break it. And he, damn him! And *him!* I'd like to kick him! He thinks he's such a shark at golf." Todd wiped his neck. "Mrs. Grady has no money to get her rights, Colonel. It's vile injustice. Tim Grady was drunk when he signed it. He was crazy! I'll break it on grounds of incompetency! I'll prove he was insane!"

Old Dawn frowned. "He was sane enough to get married, wasn't he?"

"And that's the criminal injustice of it!" Todd roared, smacking his palms. "This poor girl married him expecting to be treated honorably. Is all she gets her dower rights at common law? This poor girl," roared Todd, patting Rose's knee, "will get her rights, if Higgleson Todd knows law! This poor girl," crooned Todd, taking her limp hand and stroking it, "will know she has one friend on earth! This poor girl," he sobbed, "will get her rights!" He patted her shoulder.

"Enough of that!" mouthed Padriac Grady.

"Enough of what, Mr. Grady? Enough of what, Sir?" cried Todd, releasing Rose's hand and sliding his chair away. "Why, Sir, you startled me!" He felt his collar. "I thought it was the voice of your father!"

Rose Dawn stood slowly to her feet.

"Is this what you called me in for, for *that?*" she whispered. "Why I—I would not touch one cent of Mr. Grady's money! I'd sooner work my fingers to the bone." Was it acting or nature that she sobbed? "It's enough to be free," she whispered.

Beyond the door Spike and Stubb tried to bar the entrance of a puffy lady. Mrs. Higgs poked them out of her path with valiant elbows.

"I can't go in where they're scheming and plotting and planning and concorking something against us?" she shouted. "Vamoose! Whose funeral is this?" She broke through the door. "What's this?" she yelled; so loud that certainly only her own voice could she hear. "What's this I hear?"

"What do you hear, ma'am?" retorted the old Colonel. He held that all white women should be regarded as ladies till they begin to scream, but he did not like Mrs. Higgs. "Speak more quietly, please, ma'am."

"I'll peak more squietly!" howled Higgs, losing all notion of the formation of words. "What's this?" She made a snatch at the will. Old Dawn barred her, his grim finger pointing to the door. "What are you sticking and picking and pawing and poking your ugly old finger at me for? Don't you know better manners than to point at a lady!"

"Out!" commanded Colonel Dawn.

"What are they doing to us, dearie?" the woman demanded of Rose, paying no heed to the old Colonel's stern command.

"Grady's money goes to Bellbender and Padriac," Todd growled. "Rose is frozen clean out. That damned Wiggs!"

"O—o!" Mrs. Higgs drew out the exclamation. She wrinkled her little blue eyes. "O—o, so—o!" sang she, with many a sonorous tremor. "This is your doings, Padriac Grady! I've suspected and watched your sneaking, smooth, hypercritical ways! You'll go where Tim Grady lies if you don't watch out—"

"Mother!"

Something like steel gripped Higgs's arms. Before she could say Jack Robinson three thousand times, the door closed behind her, and she was out. She kicked and hammered at the panels. Round little Stubb and lofty Spike gripped her fast by the elbows. They led her away.

For a long time after Todd, Padriac, and Rose, too, had gone forth, old Colonel Dawn sat motionless. The memory of Rose's lovely face yet lingered, smiled at him from the shadows, drowsed in cobweb corners. This was the woman brave John Dawn had loved above all other women, had loved alone of women. Old Dawn pulled a picture out of his desk.

Spike and Stubb, hearing no answer to their knocking, found him with his head on his arms.

LIII. DELEON BITES IRON

"AH, Mrs. Higgs," said Mrs. Weinvoll. "Do you know that Hoag woman?"

"I know *of* her," returned Ma Higgs distantly, not inclined to unbosom herself too freely to Mrs. Weinvoll, of Milwaukee. Their social spheres were far apart. "I know *of* her," Higgs repeated haughtily. "I don't know anything good or decent or respectable about her," she admitted.

"Neither do I," said Mrs. Weinvoll, ruffling her kangaroo body.

"She lets her daughter run wild and free," said Higgs, "like I'd never let no daughter of *mine.* You know Bunnie runs around with that Thornwood Clay? *He's* no good. I knew his father. I helped push him out of my Westchester county home, Dawnrose, last Christmas Eve. Isn't that disgrace enough?"

"With Thornwood Clay?" said Mrs. Weinvoll. "But I thought—"

"Many the time! And I've saw her running around with Deleon in McGinty's blue racer many and many the night. Ah, once I caught them kissing!"

Weinvoll nodded. "Shame to her and her mother! Shame to her mother that don't keep better watch! I *don't* see how she bears the light o' day!"

"A mother's duty never ends," said Higgs. "Mine hasn't with my Rose. Just once I closed my eyes, and she up and off and married that John Dawn. Let him rest well. I say no evil of the dead. But it was her loving ma married her to old Tim Grady. My dearie has me to thank for that, that I made her wife to old Tim Grady! Even if she was not wife to him one single hour."

"No, ma'am?" said Weinvoll. And her eyebrows raised.

They talked of much which ladies may, and much which ladies mayn't. Ma Higgs unbent, for her snobbery was not deep. Too many snobs had snouted her for her to feel uppish very long.

Milwaukee bent over creakingly to tap Moline's knee. Faded brown head met streaky yellow head, combining as equals. Those gold curls of Rose Dawn, how they had faded to Ma Higgs's streaky yellow! Her clear blue eyes to those dim small pupils!

The voices of the ladies were like tintinnabulation of the prophetic bells of Hell. Two minds with, but a single thought, two tongues which beat as one. As in the Golden Days, the lion lay down with the lamb, the hyena with the bat. Men find such concord only in liquor, women in talk.

"No, ma'am!" said Higgs. "I've watched her well, the pretty dear!" "So much like her mother," murmured Weinvoll. "Indeed, we could be mistaken for sisters," said Higgs proudly.

Lovely, lovely Rose Dawn, most beautiful of women! And you, you old buzzard, old Higgs!

"True you can pat yourself on the back, Mrs. Higgs, for you have a wonderful daughter, and she's all due to you. But that Hoag woman! Do you know where her daughter was on *that* night?"

"I know. I saw her dancing with that Deleon. O, didn't she simper and smile and grin and giggle and twirk and twiggle to him though!"

"But you and your daughter left early, Mrs. Higgs. (Well might Mrs. Hoag wish she'd done the like and the same!) Has she no mother's care at all, Mrs. Higgs?"

"Strict she pertends to be, Mrs. Weinvoll. But if *my* daughter was what *her* daughter is, Mrs. Weinvoll, I'd lay me down and die!"

"What did Bunnie do?" Mrs. Higgs gasped, brightening.

"I see her like as if she was before me, in her pale, light-colored, white gown; and with a white rose in her hair like any boughten woman. Often have I watched her sneaking in and out, a-taking kisses from that Deleon. I steered Rose away from him in time!"

"No, Bunnie was all in red that night," said Weinvoll. "Thusy was wearing white. You might have known it, Mrs. Higgs, if you'd but seen the color of that gown! Stark red! Naked red! But was her mother watching her, Mrs. Higgs? No! Her mother was cutting up at, the table with Mr. Grady, and I had to sit there myself to keep her straight!"

"So prim and stern and black Mrs. Hoag looks," said Higgs. "And you say, Mrs. Weinvoll, that her daughter is—?"

"True word you spoke, Mrs. Higgs! I don't talk about any one behind their backs. But it is true as I am breathing that Bunnie Hoag was out that night with Deleon in a place which shall not be mentioned! People heard her crying down by the shore. 'Gay! O, Gay!' she was crying by the river banks."

"I heard her!" said Higgs. "I heard her myself before old Tim came home. 'O, Gay! O, Gay!' she was crying, like as if her heart would break."

"True enough," said Weinvoll. "And I did my Christian duty and told her mother of it. Though the little minx denied it bald-faced, yet it's true. O, how her mother was dumbfounded! O, how she put on airs! Threw up her hands! No daughter of hers, O, no! Of course not! That's what they all say," sniffed Weinvoll. "But I tell you again, Mrs. Higgs, that if *my* daughter was what *her* daughter is, Mrs. Higgs, I'd lay me down and die!"

"What's she done with her?" cried Higgs. "I thought I saw her only the other minute playing tennis with that young Larry Spencer."

Weinvoll pressed her hands in her lap. "No, indeed, Mrs. Higgs. Her mother's locked her up in her room, and won't let her speak to man or soul. Too late! Too late! She's awoken to her duty as a mother far too late!"

"Thank God 'twill never be said about me!" breathed Higgs.

"Speak of angels!" gasped Weinvoll. "Shu-h! Shu-h! Here she comes!"

Gaunt and tall, her black frock snapping about her bones, Mrs. Dusty Hoag approached on the veranda. Her dark countenance was tragic as the demons. Her hands shook. Her straggling dark hair looked as though she had torn at it.

"Yes, indeed, Mrs. Higgs, a lovely bright day!" Weinvoll cried loudly. "A day of Heaven!" cried Mrs. Higgs, equally loud. Being both well-bred ladies, they would not let Mrs. Hoag know they had called her names behind her back.

"Have you seen Bunnie?" cried Mrs. Hoag hysterically.

"No, indeed!" said Weinvoll, startling in vast surprise, as though she'd forgotten such a person as the Hoag person took breath. "Goodness, how you startled me! We haven't seen anything of you in such a time. I was just saying to Mrs. Higgs I wondered where you was. You and your daughter—" a not silent sneer here—"I've noticed you've been keeping pretty much to your rooms."

"Where is Bunnie!" cried Mrs. Hoag distractedly.

"I never knew 'er, saw 'er, nor heard of 'er," said Higgs loftily.

"Where is Bunnie!" screamed Mrs. Hoag. She fell back against a veranda chair, groping weakly. A paper fell from her hand. Mrs. Higgs delicately picked it up and read it.

"Bunnie ain't in her room?" Mrs. Weinvoll asked in good-natured concern, feeling a little sorry for Mrs. Hoag now. "I thought you'd keep a better eye on her now, Mrs. Hoag, after all that's happened."

"She's gone," whispered Hoag, staring with haggard, weary glances. "She's gone! No one has seen her!"

"Gracious!" said Weinvoll pityingly. "I knew it. She's run off with some good-for-nothing-fellow. Why don't you ask Mr. Spencer or Mr. Clay? They've got rooms on both sides of yours. Maybe she's run off with that long drink Schermerhorn. Or with that Lopez the police are looking for." Mrs. Hoag didn't listen to these sympathetic suggestions. "Read that!" she said with a hard cough, pointing to the paper which Mrs. Higgs had already read. "She left it," said Hoag, pressing her hand to her scrawny throat. "Such a quick temper she had, so brave and wild like her father! She's gone!"

Weinvoll read: "Good-bye, Mother. I loved you, Mother. I've always been a good girl, Mother—I tried to be. O, I loved you, Mother. Say some prayers for me. Give my beaded georgette to Cousin Sally and my picture in the little frame to Larry Spencer. Good-by to you, my Mother!"

Mrs. Weinvoll fanned herself. "You don't think—?" she queried meaningly. Back and forth she rocked on her broad hips. "Surely you can't suspect, Mrs. Hoag—"

"There!" sobbed Mrs. Hoag, pointing with black bony arm to the river. "There!" she shrieked at the treacherous dark waters. "She never could abide punishment. Always so quick and fierce and hot she was that way. O, God, God!"

Higgs twirked her neck. "It's better so," said she. "Them who can't manage their own children, God will carry them away."

"Ah, Mrs. Hoag," said Weinvoll, "a true word Mrs. Higgs has spoke! Better had she died in all her pretty innocence, than that she is what she is! I speak plainly."

"O, my Bunnie! O, my little black-eyed baby! I didn't mean to hurt your little feelings! I thought it was for the best. How I've watched—how I've prayed! How bright she was, and gay, and filled with God's own deviltry."

"You'd better notify the police," said Higgs calmly. "Tell old Dawn."

"I tried to do all that's right for her," Mrs. Hoag sobbed. "How did I fail? Where did I shirk my duty? I was so careful of her, but the wildness was in her. I've punished her enough. I've whipped her when she was a little thing until my arms were tired. What did I do wrong? How have I failed?" She stumbled away, sobbing with hoarse and foolish gasps. Her bony neck was stretched. She mopped her raw eyes.

Laurence Spencer and Arethusa Weinvoll came up the veranda steps, tired and laughing, tennis rackets in their hands. Arethusa's little freckled eyes winked coyly at the big young man, her little freckled nose wiggled affectionately. Milk-white her arms and neck. And when she sat down in a veranda chair, above her rolled socks her knees showed milk-white.

Mrs. Higgs spied them first, Mrs. Weinvoll's back being turned.

"Right there before our eyes she is, that little wretch! Look there at her! Many and many's the time I've seen her out with Deleon. You don't need two looks at her to know what *she* is! It's wrote all over her face. If I had a daughter like that, I'd lock her out the door! I'd turn her to the gutter and the street!" Indignantly bustling, Weinvoll turned. "A true word, Mrs. Higgs—" Her soul writhed in racking fires. It was to *her* daughter Mrs. Higgs was sneeringly pointing. Could it be possible? Did this odious old Higgs hussy point to Thusy? Did not Hell gape? Was she not pitched down to Tartarus? "That is my daughter, Mrs. Higgs!" hissed Weinvoll.

"Wart!" cried Mrs. Higgs, losing control of her tongue. "Why, I have seen her with my own eyes, the sneaking little minx—"

"My daughter you speak of, woman!"

"No credit to you in that!" snapped Mrs. Higgs.

"I can thank *my* God," said Weinvoll, wrapping her shoulder-blades about herself, "that *she* is above suspicion! Yes!" she shrilled. "Each night I get down on my knees beside my bed, and thank *Him* that she is pure! Which is more than can be said about Rose Dawn, Mrs. Higgs!"

"Wart?" cried Mrs. Higgs, frothing and foaming. "Wart? Wart? Wart?"

Mrs. Weinvoll could have no more bent down on her fat knees in prayer than could the Woolworth building. And had she bent, no power known, not seven steam derricks, not all the king's horses and all the king's men, not that Archimedean lever which boasted to move the earth, could have lifted her up again. But still she repeated defiantly, snortling through her nose:

"Yes, each night I get down on my knees and thank *Him* that Thusy is not like Rose Dawn. *She* isn't seen flirting with Higgleson Todd or her own step-son."

"Wart!" howled Higgs. "Wart do you say about my Rose!"

"O, how surprised you are!" jeered Weinvoll. "O, how flabbergasted! O, my gracious! Doesn't the whole world know that Deleon was on the *Thorn* all night the night Tim Grady was murdered?"

Ma Higgs was within one breath of death by apoplexy, a thing fashionable but unpleasant. She tore with clawing fingers at the air. She swelled like a toad and grunted like a hogfish. Her Medusan locks rose hissing, each one a bleached yellow snake.

"And doesn't the whole world know she tried to poison *him?*" panted Weinvoll. "Doesn't the whole world know what she is? How *dare* you speak about my Thusy!"

Had not Clay and Maveen come on the veranda this moment, it is likely that Moline, Kansas, would have launched itself like a tiger at Milwaukee, Wisconsin, tearing at throat and eyes and hair, and the two cities fallen choking to the dust, gripped in that mortal fate which overtook the two calico cats.

Laurence had gone to his room to tub after leaving Arethusa. He heard his door open. Wrapping a towel about him, he stuck his nose from the bathroom.

"Spencer, for the love of God! Can you lend me some money?"

Gay Deleon had crept in cautiously. He leaned against the door, his shoulders wilting. No color in his cheeks. Nervously he fumbled with his little moustache. He was only a poor little snipe in decent clothes, all the fire, scorn, audacity, and mercilessness taken from him. His evil hour had come on him, as it had come on Thorn Clay, on Tim Grady, on Dot; as it has come on many another soul. His evil hour! Yet he'd know worse.

A poor little snipe in decent clothes. Splendid the polish of his hair; scented his hands; suave his gestures; delicate his skin. None the less, a snipe.

"I lost my last cent in the Biscayne Club, Spencer! O, the black luck! I've got to have money. I'm good, Spencer. I offered to pay you before. Listen to me, Spencer!"

Laurence put on a robe and came slowly out of the bathroom. His looks were narrow.

"Pete—a friend of mine wants money!" cried Deleon distractedly. "I want enough to get out of this damned place, Spencer! Lend me railroad fare. You're a good fellow, Spencer. I always liked you, Spencer.—Spencer!"

"So you're going to leave us?" Laurence asked ominously.

"I don't like the way people act," whispered Deleon. "No, I don't like it! I want to leave Biscayne. A hundred, Spencer. Only a hundred!" Laurence paced slowly across his room. "I won't talk to you," he said shortly. "Get out!"

Deleon advanced a pace. Softly he stepped, and desperately. "I tell you I've got to have it, Spencer!" he said dangerously. "No other way this time, Spencer. I've got to have it! I'm not talking lightly." His tone became wheedling again. "O, be a good fellow, old Spencer!"

Laurence pointed to his bureau. "I've got twenty dollars or so in there, Deleon. If you're brave enough to stick me up for that, just you try!"

"I'm not trying to hold you up, Spencer."

"I know that well. Your greasy friend Lopez tried it once. *He* learned his lesson! You think because this is bad—" Laurence stretched out his stiff left arm—"I don't know how to fight. I killed the man who broke that arm, Deleon! I killed him with my hands!"

Gay Deleon made a desperate leap towards the bureau drawer.

Laurence fell on him, hurling Deleon over the room and bang into the wall. "Look, Deleon!" he said to the cowering gambler. In the opened drawer lay a service pistol, heavy, dull, and blue. "I'm a peaceable man, but I've seen war! Four notches on that gun. Count ''em!" Deleon backed away, not liking to see that thing of steel. Laurence closed the drawer. "I've seen war, I say, Deleon! I'd not stop one second if it were my life against another's. Don't forget that, Deleon! I'd kill a man without compunction, if I had to, Deleon! Bah! I don't need a gun. My fist is enough for such a poor thing as you. Get going!"

"You dirty miser!" spat Deleon, feeling safe from the gun.

Laurence swung back his fist. Immediately he was shamed. He would as soon have struck a toad. Deleon saw he was safe from a blow, too. "You penny-pincher!" he snarled, backing out the door. "I hate you!" "Hate away," said Laurence, slamming the door in Deleon's face.

In the hallway two men laid hands on Deleon. He looked to right and left, shivering. The hallway lights were gloomy. Deleon sobbed. "We're looking for you, Mr. Deleon—" "Under warrant sworn by Colonel Dawn!"

"What's this? What's this?" screamed Deleon, as Spike and Stubb snapped gyves upon his wrists. O bitter iron! He raised his wrists and bit it.

"You are arrested, Deleon—" "For the murder of Tim Grady!"

LIV. MESSENGER OF THE BLACK KING!

BESIDE black Tom's squatting haunches, the cabbage palms stir gently. O, dreadfully they move! The wind is sick. Thinly rustle the wings of death. Thinly stir the cabbage palms.

The Negro casts his white glance downward. Dreadful those rolling eyes! In the trembling hearing of him, the black king, sounds a rustling rattle. Clear, dusty dry, staccato: "Beware! Beware! I am the messenger of the Black King!"

Two ruby eyes staring from a swaying head. Lipping tongue. Waving coils. Jaws yawning wide and foamy. Golden red those eyes, clear as ruddy wine, hard as red granite stone, lovely in their burning steadfastness as the dear eyes of Lilith. O, venomous breath! O, hooked fangs! O, creeping messenger from a greater King than black Tom Jefferson!

"Beware! I am the messenger of the Black King!"

Tom hurls his great bulk through the air, tearing at the winds. Sharp beneath him strikes that poisoned head, hard as a hurled dart. Wrathfully rattles quiver. An insatiable mouth gapes up at him. All the sopping grasses are beset with eyes. The winding vines are serpents.

Panting, choking with jungle fear, clashing his canine teeth, Tom swings aloft, apewise, branch to branch. He dares not touch that sinking mire again. From vine to vine, clear above the bubbling scum and the sharp spears of grass. Quagmires suck, thirsty for him. Birds scream. The air is poisonously still.

On the stone road, men go up and down. Their hard eyes seek the wilderness beside the road. Tom does not fear them now, does not fear an airplane roaring up towards him from the ocean. Does not fear the dogs. At the edge of the swamp he crouches. He draws a canopy of bladed grass about him and lies flat to earth. Men pass not ten yards away. Patiently he waits for night.

"Beware! Beware! I am the messenger of the Black King!" Sounds again that rattle behind him.

LV. SHADOWS OF THE ROPE

WIGLEY ARSEN, hearing in Jacksonville of Deleon's arrest, stopped off to wire the *Morning Mist.*

"The *Mist's* special correspondent," he telegraphically lied, "interviewed Deleon in his cell. He was hard, unrepentant, and defiant; and his eyes glittered as he talked. He was supplicating, whining, and craven; his eyes wavered as he protested his innocence. He was silent, refusing to answer all questions. He was terror-struck, and as he paced up and down his narrow cell his eyes fell to the floor, where he left them."

Already in a million homes and twice as many ash-cans reposed copies of the *Morning Mist* with scare-heads spitting the name of Gay Deleon in loathsome letters. They declared he lay chained to the floor of his cell with anchor cable, while a company of militia guarded him, and a horde of ten thousand Southerners, bent on lynching someone, howled about the jail.

Black, grotesque drawings, done by thirty-dollar artists in back-rooms of New York, showed him writhing in his chains. Showed rats and cockroaches nibbling his crusts of bread. Showed a gibbet being erected outside his cell window, blotting out the lean sunlight, decked with swaying chains.

The editors of the *Mist,* hating Deleon for reasons of their own, filled two extras with Arsen's dispatch, leaving enough for the Sunday supplement. Reporters rushed to all the best New York clubs, ascertaining just when Deleon had been kicked out of them, and who had done the kicking.

Thus the *Morning Mist* after Deleon's arrest. But when Arsen and Ike arrived in Biscayne, this telegram was waiting: "Deleon innocent hereafter." The *Morning Mist* had been overset in the night. It wept great salty tears for Deleon. It wrung its hands and whooped and sobbed for Deleon. It called up the Constitution, Magna Charta, and Washington's Farewell Address in defense of Deleon. It stated ringingly that if Deleon should die, then four million New York Democrats would know the reason why.

This *volte-face* ensued after the secretary of a certain man (whose name is great in the nation) had cursed out managing editor MacErcher as heavily as a telephone may curse. MacErcher cursed Bill, the city editor. And Bill cursed Dubby, the cub. And Dubby kicked the pimpled, inky office-boy, silently, but with great skill. The office-boy strangled the office cat. So it's an ill wind that blows nobody any good.

All this may have been because Wiggs had been retained to defend Deleon, and Wiggs was a terror at libel suits. But quite likely it was because the Arty Girl's father (whose name is very great in the nation) owned the *Mist*. Wigley Arsen and Ike Duval went at once to see Colonel Dawn on arriving in Biscayne. Old Dawn gave Arsen more respect than Ike, since Ike was only Justice, while Arsen was Fame. "I've never been interviewed before," he said. "Like the first time you're married, or the first time you're buried, it seems more important than it is."

In the jail below lay Gay Deleon. Past the windows, in Confederate Park a band was playing "Dixie." All the winter tourists from the North violently cheered. A marble General Pickens rode furiously on a fat truck horse. A bronze Seminole Indian smoked a cigar.

Ike Duval looked at old Dawn suspiciously, being suspicious of all men. The Colonel grew uneasy beneath that solemn stone glance, thinking of his sins. An illegal bottle of gin his office desk weighed on him. He remembered once having accepted a box of grapefruit from Boosten Claude for refusing to arrest Claude after that small, irate man tried to shoot up Biscayne.

"Ol' Boosten didn't mean to hurt anything," Dawn had explained it to his conscience. "What if he did break a couple of plate glass windows and pot the garbage man? He paid for them." And Dawn thought back to other sins, far back as fifty years before, when he had crept forth in the dark of the moon to rob farmers of green pineapples and sour melons. He wondered if Ike Duval's glance meant he knew of that. Old Dawn thought of his life as a shameful thing, abhorrent, spotted with hidden sins. He wondered if he should not have been himself behind the bars long ere this; if in him the gallows had not been cheated of a legitimate burden.

Suspiciously Ike scowled; heavily spoke. "Where do I spit?" he demanded, shifting his tobacco. "Located the nigger yet, Colonel? Used to know him myself. He's a bad egg."

"Tom's run for the swamps," said old Colonel Dawn. "Unless some of the swamp niggers help him out, he's a goner. No white man knows those trails. Why, eighty years ago in the Seminole War whole troops of soldiers were sucked down together, sometimes not one man getting clear. The dirty Creeks'd sneak along and scalp 'em before their heads oozed under."

"A nice country!" muttered Wigley Arsen.

"In the swamps a man's got to look mighty alive," said old Dawn quietly. "And after a week he's apt to look mighty dead."

"He ought to give himself up," said Arsen. "*He* didn't kill Tim Grady."

"Give himself up after his attack on Mrs. Grady? Would you do it? No, Sir! He'd only hang for Grady, but for Rose Dawn he would burn! Not that I'm blamin' the nigger. Any man would have wanted to put his hands on Rose Dawn if he were around her very long. And if Tom had been white, no one would have much minded. Can the God blame him who made men like that about women? Well, when Tom is caught all *I* can do is give him white man's justice."

"What sort is that?" asked Arsen curiously.

In Confederate Park the band had struck up "Cannibal Isle."

Arsen looked out the window, vaguely stirred by the music and the heat of afternoon. Among listeners slowly strolling through the park, Arsen saw Rose Dawn. Between sleek trunks of royal palms he watched her golden curls. For a moment he kept still, thinking of her and the music.

Padriac Grady, Boosten Claude, and Higgleson Todd fluttered thick about her. Hats off, they bent to whisper. Behind them stood van Chuch, sullenly expectant. Now she passed from sight. The music closed. Arsen could have cursed the great palms which hid her from him, though they were loveliest of all breathing creations, and the woman but the shadow of a day.

Old Dawn looked at Arsen with wise penetration.

"You look ill, Mr. Arsen," he said, "Or perhaps you are in love!"

"No! O, no! No, indeed; not hardly!" Arsen denied, waving away the horrible thought. "In love with the tropics," he added lamely, flushing red.

"I know that sort of love, too," said Dawn. "But it bears a woman's name."

Rose Dawn had come again into view, just for a moment, with sunlight through gold-flecked shadows strewing her face. Old Dawn stared with hoary wisdom at Arsen, shaking his head. His voice was muffled.

"A beautiful woman," he whispered. "Like the tropics. They get hold of a man. Here!" He extracted the illegal bottle from his desk. "Have a drink!"

And out here in Confederate Park stroll various people. Van Chuch, Rose Dawn, Tim Grady's son are here; and Mrs. Mallow, with simpering gestures. The Queen of Spades! She steps on a toad and squeals, overcome with that horror of creeping things which is instinctive in all female women. No man offers to help her or the toad. Mrs. Mallow prances up to Todd. "O, you dreadful, dreadful, Mr. Todd! Who is that little blond girl who goes around with you so much?"

Todd mutters, casting his eyes apprehensively around for Mary Dubby. He is finding Miss Dubby is not so easily subjected as she was in his legal offices. That may be—not to crack the wind of the poor phrase, running it thus—because his offices to her are not legal.

Old Colonel Dawn, Ike Duval, and Wigley Arsen drank from the illegal bottle. Night dropped on Confederate Park. God's awful eye had blinked. The golden curls of Rose Dawn were hidden. The music was stilled.

A grinning black man knocked and entered.

"Lady to see you-all, Cunnel." He bowed, did a shuffle and scrape, and jig-stepped sideways. "Who is it, Twombly?" asked old Dawn, quickly hiding the bottle.

"Ptolemy?" repeated Arsen, misunderstanding. "Twombly, I said. Tell the gentleman your name, Twombly."

The Negro scuffled, snapping his fingers happily. "Twombly Carruthers Fitzmaurice Black!" he sang, as grinning mouth touched his ears.

"All those names to distinguish him from the other ten million blacks?" asked Arsen, lifting his brows. "I suppose his father gave him the last name, while his fond mother gave him all the rest."

"No, Sir," said old Dawn, shifting his feet. "His mother gave him the last name, but the others were his father's."

Twombly danced out the door, admitting Mrs. Mallow. That lady was in a boiling fury. She had forgotten all her pouting graces; her hat was askew. Musically after her skated Twombly Carruthers Fitzmaurice Black, cracking his fingers, twisting his body from the hips. Mrs. Mallow jounced him with her elbow. On skittering heels he toppled, flopping against a desk. He continued his jazz melody with fingers beating the wood.

Mrs. Mallow sputtered like a short circuit; she fizzed like a fuse.

"I want you to arrest Thornwood Clay, Colonel!" she shouted.

She stamped her foot. Her glittering eyes were small as shiny dimes. Gravely old Dawn looked at her. "Anything else, ma'am?"

"Ask him where he was the night Tim Grady was murdered!" she shouted.

If Mallow's face had ever been lovely, such beauty was departed. The lamented Messers Marsh and Mallow must have stirred on their earthly pillows, wondering why they ever so joyously ate her arsenic and oysters. Ah, beauty, where is thy sting? "Clay'll toss me down for that Grady girl, will he?" she cried. "He thinks he can kick me off! Ask him where he was!"

"Where was he, ma'am?"

"McGinty drove him and me to Daytona!" she shouted, hauling at her hat. "I want Thorn Clay arrested for abduction!"

Old Colonel Dawn thought gravely. "A boat leaves for Havana at six tomorrow morning," he said, interlocking his knuckles. "You'll take it!" Mrs. Mallow gasped. "Trying to frame me!" she panted. "Frame me because I'm not so young as I was? Why don't you frame another woman I might name? Afraid of her yellow curls, are you? Afraid of Rose Dawn Grady's pretty eyes? Wait ten years, and you won't be so easy on her, Colonel Stoughton Dawn!" She wagged her finger violently. "I stood trial for Marsh and Mallow—make her stand trial for Tim Grady! The whole world knows she hired Gay Deleon to kill him! The whole world—"

"Six o'clock," said Dawn, growing white. His black brows were one line above his burning eyes. "Don't let me see you after that!"

"Do your duty and arrest Rose Dawn! I'll tell the world—" But Mrs. Mallow did not stay. She saw a glance in old Dawn's eyes she was dreadfully afraid to brave. Wilted of plume, she went out the door.

Though forelooking is as unproductive in historians as in Sieur Nuits, still we'll say that Mrs. Mallow took the boat. She packed her perfumes, her corsets, rouge-pots, flapper frocks, hair, and teeth, and went in the small dawn. Maybe she still flourishes in Havana. 'Tis said that there they like 'em fat.

Suddenly men were shouting out the window, down below. Towards the jail they were running. Far away on the town streets, rushing through the park, swelling by the river, rose a jubilant cry. Something crashed to earth beneath the window. Men panted. Blows rained. A ghastly voice groaned: "O, white gen'men!"

"They've caught Tom Jefferson!" said Arsen in solemn tones.

A pack of men were writhing down on the ground, in the blackness, in the shadows of bushes, beneath the window of the cell of Gay Deleon. More runners panted up, their breathing harsh as dogs.

"What's the matter down there?" old Dawn roared, leaning far out the window. "You, Boosten Claude, what are you doing to my boy?" "Your boy, Colonel?" muttered Claude. "Well, that's right!"

A roar of good-natured laughter swelled from the crowd.

"It's only the Colonel's Twombly!"—"It's not Tom. Poor old Twombly!"—"Good boy, Twombly!"—"He ain't done nothing. Let him go."—" 'S long's we got him, might as well have a little fun."—"Let's pertend to string him up for fun."—"All niggers look alike to me."—"Rope! Rope! Rope!"—

Old Dawn leaned forth, his fierce eyes fixing individuals of the mob. Each man who saw that glance upon him tried to hide behind his fellows. "Who touches that boy will die!" roared old Colonel Dawn. "I keep the law in Biscayne! You touch him, and you'll die!"

With his glances on the ground Boosten Claude walked away. The others followed him, hurrying furtively. Twombly was still whimpering. White men's mobs are bad medicine for black boys, even when the white men laugh.

Old Dawn still pounded the window-ledge, breathing deeply.

"Great Greece, Colonel," Arsen mumbled.

"What is it, Sir?"

"You look just like Anthony when he is fierce and angry."

LVI. DEATH TO THE DOG!

BLACK TOM has broken free! He has slipped through the cordons of the posses. Northward he pants and stumbles. The hounds howl after him. O, the love of women, Tom Jefferson! O, the blood of men!

Crawling along by starlight, cowering in brush and thicket by day, eaten by ravenous mosquitoes and scorching suns, seeing the hard-eyed men pass up and down unendingly with guns upon their hips. Their mouths are thin. Dogs yap. Telephones and church bells ring over the countryside. Behind him the grewsome swamps, the cold reptilians.

His feet clog in sand, tangle in bristly undergrowth, stumble over coral crooked as lava, sludge through tomato fields and citrus orchards. Up about him like danger fires lift the smoke of habitations. All day he has lain in an irrigation ditch which cuts through grape-fruit orchards. Golden globes of fruit hang in green bowers, ripened for picking. Dawn, towering swift and yellow, found him here. He waits the cloudy night.

Two men have been moving about the orchards since morning. Their voices are gruff. They stir as slowly as fish in water. All the world seems a dream. One stands near the ditch, looking down at the brown waters. Hidden under overlapping grasses beneath the hollow of the bank, Tom is not two feet away. Earth clods shake on him at the men's tread. The man casts a pebble. Ripples lap Tom's nose.

"When do you reckon they'll catch the nigger?" "Before night."

Boosten Claude, owner of the orchards, walks out. At his heels scampers a little white wooly dog. "Shut up, Mutt!" Claude's lips are hard, his eyes red. He has been up all night. A pistol hangs at either overalled hip.

"Any news of the nigger, Mr. Claude?" "He's left the swamps. We'll get him before night." "When you do, I'm laying off work, Mr. Claude."

Their voices to black Tom are faint as bells. Over the hills a bell is ringing. Haze lies on the swimming yellow day. Creation sleeps.

The white wooly dog is short-legged, shrill, weak, inquisitive, an imp of canine beasts. No dog for a man.

"Lie down, Mutt! Look pretty. Get out of my feet, you whelp!"

Mutt looks toward the ditch with yipping blasphemy. He scampers up, stretches out his paws, and yips. Howling, he turns and flees back to his master. His white wool bristles, his soft ears flop; his little pink eyes spit fire.

Thickly as the mud he lies in, the heart of black Tom oozes. With all black oaths, senseless grummerings older than speech, Tom curses the little cur. Curses him by the gods of fire and death and poison, by the alligator and the snake, by the jungle and the fen. Damns his sire which was a rabbit, his dam which was a skunk. Damns his offspring, which will be weasels. Damns him wool and hide and hair and bark and snarl. Damns the fleas upon his back.

Boosten Claude wanders nearer to the ditch. Mutt darts out from between his legs, frothy with snarls, and whines back again.

"Shut up, Mutt!" Claude peers up at a tree. "Boys, it looks like scale's been on this tree."

He climbs, pushing aside prickly branches, shielding his face with his arms. He disappears in the dark green leaves. Once more Mutt trots warily toward the ditch, growling sharply. He prances and frisks, wiping forepaws on the grass. For his bulk, Mutt's voice is louder than a lion's. He growls with ominous teeth. He frisks in the grasses by the ditch's bank. He dares to nip at Tom's wretched face. Growing brave, he snaps at his eyes. "Take a look at Mutt, boys!" Claude cries from the tree. "Reckon he's spotted a snake, the little devil!" Claude begins to descend, feeling his way cautiously. "Sic 'em, Mutt! Go after 'm, boy!"

Out of the weedy waters snaps up a giant black hand, huge as the little cur. It strangles that yelping pipe, closes the breath within that throat. Mutt's feeble body, thin as a sparrow beneath the fluffy coat, writhes in death convulsions. Legs claw vainly. Eyes pop out. No whine. Clawing legs dangle limply. Eyes, grotesquely goggled, bloody with veins, are veiled with mortal film. Tom shakes that rag. He flings it in the ditch. Up, and running! Staggering between the trees of golden fruit! Away!

"Mutt!" thunders Boosten Claude. His tone is a scream. "Look, look, look! There he is! On him, boys! Don't let him get away!"

Tom has leaped a low stone wall. He stumbles through grasses. He stretches out his arms towards the swamps. Voices beat. Shots follow him.

LVII. THE ROLLING DICE

FOR the first time since Florida arose from the coral sea, the Biscayne jail housed a white man neither Republican nor drunk. Spike and Stubb kept guard before the hot iron doors. Curious men, having nothing better to do, paused to stare simmeringly, their tongues lolling. Threat of lynching still ran in the air. Men's whispers were not pleasant.

A small boy was perched in a tall palm by the jail. He had not come down for breakfast, and seemed in no hurry to come down for dinner.

"Climb down—" "Out o' that!" the officers ordered him valiantly. Their answer was a jeer. Only a monkey could have climbed that palm. Stubb tried it, but his fat legs slipped on the unwrinkled bark, and he slid down on his hind end in the midst of a nest of ants.

Spike picked up a grapefruit from the gutter. Old and brown it was, and rotten ripe, and crammed with sizzling juice. His stiff hair bristling with anger, Spike hurled it at the imp in the tree. The dauntless weanling dodged, caught the missile at the top of its parabola, and threatened to hurl it back again. The officers retreated inside the jail.

All the youngster could see was a blank brick jail wall, unutterably red and hot. But he continued to gawp as though it might unroll. His mouth was parted, wet at the corners with saliva. An ant crawled down his neck. Anon below passed one of his compeers, bare-footed, staring-eyed, gap-toothed, and freckled. Thereupon the imp in the tree gibbered and swayed and shrilled. Made faces, shook the palm fronds and yaw-hawed, giving expression to spiritual exaltation with thumb at nose. His friends stared up wistfully, as at a divinity. The imp grinned and tried to wiggle his ears.

Spike and Stubb paced slowly back and forth past Deleon's cell. Their faces were watchful and doomed. Deleon did not look up at them. He sat humped on his steel cot. Not at the barred blue window did he stare, but at the gray floor. His hair was no more sleek as a wet cat's, but fallen in long tousled strands about his forehead. One of his moustaches yet pointed upward with the old time arrogance, the other drooped unkempt down. To the tall gallows one pointed, to the pits of Sheol the other. A scum of black beard gave his sleek cheeks the look of piracy, made him look tough as old leather.

Truly not the same Gay Deleon who snared women's hearts. His linen was soiled and wilted. His white buck shoes were smudged. His pants—what word can express it?—his pants were uncreased. He was true prototype of those hardened, unconfessing, unrepenting baby-stranglers whom old ladies love to visit in prison, feeding them chocolate drops and Bible tracts.

Twice night and a day had passed him by in jail.

"O, God!" at first he had screamed; but his throat grew harsh. He had wept; but his tears ran dry. He howled; but breath failed him at the last, and he could only hoarsely croak.

Fallen to silent despair, a brooding stupor. He stared at the cement floor. Once he had knotted his cravat in a silly noose, and swung it to a window bar. But he saw Gay Deleon hanging there, and in frenzy he tore the cravat apart. When food was brought he contemplated the knife. How easily, with what little pain—O, pain, more horrible even than death to Deleon!— might he drain out blood from his wrists, play the high-born Roman, lie down to fading sleep.

Gay Deleon was no Roman. No courage he knew to end his stinking life. Death might be best. He pondered on what he dared to ponder. But self-appointed, by his own hand released, he dared not face the howling night.

To you, Deleon, as you visited mercy, mercy shall be visited again. Now, in your black hour, think of them on whom the black hour has fallen. Of old Thorn Clay, and many another ruined gambler. Of Dot, and your women. Deleon had known such despair before, had known all the dire horrors of the losing gambler. Yet but a turn of one rolling die, and he would be Deleon again. The hills would not be high enough for him. But a turn of the dice—

He could hear Spike and Stubb down the corridor rolling out dice on a hard floor. Rattle and click! Grumbling oaths. Deleon raised his ears and listened.

And now back and forth in front of him the policemen tiptoed, fixing him with stern glances. Their loud voices died. They were portentous with silences. So went the hours. Deleon was consumed with remembrances.

Curiously, it was young Spencer whom he hated, perhaps because Spencer's had been the last face he saw while free. A man must make his devils visible, must have one soul on whom he fastens the supremacy of his odious passion. "I'll get him! I'll pay him back!" Deleon raved. He raved. He was not in position to get anything, save to get it in the neck.

The officers were staring grewsomely in at him. Their hands clasped those bars which might not be shaken. They stared as two ruffled owls into the den of a rattlesnake. They spoke as to a thing which stank. "Mrs. Grady has got permission—" "From Colonel Dawn to see you, Deleon."

Deleon started up from his squeaky cot, striving to slick back his hair. He shook his clothing, rubbed his chin bristles, even in his despair en-deavoring to look again the gallant cavalier. He mumbled a sickly "Hello!" to Rose Dawn, who stood white and still before his barred door.

The watching officers drew away. Deleon grasped his irons and strove to smile, looking much like a monkey. Rose stood on uneven hips, one hand at her breast. Deleon's loss of morale was terrific. She did not smile back. Deleon moistened his lips.

"Good of you to come, Rose," he said, his tongue thick. "You always were tender-hearted. *You'd* not forget."

Rose paused. She could not look at him. "Padriac has telegraphed Mr. Wiggs to defend you, when—when—"

Still she could not look at him. Deleon was visibly heartened.

"That's fine of young Padriac!"

Down the corridor again he heard sound of rolling dice. Life was not so bad. Always a chance. "Very fine of young Grady!" he said again. He picked up his cravat and put it on. Shook wrinkles from his coat. Again brushed his hair. "Why not have him see about bond for me?" he whined. "If Grady wouldn't do it, Schermerhorn might. He always was a fool."

Rose was constrained. "I didn't know bond was taken—for *this.*"

"But I'm not guilty, Rose! I didn't do it!"

Rose cast an uneasy glance about. No one was within hearing. Spike and Stubb were crouching in the entrance, their dicer's oaths heavy. "Didn't you, Gay?" she whispered in trembling voice. She stared at him from the blue silences of her eyes.

Deleon shook his bars. "Rose! Rose Dawn! You don't believe that! What do you mean, Rose?" He struck his fist against the bars, wincing for pain. "It's a frame-up!" he shouted. *"Somebody put this thing on me!"*

Rose did not answer. Deleon fell back from the bars, dropping down on his cot. He shook with harsh sobs. He covered his face. He beat the stone floor with his heels. Rose watched him with that same cold bright glance, cold glance, or hot. Something in her eyes of sultry ocean heat. "I'm sorry, Gay," Rose whispered compassionately, when the silence had endured long.

Deleon brought his hands down from his face. He began to weave his knuckles. His thoughts must have been very bitter. He rubbed his face, and groaned. With fierce gesture he tore off that strangling cravat. "Sorry!" he jeered thickly. "You—you got me in this yourself! *You know who killed old Tim Grady!* O, God! Thank God I never fell for you!"

Rose Dawn drew back, clear across the width of the corridor.

"Wait! Wait, Rose Dawn! You shan't go till I have damned you more than John Dawn did when he went to war."

A whisper. "What do you know about that?"

"What do I know? Ha! He wrote you he was sick of you and wanted to go away! I know! Told you to come to me! Ha, ha, ha, ha!" Deleon gasped with terrible laughter. "What are you crying for? I know, I know! How? Ha, ha, ha! Why, damn your blue eyes! How do I know! *I dictated that letter myself, and John Dawn's name was signed by Pete Lopez!"*

"What?"

"Wait! Wait! You'll put something over on me? I'll put something over on you! We were drunk one night, Pete and I, and I swore I could get you. Sent that letter to you—sent one to John Dawn, telling him to get the Hell out, and Pete signed your name to it! Ha, ha, ha!" Again the strangling mirth. "We knew you'd had a lovers' quarrel, and Dawn was always a hot fool. Damn it, Rose! You'll put something over on me, Rose! Remember I sent John Dawn to where he won't come back. I've won from you, Rose Dawn, whatever stakes you play for!"

"You're crazy mad," Rose whispered.

"It was a joke! But I'd not marry you—you hadn't any money. I could have had you, Rose Dawn! But I didn't want you. I don't want you. I don't want you! *I don't want you!* You—You—Ah, God! Ha, ha, ha! One trick! Hot-headed old John Dawn! I'll slap his face in Hell. Get away! Get away! There 're a thousand women like you. Do I care for your damned tears? I have been drowned in tears! I'll shout it to the world who killed old Tim Grady!"

Long after Rose had gone Deleon continued his mad shouting, pacing up and down his narrow cell with panther quickness.

Out by the door hushed oaths.

"A natural, bones! Little seven out of Heaven! O, the ladies love you, Richard! Shoot the works, Spike!"

The rolling dice! Deleon hearkened. Fate must not be despaired of. A lucky toss, and these bars would be opened. He would have money in his pockets. The world was his. There were other lovely women than Rose Dawn. O, money and women! O, the jaunty heart! O, the rolling dice!

That night Gay Deleon vanished out of jail. Out of the bars ineluctable, out of the steel doors. Spike and Stubb stood stalwartly to swear he had gone as goes blowing smoke. But the thing is, he was gone.

LVIII. HOWLING GHOSTS

ARETHUSA WEINVOLL and Mary Dubby sat on the Poinsettia's veranda late that night. This was the night men hunted for Gay Deleon. The girls' arms circled each other's shoulders. Arethusa, who was no dunce, suspected Miss Dubby of being a very good stenographer, suspected her, in fact, of being everything she might be suspected of being. But Arethusa was daughter of this up and jumping generation, and didn't believe in respectability.

Arethusa boasted of her immoralities as proudly as a little boy boasting of the cats he's killed. With many night-hid blushes she whispered the name of Gay Deleon. Mary Dubby, however, was very respectable.

Arethusa grew hysterical as she reflected on Gay's fate, not knowing that prisoning doors had opened up and freed him. There was her knight, for all she knew, incarcerated in unknightly donjon keep and fortress vile, to wit, the village hoosegow. And, from all authentic gossip, in a fair way to hang; a most unromantic attitude to take.

"He's guilty!" wept Arethusa, twisting a handkerchief. "He must be. He has such calloused eyes. Yet I can't help thinking it was done all for me."

"Perhaps not," Mary conceded, feeling for a pencil in her hair. She smashed a mosquito on her stockings, and chewed a little gum, keeping her arm about Arethusa and gazing out at the black night.

"I hope not," said she.

"Of course he is!" cried Arethusa, rising to Deleon's defense.

"O, he did it, all right. You can't understand the agony, Mary. Each breath is a gnawing cry crushing my heart. Each drop of blood in my glands is hysterics. And I dare not say a thing to mamma."

"If *he is,* then *she* is!" said Miss Dubby hatefully. She did not like the way Higgleson Todd ran after Rose

"Whatever happens to him will happen to Rose Dawn Grady—O, I hope so!"

Arethusa gasped. For any other woman to hang with her homicidal lover was not endurable. One woman suffering for a man is tragedy, two is bigamy. Arethusa wept.

"Why do men do such things, Mary?"

"Deviltry is born in all of 'em," said Mary. "If they don't kill some one, they beat their wives. Or give dictation with their feet on the desk."

Arethusa dried her little freckled nose. Her milk-white arms gleamed in the night. She rested her chin in palms. Old Colonel Dawn, leaping furiously up the veranda steps, eyed her keenly. "If he wanted me, I'd go with him to the ends of the earth," said Arethusa softly. "I'd hang in his place. For I love him!"

"No sense in being foolish about it," said Miss Dubby practically.

Arethusa clasped her knees. "And I know Gay loves me! For he told me he did. Don't say a thing of this to mamma, for Heaven's sake! She thinks he's been going with Bunnie Hoag. And two days ago mamma and that odious old Higgs woman had a dreadful quarrel about it, just after Bunnie ran away."

"I know how to mind my own business," said Mary. "I won't say anything."

"It's queer to be in love," said Arethusa, sighing deep.

"I don't know," said Mary. "I never was."

Higgleson Todd slipped out of the hotel and sat on the steps with them. He smoked cigars. He was glad of the darkness. In the light he did not care to be seen with Mary Dubby. Yet she was a pretty, frail thing. Todd glanced at his watch. Soon he would go to dance with Rose Dawn.

"Where has Bunnie Hoag gone?" Mary asked after a pause.

"I don't worry about her," said Arethusa listlessly. "She's a little fool. She's crazy about that simple-minded Laurence Spencer."

"You don't think anything has happened to her?"

"Goodness! I don't know. I don't care."

Old Dawn came forth again, and being blind for the sudden darkness, stumbled over them. "I beg your pardon, ma'am. Miss Weinvoll, isn't it? And Mr. Todd."

The Colonel peered at the three of them. Todd grew vastly uneasy, for the old man's black eyes were sharp. "And who is *this* young lady?" asked Dawn with an old man's geniality. "I don't remember seeing her pretty smiles before."

"O, this is Mr. Todd's—" said Arethusa.

"My wife!" roared Higgleson Todd, quite out of balance. He was thinking of a man named Mann. "This my wife, Sir!"

"I beg your pardon, Sir!" snorted old Dawn, walking away, not knowing how he had offended the gentleman from the No'th. He turned from the darkness. "If any of you see Deleon," he said, "don't let him get away!"

"Two," whispered Miss Dubby cryptically, laying down her second finger. ("Two what?" stuttered Todd.) "O, just counting," smiled Mary Dubby. "Glad to see you've got that far," Todd grunted.

Arethusa sat alone after Mary and Todd had left her. Long past midnight she sat. Light went out in her mother's room. Many other lights in the hotel. At the Deepsea Club, people were dancing. Far from the bay front Arethusa heard the music tinkling. A few idlers still walked around the verandas, strolling to the tune of soft whispers. And silence.

From the darkness of vines near the veranda a low voice spoke to Arethusa. "Arethusa!" She startled, clapping hand to mouth. "Don't say anything! Be quiet! They're looking for me!"

She followed a beckoning hand, and crept down into the darkness. A car stood waiting. South it went, on the road past the cypress swamps.

And that night Wigley Arsen walked down alone to the *Thorn*. He had with him the serpent knife, borrowed from old Colonel Dawn. A curious idea had come to Arsen of tracing the murderer's emotions step by step. Of handling the knife with him. Of creeping down the deck with him. Of thrusting his arm through the little porthole with him. Of striking down the murderous blade with him, though what he struck at should be no more than bed pillows. It all would be good for a feature story in the Sunday supplement of the *Mist*.

The *Thorn* lay untenanted, a white ghost ship in black waters. The river ripples rocked her. Her masts were tangled in the starless night.

Red the Sailor sat by the gangplank, smoking. *"I* wouldn't go on her nohow," Red warned Arsen. "No, Sir-ee! She's ha'nted!"

Arsen tried a lofty laugh. University men do not believe in ghosts. But Arsen strode up the gangplank slowly. His feet grew leaden. Dark was the night. He heard the breath of shadows. He saw great empty Nothing.

"What do you mean, haunted?" he called to Red.

"Ha'nted with a ghostie," said Red. "E'ry night, come six bells o' the evening watch, I hear that ghostie screaming! A noise like this—'E-e-e!' " Horribly Red the Sailor shrilled, making Arsen quiver.

"When I hears that, I up and walks away," said Red the Sailor, with the wide gaze of a little child.

Wigley Arsen stood square in front of the little porthole of old Tim Grady's cabin. Blackly that round window shone in the night. Arsen fingered the carven serpent of the heavy knife, fingered the sharp blade. It was good for any ghostie. It was fire unto his hands.

Arsen was brave. All men are.

"You're a fool!" he called to Red the Sailor. And put his hand upon the port-hole glass!

From that dreadful cabin rose a moaning, more dreadful banshee sound than ever heard before on land or sea! A lonesome shriek! It was no wind. It was no living thing; was the voice of sentient soul tossed in torments. It was the screaming of the damned!

"Don't!" shrieked Red. "O my God, watch out for ye'r soul, man living!" He fled down the dock away from the ghost-white *Thorn*. He tore at air. His face was white as lightning.

Once again from the cabin of the dead man rose that scream, and the soul of Wigley Arsen turned jelly in him.

" 'Tis a bloody, bloody moon! I fear for it!"

Arsen caught a sight of something terrible and gray behind that porthole. The knife slipped from his hand. He heard its weighted point thump in the deck. He was aquiver. His spine was snow.

"Arsen! Arsen!" rose that scream.

Wigley Arsen backed away down the deck, muttering. "Don't scare me! You can't scare me! I'm an intelligent man. I'm not frightened at anything.

I know you're human. I'm not afraid. This is a hoax. I'm not afraid." In singsong he spoke, but his voice died away. He tried to summon it again, for it was sweeter than the angels. "I'm perfectly calm, I assure you," he silently mouthed. "I'm going to investigate this. I represent a great newspaper, and we'll not be fooled. I don't believe in ghosts. You can't frighten me, I assure you."

The water rippled. The trees rustled. The wind groaned. Arsen's feet tripped over the gangplank, and for the instant he thought Hell had him by the heels.

"O, Arsen! Murdered for a woman's love! Don't strike me with that knife!"

"Get away, Tim Grady!" Arsen screamed. "You're no friend of mine!" He leaped over the quay as though his feet were winged. Beyond his shoulder he saw a thing all white fluttering on the *Thorn.* Arsen overtook the fleeing Red. He passed him as though Red stood still. He hardly touched the ground. He caught up with his own shadow and left it behind him.

Wigley Arsen did not pause to breathe till he was in the Deepsea Club, and laughing crowds of dancers were about him. But still he heard that scream, and would hear it forever after—

"Murdered for a woman's love! Don't strike me with that knife!"

LIX. WOMEN AND WHISKY AND WRATH

MANY danced in the Deepsea Club that night, but Rose Dawn was not among them. Early into the morning the dancers scuffled, to the croaking of viol and the cricketing of violin.

"I don't know what's possessed Rose," said Mrs. Higgs to Todd.

"She's been so queer and cold of late, and she looks at me so funny. She snuck off some place this afternoon, and it's *my* private opinion she snuck off to see Deleon in jail. If she did—! If she did—!"

The old buzzard closed her jowls and wagged her head, silently promising tortures unheard of for her lovely daughter. "And since then she's been sitting in her room looking like she's dead. If she'd only squall, I'd understand it. You expect a lady to squall. But just sitting still, not talking or saying a word—it ain't human. I'll make her come! I'll send for her. She'll mind me!"

What commands, threats, or exhortations Mrs. Higgs used to draw Rose to the dance are a secret with Mrs. Higgs. But Rose came, at a late hour. Old Colonel Dawn, ruthlessly carrying on the search for Deleon, looked in and saw her. And stood apart, where she could not see him, gravely watching her.

On piers the Deepsea Club extended over the waters of Bay Biscayne. Black as black jewels waves sparkled below, twinkling duskily between floor cracks. Rose leaned over the bayward railing, staring deeply down at the tides. She was in a gown of purple more spangled than the starless night. Her shoulders moved. Old Dawn surmised she was quietly, stilly sobbing. But no sound came from her throat, and no tears in her eyes. What passions warred behind that softly stirring bosom? What thoughts tossed beneath her golden curls? Rose dreamed. Waters tossed. Music silenced.

A motor-boat went down the bay—"Put! Put! Uf!—Put! Put! Uf!—Put! Uf!—Put! Put! Put! Put!—" rough, uneven dissonance. Old Dawn thought of a ragged stone's dimensions made audible. Far out past the coral reefs sounded the ocean.

Behind her stood Padriac Grady, not daring for some reason to approach and break into her musings. His hands worked. In the darkness Padriac bore some resemblance to old Tim Grady. Something in the gleam of his gray eyes; something in the thrusting forward of his neck; something in the untidiness of his dark red hair mirrored his father.

With a start he moved toward her, cautiously, a little uncertain of himself. Rose seemed unconscious of his presence. Hushed she was as the night, hushed as an immortal in alabaster. She was Astarte, cold as the virgin moon. She was Aphrodite, queen of oceans of passion. Whichever, she was a goddess.

"Wonderful night," said Padriac thickly, paying no heed to the night.

Rose did not hear, so deeply she looked at the black swimming tides. Her soft breast pressed against the wooden railing, and stirred, and shook. Padriac Grady wished to his God that he were even as that wooden railing.

Mrs. Higgs marched up, waving a crimson feather fan. She linked arms with her daughter, giving Padriac virulent looks. Her brassy hair looked lemon in the dark. Above her low-cut gown her puffy flesh jiggled like jelly. "What are you after now?" she demanded of Padriac. "Do you think you can keep us by a grin from getting our rights?"

"What is the matter?" cried Rose, waking up.

"I'll say my say when I have my say to say," declared Mrs. Higgs furiously. "If you had half the sense I've tried to put into you, you'd know we got to fight for our rights in this world. For *you,* Mr. Padriac Grady, I'll say right now we're not going to stand for you and Bellbender getting everything. We'll fight you to the last. Did we throw away our youth and beauty? Did we marry old Grady to get a soup bone?"

Mrs. Higgs talked for five minutes, fanning herself passionately.

"What did you say?" Padriac asked, looking at her evilly. Mrs. Higgs began again.

"Understand me, Mrs. Higgs," said Padriac coldly. "My father's will was none of mine. Are you blaming me for it? You can sue till the moon grows black, and I won't try to stop you. Do you think I'd stand in the way of Rose for a few dollars?"

"Well, now, that's different," said Higgs, eyeing him keenly.

"It's silly to quarrel over money," said Padriac. "Indeed, that's what I declare and affirm," said Mrs. Higgs heartily. "I never think of the dirty stuff. So you won't fight us when we break the will and get our rights! But that red-headed minx, that Maveen, *she'll* do it! And so will Bellbender; he'll want to give that money to the dirty heathen. Not that I begrudge you what your farther left you, Padriac. I reckon you worked for it. But Rose and me ought to get the rest."

Padriac touched Rose's naked arm. "Rose, you're not angry at me?" he whispered. His fingers shivered.

"Money?" she asked, as if in a dream. "Money? Money! Are you still talking of money? Why, before I'd touch the money of Timothy Grady, I'd throw myself in the sea!"

"What's got into you, Rose?" snarled Mrs. Higgs, as Padriac walked away. "It's all right to talk about fighting the will, but we can't do it. You got to be nice to Padriac. You got to! I see that look in his eyes, dearie; he'd marry you in the crack of the whip. And he's a real nice young man."

Rose Dawn opened her mouth to speak bitter words. But filial obedience and long subjugation to her mother kept her silent. "I'm tired," was all she said. "Very tired tonight, Ma."

Mrs. Higgs whimpered, knowing Rose was close to tears and knowing well how she could stop them. "I've tried and endeavored to do my best for you, dearie," she lamented, "all my life long. I've been farther and mother both to you. I brought you up out of nothing. Where'd you been if it hadn't been for me?"

This rhetorical question Rose could not answer.

"And now to have you turn away from me this way, to know you're wanting to live your own life apart from me, to know you're thinking thoughts your Ma can't share, to show yourself so selfish, not thinking of all I've done for you—O, it's hard, dearie. It's bitter hard! Some day you'll know. I hope to God you'll know! I hope to God you'll suffer as I've suffered! Bitterer than a dog's bite is the sneers of an ungrateful daughter!"

"I didn't mean to make you feel bad, Ma," cried Rose, her tender heart hurt that she had hurt another. "I'm sorry if I said anything, Ma."

"O, an ungrateful girl have you been all your life long!" whimpered Mrs. Higgs. "You ran away and married Dawn. And even after he was good and dead you was still thinking of him. It was all I could do to make you marry Grady. Yet it was for your own good. And what thanks do I get? What thanks? O, dearie, you can't know—"

Mrs. Higgs released that stream of red-eyed tears which never failed to move Rose Dawn. But something she had said had made Rose hard. Without a word she turned and looked at the black waters again, which were saltier, and deeper, and more drowning than the utmost tears of Mrs. Higgs. Mrs. Higgs stopped her sobbing and peered cunningly at her daughter. The strange indifference Rose showed to her caterwaulings frightened Mrs. Higgs.

"You don't know how I've slaved and toiled and sac'ificed to make you what you are, dearie," she sobbed.

Rose looked wearily at the waters. "I think I do," she said.

Now thunderously uprose the moon. A waning half moon decrescent. Haze clouds crimsoned it. Lightnings muttered. The deep spoke of rain. Far tides rippled on Bay Biscayne. Drooping cypresses bent to the waters with tears. Upon distant keys palms spread their fanlike crests. Motionless they stood, and pondering, heads slanted in grave listening. It seemed they hearkened to the outer ocean. And still the lightnings muttered.

Old Colonel Dawn watched Rose within the moon's small light. He spoke to Padriac. "Leaving for the No'th soon, Mr. Grady?" Padriac also looked at Rose. "I don't know," he said. "I'm in love with your tropics, I think."

Old Dawn smiled without laughter. He had heard that before.

"The beauty of them gets hold of a man," said he. "They're likely to steal his soul."

"I'd never thought of it that way."

"I know!" whispered old Dawn. "Take Boosten Claude. His father's father came down with the Yankee troops, and stayed. First for a month, and then for a year. He was buried here.

"Each year along the time of spring he'd stand on the shore and look no'th, snuffing the wind. 'Pussywillows coming out—daisies'll soon be by the Weirs,' he'd say. 'I'm going back, Stoughton. I'm going back!' But here he is till judgment.

"Boosten's father used to talk of going back, too. But the heat had got in his bones. First time Boosten ever saw snow was this winter, and he's shivering yet. And Boosten's son, if he ever has one, 'll die if he goes no'th o' Forty. Yet Boosten isn't half the man his grandfather was."

Padriac Grady stared sulkily at old Dawn. "I'll not be like that."

"The tropics always remind me of a pretty woman," said old Dawn. "A woman you may see for only a minute in the street, but can't forget for years and years. You'll want her so hard she keeps you from your sleep o' nights and your food o' days, and you'll hope there's a Heaven where you can meet her again. I've seen a few like that. And the older a man is, the harder it is to forget."

"I'm not afraid of the tropics," said Padriac coldly.

Old Dawn nodded sagely. "Love's queer. One kind of love's not satisfied when a man marries. In the spring we see blue eyes; or perhaps a flash of this Southern sky. I've brought a son into this world, and I've outlived him. I'm growing old. Yet I remember women!" Old Dawn lit a cigar. "A man loved her once—"

"Loved whom?" asked Padriac dully.

"Loved the tropics. Who can blame him? John Dawn loved her. She stole his soul."

Old Dawn walked away, stumbling a little. Rose Dawn's spangled dress gleamed against background of starless purple night. Now the lightnings muttered. Now the black clouds rolled. Long sat Padriac, looking at her. He felt the thirst for drink.

The music died away, and the dance was ended.

Rose Dawn startled. She saw Laurence Spencer and walked towards him. "I want to speak to you professionally, Larry."

The young man bowed; he had never been consulted before professionally.

"I can't sleep, Larry," she whispered. "Something's wrong with. me. Can you tell me some drug which will make me sleep—soundly?"

Laurence tightened his cupid mouth. "Opiates are dangerous things," he said. Looking close, he saw indeed shadows beneath her eyes. "You oughtn't to keep such late hours," he said crossly. "It gives wrinkles to any woman."

"Wrinkles?" asked Rose, touching her brow.

"O, wrinkles come after twenty-five. You can't stop 'em. Be careful, or they'll make you lose the lure, Rose! They'll wreck that beautiful, innocent look of yours, Rose."

After Laurence walked away, Wigley Arsen approached, to pay his evening devoirs to lovely Rose Dawn and perhaps to escort her back to the hotel.

Out of the shadows stalked up Padriac Grady, breaking into Arsen's good-nights. Grady's dark hair was rumpled to a peak. Even in the dim light his face looked naturally florid. He wavered and staggered. His eyes were fierce.

"What are you doing with Mrs. Grady!" he demanded in loud voice.

"Why, Paddy; what's the trouble?" asked Arsen nervously.

"Trouble yourself to answer me!" Padriac spoke thickly, lowering.

"Well, Paddy—"

"I'm Mr. Grady to you. Remember that!"

"Well, Mr. Grady," Arsen stuttered, growing red and cold. "I brought Rose home—" "Mrs. Grady, damn you!" "Why, Paddy, don't you remember the old days in New Haven—"

Padriac raised his hand. His breath hissed. With inarticulate roar he ran his fingers through his hair, rumpling it further. Arsen was appalled. He deemed he saw ghosts. It was the very image of old Tim Grady come to life again! In the darkness, roaring, shaking his fists old Tim Grady come back from death again! And Arsen remembered that cry he had heard on the *Thorn* earlier tonight, the cry of the dreadful dead!

"Speak quick!" snarled Padriac. "None of your bounding insolence to me! I'll not stand for it!" Arsen stuttered. He drew back. "I've watched you long enough," said Padriac ominously. "I've had my eye on you long enough! Did you say 'Paddy'?"

He lifted back his fist, straight behind his shoulder. Pace by pace Wigley Arsen stumbled back. Pace for pace Padriac followed him up.

"Out till this hour of the night with Rose!" he shouted. "Get off! Get away! Get out! Get out, before I forget I'm a gentleman!" "What—" "I'll strangle you!" foamed Padriac. "I'll strangle you!"

The roaring voice of old Tim Grady! Devils in the rain!

Arson's heel caught on the steps, and he stumbled and tumbled down. Grady's fist swung at him, just missing. Arsen sat down in a puddle. Cast away, cast out, as had been old Thornwood Clay.

Arsen had not raised voice then. No one raised voice now. Out into the roaring rain, the tropical night, the rushing gutters of the street. Thrown like a dog into the mud. Arsen sat in the puddle till he knew that it was wet. He slunk away, gasping curses, utterly confounded. Rose had gone inside the Poinsettia, cold and still. Cold and still as steel. Cold as white heat.

After several unsteady lurches, Padriac hiccoughed and followed her. Padriac Grady had got drunk.

Women and whisky and wrath!

LX. THE DREADFUL HOUR

ON you, Gay Deleon—gay Gay Deleon—has come your dreadful hour! Think now of Weinvoll, rotting behind bars for a sin you did! Think of old Thorn Clay, starving in the cold! Think of mighty Dusty Hoag, shot with lead through the mouth! Think of old Tim Grady! Think of Dot, of your women! Think of John Dawn! Yes, think of death!

The roulette wheel spins in the Biscayne Club; the ball clicks; fortune flickers; men watch with cold dead eyes.

Dead men, the living-in-death. They have no hope, and no hereafter, but money, which is soon spent.

Jake the croupier has face of limestone and pale long yellow hair. He wears a short green baize kirtle. Steadily he handles his rake. All men about the wheel are in evening dress, save for a uniform or two. A man without a white shirtfront has no business gambling. At all places else, the Royal Poinsettia, the Deepsea Club, ballroom, billiard-alley, or boudoir, knickered tweeds are supreme. But here the Angel Azarael might not enter without dinner coat.

Deleon came in. The old black door-attendant tried to push him forth again. "You can't come in, sah!"

But Deleon came.

Men turn in curiosity. A glance, and they are back at the table, restlessly stacking their chips. Jake does not turn up his chalky face, but deep lines in it harden. A droop comes to his eyes. As the wheel died two or three men spoke to Deleon, keeping at respectful distance.

"Out on bail?" groaned Urban Wiggs, that fat dull fool. "Hear my father will appear for you. Damned shame!"

Somehow Deleon had managed to get shaved and bathed, and into dinner clothes. The click of the wheel brought lights to his black eyes. He threw back his head. The rolling dice!

Once again the bravura, the king of fickle fortune, the lord of women. He should have worn cape and rapier, walked with plume in his hat. For the instant it might be seen why many women, fair and high and holy, plain and low and bad, loved Gay Deleon. Poltroon, no doubt of it; sharp, unveracious, unprincipled, unsteadfast, fickle as water. Yet a pretty thief of hearts, a knave of good sharp deeds, a lord in his own right by the law which says any scoundrel, but no merchant, is a gentleman.

"Bail!" Deleon sneered to fat Urban Wiggs. He chuckled fearfully. "Two—fool—cops! Two fool cops, shooting craps in the jail. I got in their game with sixty cents, and cleaned them right."

Deleon stifled with laughter. "And then I rolled them for the keys!" He giggled. "I come back!" he boasted. "Luck doesn't run against me forever!"

"They'll be looking for you," said Urban Wiggs grimly.

"Let them find me! If I had money—" Deleon cast a wad of dirty bills to Jake. He was indifferent to the hushed hostility. He was free, and his luck would turn. He had money in his pocket. The rolling wheel!

The wheel spun. Silently sat Jake with his cold stone face. Not once did Deleon win, though he scattered bets like rain. Buoyancy left him. In a monotone he cursed all devils. His glance was steady and blazing. Over and over he counted the chips left him. They dwindled. None were left. Not one.

"Lend me some money, Wiggs!"

Urban sneered, wagging his head. He stuck his fat hands in his pockets, turning the broad of his back to Deleon. "You're done," he said. "It's a three!" screamed Deleon. "Watch it roll! I've got the hunch!"

And three turned up. Two more numbers Deleon called, feeling prophetic fervor in him. But he wasn't betting. The bettors watched Deleon curiously. They were superstitious, or they would not gamble. The stony croupier smiled. He did not believe in second sight.

"It's a nine!" cried Deleon, working his hands in spasms. "God! If I had money! Nine! ... It's winning . . . winning . . . winning. ... It's nine! What did I tell you? I might have made a million dollars! Lend me money, Wiggs!"

The floor seemed to rock and reel beneath him. The hunch surely came from Heaven, from that God who is providential to gamblers. His luck had turned! His luck had turned at last. But if he should not seize it—"Lend me money, Jake!"

That stone man said nothing. After a long time his wrinkles cleft into a grin. "Not just yet," he said wearily. "You get out!"

The wheel was a spinning top. Its whirring song madly denied Deleon. Smiles of winners. Hissing breath of losers. Crackling green money. Chip clicking on chip. A drunken man who bawled continually: "All right! All right! I'll pay!" and kept fishing from his pockets tobacco coupons.

White magic in the air. The rolling dice! Money! Silent voices screamed to Gay Deleon: "You might have won, Gay Deleon! Why don't you gamble, Gay Deleon! We're with you, Gay Deleon!"

His fevered blood burst; his heart. His lungs could not contain his breath. The mob scowled at him. The sight of the broken is pleasant to neither lucky nor unlucky. Win or lose. . . . win or lose, but each man, pray God, the gentleman! Let him blow out his brains in his own way, and not spatter his friends' dress shirts.

Jake lifted his basilisk eyes. Pale were they as the moon, their lashes colorless. "I said to clear out, Deleon, and let the gentlemen gamble!"

"Lend me money!"

Urban Wiggs's broad back was maddening to Deleon. He beat his fists on it. He gripped Wiggs by the collar band. "Don't! Don't!" Wiggs groaned, near to apoplexy. "Don't knife me, Deleon!" "Lend me money! I can win!"

Hands seized him hard. A blow smote him on the ear. He was kicked down steps. "Clear out, you dirty mucker!" Loud clapped the gates of Hell behind him. He lay in the gutter.

Creeping along down dark streets, he found McGinty's swift blue racer. Deleon's hands shook on the wheel. Glances cast on him by passers-by terrified him as he crouched low. Courage had gone out of him. He saw ghosts creeping in foul alleys. He was in the grip of cold spasms.

But one more hope remained. Always hope. By devious unlighted ways he drove to the Poinsettia. He crept up a back way to Laurence's room. No one saw him. Or if one did, it was only a black maid whose silence Deleon rewarded by smile or kiss.

Laurence was away dancing at the Deepsea Club. Entering the unlocked door, Deleon felt about in the blackness. Spencer should have money; he always had it. Deleon could find nothing. He sought the bureau, and in a drawer found Laurence's pistol, heavy and black. Deleon pocketed this. His stealthy fingers played music on the walls. Hatefully he tore all things his hand could find, dumping out drawers on the floor, stamping on them. It was a childish act. He smashed a picture. But he found no money.

Deleon pulled at a closet door which held firm against his tugs. With cold fright Deleon hesitated, laying ear to the panels. He heard the hushed pulsing of the vaporous night; a hissing soft, continually breathless as the sound of rain on leaves. Creakingly the door gave, it began to swing ajar. Black were the shadows in the unlit room! In the widening crack Deleon saw the gleam of eyes. O, dreadful hour! Shape of doom!

"Who are you?" thinly moaned the shivering night. *"Who are you?"*

Deleon fled. He scrambled from the window and dropped down a sturdy wisteria to the grass. Amidst bushes he lay, gasping. Roaringly his heart pumped great floods through the portals of his ears. He dared not look above. A bird screamed at him. Shadows shook their snaky hair.

He crawled away on all fours, whining in his throat. On the steps of the hotel veranda he saw Arethusa Weinvoll sitting alone, her chin in her palms, looking up at the black clouds. Faintly he heard the music of dancing at the Deepsea Club. Arethusa turned her head, and her milk-white breast flashed silver for an instant. Deleon scrambled silently through the bushes along the veranda, and hid near the steps.

For minutes he watched the girl. She did not stir again. Late strollers clumped about the porch, their whispers dwindling thin as smoke. Minutes passed heavily while Deleon watched. Arethusa was rich. But more, she was a woman.

Lovely she seemed in the darkness, white and soft and young. His heart lightened; he brushed back his hair. Life is not to be despaired of. Money and women! Softly Deleon whispered:

"Arethusa! Be quiet. Don't say anything. Come away with me!"

She went in the blue racer with him. Nothing she asked; but they spoke together in many whispers. Such drowsing converse was theirs as throaty pigeons know. Her shoulder beneath his arm warmed Deleon's heart. He even dared to hum a tune, in this, his dreadful hour!

Dark night! Trees closed over the spinning road. No sky shone through. Southward went the blue racer under branches forming a tunnel. Trees whispered; they sawed their ominous boughs. Southward Deleon drove down the white road beside the cypress swamps. He passed a squad of men with guns and ropes in their hands. Dogs leaped from before his head-lights' spears.

"If you see the nigger Tom—" the cry died behind him.

Steam in the air. Dark night. Awaited him the Black King!

Up came the burning moon in haze. A gibbous cheek, half a face, the red eye of the demon! Clouds flurried past in horror. Up stood the burning moon in mist.

By the road's edge Deleon halted, by the margin of the cypress swamps. Shrilly hummed myriad insects. Hoarsely boomed the ancient sea. The swamps so near seeped! seeped! with a treacherous sound of tears. A bush stirred. A bush, beside his hand was stirring.

Down the black way behind, dogs began to bark. With rustle loud as rain an owl broke through branches. On shadowy, silent wings it fled towards the moon.

"Beware!" its pinions whispered. "Beware of the Black King!"

Deleon did not hear. The girl lay in the bend of his arm. Kisses they gave, and took again, as though their thirst burned creation. Deep, as though the sea were turned to lips. Slow, as though the world would never end.

O, dreadful hour!

The bushes crashed. Out of the black uprose the black king!

Out of the black giant Tom Jefferson. Away and deep the dogs. Huge, famished, terrible as a panther, with gaunt and flaming eyes, with knotted arms, leaped giant Tom. Deleon did not have time to scream. The giant had grabbed his pistol.

Madly Deleon writhed and tore. He threshed his feeble fists. Now he was dangling in the air like a spider, dancing like a man who hangs. Stars reddened. Roared the void. Death had him by the throat.

"And you, you pretty crying thing—"

Arethusa screamed. She tore her cheeks. Leaping out, she fled down the stone road. Great death upon her trail. Screaming yet! The black king had overtaken her. . . .

"Wo-o! Wo-o!" bay the dogs.

"Who-o! Who-o! Woe to who?" cries the rushing owl.

Rain comes.

Yet sounds the sea. It will sound forever.

Down the road, creeping into the edges of the swamps, bare murky yellow torches. They are smoky stars. Rain falls on them. They dip in and out amidst trees and grasses. Men shout to one another as they thresh about. Their eyes gleam whitely. Their hands shake. Now one has fallen in a slough. Men rush together, forming a chain to drag him out.

Vacantly twitter birds disturbed in sleep. They rustle away on whirring wings. Little beasts run with a soft pat! pat! Mosquitoes drone into the rain, and die with draggled wings. Things crawl and writhe within the foul nocturnal quags. Loudly booms the deep, triumphant baying of hounds. They whine around bushes, dive into dark recesses with slavering tongues.

Boosten Claude runs down the road, waving a torch aloft. Shadowy saffron circles flare before him, but they vanish out. Claude's knife-face is steel. He bellows deeply to his men. His voice is drowned in echoes. Torches dip in answer to him through the woods, through the morasses.

"We've got the line about him. We'll get him in the morning!"

There in the bushes lies Gay Deleon. One foot (those dancing feet) is twisted beneath him. His head lies on the stone road (it has known softer pillows!). Bloated mosquito clouds whine in the rain. They sing a requiem.

"Don't touch it, men! Call off that damned hound! You, Arsen, take charge of this girl. Make her stop her screaming."

Screaming yet, Arethusa sits on the rain-soaked road tearing at her hair.

Gay Deleon, the debonair! A hundred women loved him. Come to this!

For all your sins, Gay Deleon, let us pray. You loved life; the way you went was sweet. To yourself you were no villain. Each man unto himself is no villain. Ah, gay Gay Deleon, your dreadful hour! For all your sins, Gay Deleon, we will pray.

Loudly yammer the belling hounds. From branch to branch Tom swings himself away. Dogs cannot follow on those scummy pools below. But still he sees the torches flaring, twinkling in and out. Still he hears the shouts of men as they enlarge their courage, shouting each to each. Still he sees them crawling down the road, long guns in the crooks of their arms, their eyes lean.

The great rain falls. Soon it will be gray day.

An owl whirls by with great yellow eyes. "Beware! Beware of the Black King!"

Its wingtips sting his face. Gaunt, silent, hard of glance, the posse men stand about Gay Deleon. They are a tribe of bitter warriors gathered at the bier and pyre of a king struck down in war. Flickering shadows leap. Saffron smokes flare and flaw. Lean yellow tongues of fiery pine-knots sizzle thinly.

"I always liked him," says Boosten Claude. "I never really wanted to shoot him. Now God have mercy on his soul!"

The torches, held in a circle, stand as candles of the death-night watch.

LXI. "BREAK! BREAK! BREAK!"

THE little Weinvoll girl says it was young Spencer," said old Dawn. "But she's hysterical, Boosten. And she's a born liar. She couldn't tell the truth."

"We've got the nigger in a net," said Claude grimly. "He can't break free!"

Old Dawn put fists on his desk. "Let the law take its course when you get him, Boosten. I'll not tolerate anything else!"

Claude sucked in his breath. "Better take a vacation, Colonel," he said with haggard laughter.

"I say the law will be obeyed!" cried old Dawn, springing up.

"And I say I don't give *that* for your law!"

Fierce the straight black brows of old Stoughton Dawn. Invin-cible his glances. "Boosten Claude," he said softly, "the Dawns don't take their words in vain. I've sworn to keep one law for black man and white. I'll keep it!"

Boosten Claude shifted his gaze. "Why did the Weinvoll girl try to ac-cuse young Spencer, you think, Colonel?"

"The natural born habit of a liar in lying."

Laurence Spencer was aware of whispering glances on him that next morning. When he came to the beach at noon, a small earth-quake arose. Bathers followed him curiously. An old gentleman wheezed, and threw down his newspaper, and put on his glasses, and plunged out into the safe sea.

"It's said he killed Deleon!"—"Good riddance."—"And that little Bunnie Hoag's been missing three days. Do you think—?"—"No! Do you?"—"No. It's not possible."

Mary Dubby, shy in a little bathing suit, sat down by Laurence at the edge of the rising tide, and chewed gum. She dabbled her heels in the surf foam. She conversed kindly with Laurence. Asked him what made the sea so sad. Asked him why the sky was blue. Asked him what was a Portu-guese man-of-war which on the white sand expired through all its purple streamers. Asked him if cocoa came from coconuts.

The rising tide lapped at their knees. Laurence remembered he was a Harvard man, and told her everything.

Mary asked why he hadn't shot Deleon, as William Hart does. Asked him why he hadn't smashed in his head with a rock, as Douglas Fairbanks does. Asked him why he hadn't leaped on his back and bitten off his ears, as John Barrymore does. Asked him if he believed in love. Asked him to fish for a sand-chigoe which hopped down her back.

The rising tide washed out the sand from beneath them. They scrambled up. Mary Dubby had been filled with a very definite idea. She knew Higgleson Todd, floating out in the waves, his great paunch looking like a watermelon in striped green suit, was watching her. Mary seemed very fair in her little silk costume, so much like a silk handkerchief. Her hair shone yellow. Higgleson Todd had a passion for blonds. He grew jealous, as Mary had hoped.

With a grunt and splash he turned his mountainous girth and paddled for shore. "You know Mr. Spencer?" asked Miss Dubby, by way of introduction.

"Hello, Mr. Todd. I didn't know this young lady—" Laurence was unaware of Mary's name. He hesitated about calling her a lady, but thought Todd might expect it. "I didn't know *she*—"

"Didn't know she's my wife?" asked Todd unpleasantly.

Laurence turned, irritated by Todd's tone. It was the first time (though I hope not the last) he was not a gentleman.

"Three," murmured Mary in a voice of silent triumph.

"Three what?" grunted Todd.

"I've been reading some of your law books, Mr. Higgleson."

"You startle me," sneered Todd. "Do you know your alphabet?"

"And I've learned it's law that if a man introduces a girl three times as his wife, she *is* his wife, just as good as by church and book. First there was Mr. Padriac Grady, and then Colonel Dawn, and then—"

"Dictation!" howled Todd, out of his wits. "You sap!—No, no! Good girl—Mary! Where are you going?"

"We might as well go to the church and make it religious," said Miss Dubby. "It's legal already."

"Dictation! Dictation! Dictation!" gasped Todd, running after her.

And never thereafter did Mr. Higgleson Todd call Mrs. Higgleson by the unkind name of sap.

Laurence saw Maveen on the beach with Schermerhorn; she returned his greeting with casual smoke from her cigaret. Disconsolately Laurence sat down on the sand, listening to the sea. "Break! Break! Break!" roared the threshing surf. Laurence put his hand to his heart. He was not surprised to find it unbroken.

"What's the use of love?" he thought.

And then he thought of little Bunnie Hoag. And then of Rose Dawn.

In far New York, the *Morning Mist* was weeping for Deleon. Thanks to Arsen being on the job, it wept five minutes before any other paper. Wrathfully the *Mist* scorched those scurrilous, lying, libelous metropolitan papers which had ever intimated Deleon killed Tim Grady. The *Mist* was answered by marked silence, obviously a sign of guilt. That the *Mist* had been first to accuse Deleon diminished not the least its upright, self-right, all right righteousness.

It questioned who was this Laurence Spencer. Was he not son of the vivisectionist Dr. Russel Spencer? Not son of Mrs. Spencer, who had been a Boston Sears? How could good come out of Boston? And he was a medical student. That clinched it. There (it is alleged) is the man who killed Tim Grady! With his alleged hand he did it. He carved Tim's alleged heart.

Everyone knows that medical students creep forth at night to kidnap ragged little slum children, using them for vivisection. Everyone knows they eat the hearts of their living patients to put iron in their blood and make their beards grow long. And worse. He was a Harvard student. The *Mist* screamed forth: "Another Harvard Man Gone Wrong!"

It published cartoons, photographs, leading editorials, and the opinions of great crime investigators. "Anthony refuses to give opinion!" it cried. The truth was Anthony had kicked the *Mist's* reporter on the heels and pushed him out the door. That was opinion enough.

A page of pictures showed the *Thorn;* the Grady wedding; Dawnrose; Tim Grady at the age of forty; the eating house in Moline where Mrs. Higgs began her brilliant career; a Florida tomato; Rose Dawn in "Sin"; the ocean; and a flashlight of Coney Island in August, labeled "Midnight Revels in Biscayne."

'Tis an ill murder which blows no one good. The *Mist's* owner, the secret man behind the guns, the father of the Arty Girl, ordered an increase in Arsen's salary. Perhaps he was gladdest of all men that Gay Deleon had gone to Hell.

"I see by the papers," said puny little Citizen A, "that the Grady case is up again. I'd like to punch somebody's jaw!"

"Rose Dawn is the woman behind it," said hideous Citizen B. "Women have loved me. I know what they are."

"Sure, she did it!" said A. "Remember how she knifed that man in 'Sin'?"

"She'll be great in the movies now," said B. "Everybody goes to see a murderess."

"I don't believe a word of it!" said C. "I'd never look at her again!"

But he stepped into Gus Bliss's pawnshop, where he gave his watch for money to see Rose Dawn again.

LXII. HEART BLOOD

SOLEMN Ike Duval found Dinnis McGinty at last, up an alley. McGinty took to his heels, but in three strides Ike was stepping on them. Ike clapped heavy hand on McGinty's shoulder.

"Not so fast, my friend!"

McGinty gobbled. The oaths he released to the sunlight were many and vile. He reeked like a laboratory with low stenches. Beneath Ike's steel fingers his rum-soaked muscles were like sponge. He quivered hugely as a stranded whale.

"Cut out that there profanity!"

"I'll cuss when I . . . pl'ase, and where I . . . pl'ase, and as much and as loud as I . . . pl'ase—and ask no hilp of any man!"

In lieu of the dots, substitute the names of any devils you like.

"What are ye after-r chasing me far-r, ye flat-foot?" yelled McGinty. "I ain't doing nothing to ye. Did auld Todd sic ye on to me?"

Ike Duval released his hard fingers. "Have a cigar," he offered, trying to smile ingratiatingly. "I'd like to have a word with you, McGinty." He gave a slap to McGinty's back. "You're all right, Mac."

Justly, McGinty was suspicious. "Todd's after-r me far-r tr-rying to stick up Doc Spincer. It ain't that?"

"You and me want to be friends, Mac. Buy a drink, Mac."

McGinty pocketed Ike's five dollar bill, still suspicious. "What's this far-r, if I may be so bol-ld as to inquire?"

"Money talks."

McGinty nodded. "But I don't," he said shrewdly.

On a barrel and a soap-box in the alley he and Ike sat down. They spat. Ike pushed his derby back on his head, and pulled up his pants to show his white cotton socks. Silently he smoked, his jaws working. McGinty chewed his cigar.

"What's the game?" asked McGinty bluntly.

"I'm going to be frank with you, Mac," said Ike, trying to look frank. He paused.—"Who was the man with amber glasses?" he shouted abruptly.

McGinty drew into himself. His eyes grew cunning. "What man?"

"I'm on a trail, Mac." Ike wagged his forefinger. "I like you, Mac. I want to be frank with you. Did I ever tell you my mother was born in Ireland?"

"God rist yer mither's bones!" said McGinty, "for with ye 'er son, 'tis in sorrowment she must have gone down to her grave!"

"On the day before Tim Grady was killed," said Ike lowly, "a man with a red wig and amber glasses got off the Gold Express. *Who was that man, McGinty?*"

"Why should I know, if I may be so bol-ld as to inquire?"

"You've got a good memory for faces. I hear say you never forget a man."

"Aye, that I don't. At fir-rst I didn't know him, but when I remimbered me—"

"Who was that man beneath the false hair and the amber glasses?"

McGinty drew back. "I will not ope me mouth!"

"Watch out, McGinty! You're due for twenty years in New York State!"

"Ye have no war-rant to arrist me! I know where I can hide."

"I'll get the warrant, Din McGinty! I'll slam you in the coop! Speak up! Unclamp your trap! Who was that man?"

"I will not ope me mouth!" said Dinnis McGinty grimly. "For he did favar-r to Dinnis McGinty, and he is me fri'nd. I've clasped his hand in the clasp o' fillowship. Now may ye roar on, flat-foot, while yer belly holds wind."

"So he's your friend, is he?"

"Ay! I forgit me not of a man, inimy or fri'nd. Did he not save me pussycat at risk of his own nick? I'll say no war-rd against him!"

"So it was him!" roared Ike Duval, slapping his thighs. "I knew it all along. I've got him now. By God, he'll hang for killing old Tim Grady!"

" 'Twas who, ye fool? What are ye after-r now?"

"I'm not after you, McGinty!" scowled Ike. "I've got enough from you. Hand back that five!"

"What have I said?" cried McGinty in anguish. "I did not ope me mouth!"

"Hand back that five, McGinty! Hand back that cigar too!"

"Yer mither was bar-rn in auld Ire-land!" shrieked McGinty. "She was bar-rn in Edinboro!"

All day the face of Solemn Ike Duval was dreadful as a hangman's. All day Solemn Ike Duval nursed secret determination to his breast, as a girl might nurse a sweet shameful love-child. But Solemn Ike Duval remembered the boldness of that man who had risked high death for a black cat, who had flicked his thumbs at danger a thousand times, whom Solemn Ike Duval had seen times without end make love to death as other men make love to love. And courage left Solemn Ike Duval.

That afternoon he was one of seven men who went down to the *Thorn,* searching for that ghost which had screamed at Wigley Arsen. They went massed. Each man liked to feel the sturdy bumping of his neighbors' shoulders. At the plank they straggled out in single file, Schermerhorn, old Colonel Dawn, van Chuch, Ike, and Todd, with Arsen; and Red the Sailor lingering at the rear.

"It's all foolishness," growled Wigley Arsen. "Foolishness! Why can't men be sensible? An educated man would never believe in ghosts. Red the

Sailor is superstitious. I would have investigated his story myself last night if I'd had time. *I'd* never believe in ghosts."

"Aw, Mr. Arsen," muttered Red. "Year—"

"Red claims he heard the howling," said Arsen more loudly. "He's superstitious. All sailors are superstitious. A sensible man would have investigated."

"Loud as thunder it was," said Red the Sailor. "It's a ha'nt. It's a ghostie. It yells—'O, Arsen! Murdered for a woman!' it yells."

"Pipe down, Red," said van Chuch sharply. "If there was really any cry, Mr. Arsen would have heard it. You're a fool."

Schermerhorn bent almost double, creeping like a cinema Indian. "Merry trouble, dear old fools," he said. "Hope it *is* a ghost."

They crowded to the cabin door. Silence from within was absolute. All shrill sounds of the still afternoon pierced their eardrums as they waited. But no sound from the cabin where old Tim Grady died. Old Dawn pounded.

"Who's there? Open up! We're ready to shoot!"

Arsen lagged behind, and Red the Sailor lingered at the gangplank. "Go on in," suggested Arsen heartily. "What are we afraid of?"

Schermerhorn kicked the door wide. He bent beneath the crosstree. "I'll show you gay lads what-o," he promised. "Here's what—"

Over the threshold he stumbled. His arms flopped up. He leaped forward on fours like a greyhound. Between his long legs squirmed out a little writhing figure, dodging between the arms which entangled as they reached for him. It was Greasy Pete Lopez, in his right hand (so quick and cunning) the heavy serpent knife! None dared to shoot. Steel flashed in Pete's lifted hand.

Old Dawn braced himself. His black eyes were furious. "You little hound! Get him! I'll get him!" He knocked Ike Duval aside and leaped for that squirming fellow. His old arms were tough.

The blade flashed. The knife plunged into his ribs, pulled out again.

Before he had fallen, holding hard to his breast, hoarsely gasping, Greasy Pete had dodged past Ike and van Chuch. He bounded towards the gangplank. With blood-curdling scream and threatening bloody blade he bowled Red the Sailor aside. He leaped to the dock and loped madly away, quick as those coyotes from whom he'd learned his tricks.

Ike jerked at his gun. He snapped it over his wrist. He spat out shots. Greasy Pete vanished in the palm groves. On sturdy legs van Chuch and Ike Duval beat through the palms after him, from the river to the Royal Poinsettia clear down to the bay front. But it would be a long dark day before they would see Greasy Pete again.

"So he's the ghostie's been swiping my eight-bells chow," growled Red. *"I* warn't afraid o' him. I'd like to break his neck myself. He swiped a chicken san'wich offen me last night."

Old Colonel Dawn lay on the *Thorn's* white deck, pale and still. Through shirt and coat welled a little bubble of blood, so old and thick from that old stiff heart. Arsen felt his breast, which was still fluttering. They broke off a door; and put him on it tenderly; and carried him away.

That night Arsen telephoned Anthony in New York. A hardness strange to him had fallen on Wigley Arsen, a terrified determination at the face of death. He could hardly speak over the singing wires.

"Anthony, Greasy Pete Lopez stabbed Colonel Stoughton Dawn; and he's dying. He's dying! His heart blood's going fast—"

The singing wires seemed to tremble. Arsen felt electricity tingling his hand.

"I'm coming at once!" he heard the singing wires.

Anthony Anthony coming to Biscayne, where Ike Duval awaited with the law! The telephone had gone dead. Arsen rang up again.

"Anthony! Are you listening? That serpent knife you had—"

Anthony swore. "I told you I gave it back to Tim Grady. It was his."

"Anthony," asked Arsen darkly, pressing his mouth to the transmitter. "Do you still think I'm a fool? Anthony?"

But the connection was dead.

LXIII. WHY THOSE TEARS, LADY?

ROSE DAWN was staring in her mirror. Looking for those wrinkles, perhaps, which Laurence had said would come. Dark crescents below her clear blue eyes had deepened. She pulled up an eyelid and saw veins upon the ball.

Her mother pounded on the door. "Rose! Rose! What are you doing? I won't let you not mind me. Behave yourself! Let me in!"

The door was locked. Rose waited silently. Again she looked in her mirror.

Glance for glance she was answered back. The glass held as much beauty as the gazer, though less immortal soul. Yet why speak of a soul where beauty is concerned? Many men would love no more than that image in the glass.

A soul is nothing much. It may be saved, be washed, be born again, be defeated, suffer anguish, fall in love. Beauty is much more. Men crawl on their knees for *it,* and spend money on it, and sigh for it, and want to marry it, and bleat and grunt and baa at it, and offer *their* useless souls to it. There is a gift measurable in dollars and cents; or in imported cars and chinchilla wraps, if beauty prefers to take its pay more ladylikely.

But Rose Dawn had a soul. Old Tim Grady, Higgleson Todd, van Chuch, Gay Deleon, Schermerhorn, Arsen, had loved no more than that image in the glass; had loved a lovely face which soon must wither, gold curls which soon must fade, blue eyes which soon must shadow. John Dawn had loved her. He of all men alone had loved her for her tender spirit.

Rose Dawn was crying in her peculiar whimpering way, pouring no tears, voicing no rending sobs. Mrs. Higgs had taught her long ago that it is not nice to give way to passions.

Rose smoothed her shining curls with nervous fingers, she darkened the sedgy lashes which fringed her clear blue eyes. She touched her lips with scarlet. Patted pink into her cheeks. Rubbed the shadows below her eyes. Lovely, lovely Rose Dawn! No man might know your heart was stone.

"You let me in, Rose. I never saw you so disobedient!"

Rose shuddered. She had never disobeyed her mother before. It was as terrible as the first time a man curses God.

Mrs. Higgs's frizzled blond locks appeared over the transom. She was standing on a chair in the hallway. Her little blue eyes twinkled furiously. Her wagging chin rested on the transom ledge, making her head bob up and down.

"What are you primping yourself up for? What are you doing these days? I'll not stand for it. I got a mother's rights! Let me in!"

Rose stood up, her back to her dressing table. Still afraid; but defiance grew in her, such as Higgs had never seen.

"I'm going to see Colonel Dawn," Rose said steadily to that frizzled fury at the transom. "He's dying. I want him to take me as a daughter! Ma, Ma, don't think I'm disobedient. But he's all that's left of Johnny Dawn—"

She stopped a sob. She put her handkerchief to her mouth.

"You won't!" howled Higgs. "You'll have nothing to do with them Dawns! We're through with them! I hope the whole race dies and rots, son and father! Now, you mind me! I'm going to get you married all pretty to Padriac. Let me in! Let me in! I'll make you regret this, young lady!"

"I'll never marry any one," whispered Rose steadily. "I've got my own life. It's mine! It's mine!"

"Well, of all unnatchel children!" gasped Higgs. "What is the world coming to? You impudent young one! Let me in! I'm going to take you away. We're going to leave Biscayne at once!"

Rose shook her head. She had defied her mother and found that she still lived on. Lightning did not smite her. She still retained her senses. Strange it was. From her earliest recollection Ma Higgs had taught her that things unimaginable happen to children who defy their parents. God always makes them idiots and sends them down to Hell.

"I'm going to see Colonel Dawn," she said lowly. "And then I don't care if I die." She shuddered. "No," she whispered. "My mind is made up."

Mrs. Higgs grew frightened. "All I've done for you, dearie," she sobbed, using that tearful recourse which never failed. "O, you don't know how I've toiled and slaved and sac'ificed to make you what you are. You don't know what I've gone through!" Loudly she wailed. "O, you ungrateful girl!"

"My mind is made up," Rose whispered again, not moved by these wet tears.

"You'll never know—oo-hoo!" Mrs. Higgs wept, "what it is to have the child you've loved—oo-hoo!—turn against you—oo- hoo!—and want to live their own life. All I've done—oo-hoo!—"

"I wish I had a child of John Dawn to love," said Rose. "I wish I had a brave, fierce boy-child like John Dawn."

Mrs. Higgs dried her tears quick as they had come. Her little eyes winked furiously. "You shut up!" she said angrily. "What'd have happened to your career with a baby! How'd you have earned a living for us? What'd have come of *me!* O, more poisonous than a elephant's tusk is the ingratitude of a selfish child!"

Rose stood firmly, showing no relenting. Her throat felt thick, but she would not let her mother see her cry. Her defiance had not lessened. After the first daring stand, defiance becomes easier, defiance of God or king or parent.

"Let me in! You won't? I'll make you regret it, young lady!" foamed Higgs, trying to crane her neck through the transom. "I'll tell you something 'll make you sorry! I'll wash my hands of you! I'll leave you! I'll disown you! I'll go to New York and marry Bellbender! *He*'ll respect me. Bellbender will beat me right!" cried Mrs. Higgs, losing her tongue. "Wart? Wart? You don't care! We'll buy rubles and casties! We'll eat gold plates! We'll bail in a sattleship that'll make that little dinky *Thorn* look like cheese! I'll disown you! I'll cast you off!"

"You can't disown me, Ma," said Rose quietly. "After all, I'm your daughter."

"You're not! You're not!" screeched Higgs. "Don't call me Ma again. You're nothing but the daughter of a traveling parson I got in Evansville, Illinoy; and I made Higgs think you were mine so he would marry me. All I have done for you! All I've tried to teach you right! All I've made you what you are! I'm through! You're no daughter of mine!"

Rose put her hand to her throat. "What are you saying!"

"I'm not shraying, I'm s'ieking!" shrieked Mrs. Higgs. "Bah! Bah! Daughter of a traveling parson! Might know no good 'd come of you! Oo-hoo! How I've worked for you! I've given you everything. Oo-hoo! I married you to ten million dollars. Oo-hoo!" She stopped her tears. "Let me in!" she howled. "I'll tend to you! I'll whip you till you can't sit down!"

She tried to climb through the transom. Her struggling heels kicked the chair from beneath her. Rose had fleet vision of Mrs. Higgs's gilded curls, of her little eyes popping out of her puffy cheeks, of her fat arms waving in the air. Something hit heavily on the hallway carpet. Something staggered up and began to swear. Something walked furiously away. Mrs. Higgs was off to marry the Reverend Doctor Bellbender.

Rose Dawn put her head in her hands, not crying. She fell on her bed, lying face down, mute as a woman dead. For a long hour she lay, dry of eye and throat. She had loved her mother.

She opened up her watch, staring at a little picture of John Dawn pasted in it. His dark angry eyes stared out at her. His long black hair seemed to wave in winds. He was a man alive.

Other lovers, yes. Other lovers many. But the first love, and the true love, may not be forgotten ever.

Ah, why those tears, Rose Dawn? You did not weep for old Tim Grady. Your eyes were dry for Deleon.

LXIV. NIGHT RAIN

IN his dreams old Colonel Dawn was raving. No more than a husky remnant of man, dry as a sloughed locust shell, as a peascod, he looked in the dim-lit dark. Much blood had come from that old heart. His breast was bandaged.

Heavy on the windows was the night rain.

"...Johnny! What mischief have you been up to now, boy?"

"No, no," murmured the sedate nurse, smoothing his pillow. "This is Miss Twine."

The old man half aroused, stirring his head. "I'm a nuisance," he whispered. "All old men...a nuisance... Ought to shoot 'em."

Once more the dreams for old Dawn. And awakening once more. And dreams. Fitful shadows flickered in corners. A fitful shadow was the old man's life.

"You must be brave, and fight for life," Miss Twine advised.

" ... An old man.... *He* never fought for life.... Threw it away ... a pebble.... Wild boy was Johnny... braver than brave... Let me go...."

"I remember seeing him years ago," said Miss Twine brightly, fighting in her own way for old Dawn's life. "It was in a picture called 'Hearts Afire.' "

"... Years ... years ago.... How many years has Hell?"

"I'm sure I don't know!" gasped Twine primly, straightening her cap. "I remember him as a very daring actor. He rode his horse straight off a cliff. I nearly had a spasm, and pressed the hand of a man I didn't know. But I was young and foolish then. Straight down to the water John Dawn dropped—"

"I remember. . . . No other man dared do it. . . . Horse was killed. Brave. . . ."

"Many the girl who loved him," said Miss Twine with a sigh.

"He loved . . . one."

Old Dawn fluttered his hand, and Twine understood he wanted a photograph from the table beside him. She laid it on his breast. His hand dropped over it. Twine looked at the picture's back, on which was scrawled in bold careless letters: "For the Old Man, from John Anthony Dawn." Taking it gently up, she looked at John Dawn's face. He was in naval officer's uniform. His long black hair was uncovered. His fierce eyes met hers steadily.

"... Never sorrowed for him.... The Dons ... not men of tears.... He went.... That was the end ... of it.... Brave, hard men ... the Dons.... Loved their women."

"I'll bet you were brave yourself when you were younger, Sir. O, I'll bet many the exciting time you had, and many the girl loved you!"

"... They'll remember ... Stoughton Dawn!"

He tried to lift himself on elbows, staring at the shadows, listening to the rain. "Old men ... may boast.... They knew Stoughton Dawn ... was brave.... Never flinched.... Fought the fight ... against the gates of Hell...." The old man collapsed. "Brave," he whispered. "But what good was it!"

"You look much like *him*, Sir. The same black eyes."

"... He was son to me ... in my old age.... I loved him! ... Dons not men ... of tears.... Yet sometimes I ... wish I could cry.... Tears don't come...."

"Tears are often best," said Twine. "They help the heart."

Dolorously down the windows washed the night rain. Water dripped. No lightning flashed, but somewhere was groaning thunder. Heavily boomed the sea. Night crept on silent feet. And ever everlastingly the monotonous whimpering of rain.

"I've forgotten what happened to him," said Twine. "Such a long time ago. He was torpedoed on a subchaser, wasn't he? It was too bad."

"...They don't ... remember old wars long," old Dawn whispered. "I've seen the fight myself.... I ... was a soldier! ... Carried the flag ... at Chickamauga.... You've heard of me ... the boy in gray.... Drummer-boy Stoughton Dawn ... led the charge ... once...."

"Surely I've heard of you," Miss Twine lied consolingly. "Does the world ever forget brave things?"

Old Dawn was pitched back again into delirium. He cried again for the charge. He shouted exhortations to old ghosts. And there in the darkness, there in the night, there to the sorrow of the beating rain, dead men died again about him!

"... Down the mountains.... Push them down! ... Who stands by me? ... Who'll go with me? ... Stand up! ... We're fighting yet! ..."

Twine began to sob. About that old man trooped the old dead. Silently the ranks went by, gray and gray, to the sound of music. Where are you, Stoughton Dawn? The drummer-boy is missing in those wraithy regiments.

"... Down on them with the steel! ... We'll fight our way clear yet! ... I say ... no man will stop us.... Who ... who goes with me? ..."

Unto the dead that cry! Arise, you dead, and drink the crimson wars!

Twine spoke softly. "That's the way to fight! Fight for life now."

Old Dawn tossed. He awoke. He whispered again for the picture.

"Like that ... when he went down... I'll see him soon!"

"Don't say that!" cried Twine piously. "I hope not! You must never give up."

"Give up ... the ship.... Johnny didn't give ... it up."

"I'm sure he didn't," said Twine, settling the old man back on his pillow as he strove to rise. "I'm sure he did his duty. So many men did their duty."

"... Sea-wasp ... off Finisterre.... That is Land's End....Then the deep water!"

"So many young men drowned."

". . . Drowned in the. . . . Sub got him . . . fighting gun for gun . . . to help a sinking . . . ship. . . ."

"You mustn't tire yourself." Twine patted coverings about him.

"It was very brave of him, I'm sure." She wiped her eyes. "*I* knew a man who died."

"Didn't want to live. . . He . . . never cared."

Silence, and the rain. Hoarsely beating, the bitter sea.

"But *she* was famous . . . when he died. . . . Widow of John Dawn . . . the brave. . . . Good advertising. . . . Her gold curls. . . . Wrote about 'My Hero Husband.' . . . She had sent . . . him out to die. . . . She wanted Gay . . . Deleon. . . . Did I see . . . her sitting at my side? . . . Johnny sat here . . . for a little while. . . . I have been dreaming."

"She is a beautiful woman," said Miss Twine. "Though blonds are fickle."

"Famous now, and rich. . . . I know she wanted to be rich. . . . God . . . knows why she's famous now. . . But I know why she's rich. . . ."

And Rose Dawn came softly through the door. She lifted up a black veil. Her eyes were red-rimmed. Miss Twine went towards her with a hand on lips. Rose knelt by the side of old Dawn's bed, clasping his hands between her palms.

Haggardly old Dawn stared at her. "Girl . . .girl . . ." he muttered.

"I had to come for *his* sake," Rose whispered, touching his withered old hands to her soft cheek. "We loved him, you and I. We knew!"

". . . You loved him! . . . You! . . . You wanted Deleon . . . . You . . . sent him out . . . to die . . . Girl . . . girl! . . . You didn't know . . . "

Rose put his hands to her lips. "It was a lie!" she sobbed. "I've loved him true. Only him. Believe me! You know I did. If you see him—before I do, ask him. He knows it now!"

"Girl . . . girl . . ."

"I love him!"

"Yes . . . you might . . . ."

"Believe me! It was his fierce temper sent him away, believing a lie. A lie done by Gay and Lopez, who hated him because he was so proud." Rose spoke swiftly and hysterically, not knowing if the old man listened. "Believe me!"

"You are very lovely . . . girl . . . The way your eyes . . . shine . . ."

Rose sobbed. Her tears were warm on his cold hands.

"I believe you . . . girl . . . Too near the time . . . when all is seen . . . to doubt . . . truth . . . Yet I have hated you . . . or tried to . . . Forgive me . . . ."

"Why, nothing to forgive," Rose whispered. "All, all the time, we make mistakes. We don't know the truth. So many mistakes! And then we're sorry for them. Sorry through years and years! Will you—will you call me daughter?"

"Why, yes, girl . . . Rose . . . daughter!"

"Will you let me kiss your forehead?"

The old man slept. He ceased to toss. A deep and dreamless sleep. Twine noted his pulse and temperature with satisfaction. Hour past hour Rose sat and held his hand. Tardily she arose, and drew on her black veil, and went out.

"He seems to have turned the crisis," Miss Twine whispered. "It needs some one to love you to make you want to live. I knew a man who died—"

So the night died. Twine yawned, consulting her watch to mark the slow minutes till seven of the morning.

Weary the rain. Dolorous the ocean. Eternal the night. With the dawn the rain died down. With the gray dawn, which lingered slowly.

Twine was aware of a shadow in the room. She startled, for she had heard no sound. A man stood with folded hands. He stood silently, and silently advanced towards the bed. Long midnight vigils had strengthened Miss Twine's heart. But the man moved so softly, and the room was so dark, that she was afraid she, like old Dawn, beheld the dead.

"You are some relative?" she asked. "You mustn't disturb him now!"

Black were the man's eyes as old Dawn's; his face thin; his dark hair close cropped. Miss Twine was uneasy beneath his fierce look.

"I've flown all night," he said, "twelve hours through the rain, from the Battery to here. Are you going to stop me?"

He sat down, stroking old Dawn's hand. He felt the slow pulse, listened to the heart. Miss Twine nodded assurance to the silent question in his eyes. "He's doing nicely." Old Stoughton Dawn awoke.

He whispered in a voice no louder than mist. "What's this? . . . Johnny. . ."

"No dream. It's me. I'm here, Old Man. I'm here!"

"Johnny. ... I can hear you . . . but I'm dreaming. . . . Dead. . . ."

"Hush, Old Man! Feel my hand. It's warm. I've come back, Old Man. Not dead—not dead, though John Dawn's dead. Listen—they call me Anthony!"

Grayer rose the morning. Rain clouds drifted clear from before a little sun. The world steamed with rain. In the gutters twittered early sparrows.

"She—she loves you yet," old Dawn whispered. "She was . . . here. . . I called her daughter. . . . She always loved. . . ."

Anthony covered his eyes. "I've learned," he said. "O, God, the liar's trick that made me go away from her! I've watched her. But I'm not worthy of her, Old Man. The dead are better dead. I can't come back!"

"Go back to her," whispered old Dawn.

"No!" Anthony's jaw was set. "No! She might forgive the dead; but me—"

Old Dawn fell into sleep with the morning. Silently Anthony arose.

"Nothing like a relative to cheer the sick," said Twine. "Blood is thick—"

"There is no blood!" said Anthony, stroking his white face.

Miss Twine turned away from his dark eyes, which seemed to look on death.

LXV. "GOOD-BYE, MY LOVER!"

LAURENCE SPENCER sat writing a poem. He wrote: "To Maveen." Crossed it out. Wrote: "Song of Farewell." Crossed that out. Wrote *Memini Mihi* and looked at it with pleasure.

" 'Remember me.' *That* will hurt her. Though I may have used it before."

Doubt came on him; the night was late, and shadowy with doubts. He thumbed a Latin dictionary. *"Memini mihi*—I remember me," he read.

Laurence crumpled the sheet and began a new one.

"Memento mihi," he wrote. So much for the title. The rest was easy.

"O, to you, the all unfaithful, in the vasty darkness wraithful," he wrote. He tore that up. "O, to you, the all remembering, in the sunset's fading embering," he began again. He swore decently and took a new sheet. "O, to you, the unforgotten when the dawn with dew is rotten—"

Laurence looked at this with evil eye. "Rotten!" he swore. He foraged around for inspiration; but all he could find was two empty candy-boxes and a small half-pint of gin. "Who's been eating my candy?" he growled. "Who the Hell?" He walked around, finally sitting down once more. He wrote—

"Long I loved you, true and tender—
Dead the heart which you have riven!
Take back the kisses you have given,
While I stalk away in splendor!"

Laurence spoke this verse aloud in a crooning wail. Horribly he moaned. "That will make her think!" he said, as he wiped his wet eyes.

Then, being angry with himself, he tore the verse to tiny tatters and scattered them on the rug. He began to pack his bag, throwing in fistsful of ties and socks, cramming them into the bags' open maws as though the bags were fledgling crows.

A Negro maid was humming a song outside his door. Only three nights before Deleon had gone out that door. Laurence imagined he could see Deleon's slinking form shadowy in dark corners.

"Good-bye, my lover . . . hum-m . . . tra-la . . . hum-m . . . hum-m. . . . Good-bye, my lover."

Sweet that mellow Negro tune, wordless and droning. A knock, and the black maid put her shining face inside the door. "Lady, 'm, say she lak see you, Mist Spenca, 'm."

"I'm packing," said Laurence crossly. "Tell her I'm packing."

The holy smoke closed the door. Down the corridor, drifting faint, died her song. ". . . Hum-m . . . tra-la . . . hum-m . . . Good-bye, my lover; good-bye. . . ."

Dark rain lowered without. Thick landward clouds were pouring up from ocean. Thirteen days of rain, said all wise old men. Thirteen days of rain, and storm at sea. Let the hurricane flags be lifted in the Caribbees! Let the great tornadoes gather! Let the sailors' women weep.

Maveen Grady was waiting in the lobby below. Singing low, the maid came down to her. "What did Mr. Spencer say, Jezebel?"

"He doan say nuffin'," explained the dark lady. "Hum-m . . . tra-la. . . ."

"Stop that whine! Did you tell him I wanted to see him?"

"No, 'm. I say lady, 'm, lak see him. Ain't got no time fo' ladies, he say."

"Tell him Miss Grady wants to see him. Tell him I'm sorry—"

She broke off, walking up and down. "No, don't tell him that. Tell him I'll see him."

"Yes, 'm. I'll tell 'im, 'm, you-all lak see 'im . . .Good-bye, my lover . . . hum-m . . . tra-la. . . . He busy, and he ain't got no time fo' trifling. . . . Good-bye. . . ."

"Stop that crazy song!" screamed Maveen. "You'll drive me out of my wits!"

"Yes, 'm," said Jezebel. "Yes, 'm, I'm going, 'm. Doan hit me, 'm. . . . Tra-la, tra-la. . . . Good-bye, my lover. . . ."

She approached Laurence's door again.

"Lady, 'm, still want to see you-all, 'm. She prowling aroun' downstai's. She Mrs. Grady."

"Mrs. Grady?" asked Laurence, feeling his heart tremble.

"Yes, 'm. One with green dress and red hai'."

"Tell her I'm in a hurry to catch my train."

"Yes, 'm. She say she bust ma head if you doan come down, 'm."

Laurence continued viciously to cram his bags. Jezebel slumped away, not caring much if her head should be busted or not. Singing, far away, dying: "Hum-m . . Good-bye, my lover, good-bye!"

Fat rain spattered. The ocean in fierce fear thundered at the shore. With that one astounding surge it subsided again to its low crooning.

Maveen walked up and down the common-room of the Poinsettia. Lights went out. She walked up and down. The night-clerk yawned at her, not silently, but with tears. She walked up and down. Rain poured. Bong! went a clock. Maveen wanted to tear something to pieces; perhaps more, she wanted a drink.

"Telephone Mr. Thornwood Clay's room," she told the clerk. "No, I don't want to speak to him myself. It's nothing important. Just tell him I'm willing now to marry him. That's all."

The clerk yawned off the message.

"Hum-m . . . tra-la. . . ." sang Jezebel.

Laurence had continued his packing with a shrug. Much may be lifted from shoulders with a gesture when one is twenty-eight. Other girls were in the world, even other red-haired girls. Laurence wondered if he cared for red hair. How about golden curls? How about the dark ringlets of little Bunnie Hoag?

What was love? What was a woman? Didn't an amoeba experience love's passion when it split and wiggled joyously away as two amoebas? What was woman more than the female of the species *Homo erectus sapiensque loquaxque?* What was woman more than woman? What was love more than Love?

A woman was an anthropoid, like the monkeys. (Laurence thought of Arethusa.) A mammal, like the whales. (He thought of Mrs. Higgs.) A vertebrate, like the fishes. (He thought of Mrs. Mallow.) The great angels ringing Heaven's fire might be zoologically lower, having six appendages like the insects, but no one wants to marry an angel. Laurence settled on this conclusion: Woman was only one step above the Simiidae, the ape, the gorilla, the chimpanzee, and the dog-faced baboon.

He remembered little Bunnie Hoag, who had run away without one word of farewell. Laurence was suspicious that she had run away with a bell-hop who had disappeared about the same time. Yet she had pretended she loved him. She had left a Harvard man, the grandson of a Sears, for a wop with a pimple on his nose. Laurence felt his eyes moist for shame and for her dear dark curls now lost.

On hands and knees he gleaned the floor, striving to gather again that verse he had torn up. Vain. He sat down and wrote another verse, reading it when it was finished in mournful monotone, letting his tears roll—

"You have left me eating the husks and the ashes,
Drunk with the salt of the bitterest lees.
And now for another your gayety flashes;
You take his embraces, you sit on his knees.
Your little heel cares not the hearts which it mashes."

Laurence intended to write a sixth line, but the rhymes of which he could think were "freeze," "cheese," and "fleas." He entitled this little heart-throbber "To Bonnie, the False." He tried to resume his biological thoughts. What is love? What is a woman? Woman is but—the universe. Knowledge comes, but love lingers. So it does at twenty-eight.

Laurence was nearly done with packing. He slammed open his closet door, which had been closed for days. As he stumbled about inside, his foot kicked something soft. There lay Bunnie in her little red dress, asleep on the floor.

He touched his hand to her forehead. He picked her up in his strong arms and swung her high, her dark curls falling on his shoulder. Her eyes slowly opened. Still Laurence thought he was seeing visions:

"I ran away," she whispered. "Mamma was going to punish me. I'm hungry."

"You've been hiding in that closet over three days!" Laurence gasped.

"Don't know how long," she nodded sleepily. "Couldn't find anything to eat except candy. What have you got to eat, Larry? I could devour stacks of fried eggs. It was exciting at first to hear mamma crying in the next room. I was afraid she'd feel bad. Some man came into your room late last night and started to open the closet door, but he ran out the window. I haven't dared to come out. O, I'm starved! I wish I had some chicken a la Maryland."

"I'll have to give you back to your mother, Bunnie," Laurence whispered, nuzzling her scented hair.

"Don't you dare!" She kicked a sleepy foot against his thigh. "She'll spank me to death. You've got to take me away with you, and we'll be married."

"And live happily ever after, Bunnie!" whispered Laurence, holding her close. He felt solemn and awful; and he had a vision of dozens of little dark-curled children running about the floor. For Laurence was a gynaecologist. "You'll be my wife!"

"Yes. I wish I had some mulligatawny, Larry. I wish I had some soup."

He seated her on his knees. "I've got something to read to you," he said softly. "It's called—'To Bunnie.' It's a poem."

"After a while," she said. "But now you must get me a great big enormous dinner from shrimp cocktail to cheese. And bushels and bushels of steak with mushrooms!" She clapped her hands imperiously. "Hurry!"

Laurence was delighted. It pleased him to be ordered around by women. He pressed her close.

LXVI. DEEP TIDES DROWN

ONE night of weltering stars had come in those thirteen days of hurricane. The ocean was thick as cold oil. No surge ran on it.

McGinty drove Anthony down beside the ocean. "Look ye, Mister-r Anthony! Did man iver see the like?"

Green fire coiled in the ocean depths. Slow ripples turned with light fair as the moon. Roller climbing heavily on roller shook out sparkles of emeralds. More than light of moon or of the doubtful stars, that cold green fire.

Wanly writhed the phosphorescence of the ocean, of the *Noctiluca,* flames of night. More numerous their infinitesimal bodies than seconds in eternity. Some mystic delight ravished their spirits to thin luminous flames. Their joy consumed the utter ocean. Heavily rolled the ocean, flaking to absinthe wine.

"Out beyond," said McGinty, casting his arm afar, "on Malimus Isle bides Gr'asy Pate, who struck the stroke at Colonel Dawn; and who ye're looking far-r far-r other reasons, I'm a-thinking, Mister-r Anthony. I till ye that because ye're a fri'nd o' mine. Do what ye will with it."

"He's got away, McGinty?"

"If Pate's got away, 'tis to there he's got. He has been a-biding his time, and now he's chased from off the *Thorn.* He has no place to turn! Ay, to there, to Malimus. We had it plotted—Gay, Pate, and me. 'Tis an isle of Hell, is Malimus! It belongs to auld King Garge; may divils rot him! 'Tis far-rty mile away by sea, or more or less. But there can ye git the liquor."

On the strand beside the glittering emerald ocean, a group of night bathers had built a high bonfire. Huge flotsam logs of driftwood burned in mighty holocaust. They laughed with roaring shouts for the tickling of the fire. Sparks rocketed up from them. The great logs hissed as flame ate their gnarled hearts. They twisted tortuously, and cracked in thousands. In glorious embers they fell to dissolution.

"Ah," snarled Dinnis McGinty, halting his car and looking long at those dim red figures moving about the great bonfire. " 'Tis the Gradys. There is he, that r-roaring rid-hid Paddy, image of auld Tim Grady. And there's the girl, and Mister-r Clay. 'Tis said they're being married. But who is that? And who is that who's walking out to sea? 'Tis Rose Dawn going out into the ocean!"

Three figures about the flawing fire, shielding their faces from the smoke. Wet bathing suits clung closely to Padriac and Clay. Padriac kicked a log into the fire's heart. Crimson shone his arms and face, diabolical and giant-strong. Once he looked up across the fire at the car where Anthony sat. His gray eyes were green as a cat's, shining with the ocean.

Rose was treading the sand, and now the inshore ripples. She stepped more deeply into slumberous green waters. She hesitated, dabbling her feet. It seemed presentiment of near disaster came to her heart. Yet the waters were lovely and bright. The waters were gleaming and warm.

Watching her, Anthony grew afraid, grew sick with dismal foreboding. No fear had he ever known before, not of himself and death. But Rose Dawn moved with such cold purpose; and there was something fatal in her manner.

"I'm going out!" she cried. "I'm going out!"

And it was as though she meant her bright light would go out. Who would go with her there? Ripples shook with quivering lights as she waded farther in. She was a goddess of the sea in those unearthly waters, walking in her element. No cold sea beast would dare to harm her, no waters smother and drown.

Her white arms lay extended over the ocean. A bubbling lane of fire trailed after her. Softly lapping, softly lipping, a comber kissed her breast, cascading it with jewels. Far and far into the night, into the cruel ocean.

Anthony heard a land bell begin to toll, as toll sea-dirges.

Breast to breast she met the sea. Pausingly she struck the tide with glistening arms. It was a vision of a dream; no life lived in this heavy world. No one could die. In another world she drifted away. Lowly thunder clapped. The hushed bell ringing, ringing, brought back muttering from the hanging clouds. And now Rose Dawn was deeply out. Far and far into the night, into the cruel ocean.

Faint came her voice beyond the veils of night. ". . . Deep water. . ."

Far and far into the night, uneager for the shore, she slowly passed. Old ocean wrapped her in clear billows. Her head was but a little flame which failed and died away out on the horizons.

The grassy fires of the sea grew dim. The stars were overcast; yes, many a star was overset. Swift as a curtain fell the blackness. The ocean was invisible, and black and round the world.

" 'Tis not Din McGinty would like to go that way. The auld sea is deep!"

That way for you alone, Rose Dawn, out in the drowning sea?

The land bell rang its dirge. "Gone!—Gone!—Gone!"

Far from the hidden waters came one cry.

Anthony leaped. Sands clotted his feet; he tripped over grass and flotsam and weed; the hard white shore beach was beneath his feet. He tore off coat and shoes, and threw himself into the black water.

Padriac was already beating out ahead of him, thick with drink, but strong and sure. Again came Rose Dawn's faint cry over the desolate wastes of ocean. It drove both men to fury. Anthony heard Grady's great gasping breath.

Cold waves passed over Anthony. He threshed on, sucking wind at the fourth stroke. He knew these seas, these tides, these drownings. These were salt of his blood, these tropic seas. Half clothed, he overtook Padriac, who swam with head too high. Their beating hands touched. Stroke for stroke they whipped the sea.

Anthony drew ahead, stroke for stroke. He pulled at the waters furiously. He tried to skim along them. O, leaden arms and feet!

No cry now at all. An eddy bubbled in the deep ahead of him. Sucking air, Anthony dived far down. Down, down in the restless strangling black he caught hold of a woman's hair, tangled like weeds. Upward with bursting heart he thrust for the precious air and the dark light of night.

Sobbing for breath, he trod waters. Rose Dawn's eyes were closed as if on everlasting dreams. Her dear gold curls trailed over her forehead. Up and down with dragging feet her body rocked in the slow ocean stir, her head lying on Anthony's arm. The sullen ocean, blackly washing over her breast, was more sensate than she.

"Gone!—Gone!—Gone!" the dirge bell rang.

Suddenly the under tides sucked at the swimmer. The ocean was shaken with thunder. Anthony clung to his love in the drowning tides, fighting back with insane fury the strength of the vast deep. He held her head upon his arm and fought towards the shore. Salt was in his eyes and on his lips, but it was not salt of the sea.

Near shore Padriac swam up to him, sputtering: "Let me have her!"—"Away!" gasped Anthony. Grady struck at him, striving to pull the girl away. They passed blows in the water. Padriac went down in a swirl. In his arms, lifting her high, Anthony brought her up the shore.

For an hour giant logs crackled. Their cinders dulled. Down roared cataclysmic rain. The world was drowned. Thunder muttered. Far from the town beyond Bay Biscayne, church bells were clamoring: "Gone!—Gone!" Anthony raved at them. For an hour he fought for Rose Dawn's life.

The sea had loved her tenderly, and death had loved her tenderly. Had loved her eyes, which were the tropics. Had loved her beautiful body. They were loth, the sea and death, to let her go.

"Get back," said Anthony to those around, for he saw her eyes stirring.

"What are you telling me?" asked Padriac hoarsely, giving Anthony's knees a buffet. "Who are you, giving orders to a Grady? I'll take no word from you!"

"Get back!" said Anthony, with a flash of his eyes.

Clay held Maveen beneath the shelter of his arm while the storm poured. She whimpered like a puppy. McGinty had fashioned himself a shelter of palm-fronds, and in his den he cursed and spat and growled at the great ocean. With threatening arms Padriac paced up and down the shore, damning the hurricane.

Anthony called to the girl who slept so stilly. And again he called. She made no answer. But her heart was stirring. Blood was in her sea-cold cheeks.

He whispered. "Rose! . . . If you ever loved me, Rose-girl, remember now! It's Johnny here with you! . . . I've got my arms about you! Don't you know my voice, dear little love?"

Her eyes opened faintly, and she seemed to know him. Some word she whispered. Her arms tried to tighten. But she lay cold within his embrace again.

"Forgive me, Rose-girl! Forgive me, crimson Rose!—"

Her hair was in Anthony's nostrils. His fingers felt their way up and down her cold smooth arms. The pulsing heart was stronger. Anthony knew the fight was won. He had stolen her from the sea.

Surges rose upon the stormy ocean. Winds growled; and blew loud; they screamed. The rain was heavy with tornadoes. Lightning streaking down the sea showed one ship far out, laboring ill. Rockets went up from her, dull scarlet stars fading soon. The loud winds whistled with high laughter.

The last ember of the fire was drowned. Nothing left of the giant merry logs but little crisps of ash, sodden in the sand. Chips of charred wood.

"So die the old loves," thought Anthony. "So all the old loves perish. Better had I stayed dead! Better—"

The church bells rang from town, across the bay, beyond the curtain of the rain. "Come!—Come to death!" they rang. "Come!—Come!"

Anthony lifted his dark eyes and understood that sound.

He wrapped his coat about Rose Dawn and laid her softly in the sand. "Take care of her," he whispered to Maveen. "Watch out for her well. I put her in your trust. Don't let her think too unkindly of me if—something happens."

He spoke to McGinty and went away in the rain.

"Come!—Come to death!—Come!—Come!"

LXVII. THE BLACK KING

BELLS ringing in dismal midnight. Church bells clamoring as the storm comes down. Bells ringing for the hurricane, swaying, mournful, crazed with sound.

Black clouds from out the night of ocean. The rain which beats upon the shore has not yet reached the bay and town. Air is thick and choking. No wind blows. Over the sea hang fringes of a still tornado. The waves froth, the waves toss, the waves billow high. Frantically they throw aloft their arms as they run northward. Old ocean beats his breast. Yet no wind at all is risen. The air is still. Heavily hangs the hushed tornado.

The dreadful blow hangs suspended. Clouds' iron doors, riven by lightning, hold back the hurricane. The old ocean beats his breast, fearing scorpion whips, the old remembered knouts. Whimpering rises the cry of old ocean, an ululation of many waters.

The bells! Continually swing their sad hammers. They moan to the dull thunder, monotonous, full of dolor. To no holy hour of prayer they call. Drowning bells! They ring in midnight's dreadful doom!

Hushed murmurings rise in midnight beneath that clangor of bells. Vague, muttering as the ocean, sounds the low murmur of many men torn out of sleep. Inoppugnable as hurricane, formless as chaos, the gathering mob! The mob which swells at midnight. Hear its murmuring mingling with the bells!

"Good thing old Colonel Dawn is on his bed," says X, trotting down the road.

Says Y, tucking his night-shirt tails into his pants: "Good thing. You said it, X. Old Colonel's dreadful man to go against, and he's stern set on law. Hi-hi! Hi-hi! Hi-hi!"

"God help 'im now," says Z. "Say, I was sound asleep. Ain't this a hour?"

Stars blaze hazily in the west. No stars at all in the east. On midnight streets men walk aimlessly up and down, and swirl in knots, and whisper together. Sweat trickles on their foreheads. No man looks straightforward. Their shaking fingers point southward to the cypress swamp.

Van Chuch and Todd are up and on the streets. They walk about, oppressed by the dreadful murmurings. The air they breathe is lourd. Heavily lies the eastern hurricane. Mutters the ocean. Toll the bells.

"What the devil is happening, Todd?"

"Don't ask me, van Chuch. Don't ask me."

Shadows of midnight stretch out lean claws. The eyes of the darkness are bitter; its countenances foul as reptiles. Far away from the cypress swamps sounds one stilled scream, inchoate, terrible in its pain.

A rat of a man runs out of an alleyway, slinking, skulking, the dirtiest shadow of the dirty night. Rat he is, or snake; or perhaps (as he calls himself) coyote. His breath foams. His eyes burn fiercely. He has vanished out on the swamp road. In his quick right hand is something sharp, the heavy serpent knife!

"Stop him! Get him! That was Lopez, as I'm a living man! Where was he hiding? Where's he gone? What's he doing now?"

"We'll get him yet," says Todd. "I have a thing or two I want to pay him back. O, damn those howling bells! You might think that God were dead."

"What's happening, Todd? Why are they running?"

"I don't know, van Chuch. But I say to you, van Chuch, that I don't like it.—Hey, you, stop a minute! What's the excitement? Where are you running?"

Men go past on steady, doglike feet. Many carry guns, pistols; some have lengths of rope, ship-ropes, packing-ropes, clothes-lines. They gasp. Small boys follow the men, shrieking and laughing to each other. The little son of X wears only a nightshirt and a woolen cap. Every one takes the road to the cypress swamps. Under tunnels of trees they disappear, going the way that Pete Lopez has run. The air is vibrant long with their hoarse breathing.

"Let's follow 'em, Todd!"

"Say; say, let's tell old Dawn of this. He ought to know what's up."

Now the bells swinging, swinging, gaining rhythm, gaining passion. Other bells, far beyond the reaches of the outmost winds, take up that rolling song. Insane their tongues, a chant of madness, a horrible song in the ghostly hour when the hid sun sweeps past the nadir. It will echo down to Hell, the music of those brass church bells! Hark to their cry!

"They've got the nigger Tom! Run—run—run, all you men! Come—come—come! They've got black Tom!"

Fear walks the deep. A night-giant wave breaks on the hidden shores. Creation trembles with a groaning. Dully the thunder rumbles. Rain has struck beyond the bay on Key Mimayne. Lightning shows a ship far out, laboring ill. Rockets go up from her, dull scarlet stars. . . .

Rifles bark, sharp as dogs; not with the brave laughter of a volley, but yelpingly, fired by cowardly hands which lie in ambush, bickering from the dark.

"They've caught black Tom!"

Cook has left his kitchen, and loafer his lamp-post. Barber has dropped his shears, soda-sizzler his shaker, teamster his reins, lawyer his books. Bridegroom has left his sweet young bride, old man his old wife. Priest and pander, blackguard, banker, bum, bootlegger—they run towards the cypress swamps. Cars sweep with a roar on the night roads, swift streaking cars, little wheezing cars, slow elephant trucks picking up running men.

Men wipe their lips as they hurry, for like slaver on them is that salt fierce taste.

Hoarsely clamor bells. Hell hears. The hidden hurricane threatens the day of doom.

Farmers in lonely dwellings hear those tocsins ringing, and leap from bed. Fishermen leave their huts beside the dark sea. Menials in respectful black hurry half-clad from the gardened palaces of the exclusive rich. Ocean captains leave their cabins. From far as bells can ring men are gathering.

"Come—come—come! They've caught black Tom, who ripped the soul from Deleon!"

Bear up the fiery cross, and wave it as a banner! Fierce hurricanes of death, unleash your ravening whelps! Spew up, old ocean, dead men's bones!

"Come—come—come! They've caught black Tom, who did to death Tim Grady!"

Hark to the roar! The air is drowned!

"Come—come—come! They've caught black Tom, who put his hands on beautiful Rose Dawn!"

O, whimpering seas. O, hurricanes!

"Come—come—come! They've caught black Tom, who wronged your maiden Arethusa!"

Guns flash as spears. The clappers of the bells are growing hot.

"Come—come—come! They've caught black Tom, who slew two of your posse men, and shot Boosten Claude through the heart!"

Clap shut your eyes. Stifle your heart.

Out of the cypress swamps, out of the fastnesses of the black king, boils the tumultuous mob. It rolls along a great gory dragon, foam in its jaws.

And what is this giant which stumbles along, falling, kicked up, hauled up from the mud and dust? What is this thing which looks like man? What do the boots kick? What feels the crashing cudgels? What is this stricken by the smudgy tossing torches? Whose wrists are strangled deep with barbed fence wire? What is this thing which groans?

Black Tom! O, son of the great kings! O, warrior of the hosts of spears! O, leader of the lances in the jungle! O, Ethiopia, Thinite gods! O, fierce and mighty heart!

Hoarse roars the clamoring cry. Brazenly beat the bells. They are one, those dreadful thunders, the solemn sound of death.

O, learned man! O, gentleman! If you knew more, you would know less. If you knew less, you would know more, black Tom, king of men. Black Tom! Tom Jefferson, M.D.! Doctor Thomas Jefferson!

Dancing along at the head of the mob, like the lipping tongue of the dragon, who is this fierce frenetic man? Who is this shouter? Who slashes air with steel? Who pants with crazy laughter?

Pete Lopez, Greasy Pete, seer of the stars! He leaps on high, and swirls and dances, for seven devils out of Hell burn in his crazy heart.

Death—death—death to the dog!

"Got a rope?"—"Take that, you smoky gorilla!"—"Out o' the way, sonny. 'S ain't no place for little shavers."—"Where's old Colonel Dawn?"—"We'll tend to him if he butts in!"—"God! Let me at him! God!"

High above all an old man's shrill senile cackles, the voice of a small boy consumed with giggles.

"Easy, boys! He won't last."—"His eyes is closin' already. Give 'im air!"—"Whose party is this, anyhow! Hell!"—"Get away, buddy, I tell you!"—"In the name of the crucified thieves!"—"Name o' Jesus—"

Spike and Stubb, strong and stern, stand in the road against the terrible mob. Their broad shoulders are set. They raise aloft their arms. "Stand back!"—"Hand over your prisoner!"—"To the law!"—"In the name of Colonel Dawn!"

Men swirl about them. Spike goes down, and comes up with bloody head, battling ten men at once. Stubb hits about him blindly, with two men riding on his great broad shoulders.

"Break away!"—"Surrender your man to the law!"—"We warn you!"—"In the name of Colonel Dawn!"

"To Hell with all your Dawns! We got this nigger now!"

The dragon rolls to the side, overflowing on a muddy field. It smashes down a wire fence. It sops in muck. It sprawls, stumbles, rolls over a ditch. With panting tongues it gathers towards a lean burnt pine.

Pete Lopez jerks off coiling strands of barbed wire from the fence. Men gather firewood, draff and stubble, piling it about the lean burnt pine. A dreadful pyre. And now men brace their feet and haul the barbed coils steadily round and round the pine and the dying giant.

The wood begins to crackle. Flames twist.

"God be merciful!" screams X. "I can't watch it!"

He takes sure aim, and shoots.

Compassionless, and altogether beasts. Not altogether, for other rifles rattle from the dark.

And now with a loud cry, van Chuch and Todd are staggering over the muck, supporting old Colonel Dawn between them! The fury of the old man's eyes burns hotter than the fire.

Van Chuch is fighting right and left with fists. He strikes out with roaring ocean curses. The blood of war is in him, Berserker rage of the brave lords of the sea. Y rushes up to meet him. Y is a simple grocer, thick of thought and speech; but now turned to a red beast. Van Chuch's fist catches Y at the chin, and he crashes back into the crackling fire.

And Todd has lifted up a fence rail, and he clears a circle about him. He grows young again, and shouts a college football cheer. "Hold 'em— Hold 'em, Michigan! Get back! What are you doing to the law? The law!" He swings his great fence rail till his bald head is all asweat.

And Spike and Stubb have taken out their billies and they knock men aside. Spike hurls himself on Z, who falls before he's hit, bellowing like a slaughtered cow.

"You swine! You bestial cattle! O, you red dogs of Hell!"

Old Dawn's finger points to man past man. His terrible glances consume them. He shakes with soundless fury. The madness of the Dawns, the anger of the men who do not forget! The dragon melts, and falls in shards. Men stumble and crawl and fall away. They drop their rifles in the stubble. They hurl their torches far away, crimson arcs against the storm.

Greasy Pete Lopez, running hard with fear, lets loose a frenetic cry. For Anthony is coming, leaping towards the breaking mob. Eyes of the dead! Eyes of dead John Dawn! Has the hurricane released him? Has the ocean let him go?

Wet with the rain and the sea, fierce Anthony stands by old Dawn. His arm goes about the old man's shoulders. The dragon has become a thousand worms, slinking away, crawling away into the merciful dark. A sob arises, hoarse as the sobbing ocean.

"You thought the Dawns were dead!"

The bells are silenced.

Out of the night clouds smash down the first hot bullets of the rain.

"Let us pray," whispers an old, old man.

They jerk off their hats, kneel down, and pray as the rain crashes.

But you, black Tom, king of men, hear not their murmuring voices. For you the voice of Death, which is the Black King. For you the voice of Immortality, which is the White King. For you the voice of your dreadful God, who is the King of Kings!

LXVIII. NEW MOON

BLACK dawn stirs. The rain grows faint. Cloud cannot be marked from cloud, for all the world is a pall of mist more terrible than darkness.

Down on the *Thorn's* wet decks men creep again in search of the hunted. They stir like shadows in the dismal murk. Their feline feet are soft with doom. Seven men once again in search of the hunted. They watch warily. Their hearts tremble. They hold fast to guns in their pockets.

Beware, Anthony! Beware, John Dawn! You do not hear their silent approach. But the mast of the *Thorn* casts reflection on the waters like a gallows.

Ike Duval goes first of all those men. His stone jowls crunch; his eyes are narrowed. After him follows Padriac Grady, muttering and a little drunk. Van Chuch is hushed and stern, somewhat saddened, somewhat morose. Todd has set his teeth as brass, and his great bald head shines inhumanly. Arsen is there, and Spike and Stubb, right and left fists of the law are they, and they know how to smite. Manacles clangle in their pockets.

Through all her sharp length the *Thorn* is rumbling. Her heart sings for the ocean. Pale smoke flows from her stack. Her bow is pointed down surging Black River. Half an hour more—

Too late, Anthony! Too late. The cruel dogs are on you!

They did not find him in the engine room, nor in the white-and-gold cabin. Cunningly they opened all doors, watching for sudden shots. They fell on him at last, seeing him by a red lightning flash, in that place where he would be least expected, old Tim Grady's cabin.

Ike Duval burst in the door and caught Anthony by surprise before he had time to lower hand to pocket. Gun level, Ike Duval advanced. He felt over Anthony's pockets. He thrust the muzzle of his gun against Anthony's heart.

"Anthony Anthony, you are arrested for the murder of Timothy Grady!"

Anthony said nothing.

"Get McGinty, boys!" roared Ike. "He's down in the engine room. I'll handle Mr. Anthony. You, Anthony—don't laugh at me! I've got you dead. You came to Biscayne in disguise on the day Tim Grady was murdered. You stayed to kill him. And in the morning you went away. I've traced you, Anthony! I've traced your every step. Step up, Stubb! Put the irons on him!"

"Anthony! Tony! Why did you do it?" cried Arsen. "I always thought you were one of my friends." He shook his head and pulled his brown moustaches.

River waves threshed against the *Thorn's* plates with a frothy wash.

"I came here," said Anthony slowly. "I had to see Rose Dawn! Something you told me in New York once, Ike, made me learn the dirty trick Pete Lopez had played on me. I had to see Rose Dawn! But when I got here I couldn't speak to her. I went away again."

"But you stayed to kill Tim Grady, Anthony!" said Ike, thrusting his heavy face into Anthony's. "If not you, then Rose Dawn—"

"I'll kill the man who says a word against Rose Dawn! Stand back! I'll kill him with my hands!"

No one said anything against Rose Dawn.

"*I* never said anything," muttered Arsen. "MacErcher and Wiggs and the whole world might lie about her. But I'd never believe it."

Padriac Grady stumbled around with steps which were like Tim Grady's heavy ghost. "You seem to be pretty damned intimate with her," he growled. "Who are you, anyway?"

"Put the irons on him, Stubb!"

They were wary. They were afraid of him, for he was a desperate man, and they knew he would stop at nothing. They were pressed for breath. The little cabin where Tim Grady had died was dark.

Sheet lightning flashed red, fearfully carmining Anthony's face. Storm beat on the roof, washing heavily down the decks. The *Thorn* rocked, mad with fear of great hurricanes which struck the outer ocean. Again lightning flashed red.

"Something more important than Tim Grady for me now," said Anthony. "I'm going to get Pete Lopez! You think I killed the old man?—He killed himself!"

Higgleson Todd looked curiously at Anthony; he was shrewd, and accustomed to tearing the truth from lying witnesses. Again lightning, Arsen shivered. Padriac Grady breathed heavily. It was an ominous sound in that room where Grady died.

"What are you trying to say, Anthony?" asked Todd.

"Tim Grady was terrified that night," said Anthony. "Something happened to him at the last, making him more afraid, making him hate Rose Dawn. He tumbled back into his cabin, onto that bed there, and reached for the will drawn by Wiggs. As he signed it, and put out his light—it's clear enough now, if you look—his hand or his head knocked down from that shelf right above him his books, and his papers, and his diary. And down came that weighted knife! It's plain enough."

Spike and Stubb nodded as solemnly as elephants. "I'd always suspected something like that," said Stubb. "Had killed him," finished Spike, bound to say his say.

"It seems reasonable," said van Chuch at last. "I've handled that knife once or twice, and I remember bow overbalanced its blade was."

"Could it fall hard enough without a hand?" asked Todd, his eyes narrow.

"It was sharp," said Anthony. "It fell hard enough."

Spike and Stubb wrapped their coats about their ears, and went out into the rain. Todd wiped his head, nodding slowly. Padriac Grady leaned against the post of the cabin door, sullenly scowling. Anthony called through the little porthole to Arsen, who was slumping away down the deck.

"No hard feelings, 'Wig.' Here's my hand."

Anthony tried to put his hand through the porthole, but it could not open wide enough. Todd noted that. No hand could have gone through there, not even Pete Lopez's womanish hand, not even the slender hand of Rose Dawn.

Below decks the ungeared engines rumbled.

"You did me a good turn once, Ike," said Anthony, "when you told me about Pete Lopez. Are you my man?"

"I am, Sir! Yes, Sir!" Ike touched his derby. "I'm going out, if you're going out, Mr. Anthony, to get that Pete Lopez."

Padriac was last to leave. His eyes were wrathy; he clenched his fingers. "Who are you?" he asked with a trace of fear. "How do you get the right to take out my ship! What hold have you on Rose? You seem to own the earth, and all that's in it!" He walked down the plank; on the dock he turned. "I've a good mind to stop you!" he threatened unconvincingly. "You butt in where you haven't any business. Who in God's name are you!"

Mad tornadoes sweeping up from ocean! And the *Thorn* stands ready for the sea. Bravely shine her lights. But the sea is black.

Thundering surges crush the coral shores. Black River is a froth and foam, palms bending on its banks. All of oily shallow Bay Mimayne is turned to the sky. Her floors are swept clean. The deepest fish are bruised and beaten.

Hurricane! Pray for the dead.

Over the coral keys sweep billows, roar on roar, blow on blow, combers unendingly, tottering the universe. Key Mimayne, shutting off bay from ocean, is drowned deep. Wrecks float over its low shores.

Van Chuch clings to a pile on the quay as the *Thorn* sheers away from the dockhead. White ripples wash between. Those waters widen.

"You're mad, Anthony!" van Chuch bellows. "No man would take her out with twenty hands below. And you have two. Don't you know the ocean?"

"Know . . . it well!" drifts back the cry. Anthony stands at the wheel, his eyes straight ahead to the scourged horizons. "It tried to get me once . . . van Chuch. . . . But here I am!"

"Ay, there you'll not be long!" growls van Chuch, wiping rain from his face.

The *Thorn's* engines spit contempt at destruction. River tides battle with it, giving it no headway. Red and green her sidelights. Masthead lights grow yellow as dawn increases, as the dull day comes. Unbent to the winds Anthony stands, staring far out at the ocean.

"Somewhere between here . . . and Malimus . . . is Pete Lopez . . I'll get. . ."

"Are you coming back?" screams van Chuch, cupping his hands and straining outward. "Are you coming back, Anthony?"

". . . Back from Malimus . . . with Lopez. . . . Tell Colonel Dawn . . ."

"What?" shouts van Chuch. "O, this damned rain! I can't hear!"

". . .Tell Rose Dawn that when I . . .come back. . . "

"I'm listening, Anthony! I get you, Anthony! Give me the message!"

Drowning winds. Lightning strikes a tree near shore. Blue smoke goes up, and the shriek of living wood.

". . . Rose Dawn . . . . If I do come back. . . . Tell her if I do . . . come back . . ."

"What shall I tell her?" van Chuch bellows. "I can hear yet, Anthony! Anthony! Anthony! Look at that tornado! Man, you're raving crazy! Death—"

Faint is Anthony's voice now. The wind tosses it. ". . . Not fate I . . . should die thus. . . . Not the utter ocean . . ."

Howls the southeast wind. Van Chuch shouts again as a smash, of storm almost topples him to the swirling waters. Trees crash. Van Chuch falls to his hands and trees, sprawling down the banks of the river. The *Thorn* rocks in the waters of the bay. She stands outward to the ocean.

Past the storm clouds, which fly frantically north-northwest, comes beating up from out the whirlpools of the innermost Carib seas, from out the wastes impassable where winds have birth, the illimitable hurricane! The hurricane wind racing at two hundred miles an hour! The sky is ripped to tatters. On those threshing wings is borne the wrath of the unregenerate void, the stark fury of the fates. Old ocean stands on edge, in a mighty cliff of waters. Old ocean shrieks; its bowels are ripped from it.

"Anthony! Anthony! That's death! What will I say—What will I say, Anthony, to Rose Dawn?"

Whispers on the wind. Van Chuch does not know if they are words or silence.

". . . *Rose Dawn.* . . . *She is the Rose.* . . .*I am the* Thorn . . . *Good-bye to her.* . . . *Good—*"

For hours van Chuch watched, his arms wrapped around a cracking palm. The *Thorn* had passed the keys. It was ground in the jaws of the deep. Oceans were above it, deep as those oceans below.

Now sparked its lights out. All sign of it was gone.

Van Chuch knew some one stood beside him. Rain-drenched, shuddering and sobbing, there stood Rose Dawn. Van Chuch threw his arm about her, for she seemed ready to leap into the waters. They were hurled to earth as the palm tree broke.

"If he's gone, I'll go with him!" Rose sobbed. Over and over, while storm swept down the sky and floods of rain washed on them.

"If he's gone, I'll go with him!"

"Steady! Steady!" said van Chuch. "Easy all!"

Within the night of noon the storm clouds broke. In the west shone one clear streak of blue, blue as the eyes of Rose Dawn. Upon that blue a curly crescent of pale stormy moon, yellow as the curls of Rose Dawn.

The hurricane fled muttering away. From the sea a light. The *Thorn* was coming home! As the long hour passed, her white lean length was visible more clearly. Anthony stood yet at her wheel.

Sturdily van Chuch patted the girl's back, with heroic clumps.

"Steady, girl! Easy all!"

That upturned moon of noon, he saw, was like the upturned lips of Rose Dawn.

FINIS

RAMBLE HOUSE's

HARRY STEPHEN KEELER WEBWORK MYSTERIES

(RH) indicates the title is available ONLY in the RAMBLE HOUSE edition

The Ace of Spades Murder
The Affair of the Bottled Deuce (RH)
The Amazing Web
The Barking Clock
Behind That Mask
The Book with the Orange Leaves
The Bottle with the Green Wax Seal
The Box from Japan
The Case of the Canny Killer
The Case of the Crazy Corpse (RH)
The Case of the Flying Hands (RH)
The Case of the Ivory Arrow
The Case of the Jeweled Ragpicker
The Case of the Lavender Gripsack
The Case of the Mysterious Moll
The Case of the 16 Beans
The Case of the Transparent Nude (RH)
The Case of the Transposed Legs
The Case of the Two-Headed Idiot (RH)
The Case of the Two Strange Ladies
The Circus Stealers (RH)
Cleopatra's Tears
A Copy of Beowulf (RH)
The Crimson Cube (RH)
The Face of the Man From Saturn
Find the Clock
The Five Silver Buddhas
The 4th King
The Gallows Waits, My Lord! (RH)
The Green Jade Hand
Finger! Finger!
Hangman's Nights (RH)
I, Chameleon (RH)
I Killed Lincoln at 10:13! (RH)
The Iron Ring
The Man Who Changed His Skin (RH)
The Man with the Crimson Box
The Man with the Magic Eardrums
The Man with the Wooden Spectacles
The Marceau Case
The Matilda Hunter Murder
The Monocled Monster

The Murder of London Lew
The Murdered Mathematician
The Mysterious Card (RH)
The Mysterious Ivory Ball of Wong Shing Li (RH)
The Mystery of the Fiddling Cracksman
The Peacock Fan
The Photo of Lady X (RH)
The Portrait of Jirjohn Cobb
Report on Vanessa Hewstone (RH)
Riddle of the Travelling Skull
Riddle of the Wooden Parrakeet (RH)
The Scarlet Mummy (RH)
The Search for X-Y-Z
The Sharkskin Book
Sing Sing Nights
The Six From Nowhere (RH)
The Skull of the Waltzing Clown
The Spectacles of Mr. Cagliostro
Stand By—London Calling!
The Steeltown Strangler
The Stolen Gravestone (RH)
Strange Journey (RH)
The Strange Will
The Straw Hat Murders (RH)
The Street of 1000 Eyes (RH)
Thieves' Nights
Three Novellos (RH)
The Tiger Snake
The Trap (RH)
Vagabond Nights (Defrauded Yeggman)
Vagabond Nights 2 (10 Hours)
The Vanishing Gold Truck
The Voice of the Seven Sparrows
The Washington Square Enigma
When Thief Meets Thief
The White Circle (RH)
The Wonderful Scheme of Mr. Christopher Thorne
X. Jones—of Scotland Yard
Y. Cheung, Business Detective

Keeler Related Works

A To Izzard: A Harry Stephen Keeler Companion by Fender Tucker — Articles and stories about Harry, by Harry, and in his style. Included is a compleat bibliography.

Wild About Harry: Reviews of Keeler Novels — Edited by Richard Polt & Fender Tucker — 22 reviews of works by Harry Stephen Keeler from *Keeler News*. A perfect introduction to the author.

The Keeler Keyhole Collection: Annotated newsletter rants from Harry Stephen Keeler, edited by Francis M. Nevins. Over 400 pages of incredibly personal Keeleriana.

Fakealoo — Pastiches of the style of Harry Stephen Keeler by selected demented members of the HSK Society. Updated every year with the new winner.

RAMBLE HOUSE'S OTHER LOONS

The End of It All and Other Stories — Ed Gorman's latest short story collection

Four Dancing Tuatara Press Books — *Beast or Man?* By Sean M'Guire; *The Whistling Ancestors* by Richard E. Goddard; *The Shadow on the House* and *Sorcerer's Chessmen* by Mark Hansom. With introductions by John Pelan

The Dumpling — Political murder from 1907 by Coulson Kernahan

Victims & Villains — Intriguing Sherlockiana from Derham Groves

Evidence in Blue — 1938 mystery by E. Charles Vivian

The Case of the Little Green Men — Mack Reynolds wrote this love song to sci-fi fans back in 1951 and it's now back in print.

Hell Fire — A new hard-boiled novel by Jack Moskovitz about an arsonist, an arson cop and a Nazi hooker. It isn't pretty.

Researching American-Made Toy Soldiers — A 276-page collection of a lifetime of articles by toy soldier expert Richard O'Brien

Strands of the Web: Short Stories of Harry Stephen Keeler — Edited and Introduced by Fred Cleaver

The Sam McCain Novels — Ed Gorman's terrific series includes *The Day the Music Died, Wake Up Little Susie* and *Will You Still Love Me Tomorrow?*

A Shot Rang Out — Three decades of reviews from Jon Breen

Mysterious Martin, the Master of Murder — Two versions of a strange 1912 novel by Tod Robbins about a man who writes books that can kill.

Dago Red — 22 tales of dark suspense by Bill Pronzini

The Night Remembers — A 1991 Jack Walsh mystery from Ed Gorman

Rough Cut & New, Improved Murder — Ed Gorman's first two novels

Hollywood Dreams — A novel of the Depression by Richard O'Brien

Seven Gelett Burgess Novels — *The Master of Mysteries, The White Cat, Two O'Clock Courage, Ladies in Boxes, Find the Woman, The Heart Line, The Picaroons*

The Organ Reader — A huge compilation of just about everything published in the 1971-1972 radical bay-area newspaper, THE ORGAN.

A Clear Path to Cross — Sharon Knowles short mystery stories by Ed Lynskey

Old Times' Sake — Short stories by James Reasoner from Mike Shayne Magazine

Freaks and Fantasies — Eerie tales by Tod Robbins, collaborator of Tod Browning on the film FREAKS.

Six Jim Harmon Double Novels — *Vixen Hollow/Celluloid Scandal, The Man Who Made Maniacs/Silent Siren, Ape Rape/Wanton Witch, Sex Burns Like Fire/Twist Session, Sudden Lust/Passion Strip, Sin Unlimited/Harlot Master, Twilight Girls/Sex Institution.* Written in the early 60s.

Marblehead: A Novel of H.P. Lovecraft — A long-lost masterpiece from Richard A. Lupoff. Published for the first time!

The Compleat Ova Hamlet — Parodies of SF authors by Richard A. Lupoff – A brand new edition with more stories and more illustrations by Trina Robbins.

The Secret Adventures of Sherlock Holmes — Three Sherlockian pastiches by the Brooklyn author/publisher, Gary Lovisi.

The Universal Holmes — Richard A. Lupoff's 2007 collection of five Holmesian pastiches and a recipe for giant rat stew.

Four Joel Townsley Rogers Novels — By the author of *The Red Right Hand: Once In a Red Moon, Lady With the Dice, The Stopped Clock, Never Leave My Bed*

Two Joel Townsley Rogers Story Collections — Night of Horror and Killing Time

Twenty Norman Berrow Novels — *The Bishop's Sword, Ghost House, Don't Go Out After Dark, Claws of the Cougar, The Smokers of Hashish, The Secret Dancer, Don't Jump Mr. Boland!, The Footprints of Satan, Fingers for Ransom, The Three Tiers of Fantasy, The Spaniard's Thumb, The Eleventh Plague, Words Have Wings, One Thrilling Night, The Lady's in Danger, It Howls at Night, The Terror in the Fog, Oil Under the Window, Murder in the Melody, The Singing Room*

The N. R. De Mexico Novels — Robert Bragg presents *Marijuana Girl, Madman on a Drum, Private Chauffeur* in one volume.

Four Chelsea Quinn Yarbro Novels featuring Charlie Moon — *Ogilvie, Tallant and Moon, Music When the Sweet Voice Dies, Poisonous Fruit* and *Dead Mice*

Five Walter S. Masterman Mysteries — *The Green Toad, The Flying Beast, The Yellow Mistletoe, The Wrong Verdict* and *The Perjured Alibi.* Fantastic impossible plots.

Two Hake Talbot Novels — *Rim of the Pit, The Hangman's Handyman.* Classic locked room mysteries.

Two Alexander Laing Novels — *The Motives of Nicholas Holtz* and *Dr. Scarlett*, stories of medical mayhem and intrigue from the 30s.

Four David Hume Novels — *Corpses Never Argue, Cemetery First Stop, Make Way for the Mourners, Eternity Here I Come*, and more to come.

Three Wade Wright Novels — *Echo of Fear, Death At Nostalgia Street* and *It Leads to Murder*, with more to come!

Eight Rupert Penny Novels — *Policeman's Holiday, Policeman's Evidence, Lucky Policeman, Policeman in Armour, Sealed Room Murder, Sweet Poison, The Talkative Policeman, She had to Have Gas* and *Cut and Run* (by Martin Tanner.)

Five Jack Mann Novels — Strange murder in the English countryside. *Gees' First Case, Nightmare Farm, Grey Shapes, The Ninth Life, The Glass Too Many.*

Seven Max Afford Novels — *Owl of Darkness, Death's Mannikins, Blood on His Hands, The Dead Are Blind, The Sheep and the Wolves, Sinners in Paradise* and *Two Locked Room Mysteries and a Ripping Yarn* by one of Australia's finest novelists.

Five Joseph Shallit Novels — *The Case of the Billion Dollar Body, Lady Don't Die on My Doorstep, Kiss the Killer, Yell Bloody Murder, Take Your Last Look.* One of America's best 50's authors.

Two Crimson Clown Novels — By Johnston McCulley, author of the Zorro novels, *The Crimson Clown* and *The Crimson Clown Again.*

The Best of 10-Story Book — edited by Chris Mikul, over 35 stories from the literary magazine Harry Stephen Keeler edited.

A Young Man's Heart — A forgotten early classic by Cornell Woolrich

The Anthony Boucher Chronicles — edited by Francis M. Nevins
Book reviews by Anthony Boucher written for the *San Francisco Chronicle,* 1942 – 1947. Essential and fascinating reading.

Muddled Mind: Complete Works of Ed Wood, Jr. — David Hayes and Hayden Davis deconstruct the life and works of a mad genius.

Gadsby — A lipogram (a novel without the letter E). Ernest Vincent Wright's last work, published in 1939 right before his death.

My First Time: The One Experience You Never Forget — Michael Birchwood — 64 true first-person narratives of how they lost it.

A Roland Daniel Double: The Signal and The Return of Wu Fang — Classic thrillers from the 30s

Murder in Shawnee — Two novels of the Alleghenies by John Douglas: *Shawnee Alley Fire* and *Haunts.*

Deep Space and other Stories — A collection of SF gems by Richard A. Lupoff

Blood Moon — The first of the Robert Payne series by Ed Gorman

The Time Armada — Fox B. Holden's 1953 SF gem.

Black River Falls — Suspense from the master, Ed Gorman

Sideslip — 1968 SF masterpiece by Ted White and Dave Van Arnam

The Triune Man — Mindscrambling science fiction from Richard A. Lupoff

Detective Duff Unravels It — Episodic mysteries by Harvey O'Higgins

Automaton — Brilliant treatise on robotics: 1928-style! By H. Stafford Hatfield

The Incredible Adventures of Rowland Hern — Rousing 1928 impossible crimes by Nicholas Olde.

Slammer Days — Two full-length prison memoirs: *Men into Beasts* (1952) by George Sylvester Viereck and *Home Away From Home* (1962) by Jack Woodford

Murder in Black and White — 1931 classic tennis whodunit by Evelyn Elder

Killer's Caress — Cary Moran's 1936 hardboiled thriller

The Golden Dagger — 1951 Scotland Yard yarn by E. R. Punshon

A Smell of Smoke — 1951 English countryside thriller by Miles Burton

Ruled By Radio — 1925 futuristic novel by Robert L. Hadfield & Frank E. Farncombe

Murder in Silk — A 1937 Yellow Peril novel of the silk trade by Ralph Trevor

The Case of the Withered Hand — 1936 potboiler by John G. Brandon

Finger-prints Never Lie — A 1939 classic detective novel by John G. Brandon

Inclination to Murder — 1966 thriller by New Zealand's Harriet Hunter

Invaders from the Dark — Classic werewolf tale from Greye La Spina

Fatal Accident — Murder by automobile, a 1936 mystery by Cecil M. Wills

The Devil Drives — A prison and lost treasure novel by Virgil Markham

Dr. Odin — Douglas Newton's 1933 potboiler comes back to life.

The Chinese Jar Mystery — Murder in the manor by John Stephen Strange, 1934

The Julius Caesar Murder Case — A classic 1935 re-telling of the assassination by Wallace Irwin that's much more fun than the Shakespeare version

West Texas War and Other Western Stories — by Gary Lovisi

The Contested Earth and Other SF Stories — A never-before published space opera and seven short stories by Jim Harmon.

Tales of the Macabre and Ordinary — Modern twisted horror by Chris Mikul, author of the *Bizarrism* series.

The Gold Star Line — Seaboard adventure from L.T. Reade and Robert Eustace.

The Werewolf vs the Vampire Woman — Hard to believe ultraviolence by either Arthur M. Scarm or Arthur M. Scram.

Black Hogan Strikes Again — Australia's Peter Renwick pens a tale of the outback.

Don Diablo: Book of a Lost Film — Two-volume treatment of a western by Paul Landres, with diagrams. Intro by Francis M. Nevins.

The Charlie Chaplin Murder Mystery — Movie hijinks by Wes D. Gehring

The Koky Comics — A collection of all of the 1978-1981 Sunday and daily comic strips by Richard O'Brien and Mort Gerberg, in two volumes.

Suzy — Another collection of comic strips from Richard O'Brien and Bob Vojtko

Dime Novels: Ramble House's 10-Cent Books — *Knife in the Dark* by Robert Leslie Bellem, *Hot Lead* and *Song of Death* by Ed Earl Repp, *A Hashish House in New York* by H.H. Kane, and five more.

Blood in a Snap — The *Finnegan's Wake* of the 21st century, by Jim Weiler

Stakeout on Millennium Drive — Award-winning Indianapolis Noir — Ian Woollen.

Dope Tales #1 — Two dope-riddled classics; *Dope Runners* by Gerald Grantham and *Death Takes the Joystick* by Phillip Condé.

Dope Tales #2 — Two more narco-classics; *The Invisible Hand* by Rex Dark and *The Smokers of Hashish* by Norman Berrow.

Dope Tales #3 — Two enchanting novels of opium by the master, Sax Rohmer. *Dope* and *The Yellow Claw*.

Tenebrae — Ernest G. Henham's 1898 horror tale brought back.

The Singular Problem of the Stygian House-Boat — Two classic tales by John Kendrick Bangs about the denizens of Hades.

Tiresias — Psychotic modern horror novel by Jonathan M. Sweet.

The One After Snelling — Kickass modern noir from Richard O'Brien.

The Sign of the Scorpion — 1935 Edmund Snell tale of oriental evil.

The House of the Vampire — 1907 poetic thriller by George S. Viereck.

An Angel in the Street — Modern hardboiled noir by Peter Genovese.

The Devil's Mistress — Scottish gothic tale by J. W. Brodie-Innes.

The Lord of Terror — 1925 mystery with master-criminal, Fantômas.

The Lady of the Terraces — 1925 adventure by E. Charles Vivian.

My Deadly Angel — 1955 Cold War drama by John Chelton

Prose Bowl — Futuristic satire — Bill Pronzini & Barry N. Malzberg .

Satan's Den Exposed — True crime in Truth or Consequences New Mexico — Award-winning journalism by the *Desert Journal*.

The Amorous Intrigues & Adventures of Aaron Burr — by Anonymous — Hot historical action.

I Stole $16,000,000 — A true story by cracksman Herbert E. Wilson.

The Black Dark Murders — Vintage 50s college murder yarn by Milt Ozaki, writing as Robert O. Saber.

Sex Slave — Potboiler of lust in the days of Cleopatra — Dion Leclerq.

You'll Die Laughing — Bruce Elliott's 1945 novel of murder at a practical joker's English countryside manor.

The Private Journal & Diary of John H. Surratt — The memoirs of the man who conspired to assassinate President Lincoln.

Dead Man Talks Too Much — Hollywood boozer by Weed Dickenson

Red Light — History of legal prostitution in Shreveport Louisiana by Eric Brock. Includes wonderful photos of the houses and the ladies.

A Snark Selection — Lewis Carroll's *The Hunting of the Snark* with two Snarkian chapters by Harry Stephen Keeler — Illustrated by Gavin L. O'Keefe.

Ripped from the Headlines! — The Jack the Ripper story as told in the newspaper articles in the *New York* and *London Times.*

Geronimo — S. M. Barrett's 1905 autobiography of a noble American.

The White Peril in the Far East — Sidney Lewis Gulick's 1905 indictment of the West and assurance that Japan would never attack the U.S.

The Compleat Calhoon — All of Fender Tucker's works: Includes *Totah Six-Pack, Weed, Women and Song* and *Tales from the Tower,* plus a CD of all of his songs.

Totah Six-Pack — Just Fender Tucker's six tales about Farmington in one sleek volume.

RAMBLE HOUSE
Fender Tucker, Prop.
www.ramblehouse.com   fender@ramblehouse.com
228-826-1783   10329 Sheephead Drive, Vancleave MS 39565

Made in the USA
Monee, IL
26 February 2020